Lies and Retribution

Text © Anthony Paul Bateman
2016
All rights reserved

No part of this book may be reproduced, or stored in a retrieval system, or transmitted in any form or by any means, electronic, mechanical, photocopying, printing or otherwise, without written permission of the author.

Author contact: authorapbateman@gmail.com

Author website: www.apbateman.com

Also by A P Bateman

The Ares Virus
At a US research facility funded by the military and clandestine agencies a super-virus has been created as a first strike military weapon. During its conception the anti-virus has furthered the possibilities of medical research by decades. Such is its potential, treachery has struck from within. If the virus is released, then the anti-virus will be worth billions to the pharmaceutical industry. Isobel Bartlett worked on the project and knows its potential.

After the suspicious death of her mentor, and upon hearing part of an audacious plan to make money from the project she flees the facility with the information needed to culture the viruses to seek help from a contact with the FBI.

Up against rogue government forces, she is helped by Agent Rob Stone of the Secret Service who has been tasked by the president to investigate a disbanded assassination program after his investigation led him to the bio research facility. The two are hunted mercilessly by an assassin from Washington to the streets of New York. Only when the hunt reaches the wild forests of Vermont can ex-special forces soldier Stone take the fight to the enemy.

The Contract Man
When an MI6 agent is found to be keeping records of his missions to protect himself from betrayal he unwittingly makes himself a priority target. But how do you silence the most dangerous man imaginable? Send him into hell on earth…

While Alex King is sent into Northern Iraq to tidy the loose ends of a botched mission, the archipelago of Indonesia is under communist threat from within its own military. A consortium of worried businessmen call for desperate measures and seek the services of an assassin. But what if MI6 could be duped into taking care of their problems for them? With secret links to China the communist contingent threatens Britain's trade initiatives with the largest mineral producing country on the planet.

In the shadowy world of intelligence, it seems that everybody has their price.

For Clair

For the time to write and the support throughout,

as always

1

London

She had eyes on. She was in position and she was calling it as she saw it.

"Control, this is Alpha Three Zero," she paused, her voice activated throat-mic deactivating and opening the air band.

"Alpha Three Zero, Control go ahead, over."

"Alpha Three Zero, eyes on and taking the lead. Over."

"Control, Roger, have that. Wait out."

She was eighty metres behind the target and out of his line of sight across the street. Her eyes darted to her left at the shop window displays. She kept an eye on the man, but her motions were fluid. She was aware that call sign Alpha Two One was cycling at a leisurely pace fifty metres behind her. If she made the call he would cycle past, take up a stationary position fifty metres or so ahead. He would stop and take a drink or check his phone. There were more scenarios, more counters. They knew the way each other worked.

At the end of the high-street the mobile control had both visual eyes on and an uploaded wireless link into the CCTV system operating throughout the borough. It was a non-descript four-year-old Mercedes van. It carried the logo of a locksmith on the side. Locksmiths operated all over at all times of day and night. They were in and out of the congestion zone and stopped wherever they were called to work. This van had two trained locksmiths inside. Both were MI5 operatives from surveillance group, or otherwise known as watchers. There would be no call for their locksmith skills today.

A police vehicle drove slowly past completing a continuous loop. In the rear seats, shrouded from view by tinted rear windows were two armed officers from SCO19. Both men wore body armour and dark blue combat fatigues. Both were equipped with Glock 17 pistols and both wore a Heckler & Koch MP5 machine pistol strapped to their chests. One carried a Remington .12-gauge pump action shotgun loaded with magnum 00 buck shot. The other carried a 5.56mm Heckler & Koch G36 carbine. It was loaded, made ready and held thirty rounds. It was a high-powered weapon deadly effective to four hundred metres and the SCO19 officer was rated expert with it. It had been chosen for its stopping power and ability to punch through Kevlar body armour at close to medium range.

"Control, plod are passing too slowly," the woman stepped into a doorway, her eyes on both the police vehicle and the target now just forty metres distant. "Get them out of here!"

"Control, have that. Alpha Three Zero, keep eyes on…"

The police vehicle maintained its speed, the driver sweeping slowly past. They knew the target, but their brief had been difficult – maintain a close distance for rapid reaction, but remain inconspicuous. The vehicle drove on, turned right at the end of the street and set about making another steady circuit. Another police vehicle with a separate armed driver and two similarly heavily armed officers were waiting at the other end of the street listening out for the word on the net.

Caroline Darby crossed over the road using just her periphery vision to check for traffic. She got within twenty metres of the target, kept walking past and stopped at a shop window. It was an old fashioned sweet shop. The kind that could have spelled it *olde* and *shoppe*. She looked at the display of stacked fudge. The window was tinted and clean. It was ideal for watching the target in the refection. She felt a shiver when she caught sight of the children in the shop, a group of mothers with pushchairs and toddling pre-schoolers. She watched the target again. He had stopped, was swaying slightly. The entrance to the underground station was sixty metres away. The tube was due in less than four minutes and the passengers would disembark and fill the streets less than a minute later.

"Alpha Three Zero, this is Control... Sit rep, over."

"Control, target is stationary. Repeat, stationary. Population light, under four minutes to rush hour, over."

"Alpha Three Zero, are you calling it? Over."

"Control," she hesitated, turned around and watched the target, who was shifting nervously from foot to foot. She couldn't see his lips, but she knew he was chanting, praying and steeling himself for his next action. "Sit-rep for SCO19 drive past ETA? Over."

"Alpha Three Zero, wait out..."

She could see the side of the man's face. It looked as if he had not shaved in days, his hair was lank and he looked drawn, haggard. He was different from the man they had been watching for the past three months, but it was definitely him. The life seemed to have left him this morning, only a husk remained. When they had first received the intelligence he had been a boy of seventeen. Now he could pass for thirty. And he did not look well.

"Alpha Three Zero, this is Control. Bravo One four minutes. Bravo Two, on route ETA three minutes..."

Caroline Darby looked at the street ahead of her and to her left. She turned back to the shop window and watched the group of women and children. They had paid, were handing out sweets to the children as they made their way to the door. She looked back at the man, but he was staring at her. Eye to eye. There was a moment's hesitation and she looked away. He started to unbutton his coat. She looked up to the underground exit and entrance behind the target. A group of people were at the top, more were behind. The people reaching the top fanned out in one hundred and eighty degrees heading for the square, the taxi ranks and the three streets that funnelled off the station.

"Control... Not enough time... Calling it... Armed units in! Go... go... go!" She stepped into the doorway of the shop and rammed her outstretched hand hard into the nearest woman's chest. The woman fell to the floor, taking her toddler with her amongst a tirade of verbal abuse from her companions, but she didn't hear, was already pulling the door shut as she turned around and made her way back onto the street.

Mohammed Ashkani was staring at her, his jacket almost completely unbuttoned. She could see the vest underneath. She could see the sewn pockets bulging, the wires protruding and the old fashioned mobile phone attached. She glanced to her left. No sign of SCO19, but she could hear the sirens. Ashkani looked at her, and then raised his head, his eyes almost completely white as he seemed to enter a trance. He was mouthing plenty, but it was silent.

Last prayers.

Caroline Darby was fit and slim and used to running. She had been an MI5 officer for four years and had served as an officer with the Royal Logistics Corps for two years before signing up with Army Intelligence for another four. She had made the twenty-five metres to Ashkani in a few seconds and wrapped both arms around his own as she had barrelled into him and taken him to the floor. She kept her arms around him, and by the time he had reacted and started to fight her off, she had linked her hands and was bear hugging him with all her strength. The pair rolled on the hard, damp concrete, but she held firm. He would need a free hand to operate the device, she was sure. She was thrown onto her back, but used it to her advantage wrapping both her legs around his thighs and pulling his legs to the ground. It was a ju-jitsu technique and one she had trained to do in the gym many times. Now it was real, but it was working. Still Ashkani fought, but with all he had left, which was the back of his head. He snapped his head back and after a few attempts he cracked her nose. Her eyes welled with tears and she could barely see, yet she hung onto the man for dear life.

People were starting to gather and Darby knew that she was on borrowed time until some well-meaning citizen attempted to break the pair up.

"British Security Forces! Stay back!" she screamed. "He has a bomb!"

At once the group stepped back, some just a pace or two and others sprinting away, and to her relief she could see two firearms officers from SCO19 sprinting towards them. The lead officer hesitated for the briefest of moments, he saw the vest, saw the same bulges and wires and mobile phone that Darby had seen and in an instant he drew his pistol and lunged the last few strides. The pistol came alarmingly close to her own face and as the muzzle connected to Ashkani's temple the officer fired once and Caroline Darby felt the man go limp in her arms. Her ears were ringing and she felt the thump of noise from the gunshot resonate in her chest.

"Wait, keep hold of him!" The lead officer shouted. He bent down and assessed the vest and position of the man's arms. He pulled the body's right arm from his chest and let it drop limply to the ground, all the while covering with the 9mm Glock. He then looked to change his mind and cuffed the body's wrists. "Okay, easy. Nice and slowly..." He helped Darby out from under him and rolled the body over onto its front. Darby took the officer's hand and lifted herself up to her feet. The other armed officer had taken a handkerchief from his pocket and given to her. She dabbed her bloodied nose and winced.

The second armed response unit was at their side now, weapons up and scanning everything through their sights. Running in also were at least ten MI5 and Special

Branch officers in various conditions of perspiration and rates of breathing. Uniformed police officers were starting to take control of the crowd gathering witnesses into groups and taping off the area. SOCO were taking charge of the body and two young RAF bomb disposal officers were leading a team of MET bomb disposal officers in through the cordon. The RAF boys were on hand because of their experience with suicide vests in Afghanistan.

A tall, thin man in his early fifties stepped through the huddle and looked down at the young female MI5 officer. "Bloody well done Caroline! Bloody well done! He's on his way over now," he paused. "It was a no show at Lima One. The suspected bomber didn't show. Operation stood down, watchers still in place. He's pretty pissed off that you got all the action! Said you better not have taken any unnecessary risks... What are we going to say to that?" He smiled and walked away towards the gathering of uniformed officers at the far end of the security cordon.

From across the square a young man watched. He was dark and young, in his early twenties. He was drinking coffee at a café table. It was a generic coffee house but it was a fine cup of Arabica. Black and sweet. He couldn't fault it. He had already paid at the counter so after he drained the remnants he stood up and walked across the square without looking back.

A young police officer had finished fastening the cordon tape and was walking back to his sergeant for his next set of orders. The man ducked under the cordon and strode confidently to the crowd near the body. A nearby police officer looked up, but ignored the man in his smart suit and confident gait. He skirted the body and entered what he guessed to be the inner sanctum of law enforcement officers; some armed and looking paramilitary, others uniformed or plain clothed. He looked at the woman who was cleaning the blood from her nose.

"Allah Akbar!" He shouted as he ripped open his suit jacket and pressed the button on an old fashioned looking mobile phone clipped to the front of the vest. "Allah Akbar!"

God is great.

Caroline Darby looked up at him, bewildered, catching on a second too late. The last thing she saw before the explosion and her hearing was shattered and her life changed forever was the image of her fiancé fellow MI5 officer Peter Redwood pushing through the crowd, nudging the bomber aside as he threw himself on her and knocked her to the ground.

2

Eight months later

Charles Forester had attended Iman Mullah Al-Shaqqaf's court case on many occasions. The Islamic cleric was accused of preaching anti-west, anti-Semitism and anti-Christianity from the mosque he preached from in Islington. The Crown Prosecution Service could not get the initial charges of conspiracy to commit murder to stick. Nor could they get the coercion charges through. Both young men involved in the bombing attended the mosque, however if they misinterpreted the Iman's sermons and teachings of the Holy Koran then it was not down to him or the other teachers at the mosque or that of the neighbouring mosques with which they worked. Instead the blame had been laid squarely at the feet of modern Britain and the disaffected Muslim youth within. After the neighbourhood rioted upon the discovery of listening devices planted by both police and MI5 in their mosque Mullah Al-Shaqqaf had brought his own lawsuit and won. The CPS countered with an extradition case to send Mullah Al-Shaqqaf back to his birthplace of Yemen. This case had now collapsed and Mullah Al-Shaqqaf was free to walk the streets of Britain and preach his sermons of hate from the mosque once more. The CPS was going to build another case.

The news cameras and reporters were jostling on the steps in front of the court building and Mullah Al-

Shaqqaf, sandwiched between half a dozen minders posed arrogantly, silently waiting for the noise to die down before he gave another of his notorious victory speeches. He was well practiced.

Forester studied the man's bodyguards. All were thick-set and above average height and weight. They had a seasoned look about them. Not a nightclub bouncer's well-practised hard and menacing stare, but the eyes of seasoned combat veterans. It had been suspected that they had been drawn from Islamic State fighters who had plied their murderous trade in Syria and Northern Iraq. Certainly each of them had subsequently had periods of time off the radar. Investigations had shown that they had all been part of *Brothers of Islam* aid work convoys, but the charity had lost contact with them and been unable to account for them for their duration with the relief work parties.

Forester had been around long enough to know a lost cause. He knew the odds of sticking something on Mullah Al-Shaqqaf were too high. The man had notoriety, a host of academics and legal experts behind him and the support of an enraged local population, affronted by the establishment's insult to their faith. There would be other extremists to go after and other extremists that the law would successfully prosecute and either imprison or extradite. You win some, you lose some. But Charles Forester, deputy director of MI5 had lost too much in that explosion, and he was not losing this fight at any cost.

3

Remastiani, Ural Mountains, Russia

The last time Vladimir Zukovsky had driven to the mountain retreat it had been in an old Volga Gaz-24. A modified KGB model with an extra ten horsepower over the standard model and blacked out windows. He had been honoured because at the time the army had been using Trabants. Much had changed now. Now he drove his own Audi saloon, purchased new from a showroom in Moscow. Unthinkable at the time of his last visit. The Soviet Union as he knew it had changed also. The Russian Federation was his nation now. And the satellite countries which had made up the great sleeping bear that was once the USSR were now largely independent states. The barriers had fallen and the country was now rotten to the core. Multi-billionaire oligarchs now ruled from behind the scenes, pumping money and influence into the government. Western imperialism was driving the country towards the brink of devolution. A nation where people seemed either to be dirt poor or millionaires. People who stood to make a change were killed.

Zukovsky had been a General on that last visit. Other things had changed too. Now the once great power, the KGB was called the FSB, which does not translate as Federal Security Bureau, but rather the Federal Security Service. The full name is *Федеральная служба безопасности Российской Федерации (ФСБ); Federal'naya sluzhba bezopasnosti Rossiyskoy Federatsii.*

The retreat was nameless. Zukovsky was sure it didn't exist on the map. *Google Earth* may well find it, but he knew the old Soviet maps only showed forest, tundra and mountainous rock. That was a long time ago, but he had to put map reference coordinates into the satnav as no address had been given to him. The drive had been long and he had been glad of the Audi's four-wheel drive system on the icy road. It had snowed recently. Great piles had been cleared to the side of the road and were mixed with mud and pine needles. Although the road was clear, he could tell from the vast piles of snow and ice that it would have been practically impassable a few days ago. He knew the forecast was good for the next few days so his return trip tomorrow should be uneventful.

Ahead of him the trees on either side of the road thinned out and he could see the gates just off the road on his right. He crossed over and swung the Audi into the driveway. The drive was about two hundred metres and as he made his way down towards the series of log cabins set out in a crescent he was hit with a pang of familiarity and nostalgia. They were not all necessarily good times; they had been brutal to say the least. But the brutality of communism and the state ruled by the iron fist of the KGB had given the USSR something that western decadence, civil freedoms and the free market had not. Power on the world stage. The Russian President was seen as a joke by most of the world, a man's man who cared not for what was thought about him, but that he was powerful and not to be pushed or dominated. Pictures or footage of him bear hunting with a crossbow, bare-chested riding horses or sparring with troops in albeit carefully choreographed judo grapples were sending out a message of strength. However, this was not truly the case and the rest of the world could see it for what it was. Posturing in light of two facts. Russia was not to be trusted on the world stage and could survive with such extremes of wealth and poverty for only so long.

Zukovsky could not forgive the current state of affairs. He was in Afghanistan when they pulled out. He commanded a battalion in the North. A godforsaken land that hadn't given up its fight easily. Or at all. With the systematic withdrawal of Afghanistan, the waiting satellite states had bolstered themselves and the Soviet Union had started to fall like dominoes until only the Russian Federation remained and was renamed. Many high-ranking military figures had found it unforgivable that they had not fought for the Union, or started to take it back afterwards. They were told by the leaders that they would bide their time and wait until they could fight and win. But these times had never come. The military leaders of the day were either dead or old men.

Zukovsky was an old man now. Another old man was Yevgeny Antakov, who was walking down the wooden steps of the centre cabin. Antakov stood six foot five, or used to. Now he was stooped and making good use of the wooden handrail. His once salt and pepper hair, trimmed short to military grade was now wavy and snowy white. He watched his old friend as he parked the car and lifted his left hand in greeting. Not so much a wave as an acknowledgement.

Zukovsky switched off the engine and opened the door. As he got out he stiffened. The drive had been long and this far north was colder than he had been used to in recent years.

"Vladimir, my old friend!" Yevgeny called from the bottom step.

Zukovsky noted the man walked no further, but still held the handrail. "Yevgeny!" He mock saluted, smiled as his old comrade returned the gesture, although noted, rather to his annoyance, that it was with his left hand, the right still taking his weight.

"The years have treated you well, General," Yevgeny paused. He remained still as Zukovsky walked towards him.

"The knees and hips need a good oiling, but they loosen eventually," he smiled.

The two men stared at each other fondly, then bear hugged and back-slapped. Yevgeny motioned a hand out to the woods beside him. "If this place could talk, eh? The secrets it would reveal; the lives it would know lost…"

"Time buries the past, my old friend. Who are we to awaken it?"

Yevgeny chuckled. "Oh, Vladimir. How right you are. And yet…"

Vladimir Zukovsky held up a hand. "Enough… you call me out here in the bitter cold and fail to offer me vodka before talking?" He caught hold of his old friend's elbow and took some weight as they made their way up the steps. He felt the man relax and lean on him.

"Vladimir, I have vodka. Plenty for us both," he paused. "And our guests also, when they arrive."

They stopped on the decked porch. Zukovsky looked back at the woods. The trees were bare and covered with a hard frost. The ground would be hard. He knew how hard it could get. Hard to dig, even just a few feet. There was permafrost this far north, at about four feet. He wondered whether the bodies were still preserved. There were many of them out there. The ones who had held their secrets. The ones who hadn't unburdened themselves and survived to make the one-way journey to the gulags.

"What other guests?"

Yevgeny smiled. "Like minded men, Vladimir. Like you and I, they yearn for change."

"We are old men now, comrade. What can we do?"

"Nonsense! I am old, I am broken and frail," Yevgeny nodded. "But this!" He tapped his temple with his finger. "This! Well, it is as sharp as it always was. Maybe more so. Old men have time to think, time to reflect. I have evaluated failures, learned from them. My mind is a sabre and with you to steer it towards our enemy's heart, well we will prevail."

Zukovsky nodded. Intrigue had got the better of him. It had to, he had driven two days to get here. He looked up at the car making its way down the drive towards them. It was a large Mercedes SUV, black with dark tinted windows.

"Ah, they are here," Yevgeny smiled and looked at Zukovsky. "You will find this interesting, no doubt."

Zukovsky watched the vehicle swing into the drive in a large circle and park facing outwards. Four people got out of the car. The old KGB General was right. Vladimir Zukovsky found it extremely interesting.

4

One year later
Festival Pier, South Bank, London

Detective Inspector Hodges hated these sorts of cases. First there were the voyeurs. The few who had seen something terrible had massed into a sizable crowd and were looking on at the gruesome scene with macabre interest. Smartphone cameras with instant YouTube, Facebook and Instagram uploads were clicking away with no respect for what they were witnessing, and then there was the legal aspect. Evidence was already in the public domain. A few uniformed officers were dispersing the crowd and putting up exclusion zone tape and the coroner vehicles were backed to the edge of the pier waiting to transport the bodies away.

Apart from the publicity, Hodges hated these sorts of cases because of what they gave you in terms of investigative material. The Thames was a huge body of moving water with pollution, a large tide and rainwater and drains emptying out into it constantly. Water was not the forensic investigator's friend. You lost fingerprints and the transferal of fibres and DNA. Depending how long the body was in the water would depend on what you could get. He felt sure they were looking along the lines of at least ten hours, possibly twelve of submersion. There were a few factors to aid his thinking towards this. Firstly, it was five-thirty PM and the post work drinks and meetings were in full swing. The tide was not quite halfway and on the drop. Which meant that the four bodies would have been in the water by six thirty AM, given the time of sunrise and height of the tide.

The team had got a partition in place and River Police were redirecting a pleasure boat loaded with passengers to another pier. The crowd at the end of the pier had gone back to various bars and Hodges felt that there was a little more control in place as he stood at the top of the steps and shouted down to DS Mathews who was working with the two firefighters below using a River Police RIB moored to the strut of the pier. "You got it sorted yet?"

"Nearly boss," he paused, grunted under the exertion. "That's it! They're free. Two minutes and we can start getting them out and into the RIB. We'll motor back to the pontoon and unload from there. Better get the coroner vehicles to go there instead."

"Nice one," Hodges walked back along the pier and waved at the coroner driver who was leaning against his van. The driver looked up and Hodges pointed down the riverfront. The driver nodded, stubbed out his cigarette and got inside the plain, but beautifully polished vehicle.

Hodges looked out across the river. There was a harsh, cruel wind coming straight in from the East, the direction of the North Sea. He shivered, his suit jacket doing little to fend off the cold. He would have to start wearing his coat now. Autumn had been held off by a rare but often anticipated Indian summer, but it was fair to say that it was gone now. The water must have been cold for them, he thought as he watched the RIB motor steadily towards him.

The River Police officer expertly steered the RIB into the pontoon, throttled back and threw Hodges the rope. Hodges wrapped it inexpertly around a cleat and the officer jumped off the boat, untied it and wrapped it around the cleat again, threading the end of the rope around another cleat at the stern so the boat was fully tethered portside on.

"Impressions?" Hodges asked his junior officer.

Mathews stepped off the boat, stood aside for the two men from the coroner's office as they wheeled a gurney beside the boat. "Sick bastards," he said.

"Because?"

"You see their faces, the tape around their mouths?"

"I have, detective sergeant. I'm asking you."

"Alive when they went in. Alive when they were chained in place. From their expressions it hurt a great deal and was terrifying... Also their wrists and ankles are raw. They struggled."

"Variables and methodology?"

The young officer reached into the boat and unfolded a towel. He dried his clothes as best he could, had started to shiver. "The lengths of chain were the same, so the shortest drowned first. The others would have watched. They would have known who was next."

"So an element of sadism." Hodges stated flatly.

"It wasn't a lone job."

"Obviously."

"They could have been drugged, something to make them cooperate. Maybe Rohypnol, it's easy to get. Loads of it about in bars and clubs."

"That's for toxicology to find out."

"Okay, it still would have taken at least three people. One to drive the boat, two to deal with the chains and hostages. Maybe they were at gunpoint?"

"Undoubtedly. Why hostages?"

"They died there. They were hostages until they died. Then they were bodies."

"Good." He was pleased with the young detective's progress. He always gave the junior officers on his team the chance to mind map in the field. Mathews was new to the role of sergeant. In six months or so he'd be accompanied by his own junior officer.

"Hate crime, Sir?"

"They all are."

"Specific hate crime. Vendetta perhaps?"

"Definitely personal. Maybe a message," Hodges paused. "ID's?"

DS Mathews watched the first body slouch onto the gurney. He reached around to the rear trouser pocket and pulled out the wallet. "Didn't do it out there, Sir," he said sheepishly. "I was getting a bit seasick." He thumbed through. "Hello…" He showed DI Hodges the opened wallet.

"Check the others," Hodges said.

The young officer jumped into the boat and pulled at the leather handbag wrapped around the neck and shoulder of the woman's body. He delved inside, water pouring out as he did so. He retrieved a leather wallet and threw it up to Hodges before going towards the next body.

Hodges opened it and stared at the identification card. "Shit," he said quietly, as he turned and took out his mobile phone.

5

56° N 020° E, Baltic Sea
Fifty miles Southwest of Lithuania

The sea was millpond calm. The sky was blue, as was the sea and it was hard to see where the cloudless sky ended and the sea began. Such days at sea were rare, to be savoured.

Max Clenton had been at sea most of his life. He had seen days like these, but not many. There was nearly always a cloud or small swell or airplane contrails, but not many days such as these in his experience. He had served six years in the Royal Navy until he was twenty-three. Eight years followed in the merchant navy, then ten years as a fisherman. He had crewed on trawlers and crab boats, and then captained salvage vessels and fishing boats of all descriptions. Now, at the age of sixty he owned his own boat and had done for seven years. She was a forty-seven metre open decked boat called *The Lady Majestic*. Clenton utilised her every way he could. Sometimes she would be trawling or long lining for different species of fish, other times she would be stacked with crab or lobster pots. In the height of summer, she had been used as a dive boat for mass diving lessons of up to thirty paying customers and six instructors, a spotting vessel for dolphin and whale watching and more recently in the past three years as a salvage vessel and abnormal load delivery vessel. Three standard shipping containers could herringbone on the open deck and could be double stacked depending on the weight. These deliveries would usually result in a homeward bound load being sought also. Sometimes the boat went under different names as well. Clenton had discovered that people were willing to pay more if the paper trail disappeared. Taxes and excise duty were one reason. Straight forward people trafficking was another. The European refugee crisis had opened doors for him and with a little forward thinking and common sense Clenton had found that not only was Britain an easy border to breach, he could continue to do so with impunity. The secret was to avoid being greedy and to hedge his bets. Like roulette, the luck runs out fast. Clenton would do a few loads of refugees, then simply pull out for a few weeks and stick to fishing. He would then be available for a consignment of cigarettes and tobacco. But only one, and then he would pick up alcohol from another contact. Then he would do a legitimate salvage job for a few weeks. He would file taxes and bank money and submit a set of books each tax year, making a small profit. He kept his cash flow moving and never lived beyond his means. Anything made from illicit deals and jobs went into a safe in a lock-up he had bought for cash many years ago, and he only ever used the money rarely and never to buy anything material, which could create a trail.

The cargo on this trip intrigued him though. He was making a great deal of money for taking the risk, more money than he would ever receive for a job, even if this one took him away from his home port of Looe in Cornwall for a little over two weeks. The harbourmaster there was a good friend and used to him being away for a week or two at a time, so there should be no reason for anybody to be suspicious. Besides, Max Clenton talked a good talk, bought more than his fair share of rounds at the pub and joked so openly about smuggling and fixing his fishing quotas that nobody ever suspected a thing. They saw him arrive at the harbour in the same rusted Toyota pick-up for the past ten years.

He had met the foreign gentleman a month previous and nearly snatched his hand off for the ten-thousand-pound deposit to secure his services. A further ten-thousand had been paid for expenses – fuel, crew wages, any bribe or payoff Clenton may have to make along the way and then he would meet a contact of the foreign gentleman at Parnu, Estonia. Here he would pick up the cargo and receive a final payment of fifty-thousand pounds upon its delivery. Clenton had asked the specifics of the cargo and had frowned at the size and weight. The overall dimensions were tiny compared to his usual loads.

"Russian Icons," the man had said, in a thick guttural accent which Clenton had taken to be Russian. "Small templates – images of Christ, angels or saints. Made from mosaics, silver or gold. Very fragile. They will crumble if touched. Some are pre-Christ, over two thousand years old. Others are fifth to ninth century when the Byzantine period created many of these artefacts. Many were destroyed under Soviet rule."

"And they're illegal to bring out of Russia?" Clenton had asked.

"Absolutely. Anything over one hundred years. But I will soon have documents from the Ministry of

Culture of the Russian Federation saying that I have ownership."

"So why do you need me?"

The old man had smiled. "Because these documents will only work on rich, stupid Americans... I don't plan on being around for a refund after I sell."

Clenton had laughed knowingly. But had soon stopped when the man emphasised that the freight must not be touched.

"There will be a security seal on the box. If it is broken, I will not pay the further fifty-thousand pounds and will enforce a complete refund for monies already paid. I won't be going to trading standards obviously, but I have many well placed Russian contacts, what many people would call mafia, who will make life unbelievably painful for you if I am not happy with your service..."

Max Clenton lit a cigar from an old scratched Zippo lighter and looked out from the bridge to the blue horizon as far as his keen eyes could see. There was something about the man's threat, the way it had been coldly delivered that had unnerved him. Clenton was a tough man, a career drinker and brawler. He was not easily scared or intimidated. But there was an underlying menace which had shaken him. Even now, he felt uncomfortable at the thought.

6

London

Charles Forester walked down the corridor, his footsteps echoing around him. There was always an echo on this floor. The floors below were a hive of activity with open offices, voices, ringing telephones and the occasional sound of laughter or banter, just like any offices the world over. The fact that the country's security and the direction of international policy were conducted in the building didn't stop people from discussing reality television or a dating disaster they had at the weekend.

This floor, however, always felt so clinical. Like a hospital or a court building. He doubted whether it would ever feel any different. There was a larger degree of soundproofing on this floor. All of the windows in the entire building were bullet resistant to .50 calibre. The curtains were Kevlar woven fibre and were essentially blast curtains. These were installed at the time the so called *Real IRA* were firing mortars on government buildings, including Downing Street attempting to destabilise the Good Friday Peace Agreement. The .50 calibre resistant glass was installed later, but not to deflect sniper fire, it was found to be the best insurance against parabolic microphone systems aimed from a distance for listening in. The ballistic rating was merely a bonus for the occupants.

Ahead of him, the overhead lights flicked on before he reached them, behind him, the first few were already switching off. This had been an initiative fought for by a committee to save money and encourage green measures throughout the building. In essence there were no more light switches and activity meant that the lights remained on. In The Ivory Tower, as people referred to the top tier of MI5 headquarters at Thames House, it merely made for a tension building scene in a horror movie. As with many civil service institutions, it had not been properly thought out.

Forester reached the end of the corridor and opened the heavy oak door. Below the top tier the doors were solid hardwood with glass security peep panels. They were utilitarian fire doors and many were self-closing. Many offices had open doorways with no doors at all. Not a money saving measure, merely a practical open office environment for free-flow information. Of course there were many security grades, but these were tiered and there was very little chance of a low level grade hearing or seeing something they shouldn't. The higher security clearance was always behind closed office doors. But not like this one. This door was stately. Forester had heard rumours of how much the director's refurbishment had cost, but like many matters he was either too busy to care or too sceptical to put much stock in the office rumour mill. As he opened the door, however, he was hit with the notion, as he always was, that it must have been quite true. The floor was parquet. Not effect, but actual individually laid parquet blocks, herringboned. The Security Service emblem was inlaid in the centre of the office, in what Forester assumed to be marble, although the director once told him it was polished concrete and therefore entirely affordable. Though, the man had conceded, undeniably unnecessary.

"Hello Debbie. Who's in?" Forester asked the pretty secretary behind the curved mahogany desk.

"Oh, hello Mister Forester," she looked up, but Forester knew she would have seen him approaching down the corridor. The CCTV system was both movement and heat sensitive. "Ms Chalmers is already inside." This secretary was good, others always gave away a tell when referring to Elizabeth Chalmers, Joint Deputy Director of MI5 and Director of Administration. Some would wrinkle their noses, others would almost spit out the name, but when mentioning her, Debbie had been impassive. Which was partly the reason she was the Director's personal secretary. Another reason was she was stunningly beautiful and going against both perceived stereotypes and womankind's best efforts, high level clearance secretaries are always the best looking since the Emily affairs of the late Sixties.

Back in the height of the Cold War many of the secretaries serving in both MI5 and MI6, not to mention the Ministry of Defence, were unmarried career women, usually plain to look at, hard-working and lacking both a social life or the chance to meet a man to marry and start a family. These women were often referred to by the Soviet Union as Emily's (the equivalent Russian name being a rather plain one) and often reaching their forties whereby they were spinsters and on the shelf. These women were targeted by handsome younger Soviet men and given the time of their lives both in bed and out of it. They were harvested for information and many key victories by the USSR during the Cold War were down to information gained by these men during pillow talk. Soon directives were initiated and the intelligence services were keeping their best looking staff to work as assistants and secretaries in the high level security areas. The thinking being that better looking women were more confident and less susceptible to being picked up and won over by flattery and attention. It was a directive that had remained. Cynically, these women were now regarded as style over substance, but in truth they were the best at their jobs as well.

"Anybody else?" Forester asked.

"Plod," she said. "And he's bought along his superior for, well, company I think."

"Right." Forester nodded.

There was going to be a handover by the look of it, these matters rarely went smoothly. The police were better placed for certain investigations and they knew it. The Security Service knew it too, but there was a protocol with such matters concerning national security. And an age old tradition of hierarchy. That's why you needed a degree to join MI5 and MI6, and to be able to read and write and spot the difference to join the police service. Or so Joint Intelligence liked to joke.

Forester opened the door to the office of the most powerful man in counter-terrorism and surveillance. Many thought that Charles Forester should have been given the job, but he wouldn't hear of it. As director of operations, he was in control of what MI5 did in the field, how it worked within its own remit and he could shape its direction. As director, he would be a politician more than an intelligence officer. He was in his middle-fifties and comfortable in the fact that this was his final position in a thirty-year intelligence career. He had bought his property at the right time and was now mortgage free. His two children had recently finished university, his wife had given up her work after inheriting well and they had both saved prudently throughout their careers. If the axe were ever to fall he would sit back and enjoy his retirement. He had already been offered a six figure fee to join the American university, security and business lecture circuit. It was an enviable position to be in, and the politicians knew it. The deputy director of the Security Service was both financially and professionally secure and therefore incorruptible.

Howard, the director looked up and held up a welcoming hand. Forester noted he did not stand. Forester countered this by turning to the two guests and leaving the director's hand hanging. Both men stood, offered their hands.

"Chief Superintendent Carter," the taller and significantly smarter man said. Forester recognised him as a politician. Usually it was the only way to get to the top, let alone stay there. He turned to the man beside him. "This is Detective Inspector Hodges."

"Pleased to meet you both. Charles Forester, deputy director and head of operations. They were my officers you found."

"I'm sorry. But I suppose this is where you say thanks but we'll handle it from here?" Hodges said.

"Now Inspector…" Carter started to say.

"No," Forester interrupted. "This is where I thank you, enter into a thorough briefing with you and ask you to join me in finding out what happened."

Howard leaned forward. "Now, this is highly unusual!"

Forester turned to the director and interrupted him also. "Then it shouldn't be. We are a counter terrorism and intelligence service. The Met are right here in this office, they have the best scenes of crime officers and they investigate murders every day. We are not murder detectives, but we have one in this very room. The first detective on scene no less. We can work together because right now, all I want are the bastards that did this off the streets."

Chalmers turned to him. She was severe-looking woman with thick spectacles. Her hair was tied up in a bun. She was good at what she did because there was no way she had slept to the top. "We need to operate under the control of certain protocols. It's what keeps us accountable and our remit concise."

"Well, we could debate this. We could get the Joint Intelligence Committee to bring it up in the next COBRA meeting, but what we need is to use the resources we have at this moment. We need a pathologist on the bodies now, we need SOCO on the quay doing what they do and we need the manpower that the Met can give us. At least for seventy-two hours." He turned to Detective Inspector Hodges and looked him in the eye. "Will you find the killers for me detective?"

"I will do my best," he said. "It's no cold case. If you can get the paperwork out of the way, and I'll want my assistant on it."

"Done." Forester stood. He looked at Howard, his mouth agape behind his desk. "We'll start right now." He turned to Hodges. "I will sort out security clearances for you and your team. We'll keep it limited to four on site. You will have full use of an office and communications will be free-flow to your own department. If you prefer to work out of your own offices, I will require regular updates. You'll be busy, so phone or email will be fine. I will assign an officer to work with you though. I have someone in mind, she won't be a spy in your camp, but she will be expected to keep me up to date. She has some seniority so I don't want game play and petty rubbish. Treat her as your second in command." He turned to Howard. "If that's all Sir?"

"Actually, Charles, it's not. Elizabeth and I have a pressing matter." He stood, pressing a button. The door opened and Debbie stood in the doorway. "Gentlemen, my secretary will see you out."

Forester turned to Hodges. "Security will be cleared for your return. I'll have my contact details waiting." He shook both men's hands.

The door closed and the atmosphere was tense. He knew Howard would be reeling, but he also knew the man was too proud to make an issue of it.

"Problem?" Forester asked.

"Sit down, Charles." Howard looked at Chalmers. "Do you want to lead?"

"We…" she started. "We have a security breach."

"How bad?"

"Bad," Howard said.

"Spit it out then."

"A pattern emerged. It may well have been missed but we were running a new algorithm on the system and it flagged up a few worrying discrepancies. An analyst on the middle-east desk pulled unrelated files. Only once, but he ran them and downloaded."

"But downloads flag up."

"They do," Chalmers said. "But he downloaded and re-set the system. Tech are on it, but even they're not sure how he did it yet. If it wasn't for the new programme sweep, it may well have gone unnoticed."

"Domestic or foreign desk?"

"Domestic."

"What were the unrelated files?"

Chalmers glanced at Howard then back at her opposite number. "Personnel. UC's and handlers."

"Undercover operatives," Forester's head swam. "Do we know how much was downloaded?"

Howard shook his head. "Enough. Those dead operatives discovered last night... their names were on it."

7

Forester had moved quickly. He was reeling. Chalmers and Howard had sat on the situation and time was of the essence. The analyst concerned had been signed off sick by his doctor and admin were duty bound to allow him seven days' sick leave before sending out a medical assessor. The man had not re-entered MI5 headquarters since the day he was traced to opening and downloading the file in question. That was three days ago, and Forester had a feeling he would not be seeing him in the near future.

He had used his mobile phone as he walked briskly from Howard's office and set surveillance in place. It was a single watcher unit and they would not have had the time to build in a decent surveillance cover scenario such as roadworks, doorstep market research or commandeering a property to watch from. However, MI5 had the best watchers in the world and it would not take them long to get up to speed.

Next, Forester put an agent on to the target to bring him in. The agent would need either the new Joint Intelligence Committee's non-case built (reactionary) arrest warrant, or as MI5 has no singular power of arrest, a police unit, in this case Special Branch, would assist. Forester cringed at the protocols. Operating in MI5 within the UK was akin to swimming in treacle. This year his department had halted six terrorist attacks, but it was only a matter of time before they lost ground and another nine-eleven, or seven-seven shook Britain. Of the recent six thwarted attempts only two arrest warrants were issued and the Crown Prosecution Service deemed only one as a successful prosecution, involving three men – all of Syrian decent who held fake Belgian and Swedish passports, which meant twenty-one known Jihadists with intent were free to walk around the country with impunity. Forester was painfully aware how little had been achieved by so much work. It sickened him.

***

The woman was dark skinned. A natural Mediterranean tan that you could not buy in a tanning parlour or spa. Her hair was as black as jet and hung loosely just past her shoulders. She had recently had it styled in an expensive salon. The kind of establishment where the Prosecco was free-flowing and the staff were no older than twenty-five, all of whom styled each other's hair daily before opening. She enjoyed the experience and relished being worked on by a stylist who was at the peak of their game and culture and was not ten years behind fashion like her home country. Not that defining her home country was easy. She was originally from Ukraine, but her family had moved to Chechnya to be with cousins and start a business venture. Upon reaching adulthood she had moved to Moscow and then to Georgia where she had initially enjoyed her time beside the Black Sea, the poor man's Mediterranean some called it. But the rich there were far from poor and she had seen and lived the fast life, and seen and lived the hard life too. Those early days at the coast were fun and refreshing, but soon changed. She had been introduced to sex for cash, sex for drugs and sex for survival. She had been so sure that she would die on that stretch of coastline where billionaires ruled and where the poor served and gave all they had. Until she had met a man. Yes, he had used and abused her and yes, he had been no different at first from the men she was forced to sleep with and escort to the casinos and nightclubs, but in time he had saved her. He had taken her away, cleaned her from her cocaine habit and shown her more than she could ever have dreamed of. An ideology, a reason for being. An ideal which would not judge her harshly of her past and expect no more than all of her future. But it would give her meaning and enlightenment along the path she had chosen and to her at that time, and now, that meant everything.

She had learned how to dress and it showed as she walked along the street, the damp air threatening to cling to her hair, but she was near her destination and she would flick her hair dry when she got there to avoid the frizz. She wore knee-length tan leather boots and dark sheer tights. Her skirt was suede and rode just above her knees. Her sweater was thin, cashmere and cream. It rolled high to her neck, but shaped well over her ample breasts. She wore a silk poncho style wrap over her shoulders and carried a medium sized leather bag. She would not have looked out of place in Chelsea or Knightsbridge, at a charity event or stepping out of a Bentley for some lunch at a celebrity chef's restaurant.

She was due to meet for sex in a few minutes. Sometimes she enjoyed the sex of course, on a physical level, but emotionally she needed to prepare. She had left that life behind, but she knew she had to make sacrifices also. Everyone with the cause had, and would. She had not wanted this mission, but she was not to choose. She had always made their assignations convincing, choosing to shower first and dress well, even wearing expensive silk or satin underwear. She was completing the illusion and she had needed to be as convincing and appear as willing and genuinely involved in the affair as it was possible to be. The saving grace was she had insisted on using protection, and that barrier not only gave her control but the ability to compartmentalise the intimacy also. In her mind, because of this, the act of sex had become exactly that. An act.

She crossed the road and turned into Lexington Avenue, just off Soho. She had heard that this had been a rough and cheap part of London, but as she looked at the houses, many converted into flats and apartments, she wondered if the real estate market had changed with heavy investment, or maybe these people should go live in Ukraine or Chechnya and see what rough and cheap really was.

She noticed the white van parked ahead. It was smart and clean and did not have roof racks. That meant it was not a builder's van, or any other tradesman for that matter. She kept walking, noticed the man in the driver's seat. He was dressed in a polo shirt and trousers. Neat, tidy and clean. Most probably a delivery driver. She checked for sign writing, but the vehicle was plain. Sometimes delivery drivers hire vans for various reasons. Either they have a lot of miles to cover and a lot of drops so put the wear, tear and mileage on somebody else's vehicle. Or sometimes their own van is in the garage for work or servicing. Either way, that could explain the vehicle. But what about the man? Delivery drivers have a reputation for driving too fast and parking where they shouldn't to make drops and many delivering internet purchases get paid barely a pound per drop so time is money and they are frenetic – always on to the next drop as fast as possible. They didn't tend to take long breaks to read a newspaper.

She kept walking. Past the building she was heading for and onwards up the street without pausing or glancing. Ahead of her two men were sitting in a Vauxhall Insignia saloon. Both watched the building she had just passed. She slowed her pace and casually took out her mobile phone. She faked thumbing the keypad as she walked past and took a picture of the car, its number plate and the two men in the front seats. She chuckled as she walked alongside, smiling at an apparent text or *Facebook* post. Both men watched her, men always did, but she did not so much as glance at them. Her heart was pounding. It had been close, but her training had given her the edge. It always did.

***

Caroline Darby rode with the sergeant from Special Branch. She kept her window rolled down, avoiding the smoke from another of his cigarettes. She didn't complain. She would always be the outsider; she didn't want to create more problems. Special Branch and the Security Service had to work together daily.

The man was forty-five, balding and had gained a beer gut since she had last seen him. She did not know him well, but he had been on arrests similar to this in the past. He was a good officer, but aging fast. She knew he drank a lot after each shift, and he was smoking incessantly. He was old school too and she had seen him punch first and ask questions later. She doubted he would make retirement age smoothly.

"Your watchers are facing us in a Vauxhall, ours are in a van and we have eyes on across the street in an empty house."

"Fast work," Caroline said.

"It's up for lease, we established it's empty and borrowed it for the day," the officer said. He was Welsh, heavily accented. He smiled at her and flicked his cigarette butt out of the window. "Skeleton key entry, nobody will ever know."

"Nice."

"So how are we playing it?"

Caroline had been ordered to take the lead. The target was an MI5 employee and she was there to keep control of the situation. If the target protested about an internal interview, then Special Branch would make the arrest. Personally she hoped it could stay informal. She could bring him back to headquarters without him lawyering up. Forester had mused that this would be the preferred option. "Stay back, we'll keep surveillance in place. See how it pans out, I'll call you over if I decide to make the arrest. Then I'll need you to transport both of us to the yard." New Scotland Yard Anti-Terrorist Department was where these sort of arrests were processed and the suspects held.

"Righty-ho," he said. He brought the car into a double space near the Special Branch van.

Caroline noted he left plenty of space in front of the car and turned the wheels outwards, almost at full lock. It shaved seconds off a fast getaway. The man looked like he was going to seed, but he was still sharp enough.

***

The dark-skinned woman had taken refuge in a coffee shop on Beak Street. She had ordered a vanilla Espresso. She sipped the strong caffeine hit and took out her smartphone. She dialled the number from memory. Her phone held no numbers in its phonebook. She deleted all texts and call history after each call. Like she had been taught.

"Yes."

"General, it's Alesha."

"Yes."

"I went to meet him. There is a problem," she hesitated. "He is under surveillance."

"Whose?"

"His own, I think."

"Good. We are done with him."

"What shall I do?"

"Where are you?"

"Coffee Grinds, a Starbucks style place on Beak Street."

"All right. I am sending you someone. Eliminate him."

"But… he is under surveillance."

"It is time to step things up. Eliminate them also. We will send them a message."

Alesha felt the blood run to her loins. She crossed her legs - excitement, anticipation threatening to overwhelm her. She glanced at the barista behind the counter but he was working on an order. She leaned forwards. "How do you want it done?" she whispered, trembling with excitement, urging him to go into detail.

"Brutally…" The line went dead.

Alesha pressed the call end icon and tossed the phone into her open handbag. She cursed loudly. He knew what it did to her, knew how she enjoyed the thought of it. It was purely sexual, a desire. She loved to kill, loved the sensation of all-empowering domination. To kill someone begging for their life was her ultimate fantasy. She could orgasm to the thought of it, the discussion of it. She had fulfilled this fantasy. The night she had killed the man who had turned her into a drug addict and sex slave on the Black Sea coast. Ridden him to climax and plunged a knife deep into his neck, watching him choke and drown in his own blood as she had writhed and shuddered in dizzying heights of pleasure.

***

Jeremy Hoist was forty and single. He was pale and out of shape. He had a shock of ginger hair which could not be styled and was now starting to recede. His teeth were crooked and his chin was weak. He once tried to grow a goatee to hide the weak chin, but this had grown through pinkish and wispy. He had shaved it off, creating office banter and more ridicule. Needless to say, Hoist was not a player in the dating game. He had never had a girlfriend. Not a proper one at least. He was often in the friend zone, a shoulder to cry on and occasionally, usually after lots of alcohol, he had managed a one-night stand. These dalliances always ended in disaster, with the friend zone closed also. His circle of friends had diminished, many getting married or into serious relationships and by his mid-thirties most of the people he knew had children and had entered into different circles of friendship. He was now finding himself on the fringes of everyone else's lives. Invites to gatherings dwindled, then halted altogether. He tried internet dating, speed dating, lonely hearts, but he was a realist. He was exceptionally ugly and if he was honest, he hadn't cultivated a personality to compensate.

But Veruschka had changed everything. She was stunning. How could she be attracted to him? It didn't make sense. But of course, it did. He had known early on. What he lacked in looks and personality he made up for in intelligence. He had been recruited in university. His IQ was exceptional and British intelligence wanted people like him to keep the seats behind the desks warm and analyse and interpret the data.

He knew, or rather he suspected he was being manipulated from the very beginning, but he was also with the most beautiful, the most sensual woman he could ever imagine. A man with no friends, no life outside of work, a man forced to buy sex once a month after payday from a brothel near his home. At first he used snippets of information and his work at MI5 as a hook for Veruschka. He wanted to be important and admired. He thought he could control it, manipulate the data, but he was weak and the people were clever. Not IQ clever, just deviously smart. Before long Hoist had been introduced to Veruschka's uncle. Hoist knew that the man wasn't her uncle. He knew that they were more intimate than that. It enraged him at first, sickened him, but he moved past it quickly. As long as he could be intimate with her, he could forgive, forget or at least be oblivious to it. She must have genuinely liked him – she was so convincingly passionate.

Her uncle went by the name of Vladimir. Hoist did not know if that was his real name or not. He suspected so. He was an old man, but fit and smart and Hoist suspected he was ex-military. Vladimir was quite specific in his demands and expectations. He wanted certain information and he was clear what would happen if he did not receive it. He had many of the couple's assignations recorded on both film and audio. When played back, perhaps edited to a degree, the evidence was damning. Hoist was a traitor. Plain and simple. He was also a poor lover on film, a fact that he rather curiously was less keen on being made public than his treachery towards the Security Service and his country.

Hoist sat in his bath robe. He had showered. Veruschka always insisted upon it. He had used aftershave and deodorant also. He hated this part. He knew what he was doing was wrong. But it was like a drug. He could not resist her. He looked at his watch. She was late. Unusually late. He had given them the ultimate information. Had he been discarded?

The doorbell rang and he flinched. He got up and walked excitedly downstairs to the door. The flat was a maisonette. He kept his bicycle next to the door and there was a cloakroom adjacent to the stairs. He opened the door and recoiled as it was pushed inwards. The woman stood there, most of her body in the doorway.

"Caroline Darby," she said. "General Intelligence Group. You know why I'm here."

"Oh shit…"

"Exactly right," she said. "Are you going to talk to me, or do I get my Special Branch pal here to take you down to the yard?"

Hoist looked broken. He swayed, his bath robe opening in the breeze through the open door. "I… I…"

"Cover yourself up. Christ, it must be cold. Get back upstairs," she said, turning to the Special Branch officer she nodded. "Come on in. Get a brew going while he gets himself dressed."

Caroline climbed the stairs behind Hoist. When she reached the top Hoist was standing meekly by his open bedroom door. She pushed past him, looked around the room, checked the wardrobe. "Anybody else in here with you?" she asked, walking back onto the landing. "Anything here I should know about?"

"No," he replied docilely. "I'm alone."

"Get dressed. Don't be alarmed, I'm going to watch," she said. "So make it bloody quick."

***

Alesha looked at the man beside her. He was thin, hard-looking and dark. She did not know much about him except that his name was Betesh, he was a Yemeni by birth but grew up in Birmingham and he had been fighting for ISIS in Syria. He never looked her in the eye and she was sure that he hated her. She recognised that he had a problem with women in authority and she relished the chance to demean him.

"I want you to go in first," she said. "Don't kill him. Just subdue him."

"What will you be doing while I do this?"

"I will be sending a message to British intelligence."

"How?"

"You'll know when you hear it," she said. She checked over the Scorpion machine pistol. It looked like a child's toy bought from a beach shop next to the buckets and spades. It was tiny, chambered the 7.65mm pistol cartridge and held twenty rounds in its magazine.

"The General said that the British pig should die," Betesh said. "He was to be of further use to us, but now that they are on to him he wants him silenced. Why do you just want me to subdue him?"

Alesha smiled. "I have had to sleep with that pig, as you put it," she grimaced. "I want to cut off his balls before I kill him."

Betesh shrugged. Nothing could shock him, he had butchered children in Syria. He checked his Makarov 9mm pistol and tucked it into his jacket pocket. It was a compact weapon, an old Soviet copy of the Walther PP.

Alesha felt a wave of elation flood over her. She crossed her legs and took a steadying breath. She had wanted this for a long time. It would be brutal.

8

Kazan, Russia

The room was dark. A single lightbulb hung from a ceiling rose high above the man's head. He was seated on a wooden chair. His ankles were taped to the chair legs; his hands were bound with the same tape behind his back. Urine, blood and faeces pooled on the floor. Under the chair a grate would take it to the open drain after the room had been sluiced.

The man had been beaten and systematically tortured for sixteen hours. There was a skill to extracting information and that skill had been practised and learned over years. It wasn't the infliction of pain that was difficult, it was reading the signs, extracting the information in the right order and piecing it together. Naturally the prisoner would lie. And those lies could be broken down and replaced by the truth, but only after the correct amount of persuasion had been applied. There was a point that the lies would contradict. All the interrogations would be recorded and the answers cross-referenced. Sleep deprivation was key to this and combined with hunger, thirst and pain – as well as the fear of more pain to come – as long as they were delivered in the correct order, the formula of interrogation, the truth would out. It did not matter how strong, tough or experienced a prisoner was, the formula would always work. The only variable factor was time.

Unfortunately for the interrogator there was a set precedence with the prisoner that he had not expected. The prisoner in question was an eighty-year old man. He was former KGB and he had written the book on interrogation. He knew the tricks and he knew that the interrogator knew this too. He had almost reached the end of his life, and he was in very real danger of dying in this very room. His heart was weak. Yevgeny Antakov was near the end and the interrogator knew it.

The interrogator was a GRU major in his late thirties. He was tall and thin and his dark hair was cropped close to hide the fact that he was balding. He was a member of the Special Operations and Security Group. A secretive wing of army intelligence with a remit that ended at the president's office. The group did not recognise borders. It operated in the shadows and respected no law which stood in the way of its operations.

"Yevgeny?" The man nudged the prisoner's shoulder. He looked at the file as the prisoner tensed. "So tell me about the warhead again."

"I told you…" he was cut off as the man slapped him across the face. "All right! The warhead was sold to a syndicate of the St. Petersburg mafia. The Bratva Brotherhood."

"And who sold it?"

"Colonel Afansy. The 343rd Armoured Brigade in Odessa. He was dealt with. Permanently."

"By whom?"

"I told you…" Again he stopped as the man slapped his face. He reeled backwards. "Stop it! I am co-operating!"

The interrogator slapped him again. "You will show respect and you will answer my questions," he said calmly. "Understand?"

Yevgeny Antakov shook his head and smiled. "You do not know what I have done for Mother Russia. For the Union when we were once a great nation." He swayed a little as he said this, his eyes blurring.

The major held his head firmly and pulled up the prisoner's eyelid. He looked at the eye. He knew the life was leaving this old man. He needed him to hang on a little while longer. He bent down and picked up a bottle of water. "You want this?" He opened it and poured a little onto the man's forehead. "You want a drink?" Yevgeny nodded and the major poured some over his mouth. The man lapped at it, like a dog under a garden tap. "That's good, yes?" He took the bottle away and opened the file. He took out a picture of a young woman of about nineteen. He placed the photograph on the prisoner's lap and watched his face. He saw the flicker in the man's eyes, noted his breathing. There had been a sharper intake of breath for sure. "Your granddaughter has recently moved to America. A place at Yale university. I am sure you are proud, no?"

Yevgeny looked up at him. He knew where the talk was going, he had taken people down the same road many times. "Please…"

"I know a man in Boston. He could be with your granddaughter within two hours," the major said. "It's a small world, you know? Did you hear there are lots of rapes and murders in Massachusetts?"

For the first time since he had been taken, perhaps the first time ever, Yevgeny Antakov looked defeated. He knew he would never be free again, knew he may well be shot later this very night – his body crudely disposed of under the very forest floor he had filled during his time with the KGB. But he also knew if he could satisfy this man before him, he would save his granddaughter, his beautiful Anya. A tear trickled down his cheek as he thought of her. How he had bounced her on his knee as a baby, repeatedly thrown her high in the air as a toddler, watched her walk excitedly towards him for the first time, taught her to ride a bicycle, bought her a pony for her eighth birthday. If he gave everything he knew, convincingly, she would be safe. They would not harm her if they had what they wanted. There was no point in risking a vendetta he would not be alive to see or know about.

"Okay," he said. "I will tell you everything. But I would like a drink and something to eat first. I need my medication also… If you want me alive long enough, you will get these things for me."

"Very well," the major said and nodded towards the two-way reinforced mirror on the wall. A subordinate would see to this. He looked back at the prisoner. "You said that the warhead was from an SS-27 Topol M. This is good, this tallies with what was missing in the manifest. It is a mobile launcher. It fits in with Colonel Afansy and his service with the 343rd Armoured Brigade. I am pleased with your answer, Yevgeny. Now, tell me about former General Vladimir Zukovsky. Did you know he was a Chechen Muslim?"

"I did not."

"The man served the Soviet Union for over twenty-five years. Ten of those years were spent fighting

Mujahedeen in Afghanistan," he paused. "Fellow Muslims."

"Nobody could have known."

"His troops suffered many defeats in Afghanistan. Maybe these were not clear cut battles. I imagine that he instigated these defeats. A sympathiser of the enemy, a traitor within our own camp."

Yevgeny shrugged. "I did not know. It would make sense, now that you have told me."

"And you did not suspect that the warhead you hatched a plan to detonate in the Ukraine would instead be targeted against the west?"

"Absolutely not!"

"You were friends with Zukovsky. He was at your wedding!" The major looked up as a corporal entered carrying a tray. There was bottled water and bread and cured meat on a plate. He waved the man in and motioned for him to put the tray down on the floor. It rested near the blood and faeces and urine. "So you planned to detonate this device in Ukraine? For what ends?"

"To show that if we cannot take back Ukraine then we will leave them with nothing." Yevgeny Antakov scowled. "We are weak. Our young all want to be popstars or reality whores. The rich buy up London and own soccer clubs. They bask on billion dollar yachts in the south of France or Monaco. They take their money out of Russia and spend it all over the world. We have lost what we stood for. Vladimir Zukovsky was supposed to send a message to the world. Russia will not be toyed with. If we were not going to fight hard to get back the Ukraine, then those ungrateful dogs could melt and die there. Like Chernobyl in the north, the Ukraine would be rendered useless."

The major looked at the old man in front of him. "So Vladimir has the warhead from the SS-27 Topol M, financial independence from funds you gave him – Russian funds from old KGB accounts - and a new target. And you don't know what this target is. But you know who he was working with, don't you?"

"No, I do not."

"Oh, I think you do," he looked at the photograph again. "She has pretty eyes, Yevgeny. Maybe I can have them sent over for you to look at before you die."

9

Caroline Darby flinched at the sound of gunfire. It was a momentary reaction, but she had crouched down on the floor in the doorway of the lounge. She looked at the Special Branch officer, who had spilt his mug of tea and was looking for a place to put it. Realising the absurdity, he dropped it onto the floor and ducked down, drawing the Smith & Wesson Sigma pistol and training it on the top of the stairs.

Caroline got to her feet and made her way swiftly to the window. She looked down, then turned to the Special Branch officer as another volley of gunfire erupted. "Contact! We're being hit!" She took her mobile phone out of her pocket and started to dial.

"That's a fucking machinegun!" The officer shouted.

The door at the bottom of the stairs crashed open and the officer edged around the door frame and peered down the stairs. There were gunshots and he recoiled back, regained composure and fired three return shots. There was another exchange and Caroline could hear shouting. The intruder was screaming, but it did not register at first that it was in Arabic. Caroline was learning Farsi. But the man shouted so fast, she could only pick out the odd word. She turned to Hoist, who was standing in the bedroom doorway. He had been tucking in his shirt and had frozen with his hand down the front of his trousers.

"Get down!" she shouted. She held the phone to her ear. She was through to the MI5 switchboard. "Come on!" she yelled into the phone as she listened to the list of options.

The stairwell echoed with heavy footsteps. Caroline looked over at the Special Branch officer, who was laying on his back. His feet were moving, twitching, but she could see the ragged bullet hole in his forehead, his eyes looking blankly at her. She half sprinted, half threw herself across the lounge to the landing and went straight for the pistol on the floor. She was aware of a shadow cast over her, but she had the weapon in her hand as she turned over and fell down onto her back, her legs on top of the dead officer's torso. The intruder was at the top of the stairs, his feet almost touching her own. He aimed the pistol downwards as she aimed hers up into his face and fired, one, two, three, four, five shots... She lost count, wasn't sure how many had hit, but she had hit. The top of the man's head was over most of the ceiling and great chunks of plaster had been blown out and dropped like a snow flurry. The man had crumpled on the top stair tread. Caroline kept the weapon trained on him and got to her feet.

She lowered the pistol and turned towards Hoist, but was showered in plaster dust and debris as the machine pistol erupted at the bottom of the stairs. She screamed and lurched into the lounge. She dropped the magazine partially into her palm, checking the inspection holes. Somewhere between nine and twelve rounds remaining. She slammed the magazine back into the butt and turned toward the stairs. She could hear footsteps. Slow and tentative. She looked at the plaster wall. Bullet holes clustered near the top of the stairs, they had penetrated through the studwork. Caroline aimed at the wall and fired four shots, spacing a foot or so in between each one, dropping the aim point each time. She heard a woman's scream and could tell she had cursed loudly. Swearing was universal. You didn't have to understand, but it sounded Slavic or Russian.

There was a long sustained burst of fire and to Caroline's horror the Special Branch officer's body was shuddering under the impact of bullets. Blood and splatter hit the wall and open bathroom door and as a final insult, the officer's head and face disappeared in a pinkish mist. Caroline heard a howl, a shrill scream of almost sensual pleasure and sudden bounding footsteps. The silence which followed was eerie. Caroline knew she had four or five shots left and kept the weapon trained on the top of the stairs. She was shaking slightly, she remembered she hadn't breathed in ages and took a deep calming breath. The weapon shook a little less, but by now she knew the threat had gone.

***

Alesha cursed all the way down the street. She tossed the empty weapon into an open refuse bin as she walked past and then crossed over the road. Betesh still had the keys to the van in his pocket and she could already hear the sirens and traffic in the distance. She had a small window of opportunity to escape and she kept up a fast pace. She took off the gloves she had been wearing and balled them up, dropping them into a service alley beside a vacant shop. She got her smartphone out of her pocket and was already scrolling down her phone to dial. For a moment she could not remember the number and it infuriated her further. As usual she had deleted the last call after leaving the coffee shop, but the sudden rush of adrenalin was affecting her mind. She needed to call Zukovsky and when she attempted, she had misdialled. She continued, her pace fast enough to be overtaking people as she made her way towards Regent's Street. Her plan was to get to a department store and lose herself for a while amongst the shoppers.

On her third attempt she got through. "There's been a problem!"

"Go on."

"I took out both surveillance teams. Two men in a car and two men in a van. Betesh allowed the target to escape," she lied.

"Are you following?"

"No."

"Why the Hell not?"

"Betesh is dead. The keys to the van are on his body."

"So go back and get them. The van is hired. They will connect the dots."

"I have had to get out of the area, the police are on the way."

"Is the target still there?"

Alesha hesitated. "The target is still there, but he has armed protection. I have no more ammunition and I've disposed of my weapon." The line went dead and Alesha cursed loudly in Russian.

10

Charles Forester entered the house and stood to one side as a Scotland Yard SOCO technician clad in white coveralls and wearing a surgical style face mask brushed past him.

Detective Inspector Hodges caught the officer's arm and flashed his warrant card. "All right to go in?" he asked.

The officer pulled the mask down. "Coroner is up there with the second body," he paused. "Just don't touch anything. There's not much to do, it's pretty cut and dry, but we don't want bullet casings or fragments picked up just yet."

Forester nodded at the officer, then turned to Hodges and beckoned him up the stairs. Caroline was at the top. The Special Branch officer was in a body bag on a gurney with retractable legs. Caroline had handed the weapon over to the SOCO team, an armed support officer was standing in the bedroom doorway, his Heckler & Koch MP5 machine carbine held against his chest. Forester turned to the coroner. "I don't care about logistics, but the Special Branch officer does not ride back with the perpetrator. Okay?" The coroner nodded. Forester turned to his agent. "How are you holding up, Caroline?"

"I'm okay, Sir." She sipped some tea from her mug. She looked shaken.

"You did well, from what I hear. The SCO19 commander said he'd have you on his team any day," he smiled. "Did you get a look at the second gunman?"

"No. It was a woman though, I heard her. Russian or Slavic."

Forester turned to Hodges. "Detective, this is Caroline Darby, one of my top officers. Caroline, this is Detective Inspector Hodges. He's with the Met and he's assigned to us for the next few days at least. We've had another incident. I couldn't help think this may well be connected in some way."

"Serious?"

Forester nodded. "Four dead officers from GIG."

"Oh my God!" Caroline exclaimed. She was General Intelligence Group. She would know some if not all the officers.

"How did it go down?" Hodges asked.

Caroline looked at Forester hesitantly. Forester nodded. Caroline turned to the detective. "Special Branch had two men in a van parked fifty metres south of here. One was in the back of the van using a portal telescopic camera, the other was eyes on in the front. We had two watchers from domestic security in a car forty metres north of here on the same side of the road. I was in here with the SB officer. We heard gunshots, fully automatic small arms fire, I caught sight of the SB van getting pummelled. I couldn't see the shooter, but the rounds were tearing through the windscreen and side panel. There was blood all over the windscreen. Christ knows what it looked like in there." Forester and Hodges had seen; they'd seen the MI5 vehicle as well. Both remained silent. "The door downstairs was kicked in and then there was gunfire, I didn't see the SB officer get hit, I was dialling headquarters, but I got the first intruder." She didn't elaborate, taking another sip of tea. "I didn't see the next attacker. She had a machine pistol of some kind. She tore the place up, I fired through the wall as she came up the stairs. I either grazed her or came extremely close because she screamed and swore and charged back down the stairs. She's a vicious bitch though," Caroline shook her head. "What she did then was awful. Just shot the body of the SB officer all to pieces."

"Anything else?" Hodges asked.

"She got off on it," Caroline paused. "It was weird, she was screaming in pleasure, like, well you know, almost sexual."

"Never heard that before," Hodges said grimly.

Forester looked at Caroline. "Where's Hoist?"

"He's having a lie down."

Forester looked around the tiny flat and strode off toward the bedroom. The SCO19 officer stood aside and Forester walked in. "Get up!"

Jeremy Hoist looked at him. He was shocked at the entrance of the Deputy Director of the Security Service. He swung his legs over the bed and rose unsteadily to his feet. "I'm, I'm sorry," he said meekly.

"We're going to a safe house. Some big, tough men will be asking you a lot of questions. Expect it to be an uncomfortable experience."

"I want a solicitor," he said.

"Fine. Special Branch are downstairs and will make the arrest formally. You will be assigned a lawyer if you cannot afford one, but he or she will be a duty solicitor so not good enough to run their own practice or make partner, and they will be very concerned about entering into a defence against treason, terrorism and mass murder."

"Terrorism? Murder? People came to kill *me*!"

"You downloaded classified data."

"Someone must have logged in using my access code," Hoist interrupted. "It could have been anyone."

"CCTV has been retrieved at the correct time and at the relevant computer," replied Forester. "And people on that classified download have been killed."

"Coincidence."

"Murdered. Together. Four of my agents bound, gagged and drowned. They were your colleagues."

"They never set eyes on me!"

"Priceless. I'll see that little quote gets into the newspapers. I'll see that by the end of your trial the public will be voting to bring back hanging for treason. Since the shootings in Tunisia, Paris and Lyon there has been a surge in the public response to terrorism and you have aided terrorists in this instance."

"I still want a lawyer."

"You'll get one. But first you are going to a safe-house for a national security debrief. I cannot allow anyone else near you for security protocols. Afterwards, you can lawyer up and we'll see that the next five years of your life are a living Hell. With the premeditated murder of four MI5 officers and the deaths of five more police and security service personnel caught up in a situation of your making, you won't get bail. I'll see you rot before trial. I'll get someone on the inside to make your life hell. You'll be buggered daily with nothing more than spit and determination and you'll get beaten senseless every week."

"Look, I..."

"Save it!" Forester turned and walked back out to the lounge where Hodges was drinking a fresh mug of tea. He handed a mug to Forester, who took it and sipped slowly. "Right, Caroline I want you as bodyguard on Hoist. I'll get an officer over to back you up. We'll get him to a safe house. Use number two-twenty-five. I don't want him anywhere near headquarters, and then I'll get a team over to interview him."

"What about protection?" she asked. "Look what just happened here. I'm not going to be a sitting duck again."

Forester nodded. There was no remit for MI5 to carry weapons on mainland British soil. As far as the government was concerned the Security Service was an intelligence gathering agency, not law enforcement. "Armed SB officers will stay with you until we get to the safe house," he said. "I'll arrange for an armed Diplomatic Protection squad once we're in place." Forester's mobile phone rang and he held up a hand to the others as he turned away to take the call.

Caroline turned to Hodges. "So I take it you're on the investigation of the dead officers?"

"I am," he replied.

"Was it bad?"

"Horrendous," he said. "The worst of it is, I don't think we've seen the last of it."

"What makes you say that?"

"It was calculated. It wasn't the work of an individual, and it took time and logistics to execute," he paused, wishing he'd chosen another word. "They needed a boat, they timed it with the tide, they were able to subdue and maintain control on highly trained individuals, but as a group. I think it was a message. I think if it were a case of just wanting intelligence officers dead we would have had bodies on waste ground shot in the head. They orchestrated this perfectly, right down to leaving identification on the bodies. They wanted the bodies and the links to be found quickly and the trail to lead right to MI5," he paused. "That guy in there," he said, nodding towards Hoist in the bedroom. "He's a pawn in a much larger game. Today he was of no further use to them. Whether having him under surveillance forced their hand, or whether it was just the right time, we probably won't know. One thing for sure though, they'll try to kill him again. You should be aware of that."

Caroline nodded. She feared as much.

Forester returned to them, his face ashen. "I have to go," he said.

"Problem?" Caroline offered.

"Always," he said. "But not part of this investigation. I have to return to headquarters for a meeting." He looked at Hodges. "Inspector, my resources are yours. You're cleared at headquarters. We have to assume that the agents killed at the quay are because of the stolen data and that this massacre here today was connected. It's too big a coincidence. Special Branch have video from across the street of the attack here, they are running it through CCTV as we speak. I won't be able to hold them off. They will want this investigation now that three of their own are dead, but we cannot risk the investigation becoming segregated. We need a free-flow of data or we'll be working against each other."

"Forester!" A man stood at the top of the stairs. He wore an expensive suit and stylish black leather shoes shined to a mirror finish and a Special Branch ID card hung around his neck on a lanyard. He walked over, a semi-folded laptop in his hands, his fingers preventing it from closing like a well-read book. "Look at this. It's a download of the footage outside, taken from across the street in the house we commandeered. Going to bloody come out now that this lot has happened. I guess we can look forward to a break in and entry, trespass, God knows what else."

"Go on," Forester said tersely. This man was a police politician, their paths had crossed many times.

The man placed the laptop on the coffee table and the four of them crouched down to get a closer look. "I must warn you, it's pretty grim viewing," he paused, looking at Caroline. "You might not want to watch this."

"Piss off," she said and took a sip of tea.

Forester smiled. "This is agent Caroline Darby. She killed the gunman," he paused. "With your dead officer's weapon. It fared better in her capable hands."

"Okay, okay, I'm sorry. Davies was a bloody good officer." He held up his hands. "Let's all take a breath; it's been awful for everybody."

"Just play it," Forester said.

The Special Branch officer pressed play on the MVI file and the film started to roll. The sound of automatic gunfire was clearly audible and the footage blurred and shook as whoever was operating the camera moved it and focused in on the source of the noise. The sound of swearing and disbelief of the cameraman was continuous. The man Caroline killed was already walking out of frame, but the image of the woman was crystal clear. She was above average height, slim and well proportioned. Her skin was well tanned, olive and her hair was jet black and she had tied it back in a thick and heavy ponytail. She wore tan leather boots, a brown suede skirt to just above the knee and a cream sweater, the poncho wrap wafted in the breeze, as she casually turned and walked away from the shattered car and calmly changed over the magazine in the tiny machine pistol. She walked towards the van, casually working the action on the weapon to chamber the next round in the magazine of twenty. The door of the white van partially opened, then the driver looked to have second thoughts. It was easy to imagine the driver frantically attempting to start the engine. Easy to imagine the driver fumbling the ignition, forgetting the start-up procedure, failing to get the van started as the woman with the machine pistol drew ever closer. The tiny machine pistol spat out a flame two feet clear of the muzzle of the barrel. Again, a casual and professional magazine change and then the shots came in bursts of three or four as she worked the bullets into the body of the driver and then shot a continuous line down the length of the panel, slicing the unfortunate soul in the back to pieces. The woman turned and walked to the entrance of the building, her back to the camera now, but it was clear she was changing to yet another magazine. The sounds of Special

Branch officers fumbling for phones, swearing in disbelief and generally shouting what they should do was all the sound that could be heard. There was a faint tapping sound of the multiple gunshots fired inside, and after a minute the woman came running out of the house. The camera operator kept the frame on her for as long as he could and called out a thorough description of her for the sake of the recording. It was a professional detail by a man clearly in shock, but starting to compose himself after witnessing such barbarity.

"We've got this footage emailed over to headquarters and we're pulling all the CCTV in the area as we speak. All of the borough's traffic cameras have been requisitioned and I've got bodies at desks going through it all."

"We need to ascertain how they got here," Hodges said. "Have you checked the body for keys? The woman had pretty chunky heels. I doubt she drove. Could mean their vehicle is still nearby."

"Good thinking," Forester said. He looked at the Special Branch officer. "Commander Anderson, can you get uniform on to that? We're done here, we need to get the asset out and question him."

"I want in on that," Anderson said. "I'll get uniform directed on to searching for a vehicle, let me know where you're interviewing him." He folded his laptop and walked towards the stairs.

"Anderson, I'll need a copy of that film," Forester said.

"Of course," he replied without turning round.

"I have a bad feeling we're going to get in a tangle with this," Caroline said. "The Security Service and Special Branch have never been so closely involved as this. They are going to be on a crusade for their officers, we don't want to lose our dominance with the investigation," she paused, looking at Hodges. "No offence, but we've got the Met in on this too and it's all connected."

"No offence taken," Hodges replied. "I've got a thick file of murder cases to work on. Take the pier killings if you want. I'm here by request. I won't be sitting back and twiddling my thumbs if I'm not needed anymore."

"No," Forester said. "I want you to see this through, for the sake of my dead agents. I think we'll do better with you leading the murder investigation. I want these bastards. I want them brought to justice and I want them now."

11

Mohammed Betesh was four years older than his brother Rafan. Rafan meant beautiful, graceful and it had been no secret that their mother had doted on the youngest of the three brothers, despite the belief that the first born was always the favourite. Mohammed had never borne his brother contempt, instead he had taken the role of his brother's protector initially to win favour with his mother. Now, as the tears trickled down his pock-marked, battle scared face he knew he had failed, and his mother's love would be lost. He was the last Betesh brother. His other brother, the middle brother Jamil had been killed in Iraq by an infidel sniper a year ago.

His right hand held the pistol grip of the AK 47 assault rifle. It comforted him. It was a folding stock model, and fitted beside him in the foot-well perfectly. He had taped three magazines together to speed up his reloads. He was looking forward to using it.

He watched the comings and goings from the end of the street. The police had walked towards him and he had considered moving, but they had opened the van sixty metres in front of him with a key fob and now the vehicle was the centre of attention. The crime scene police were now dusting it for prints and uniformed officers were making calls. How he wished he could step out of the van right now and hose them down like he had those worthless, godless souls in France. He had bought them terror in Lyon like his Muslim brothers had in

Paris. And all France had done in return was bomb his heroic brothers in Syria and strengthen their resolve, keep the fight going.

He had watched the two men in suits leave the house. The taller man was clearly in charge and spoke with both high-ranking uniformed officers, the coroner and another man in a suit. They had both left in a black Jaguar saloon which had been driven by a driver who had waited with the car. The coroner's ambulance had left and was replaced briefly by another. A gurney operated by two men was wheeled out of the building, across the pavement and into the ambulance. Mohammed Betesh almost wailed as the vehicle drove away and on past him. Was his brother inside? He was in one of the vehicles for sure. He thanked God that his brother had not shared the same journey with the godless British pig he had slaughtered. He cursed Alesha at once. She had fled for her life. She should have stayed and ended the fight. She was a Russian whore and she was not a true believer. She was *kafir*. General Zukovsky was her mentor and he was a Chechen Muslim, a fellow brother. He had hidden his beliefs within a lifetime of service in the Soviet and later Russian military. He had risen to the top, but had served his Muslim brothers well. He was the ultimate undercover saboteur inside a regime which once permitted no religion at all. But his fascination with this Russian whore was a weakness. She served *him*, not an ideal. The hold he had on her was total, but her resolve was not stoic. She had too high a leaning towards self-preservation. Zukovsky had convinced his men that she was a true believer and that she would make her own sacrifices for their cause. Only now, knowing she was in fact safe and that his dear brother Rafan lay dead and cold destined for a coroner's slab, he was not so sure. He would not receive his sharia funeral, his *janazah*. His body would not be bathed, no *kafan* would wrap his body. He grimaced at the thought that he may be cremated now that nobody would ever come forward to claim his body. *Damn that bitch! Damn that bitch for fleeing without him!*

Mohammed watched the woman leave the house. She was tall, slim and wore her blonde hair tied in a ponytail. She strode confidently outside and stood beside a dark blue Vauxhall Insignia which had just pulled into the empty space left by the coroner vehicle. She opened the rear door and Jeremy Hoist walked meekly across the pavement and ducked inside the car. The woman followed him and closed the door. A passenger sat beside the driver. The car moved swiftly off and Mohammed tensed as it drove on past. He started the van and waited for the car to disappear from view before he pulled a three-point turn and followed. He knew that the end of the road was a no right turn and he could afford to lose sight for a few minutes.

He dialled on his voice activated mobile phone. "Call Rashid..." The phone dialled and after a few seconds was answered.

"Yes?"

"Coming towards you now. Dark blue Vauxhall Insignia saloon. Two men in the front, both in suits. One woman in the rear, off-side. Blonde hair, ponytail, grey trouser suit. Our target is in the middle seat. Red hair, blue jacket, brown trousers. Another suit in the near-side rear seat…"

"*Registration?*"

"Didn't catch it. Begins LD – I won't guess the rest."

"*It will be enough. They have to come past me.*" Mohammed could hear Rashid's moped revving as he moved off to intercept the car. "*I have them! As you described. I will drop back and call out where we are going, what we are passing. You catch up and pass me to take over if I get too close.*"

Mohammed smiled. Rashid was extremely competent at mobile surveillance. They would not get away from them now that he was on their tail and the moped was the best vehicle of all to use in London's traffic.

The Vauxhall made good progress. It kept to a steady speed and hit the first few lights on amber or green. Which meant at its steady pace just under the speed limit it beat all the lights and barely slowed. The driver was well trained, changing lanes when necessary and watching and reading the road, traffic and obstructions ahead. Rashid kept pace, using large vehicles for cover and joining other motorbikes and mopeds when he could. This helped reduce his profile and anyone carrying out counter surveillance drills would find it more difficult to remember him.

The car wove on through the streets until it passed Hampstead Heath and drove through a series of residential streets. It stopped outside a red bricked detached house in Amblewood Road and both the front and rear passengers and the blonde woman got out and slammed their doors shut. The target got out more slowly, but was escorted swiftly up the driveway by the woman and into the house. The driver of the Vauxhall pulled a three-point-turn and parked, its front at the entrance ensuring nobody would box the vehicle in.

Rashid accelerated past without looking at either the house or the car. He turned left at the end of the road on to Brent Street and took another left. He doubled back on himself, where Mohammed was parked up in the van with its engine still running. He pulled up to the driver's window. "It is the fifth house on the right. The blue Vauxhall is parked facing back this way. If you go down this road and turn right onto Brent Street and then right again onto Amblewood Street, you will be able to do a slow drive past without drawing too much attention."

"Good work, Rashid," he said. He watched the young Pakistani pull away on his moped and followed his instructions. When he turned onto Amblewood he saw the Vauxhall parked up ahead. He crossed the road and parked on the right. As he switched off the ignition he placed his hand on the butt of the AK47 and breathed a deep calming breath. He wanted to shout, to scream, to grieve for his brother. He wanted to avenge his brother's death. He knew he would never know who had killed him, but he knew from which agency they had been sent and that agency was in the house across the street from him protecting the treacherous, godless pig Jeremy Hoist. As soon as he had back-up, he would go in and cut them all to pieces with his assault rifle. He reached inside his jacket pocket and felt the hilt of his *Khanjar*. It was a viciously sharp curved Arabian dagger he had been given in Yemen. If anybody survived the onslaught from the machinegun fire, he would cut their throats slowly.

12

Forester rested his head in his hands. He felt tight-chested, needed air. He pushed himself away from his desk and sat back in his chair. "How many?"

The man across the desk from him was ex-army intelligence. He hadn't always been. He was once a sergeant in the Coldstream Guards. His manner was still clip and no-nonsense. "Twelve," he replied.

"No signs of violence?"

"In two cases they'd put up a fight. Blood, positive DNA but only indicating a bit of a punch up. Not shot, stabbed or slashed."

"And any evidence left by perpetrators?"

"None."

"So they have simply disappeared?"

"Vanished. No demands sent, yet."

"I want this kept quiet. Who else knows?"

"Ms Chalmers, Director Howard," the man paused. "Peters from admin, personnel section. He raised the alarm initially. Plus, two men from my section sent to investigate. David Stern and Devinder Bajway. Forensics were given the blood samples and told to match to MI5 personnel. So I guess they only know about two agents."

"That's about five people and a department too many. I'll speak to the top brass, you get everybody else in and tell them that until further notice they don't speak to anybody. If they have, then now's the time to tell us."

"Sir," the man stood, nodded and left the room.

Forester put his head back in his hands and lent his weight against the desk. His mind was swimming; he was struggling to put together a cohesive chain of thought. The white telephone on his desk rang. The interdepartmental line.

"Sir, a call request has come through from the secretary of a Major Uri Droznedov of the Russian Federation, GRU."

"I see. Usual protocols?"

"Yes Sir. Patched through the embassy with this week's code. He said it was urgent and that Major Droznedov will be waiting for your call. He asked if you would make it a priority."

"All right, put me through to the embassy."

The telephone rang for a few seconds and then went silent. Forester knew that his secretary was reading the code to the operator. There was a whirling noise for a moment or two, and then it went silent again. By now his secretary would be speaking with Droznedov's secretary. Although this was an extremely high-ranking title in Russia, mostly given to Army NCO's of great experience.

"I have Major Uri Droznedov for you, Deputy Director Forester," Forester's secretary said. *"Go ahead."*

"Charles Forester speaking."

"Hello Sir, I am Major Droznedov, GRU. Thank you for taking my call."

"You are most welcome; how can I be of help?"

"Sir, it is I who can help you. Are you recording? I think you should, but maybe not publicly, officially, if you understand me, no?"

Forester flicked a switch on the base of the telephone. "Go ahead."

13

Caroline showed the two MI5 debrief experts into the house and closed the door. Behind the door was a half inch solid steel inner door with reinforced hinges and a steel frame fixed to the wooden doorframe. Caroline closed this also, which took not inconsiderable strength, and drove the steel bolt home. This activated a total of three steel bolts evenly spaced at twenty-four inch intervals. The back door was the same. The windows were bullet resistant to 5.56mm NATO and 7.62mm (short) – the two most commonly used military calibres. The French developers claimed each pane could take five rounds before shattering and even then the composite self-healed under dramatic heat increase, the kind caused by rapid multiple bullet strikes. What resulted was a sticky spider's web that could continue to take small arms fire long after it looked damaged. The windows could also withstand up to two 7.62x51mm NATO sniper rounds. Each laminated glass pane was thirty percent smaller than the windows in the rest of the street and the frames were reinforced steel coated with white UPVC. This meant that if an intruder actually stuck around long enough to break the glass, they would stand little chance of getting inside.

The two new arrivals used to be called interrogators but after all the waterboarding that went on in Iraq the Security Service sought to get rid of the name. There had been little remit out there after the fall of Saddam's regime and the CIA, MI6 and MI5 acted with impunity. It was a dark time for the intelligence services. Caroline was not entirely sure what these people were called now, but it didn't really matter. They were experts at getting people to loosen their tongues. They wouldn't be connecting Jeremy Hoist's testicles to a car battery or pouring water on a wet towel over his face, but they were extremely persuasive and would not have to physically touch the man in order for him to tell them what they wanted to know. What was difficult for them, was that they did not already have the answer. They needed to find out what Hoist had done, not whether he had done it. This line of questioning needed to follow a formula, a pattern. Anybody will admit to doing something with enough persuasion, which was why torture was relatively ineffective. What was harder to achieve was getting a person to admit they have done something and then elaborating on it truthfully.

The woman was in her early fifties, short and rotund. She wore her greying hair in a tight bun and carried bifocal spectacles around her neck on a gold chain. She looked like a seventies school headmistress. The man was ageless, in that he could have been forty with older looks or sixty with younger looks. He did not merely look fifty. His hair greyed at the temples and graduated to jet black on top. He was well over six foot and extremely thin. His features were gaunt and drawn. His suit hung far too loosely from his coat hanger shoulders. To Caroline he looked like death. She had once referred to the man as the Grim Reaper and the person she had been talking to knew exactly who she had meant. That had been a few years ago now and she had been relatively new at MI5, but she was still wary even though she was a senior agent with the General Intelligence Group.

Alice, the safe house operator had provided the Special Branch close protection team with refreshments and was busy getting a sweet milky tea and a strong black coffee for the two new arrivals. The two interrogators could not have been more different and their choice in beverages mirrored this fact. Alice had served as an MI5 operative during the seventies and eighties. Her husband, an operative also had died in Northern Ireland in part of a deep cover operation. Now at retirement age, she had been given a handsome pension and the job of running the safe house. It paid well and provided her with a comfortable home in return for looking after MI5 operatives at debriefings or providing a secure location for clandestine meetings a day or two at a time, a few times a month. She appreciated the company and loved the distraction from retirement.

"Where is the subject?" the woman asked. She smiled at Alice as she accepted the tea, nodded appreciatively as she took a sip. Caroline suspected that the two had met previously.

"In the interview room," Caroline answered.

"How long?"

"About an hour."

"Any refreshments?"

"No," Caroline paused. "Thought I'd let him sweat a bit."

"Good," the man said. He sipped his coffee and looked at the file he had kept pinned under his arm. "DD

Forester filled me in and a courier bought this over. I briefed Barbara in the car on the way over. What would you say his frame of mind is?"

Caroline thought for a moment, rubbed her chin subconsciously. "Arrogant," she said. "The people he was involved with tried to hit him and it could have gone very differently."

"I heard," Barbara said. "Good shooting, by the way."

Caroline shrugged. "Hoist has been quiet, but I heard him with Forester, and there was no remorse, just arrogant indifference. He wanted to lawyer up. He *is* scared though."

"Good," the man said. He turned to the woman. "So, Barbara, good cop or bad?"

"Oh, bad, I think," she smiled.

"Great," the man said. "I'll go in first then."

Caroline led the way, then turned around. "I'll be in the booth."

"Okay dear," Barbara said. She stood to the side of the doorway and let her colleague open the door.

Caroline walked to the booth, a small room alongside the one-way glass panel which made up all of one wall. It was toughened glass from the same French manufacturer as the windows. This was rated to five 9mm pistol rounds and could withstand a sledgehammer. At least until the average person tired of wielding it. She looked at a small black receiver unit and lights above corresponding labels signalled that audio and three cameras were recording. It was a digital set-up, and must have either operated constantly, recording over itself every six weeks or so, or was operated by the movement inside the room by passive infrared.

Jeremy Hoist was seated at the table. He looked anxious and was tapping the table with his fingers. His leg bounced up and down tapping his heel occasionally on the rubber compound floor, but he stopped abruptly as the man entered the room. "You can't hold me here like this!" he shouted. "I want a solicitor!"

"Naturally," the man said calmly. "Firstly, allow me to introduce myself; I'm Malcom Swift. I need to get a few details from you, if you don't mind. And then we can get you a solicitor, if you so wish."

"Why wouldn't I want one?"

"Well, it's just so formal. There's no going back, you see?"

"No?" Hoist looked at him obstinately.

"Well, we have CCTV of you entering an empty office, computer mainframe time sequencing of the file in question being downloaded onto an external drive at the sole computer in that room, footage of you leaving the room and nobody else entering that room for over ten minutes. Now, that would seem to be enough to prove that you are responsible for the theft of classified information. A treasonable offence. I am reliably informed that would carry a seven-year custodial sentence."

"I'll take my chances!" Hoist snapped. "I was coerced! I was in danger if I refused."

"I understand," Swift said. "It must have been awful. For you to do that."

"Err, it was." Hoist looked bemused.

"And there is always the chance you'll get bail."

"Exactly," Hoist said.

"I'm not sure you'll be granted protection though."

"Protection?"

"Yes," Swift turned to the file and started to read. He spent a few minutes scrutinising the sheets of paper in front of him.

"What do you mean, protection?"

Swift looked down his nose at him. "From the people who want you dead, dear boy."

"But he was killed."

"One shooter was," Swift said. "But the other one, the woman, she fled the scene."

"What woman?"

Swift stood and gathered the file together. "Excuse me, I have to check something."

Hoist called after him as he closed the door behind him. "What woman?"

"He's looking puzzled," Caroline said to Barbara. "There's something to work with along that line."

"Yes dear," the woman said. "We *have* done this before."

"Sorry." Caroline looked up as Malcom Swift stepped into the booth.

"We'll give him a few minutes." He picked up the jug of coffee which Alice had laid out on the table and poured a cup. "Do you know if he smokes? There's nothing in the file."

"No, I don't," replied Caroline.

"Pity. If he does he'll be hanging out for one. I'll try him in a minute. And he's had no refreshments?"

"None."

"Good."

Alice coughed politely to announce herself. "Sorry, this has just been emailed over from Forester's office, for the attention of Ms Darby. It's a copy of the latest update from Special Branch."

Caroline took it off her and thanked her. She read the front cover and did not notice Alice withdraw discreetly. She thumbed through, then turned to Swift. "You can use this." She passed him the first two sheets which contained photos taken from various CCTV feeds. "The woman who did the shooting this morning was a Russian citizen named Alesha Mikailovitch. Thirty years of age, known prostitute-stroke-escort and former drug addict. Wanted by Interpol for the murder of a drug baron in Georgia, that's Black Sea, not United States. The drug baron was a mafia kingpin known to have committed or at least ordered over twenty murders, so I don't think it's a priority on Interpol's books but she's wanted nonetheless."

"So what was she doing with Hoist?" Barbara asked.

Caroline smiled. "Well I guess that's *your* job to find out."

"Sassy," Barbara smiled. "Let's get to it then."

14

Detective Inspector Hodges studied the toxicology report and took out his mobile phone as he read. It rang three times before it was answered. "Forester, Hodges," he paused. "I have a lead on the drug used on your officers."

"Excellent. How so?"

"There's a drug dealer on my patch who is looking to get a whole lot bigger. Drug squad nicked a couple of his street dealers a few weeks ago. They had cut cocaine with Ketamine and Gamma-Hydroxybutyrate. That's sometimes called GHB. They were selling it as a date-rape drug. Fast working on account it was packaged up in powder form inside gelatine capsules. It was so much stronger than Rohypnol. It was also too heavy on the ketamine. That's a painkiller for horses. Most of the women it was given to had it spiked in their alcohol. They didn't remember a damned thing. Two young college students are still in comas. The toxicology report is identical. I've had copies and appraisals sent over."

"Good work. Keep me informed."

"Will do." Hodges ended the call and turned to DS Mathews in the driver's seat. "Okay let's knock them up."

The bar and nightclub would open for happy hour at around six, but for the next few hours it was closed, although there were lights on inside. Nightclubs needed a lot of cleaning and restocking and Hodges had it on good authority that there would be staff inside for most of the afternoon. It was an imposing building in the daylight, a refurbished, reinvented foundry. There were parking spaces all down one side and a decked and covered smoking area at the front. Red velvet rope and brass bollards separated the entrance and waiting area from the street.

Hodges led the way and stopped at the front double doors. He thudded on the glass and waited. There was a woman inside at the bar. She looked up and saw the gathering of police officers outside, but instead of coming to the door, she walked casually behind the bar.

"Right! Get the big key on that door!" Hodges shouted and stood aside for the largest of the four uniformed police officers to bring the battering ram. It was a solid pile driver of red metal two and a half feet long and he positioned it against the join of the two doors, brought it back in one slow and steady motion and then sent it forwards with huge force, shattering the lock and smashing the doors open amid a shower of glass and wooden splinters as both windows shattered and the wood split.

Hodges strode into the foyer, followed by DS Mathews and the uniformed officers. A tall black man walked out of a side door and stood before them. He was an imposing figure at least six feet four and eighteen stone. His shoulders were rounded and his pectoral muscles were visible through his tight-fitting silk shirt.

"I didn't order no bacon. Haven't you pigs heard of knocking?" he motioned towards the shattered doors, his biceps straining at the shirt sleeves. "Somebody's going to be paying for that!"

Hodges looked around him. Two bouncers had shown up, the bar wasn't open yet, but Hodges knew that they were the dealer's security. He also knew how torn and impotent they were at this moment. Caught between loyalty to the man paying their wages and taking on the law. The law always won. Hodges knew it, the drug dealer knew it and the heavies knew it.

"Why don't you ladies go and shoot up some more steroids and pump a few more weights before show time?" Hodges suggested. "I'm going to talk to your boss. If you don't bugger off now, I'll arrest you."

"For what?" A wall of a man asked. He was the nearest and largest of the two bouncers, but neither looked as imposing, as threatening as their boss. "You've got nothing on me."

Hodges turned around. "Constable, give me your Taser." The officer stepped forward and handed over the yellow plastic Taser which looked like a toy gun.

"What are you doing?" The bouncer stepped backwards a pace. "You can't use that. I'm not doing anything!"

Hodges made the XT26 Taser ready and aimed it at the man's stomach. A red dot appeared from the laser sighting system. The man looked down at his stomach and flinched. "Now, sweetie pie, fuck off, or you're going to get fifty-thousand volts in your guts. You won't want to work those abs for a while."

"But I'm not doing anything!"

"You're obstructing the police and you're posing an intimidating and threatening presence."

"Okay!" The man shrugged at his boss and tapped his colleague on the shoulder. Both men walked through the bar and out of sight.

Hodges handed the Taser back to the officer, who holstered it and looked a little relieved. The detective turned back to the black man and smiled. "So Solomon, how's that Nigerian passport looking? The visa must be about due to renew, no?"

"What is this? My paperwork is just fine, man."

"I'm going to cut to the chase here," Hodges gestured the uniformed officers away, nodded for his detective sergeant to stand back a few paces. "Solomon, I know you had that date rape concoction manufactured."

"Drug squad didn't have shit. That's why I'm walking around free. Free to earn in a month what you earn in a year, man. I'm a legitimate businessman."

"You're a worthless piece of shit drug dealer," Hodges stared at him. "You made a drug and sold it to men who use it to get what they want from woman with no regard for their safety, health or wellbeing. You have made rape easy to commit and difficult to prove."

"I want my lawyer, man." Solomon stuck out his chin indignantly. "I want you out of here."

"No," Hodges said. "I'm going to give you one chance and one chance only. I'm not here to arrest you. I'm here for information. Your drug was used recently to subdue four people so they could be killed horribly. I want to know where it was sold, who was selling it, when the batch was made and I'm going to make you an offer and you're going to accept it."

The big man looked at the detective for a moment. There was something in Hodges' eyes, a sincerity that he found hard to ignore. "Which is?"

"A stay of execution," Hodges said.

"Huh?"

"You tell me everything I need to know, and I'll give you time to get your affairs in order. You cease your drug operation, get rid of your supplies. You destroy your stocks of this rape drug. By the time the police come back into your life you will be a clean and respectable business man."

"Or?"

"This drug has directly aided terrorists in killing four MI5 officers. By the time I've finished with you you'll be linked as an ISIS sympathiser. I know you are a Sunni Muslim. Okay, I'm sure with running a bar and nightclub, you're a completely crap Muslim, about as bad as I am at being a Christian, but the link is there. It will stick. Your mother lives in Bermondsey, right? She has cancer, am I right? She's undergoing chemotherapy. I understand she has a good chance of survival. How's the health service in Nigeria? It would be awful for her to be deported as a terrorist sympathiser, whilst you're in prison and your funds and assets are frozen."

"Bastard!"

"I haven't even started yet!" Hodges snapped. "There's your sister, your daughter from your first marriage, your new wife, your father in Nigeria hoping to come over soon. I hear he has a heart condition. No doubt our glorious NHS would be able to help that out with expensive medication, a bypass or stent."

"This is intimidation. My lawyer…"

Hodges held his finger to his lips. "This isn't the same sort of thing you've been up against before, Solomon," he said quietly. "This is spy stuff. You don't help out here and one day there's a car bomb under your Bentley. A mercury tilt switch and some left over Semtex from a raid in Northern Ireland years ago. Or a tiny drop of polonium in your mother's chemo treatment. They lost four agents, they won't take it lying down. I can get your muscle to bugger off with the threat of a Taser. Christ! We test them on each other on courses! Just think what the dirty world of espionage could do if you were found to have supplied the drug that helped terrorists kill their own."

Solomon held up his hand. "Okay!" He looked thoughtful for a moment then stared at Hodges. "What do you want to know?"

15

Hoist looked at the woman opposite him. She read the file, but said nothing. He tutted, but she did not look up. She drank some of her tea, put the cup back on the table, didn't take her eyes from the page.

"Where's Swift?" Hoist asked. "And who are you?"

Barbara kept reading for a few moments longer, then looked at him. "What was your motivation for betraying your country?"

"I haven't done anything."

"Why did you kill your colleagues?"

"What?"

"Did you drown them also, or just provide their details?"

"I didn't drown anybody!"

"But you don't deny providing their details?"

"No, err yes… Wait!" He ran a hand through his ginger hair. "Look, I haven't done anything like that."

"Oh but you have. You downloaded a classified file and days later four people with their names on that file, their personal details, are dead. Murdered."

"I didn't know!"

"Sure."

"I didn't! You have to believe me!"

"I don't have to do anything." She pushed her chair back and stood up.

"Where are you going?" Hoist asked indignantly, but she was already at the door.

"Give him twenty minutes," Swift said to Barbara as she walked into the booth.

Caroline poured a coffee. She spooned in a teaspoon of sugar, deciding it was going to be a long day. She looked at Swift, who was opening a packet of cigarettes. "So what now? You go in all nicey-nicey?"

"Something like that," he replied. "He really is a first class shit, isn't he?"

"Not big on remorse," Barbara said, pouring herself a tea. She helped herself to four sugars. She slurped loudly as she drank. She spooned in another sugar and stirred. Caroline looked away. "Oh, I'm sorry dear. Are you the sugar police? Must be with your figure. You'll get a waistline like me one day. Can't keep twenty-seven inches for ever. Twenty-five years working all hours for Queen and country takes its toll."

Caroline said nothing. She looked at the file on Mikailovitch. She had not seen her for real, but she felt a personal connection. The woman had almost killed her in Hoist's apartment, but she had fought back and forced her to flee. She was sure more than anything that she both wished she had killed her, or would do so given the opportunity. She had not killed before today, and it surprised her how little emotion she felt having killed the attacker this morning. It had simply been self-defence, and in light of what had been inflicted upon both the MI5 and Special Branch surveillance teams, she felt a satisfaction that was both difficult to suppress and so far guilt-free.

"Right, I'll go take a turn," Swift said. He walked out of the booth and a moment later he walked into the room. Hoist looked up and Caroline could see that he was irritated.

"I want a drink," he said. "And I want my solicitor."

Swift held up a hand. "I will get you a drink in a moment," he said calmly. "And please, for all our sakes, we don't want lawyers involved just yet. You'll regret it, you really will."

"Are you threatening me?"

"No. I am trying to help you," he said, watching Hoist frown. "You see, if we can ascertain what has been done, how badly it affects national security, how best to create some damage limitation, then maybe we can keep all of this under wraps. You can help us; we can help you." Swift took out a cigarette, lit it and blew a plume of smoke over towards Hoist. Hoist waved the smoke away with his hand. Swift inhaled again, blew another plume of smoke at him. Hoist wrinkled his nose in disgust. "I'm sorry," Swift said. "Can't smoke in government buildings, usually. A bit different here, so I'm making hay."

"Why is it different here?" Hoist asked.

Swift blew another plume of smoke at him. It dispersed into a cloud in front of Hoist's face. "This place doesn't exist."

"What do you mean?"

"It's a safe house. It has to be safe. There are a few all over town. We have them all over the country."

"So nobody knows I'm here?"

"A few people," Swift replied. "A very small group."

"What's going to happen to me?" Hoist asked. He looked worried, some of the arrogance gone.

Swift stubbed the cigarette out in his empty coffee mug. He blew the last lungful of smoke at Hoist. "Well, that depends."

"On what?"

"On you," he paused. "And of course how big the group gets." He looked at Hoist, who was frowning at the comment. He smiled as he stood up. "There are four dead agents. Two were deep cover operatives. Embedded in an Islamic extremist group who are on the verge of making very big waves indeed. The other two are both handlers. They have been the link between other groups like this and the information and intelligence reaching both MI5 and MI6 where people like you process it and funnel it through departments for appropriate action."

"But what would happen if the group became bigger?"

"Well, nobody knows you're here. The Special Branch boys will be stood down as soon as our own security is in place. We'll use diplomatic protection, and they don't investigate. It doesn't take a brilliant brain to imagine how hurt and disgusted some people would be by your actions. You could be lost in the system, disappeared. Look around you. This is a soundproofed room. The floors were put in during troubled times. IRA terrorists may well have ended up here for an interview without coffee. That's what we used to call an interrogation." He walked to the door, turned and looked at the man hunched over the table. "Notice the drain on the floor?" He smiled as Hoist looked at the grate under his chair. It was like a large shower plughole. "That would have been put in to sluice away blood, excrement, all sorts of horrible matter that big men would beat out of someone like you. But don't worry, we don't go in for all that anymore," he smiled. "Well, not unless we really have to."

16

Mohammed Betesh watched the car pull into the end of the street. It was a little too obvious for his liking but it would not be there long. He had received orders to wait from Zukovsky, to remain in position until the assault force arrived. He did not know who was going to be arriving, but he could see Rashid on his moped some way behind the car. He had not heard Rashid arrive, but imagined that the man had cut the engine and freewheeled into position. Rashid was proving to be an asset, a good thinker. Untested, Rashid was new to the operation but had proven himself a good fixer, someone who could get equipment and favours. He was also a good surveillance operator. He had come highly recommended from ISIS recruiters in London, some of the most extreme Islamic preachers and clerics in the country. Now Mohammed would discover if the man was also brave.

Mohammed's phone rang and he looked at the display. No name was showing, but he recognised the number as Alesha's. He waited just long enough to prevent the call going to voicemail, then accepted the call.

"Yes?"

"Mohammed, I am in position with Khalil. Rashid is behind us."

"I am surprised Zukovsky is giving you another chance," he said.

"There will be no failure this time!" She snapped. *"Besides, I have braver men with me now. Rafan died like the cowardly dog he was."*

"Whore!"

"At times I've had to be. Just like your mother, I'd imagine. Only not with goats."

"Bitch!" He shouted into the phone. "I'll see you dead for that!"

"Eyes on the prize, Mohammed. I thought you were meant to be a professional."

Mohammed breathed a deep, steadying breath. He squeezed the phone, gritting his teeth together. "What are our orders?" He smiled at the thought of slashing the Russian bitch's throat before this operation was complete.

"You follow me, of course. I'm in charge, after all. Take out the security in the car and we storm the house. Two at the front, two at the rear. They won't stand a chance."

***

Forester sat in the rear of the Jaguar XJ saloon. His driver was ex-army, had spent his career driving senior staff at the MOD. He was the best in the business and had driven for Forester for eight years. He instructed at the MI5 driver training centre in Norfolk several times a year. At the weekends and holidays he raced his classic TVR in hill climbs. One of the more affordable motorsports. As he threaded his way silkily through the north London traffic, Forester marvelled at what rapid progress they made. He had once told Forester that it was not a matter of reading the road and vehicles in front, but as far ahead as you could see. Two thousand metres or more on open roads, ten cars ahead at least in the traffic. It gave you more than enough warning to see obstructions before the cars ahead of you, and he also had the traffic light changes timed from experience on the most driven routes around London.

Forester's mobile vibrated and he took it out to see Detective Inspector Hodges' ID and number flash up. "Hello, Inspector."

"Forester, I have a lead on the drug used to incapacitate your agents. It was as I suspected, the supplier has given us the details of his two dealers. We followed the leads and there haven't been many sales of the batch matching the toxicology reports on account of the Met busying themselves with nailing this, nipping it in the bud. Those two girls lying in comas are bad PR. Forget racial crimes, armed robbery and murder, young white women from middleclass families getting drugged, raped or spiked into a coma is something that can happen to everybody's little girl. I'm on my way to his hottest tip. The dealer phoned first, ordered the man to stay put. I've got a uniform on him to stop him welching on our agreement. I've pulled a few strings on this, guaranteed him exemption from prosecution as long as he closes down this side of his business. If it goes to prosecution I'll stand by that, it's important to remain good to your word in this game."

"I understand," Forester said. "I want the person who bought those drugs. MI5 isn't interested in anyone else."

***

"Are you stupid?" Barbara shouted, smiling as Hoist visibly flinched. She threw down the picture of Alesha Mikailovitch in front of him. Casually tossing it down like a croupier dealing blackjack. "What's her name?"

"I want my lawyer!" He shouted.

"There is not going to be a fucking lawyer you little prick!" She snapped. "Look at this room! Look at the floor! Look at the fucking drain! There will be two big ex-SAS types in here in a minute to beat your sorry little face in! Now who is the woman?"

"Veruschka," he said solemnly. "My girlfriend."

Barbara laughed. "Try again."

"She is! We were having an affair."

"An affair?" Barbara scoffed. "Was she married?"

"No."

"Well I know *you're* not," she sneered. "So how was it an affair?"

"We were together."

She tossed a sheet on the table. There was another photograph and a paragraph written underneath. "Her name is Alesha Mikailovitch. She is wanted by Interpol for the murder of a rather unsavoury Russian drug baron. She's a known prostitute. A crack whore who slept with men to further her pimp's reach and business."

"That's not true!"

"Oh wake up and smell the blackmail will you?" Barbara stared at him. "So what did they want?" Hoist looked at her blankly. "Spit it out! Delay any longer and those ex-SAS boys are going to turn your spleen into something that resembles green baby shit."

"Just minor things."

"Or so it started."

"I didn't mean it to go so far."

"They never do. So how did it go? Let me guess; you meet by chance. A bar? No, it has to have a hook. Internet dating? Bit of a stretch, but I guess they targeted you first and looked for an angle. Hacked your home computer. You'll have one of course. Mainly for porn and online gaming would be my bet. So it was through the internet, right?" Hoist nodded. Barbara slid a pen and sheet of paper across the table. "Name of the site, user ID, account number, security questions. Everything we need to get into and own your account."

Hoist wrote down all she needed. He looked up as Caroline entered the room, took the sheet without a word and closed the door behind her.

"She said her name was Veruschka," he said lamely. "They trapped me. Made films of me. I just wanted to impress her,"

"Can't imagine you'd be able to do that," she sneered. "So you had a few dates, slept together a few times. Impressed her with your tales of a 007 lifestyle, even though you lived where you lived. Most probably told her it was a cover," she smiled as she saw his eyes flicker. "Then when does the butterfly sting like a bee? When does your lover drop her bombshell?"

"Two weeks ago."

"They wanted what?"

"Information."

"Be more explicit. Those ex-SAS boys are straining at the leash."

"Information from personnel. They wanted names and addresses, cover aliases, covert operation names, details of assets both at home and abroad, operations and details on mosque surveillance throughout Britain."

"And you supplied them," Barbara commented flatly. "That was a lot of information. It would take a good undercover agent months to get hold of that little lot. So you were caught with what was downloaded three days ago. This was a personnel file detailing a small percentage of undercover agents and handlers. How much more was downloaded?"

Hoist frowned. "What do you mean?"

"Well, from their shopping wish list, how much did you get for them?"

Hoist looked at her, he seemed confused by her question, unsure what she had meant. He thought he had detailed their requirements. He shrugged. "All of it."

17

Mohammed could see the driver of the blue Vauxhall Insignia saloon smoking, his window wound down half way, the smoke clearly wafting outside. The man was off guard, his instincts nulled by the belief he was perfectly safe in this quiet neighbourhood. Mohammed could see Alesha getting out of the car up ahead. That was the signal to move and he got out of the van, keeping the AK47 held down alongside his leg. He crossed the road most of the way, estimated the blind spot in the wing mirror of the undercover police vehicle and walked casually at a brisk pace. His fingers wrapped around the hilt of the Arabian dagger and he drew it clear of the curved metal scabbard. He could smell the cigarette smoke as he drew closer. He looked up and saw Alesha and Khalil nearing the driveway, Rashid crossing the road. He saw the police officer in the car sit up and take notice. Mohammed quickened his pace, reached the open window and slashed the knife across the man's neck, opening up the windpipe and severing the carotid artery on his right side. A spurt of blood hit the windscreen and splattered a pattern on the glass as the driver writhed in his seat, both hands clasped around his throat. Mohammed had his arm back outside the car before it could get bloody. He sheathed the blade with the blood still on it. It was a Yemeni tradition to never clean off the blood of your enemies. With both hands on the AK47 he joined in with Alesha and Rashid and ran up the driveway to the front door. Khalil brought up the rear. He had a Glock 17 pistol in one hand and a bag in the other.

Alesha held a compact MP5 9mm machine pistol. She aimed at the lock on the door and fired a short burst. The wood splintered, but the bullets flattened on the steel door behind and ricocheted back through the wood showering them with splinters and fragments of copper and lead. They both flinched, Mohammed screamed as a large piece of bullet fragment tore into his shoulder. Blood seeped from the wound and made a pattern like a pressed flower head on his coat. He grimaced, snatched the bag off of Khalil and delved inside. He took out three Russian grenades and two shaped charges of plastic explosive and laid them on the ground. He passed the bag back to Khalil. "Get around the back, now!" He turned to Alesha. "Go with him!"

Alesha glared at him, but relented and followed Khalil. Mohammed stood back and fired a sustained burst at one of the downstairs windows. The AK47 thundered, firing thirty bullets in a few seconds, so close to the window the muzzle flash danced against the glass and scorched the frame.

***

"We're being hit!" A Special Branch officer came bursting into the hallway, shouting into the booth. "Get down! Get down!" He had his Smith & Wesson Sigma pistol in his right hand and he was trying to dial on his mobile.

Caroline gathered her file together. Swift, who had been going softly-softly with Hoist after he had been shaken up by Barbara appeared at the door, startled by the noise. Hoist was on his feet and standing behind him, peering over the man's shoulder. Swift turned and ushered him back into the room. He shut the door behind him, the lock engaged electronically.

"We're under attack," Caroline said. There was a dull thud and she knew from experience that it was a grenade detonating against the door. It shook the house. She looked at Swift. "Give me that file, I need to shred it. Send the recordings onwards to HQ by pressing the condense and send buttons, then press delete to erase the recordings from the hard drive. Do it now!"

Swift bounded into the booth where Barbara was crouching, stunned and panicked. The two fumbled with the box. They had never done a shut-down protocol for real. Caroline ran into the office and heard another thud, this time from the rear. The other Special Branch officer was running upstairs two or three treads at a time. He looked at Caroline, his face ashen. Caroline started pushing the file documents and photographs through the shredder.

"I've hit the panic button and called through to the switchboard!" Alice shouted through the doorway. "Here, give me that and see what you can do elsewhere!" She grabbed the documents and pushed them through two or three sheets at a time.

"Any weapons?" Caroline shouted.

"Kitchen utensils, rolling pin, knives, nothing else!"

Gunshots were clearly audible and the thudding of bullets impacting on the toughened glass and metal. Caroline ran out to the hallway and into the lounge. The remaining Special Branch officer was peering around the edge of the shattered window, but it had still held firm. "Get back!" she shouted. "Get upstairs and get a window open! Get some rounds down on to them! The high ground has the advantage!"

The Special Branch officer looked at her for a moment, then decided it wasn't a bad idea and bounded up the stairs after his colleague, who by the sounds of it had done exactly that. The short, sharp reports of a 9mm pistol filled the house. The gunshots outside sounded louder with a window open, near deafening. The door thudded again, then juddered as an almighty explosion almost knocked her off her feet. She knew it was something far larger than a grenade. The doorway was askew and was shifting as someone behind it started to kick at it. Caroline ran past Swift and Barbara who were both on their mobile phones having apparently completed the security protocol to delete the hard drive of the CCTV unit. She looked around the kitchen and put a pan on the electric hob and switched it on full. She wrenched open the cupboards and took out a full one kilo bag of castor sugar, ripped it open and tipped it into the saucepan. The rear door shuddered like the front door had only moments before and the noise of the explosion was felt in her chest as the shockwave resonated through the house. Glasses and crockery dropped out of the top kitchen cupboards and shattered on the tiled floor.

Caroline took a heavy cook's knife off the magnetic rack and held it firmly in her right hand as she made her way more cautiously into the hall. She looked up the stairs and shouted. "One of you get down here, we're about to be breached! I need a weapon on the front door, it's almost down!" She could hear the door being pounded behind her in the kitchen. She looked at both Swift and Barbara, they were frozen. This was not in their remit. They were psychologists, negotiators. "Get Hoist out of there and get upstairs!" They did not need telling twice. Swift worked the keypad and Caroline could hear them shouting at him as she went into the kitchen. The door was almost in and the kitchen window was opaque, a web of shattered glass, impossible to see through, but still holding firm. It was bowed where it had been punched or more likely beaten with the butt of a weapon. There were no more explosions but the door was shifting inwards. A four-inch gap was held only by millimetres of the tips of the steel bolts. The barrel of a pistol eased inside. Caroline could tell that the person behind was forcing their shoulder and all of their weight against the door, gradually heaving it open. She quietly edged across the kitchen, backed up to the door, took a deep breath to steady her nerves, then hacked down with the heavy cook's knife across the person's hand. The pistol clattered to the ground and there was a gut-wrenching scream as the hand retracted and most of a thumb dropped onto the floor along with a surprising amount of blood. The screaming carried on as Caroline picked up the weapon, jammed it out through the gap and fired five rapid shots. There was a moment's pause and the door took a heavy rapid and sustained burst of fire from some sort of small automatic weapon. Twenty rounds or more clattering and singing as they ricocheted off the metal and through the air. She looked at the bubbling froth of dark brown boiling sugar and backed up to take it off the stove. It was filling the air with a bitter, acrid smoke that started to sting her eyes and burn her nostrils. The door gave way with a final push and dropped askew in the doorway. Caroline saw a man getting back to his feet having fallen on top of both doors, cradling his bloodied hand. A woman stood behind him. She recognised her as Alesha Mikailovitch. She was strikingly beautiful, but her eyes were fierce and cruel. She was changing over the magazine of the smoking MP5 machine pistol, panting and grinning with pleasure, arousal. Caroline remembered the sound she had made firing the bullets into the poor Special Branch officer's body. A haunting display of pleasure amid violence and death. Caroline made eye contact with her, momentarily before she flicked out the pan and splashed them both with the molten caramel. Almost four times the temperature of boiling water, sticky and slow to cool. It melted their skin and clothing and their screams were beyond a level of which Caroline had ever heard before. Or ever wanted to hear again. Animalistic, other-worldly. Alesha flailed backwards and out of view down the side of the house, the man fell onto his back and rolled onto his front. He was kicking wildly and still wailing. Caroline still had half the liquid in the pan and ran to the front door, which had given way but had fallen at such an angle as to create a difficult barrier for the intruders to breach. She caught sight of Alesha screaming past her accomplices, her hands cupping her face as she ran onto the driveway. Both men turned and looked at her, giving Caroline a chance to splash the rest of the liquid at them. The lead figure took the brunt across his chest and face and he jumped high into the air dropping his AK47 and spinning a kind of uncontrolled, unintentional pirouette. He cupped his face, and Caroline realised at that moment that both he and Alesha's hands were scalded also and stuck to the ruined skin. He screamed and reeled backwards fleeing after her. The second man looked up. He had escaped the dousing and had a pistol in his hand. He seemed to notice the pistol in Caroline's right hand and turned and ran. Caroline raised the weapon and sighted on the centre of the man's back. She cursed, lowering the pistol as she watched him run into the street and disappear from sight. She backed into the house, then spun around remembering the attacker with the injured hand. She dropped the pan on the floor, held the pistol with both hands and sighted it in front of her. She edged into the kitchen and carefully peered out of the doorway. The man had gone. Alesha's machine pistol lay abandoned on the ground, a thick, sticky black treacle covering it. She turned around and walked to the stairs. There was an eerie quiet in the house. She could hear sirens approaching, still a long way off. She climbed the stairs steadily, the weapon held out in front of her. Barbara was cowering in the bedroom doorway. She stood up as Caroline approached. Swift peered out of the bathroom, Hoist was behind him crouched on the tiled floor. Caroline eased her way into the second bedroom. Its window overlooked the garden behind the kitchen. A Special Branch officer lay slumped on the floor, his weapon on the floor beside him, a pattern of crimson holes patterned across his chest. Caroline turned to the landing. She saw the open window overlooking the driveway. She saw the second officer slumped across a bookshelf. He was staring at her, but his eyes held no life. He still held the pistol, blood had run down his arm, over the frame of the weapon where it dripped off the tip of the barrel and pooled on the floor. Alice stood next to him, her fingers resting on his neck checking his pulse. She looked up at Caroline, tears in her eyes.

The sirens were clearly audible now, filling the street. Caroline turned and saw Barbara, Swift and Hoist gathered on the landing at the top of the stairs.

Hoist stared at the dead officer, not raising his glazed and teary eyes as he spoke. "I'm sorry. So very sorry," he said. "I'll tell you everything."

18

"And you won't arrest me, right?"

"No."

"Later, down the line?"

"Oh, I'm sure I will. But not for this."

"Can I have it in writing?"

"No."

"Then I'm not talking."

"You are." Hodges walked over to the double French windows which opened out onto the world's smallest balcony. Barely enough room to stand. The windows were open a touch. Smoke from a smouldering cigarette in an overfilled ashtray wafted out of the window. He looked down on the alley below. "Or I'm going to throw you out of the fucking window." The dealer looked at him. There was doubt in his mind, not knowing if he was serious. "I've assured your boss. I've given my word and pulled more than a few strings. He's going to give up on this drug lark. Which means, sunshine, you may well be out of a job. But better that, than to be paralysed and drinking liquidised food through a straw. Now, tell me what you know or you're going out head first."

The man hesitated for a moment, then shrugged and sat down. "The deals were done here, or rather downstairs in the bar. There were other places, but this batch was new and as far as I'm aware, they were done downstairs or in the alley." He reached into his jacket pocket and took out a DVD in a clear plastic cover. "That's everyone. Solomon called and told me to put it together. There's ten nights dealing condensed into about an hour."

"Just on the off-chance; were there Arab looking men, or a Russian woman about thirty with black hair buying?"

The man nodded. "A couple of blokes might have been. Just looked like Pakis to me."

Hodges frowned at the racial slur, but moved on. "Okay. I'll take the disk. I'll have some officers around here in two days. This establishment better be clean, or you still might take a dive out of that window."

***

Forester had received news of the hit on the way to the safe house. His driver had shown why he was the man who trained MI5 field operatives in evasive and defensive driving. Forester held the grab handle, braced his feet against the front seat and pulled the seatbelt tight. The driver took the car up to eighty miles per hour on short stretches through the streets, weaved in and out of traffic and mounted the curb at one point. The big Jaguar was a top of the range model with a five litre supercharged V8 engine and the driver made good use of all of the five hundred and fifty horsepower. They conveniently caught up with and become part of the police vehicle convoy responding to the multiple calls coming from the shooting at the safe house. Armed response units, police patrol cars and ambulances weaved through the traffic with blue lights flashing and sirens wailing.

A cordon was already in place and armed response officers had fanned out around the house, with uniformed officers taking statements from eye witnesses. Houses opposite and to each side were being emptied by police. Forester rubbed his forehead in despair. It could not have become more high profile. His driver pulled the car in towards the curb, where despite having flashing blue lights behind its grill, a police officer waved frantically for him to stop. He walked around to the driver's window, who unceremoniously thumbed behind his shoulder. Forester wound down his window.

"You can't go any further," the officer said. "Can I have some ID?"

Forester showed him his card, but it merely showed he was from the Security Service, and not that he was second in command. "I have operatives in that house. Radio ahead and tell them to let me through."

The officer looked perplexed. He had clearly been told to let nobody through the cordon, but he hadn't been ready for this scenario.

"It's okay, let him through!" Commander Anderson walked up and lifted the tape. "Forester, what the hell is going on? I've lost three more officers! This is unprecedented!"

Forester looked at him. "What about my people?" He ducked under the tape and walked swiftly towards the house.

Anderson caught hold of his arm. "They're okay," he said. He watched Forester visibly relax.

"Look, this has gotten out of hand. My chief has already met with the Prime Minister."

"What?" Forester raised his voice, which was a rare thing.

Anderson flinched. "Look, what else was he to do? There's a full COBRA meeting being scheduled later today."

Forester was seething, he had yet to be informed. Joint Intelligence was a fragile status quo at the best of times, but as director of operations in the country's counter terrorism and espionage agency, he should have known before a mid-ranking policeman. He pushed past Anderson and walked briskly up the driveway. He paused briefly, horrified when he saw the demolished door and the shattered glass on both the upstairs and downstairs windows. There were hundreds of brass bullet cases over the driveway and they glinted in the sunshine, winking at him from the flower beds and lawn.

"They forced entry front and back. They must have fired hundreds of rounds," Anderson said, catching up with him. "They killed my driver," he said grimly. "Cut his throat like a bloody lamb. He was still in the car. They got both of my officers as they engaged in a firefight. They were outgunned. How can you take on automatic weapons with a bloody pistol?"

"I'm sorry, Anderson," Forester said. He looked into the house through the doorway and saw Caroline cradling a cup of tea or coffee.

"That's one hell of a lady you've got there," Anderson commented. "She slashed one attacker with a kitchen knife, damned near took his hand off, got his weapon and returned fire. She then saw the lot off with boiled sugar."

"What?"

Anderson chuckled. Maybe it was adrenaline subsiding, or a grief coping mechanism kicking in. "She put on a pan of sugar. A lot of it. Boiled it to syrup, about three or four hundred degrees Celsius according to a forensics officer who is in there now doing a preliminary. Then she douses them in it like some medieval soldier defending a bloody castle!" Anderson shook his head. "It worked though. The woman dropped her weapon and took off like she was on fire. I suppose in a way she was." He pointed to the ground in front of the door and the two steps. "See there, it's all set to, I don't know what, butterscotch?"

Forester walked up the steps. He heard the sugar syrup crack as he stepped on a patch and stepped over the doors. Caroline put her cup down and walked over. She was pale. Her mannerisms were similar to someone with the early stages of a cold; shivery and tired looking.

"Well done. Again." Forester put a hand on her shoulder. "We're going to stop this. I'm going to pull out all the stops to get these bastards."

Caroline nodded. She had never heard Forester swear before. "We've taken too many hits. Not just today… the bombing… the court cases…" A tear trickled down her soft cheek, another ran down the same path, more rapidly. "Peter's death. I'm not sure I can take it anymore," she said quietly.

"I know," Forester squeezed her shoulder. "It will be all right. I have a plan. We're not taking this, or anything else lying down anymore."

19

They were still screaming when the car drove erratically into the parking area of the warehouse that was acting as their headquarters in Newington. Rashid had driven them, Mohammed had scrambled into the front passenger seat and Alesha and Khalil had got into the rear, with Alesha guiding him. Khalil was cradling his hand. The blood was all over him, he could not see and he could not control his agonising screams. Alesha had closed her eyes in time, but her hands and face were terribly scalded and the syrup had set hard. It was still burning where the syrup was closest to the skin. She wailed, more so when she noticed her face in the rear view mirror. Mohammed was in a similar state, but had taken a good deal in his right eye. He knew he had been blinded in his right eye, but he was more controlled than the other two. He grunted in pain, but he wanted nothing more than to go straight back and rip the heart out of the British bitch who had done this to them. Rashid had driven swiftly, but kept it legal. The others had all screamed at him to go faster. Khalil had shouted that he needed hospital treatment. Mohammed had denied him this, ordering Rashid to drive back to their base. Their Muslim brothers were bombed daily in Syria and Iraq by infidels – there were no hospitals available to them for burns and shattered limbs. Rashid had remained quiet. He was unscathed. Maybe it was the guilt that had dulled his mood.

Rashid parked the car and got out. The other three all scrambled for their doors. Alesha barged past him, leaving Khalil cradling his hand and eyes and unsure which direction to walk. Rashid went to him and put an arm around his shoulder. Mohammed pushed past them both and followed Alesha in through the smoked glass door into a deserted and unfurnished reception area. A short, stout Russian with white hair and a matching white beard held the door open. He looked bemused at them. He had seen them arrive on the monitor of the CCTV system he had installed. Rashid guided Khalil in and closed the door.

"This doesn't look good," the Russian smirked. He locked the door behind them and followed the others. Khalil was wailing, he prayed to God, muttered under his breath. Cursed the British woman out loud.

Zukovsky was studying plans on a table in the warehouse loading bay. He had his back to them, his broad shoulders hunched. He was deep in concentration when Alesha Mikailovitch flung herself at him.

"Look what they have done to me!" she wailed.

Zukovsky turned around, visibly recoiled when he saw her face and the wounds she had suffered. He looked shocked. "What has happened?" He looked past her and saw both Mohammed walk in, followed by Khalil. Rashid pulled out a chair and guided Khalil to sit down.

"Orlev! See to their wounds!" Zukovsky snapped at the stout Russian. He put an arm around Alesha and guided her over towards the others. Rashid had pulled out more chairs and Mohammed was sitting down. He was tentatively easing his clothing out from the sticky, blistering mess underneath.

"I am no doctor!" the Russian protested.

"You hold a medical degree, Professor," Zukovsky glared at him. "You will have learned the basics before specialising."

"But decades ago," he started to protest, but saw the look in Zukovsky's eyes and thought better of it. "Fetch me some tepid water and towels, or some clean cloths!" he snapped at Rashid. "There is a first aid kit in the kitchen, bring it to me!" He looked at the three of them, bent down beside Khalil, who was still bleeding from his severed thumb. It was evident the man had lost his sight – both eyes were completely white, like those of a steamed whole fish. He looked at Zukovsky, who in turn shook his head dismissively. He turned instead to Alesha.

Mohammed was more proactive. The man was peeling away the layers of clothing, his teeth grit together as he rode the wave of pain and tore the blistering skin. The boils were weeping their protective fluid, the wounds raw underneath.

Rashid appeared with a bucket of water, cloths tucked under his arm and a standard workplace first aid kit. He dropped the first aid kit onto the floor and put the bucket down.

Orlev looked at him. "Soak the cloths," he said. "Then wrap the burns."

Rashid did as he was ordered. Alesha shrieked when he placed the wet cloth against her cheek. She glared at him and took the cloth from him. She bent and took another wet cloth out of the bucket and placed it against her breasts. They had been terribly burned as well. She folded the cloth so that her hands would cool as well.

"We will need cold water next," Orlev snapped at Rashid. He looked at Zukovsky, then said, "Shock could set in if the wounds were doused in cold water. They are continuing to burn and we must bring the temperature down steadily. Cold tap water next, then iced water if possible."

"There are refrigerated cans of drinks," Zukovsky offered. "You could cool the next bucket with some of those."

"That will do," the stout Russian said.

"What about me? I need a cold towel," Khalil said. "Hand me one." He looked in the general direction, but he could see nothing.

Zukovsky placed a hand on his shoulder. "Come with me," he said. "We will bathe your face in the bathroom sink." He helped Khalil to his feet and walked him out of the loading bay. They took the corridor and Zukovsky led him into one of two cavernous storage rooms.

"My thumb… it still bleeds," Khalil said. "I need to go to a hospital. I am blind, General. Maybe a hospital will save my sight?" Zukovsky said nothing. They had reached a car. It was a ten-year-old Jaguar saloon. He opened the boot with a key fob. "Where are we? What are we doing?"

"You are right, my friend," Zukovsky said. "I will take you to a hospital. But you must be sure to say nothing. And I will have to leave you. If you are arrested, I cannot help you."

"I understand," Khalil said. He was shaking, his voice trembling. "It hurts so much."

Zukovsky let go of him. He stepped back a pace, and took the Makarov pistol out of his jacket pocket. It had a curious looking hexagonal nut on the end of the barrel, into which, Zukovsky screwed in a six-inch-long suppressor. Often and incorrectly referred to as a silencer. He aimed at a point behind Khalil's right ear. At the brain stem. He fired once and the tiny pistol coughed. The ejected case clattered on the hard floor and Khalil slumped forwards over the edge of the boot. Zukovsky put the weapon on the ground and manoeuvred the body into the boot, lifting its legs and tucking them inside. He closed the boot lid, picked up the weapon and walked back to the open doorway.

20

SCO19 armed response units drove both front and rear of the convoy. Both vehicles were police liveried with blues and twos operating on top. They were Land Rover Discoveries with bull bars mounted to both protect their engines if rammed and to damage any potential attack vehicle. Each vehicle held four officers. All were armed with Glock 17 pistols, Heckler & Koch MP5 machine carbines and each vehicle was equipped with a .12-gauge shotgun and a 5.56mm Heckler & Koch G36 assault rifle. Behind and in front of these two vehicles were two black Land Rover Discoveries from the Metropolitan Police Diplomatic Protection squad. Again, each carried four armed officers equipped with Smith & Wesson Sigma 9mm pistols. Sandwiched in between were Forester's Jaguar and a plain blue Vauxhall Insignia saloon. The lead vehicle was calling out the route and police vehicles ahead were holding back traffic at chokepoints and traffic lights. Progress was swift. Forester looked at his driver, catching his expression in the rear-view mirror. The man was loving life.

Caroline Darby rode next to Forester. The vehicle in front carried Hoist, Commander Anderson rode next to him.

"Matters have become clouded," Forester said.

"They've become unexpected, I'm not sure they're clouded," Caroline mused.

"I have received news. The worse kind, I'm afraid." He ran a hand over his face. Caroline had seen him do this when he was overly tired or stressed. It was as if he were wiping with an imaginary hot flannel. "I received word from a Russian intelligence officer, an army major with the GRU. A warhead that went missing has been traced to a Russian former general named Vladimir Zukovsky…"

"An associate of Alesha Mikailovitch? I read the file," Caroline interjected. "What are we talking in terms of warhead?"

"Nuclear. Short range, high yield. Enough to make Hiroshima look like a village fete firework display."

"So in terms of destruction?"

Forester rubbed his face again. "The system was designed to be detonated in the air about two thousand feet or so above the target. If it detonated in any British city, it would be almost total devastation for a five-mile radius. However, they do not have the resources to launch it, so it would supposedly be detonated on the ground. In that scenario we're looking at approximately a mile radius. It's all to do with resistance. Buildings, bridges, hills and rivers lessen the radius. The warhead reaches temperatures six times hotter than the surface of the sun." He shook his head. "What kind of men make such things?"

"This is all related though," Caroline said. "Why else would Alesha Mikailovitch turn up on our radar? What about the dead agents?"

"Connected. There's more. We have missing agents as well. Undoubtedly connected."

Caroline shook her head. "But if they have plans to launch a strike, then why the need for killing or capturing our agents? Why the need to silence Hoist? After detonation, none of it matters."

"All I can think of for the moment is that Zukovsky does not know that we know about the warhead. This has come as a tip. Zukovsky was to be part of a terrorist strike on the Ukraine. He changed the plan, kept the funds and the warhead and started his own agenda."

"It still doesn't explain the elaborate blackmailing of an MI5 analyst, or the killing of our agents."

"I think it does," said Forester. "I think we have been given a false hand. I think we are meant to tie up all of our resources hunting for the killers of our own. Crucial man-hours searching for missing colleagues. I think we have been thrown a horrible hand – that of our missing agents – and I think the only way to win is to ignore it, not to place a bet on it. Sacrifice that hand for the sake of the game."

"It's not a bloody game!" she snapped.

"I think to Zukovsky it is," replied Forester. "Well, I'm at the table now, and I will deal a few hands of my own."

"Meaning?"

"I have been known to have an ace up my sleeve from time to time," he mused. "I'm going to meet with the Prime Minister today. A private meeting where I intend to sound him out about something. Something unprecedented. A COBRA meeting is scheduled for this afternoon after our initial meeting. I am going to treble

Detective Inspector Hodge's resources and leave him on the murder case. I don't think there are murders to solve anymore, more a case of finding Zukovsky and his associates. But Hodges is tenacious, has an incredible record, knows the city like the back of his hand and he may well find a lead that takes us to their doorstep. Special Branch can turn over the city looking for anyone they so wish. The police are already searching for our missing agents; Special Branch can take charge of that."

"But they're our agents!" Caroline snapped. "*We* need to find them!"

"And they will be found. But the whereabouts of a missing warhead is going to, and *has* to take priority. General Intelligence Group have but one remit as of today – leave no stone unturned, no favour owed. We are going to find that warhead."

***

Hodges put down his coffee and looked at the three officers in turn. Behind him was a white board with a hastily drawn mind-map. Around the edges there were a number of photographs and post-it notes. Solomon's photograph and a note of the date rape drug abbreviated as GHB linked to a photograph of his dealer. From this a number of photographs linked up. Some had a red marker cross through them. These were dead ends. Two were circled in black. These were the most probable leads. The other side of the board displayed a picture of the van abandoned near Hoist's apartment. The name of the hire company headlined, with a CCTV photograph from the company's office where it had been picked up by one of the men in the GHB link on the other side of the board. The credit card used to hire the vehicle was one of many since listed as stolen.

Two images of Alesha Mikailovitch from both CCTV and her Interpol file record sat squarely at the top of the board. The photographs next to her were both taken from an old MI5 file, and a shot of him on the mortuary slab. Rafan Betesh was known to the intelligence services. He had fought with ISIS in Syria and executed people in propaganda videos. Hodges had requested a file of known associates and was delighted to discover he had a brother. He put out an all ports on Mohammed Betesh. He knew these people valued family ties and trusted few.

On the table in front of them were several piles of paper and files which had been opened and labelled. Hodges looked up as a uniformed officer walked in. The woman held a file out for him. Hodges took it and opened it. He didn't notice her leave.

"What's that Boss?" a young female detective asked. "More from the spooks?"

Hodges nodded. "Photographs from CCTV at the safe house that was hit. That all ports call was spot on, Watkins," he said, and she smiled. It had been her idea. "Mohammed Betesh was one of the gunmen. Mikailovitch was there with two unknowns. Their images are being run on the Joint Intelligence system as well as our own as we speak. Should come back with something."

"But what's the MO?" DS Mathews asked. "What information can this guy Jeremy Hoist have that he should become a target? Twice?"

Hodges picked up his coffee and drank it down in one, tepid gulp. He put the empty cup back down on the table and looked at the board. "We're putting together a puzzle without all the pieces," he paused. "We need to use what we have to find them. To focus on the deaths of the four agents and use the information on the periphery to get closer to capturing the people responsible for their deaths. Let the spooks work out the whys and the what-fors."

***

The safe-house was a terraced, four storey town house in Camden. There was no garden, merely a single off road parking space that also made space for the four separate wheelie bins. Recycling was a chore in Camden. The front of the house was separated from the quiet street by painted black iron railings. The rear of the house double backed on to another house and another street. Here, however, was the unique factor. MI5 also owned this house and the two houses connected on every floor. It provided entrance and exits at all hours with little observation, and a handy escape route if needed.

SCO19 withdrew to the end of the street, as did one of the DP units from the Met. They arrived with little announcement, Caroline and Forester exited swiftly, opened Hoist's door and walked him briskly inside. Two protection officers followed. As planned the other DP unit would drive around the block and park outside the second house. Each SCO19 vehicle took up position at the end of both streets. Two officers from DP entered through the second house, leaving two in each vehicle and four in the safe-house.

Hoist was ushered towards a leather sofa. He sat down and looked up at Forester as he approached. "What happens now?"

"You will be interviewed again. We have to ascertain what you have said, or what you know that has prompted them to try and kill you twice."

Hoist shrugged. "They wanted information, I gave it to them. They didn't tell me anything."

Forester nodded. "We shall see." He looked up at the couple standing to the edge of the room. "Short notice, I'm afraid."

"That's all right, Sir," the man said. He had a clip manner. Ex-Army, NCO. He was a dutiful man with a long service history, unblemished. Until he suffered PTSD after Afghanistan. His wife, Michelle was the nurse who helped him recover. Both were out of the forces now, but a contact of Forester's recommended them for the medium-level security position. The couple enjoyed living in the house and neighbourhood, found the salary with board included to be the most they had ever earned and were thoroughly dependable.

"We have a debrief team coming," Forester said. "They've had a bit of a morning, it's fair to say. So if you can look after them with coffee and snacks, it would be appreciated."

"Yes Sir," the man said.

Forester turned to Caroline. "You need a break. Go home, come back here in the morning."

She frowned. "Shouldn't I stay here? Or shadow Detective Inspector Hodges?"

"There's nothing you can do here," Forester said. "Hodges will have more staff by this evening."

"If it's all the same, I'd rather stay here and listen in on the interview."

Forester looked at his watch. "Very well," he said. "I have a COBRA meeting scheduled. I have something I want to look into afterwards, but it will take me away for a while, but I'll be contactable on my mobile or email."

Caroline nodded. It never paid to pry. If Forester was willing to elaborate, he already would have. "I may well go over and see Hodges in the morning. I would like to see what progress he is making. If you don't mind, I'd like to see Commander Anderson as well. I'm worried there's too many facets to this investigation."

"There are," Forester agreed. "But it will change soon. The cards have all been dealt."

***

The sky had turned grey and cloudy. It made little difference to the drone because it flew at no more than three hundred feet, well below the cloud cover. It was equipped with eight rotor blades and powered by two rechargeable battery packs with a small power reserve unit. It made next to no sound and at over one hundred feet it was completely inaudible from the ground. Mounted front and rear were directional cameras controlled via the remote control unit. The control unit was large and strapped over the operator's shoulders enabling all the flying to be done in front of their chest. The cameras were for operation and did not record, but they operated on both wide-angle for easier control and pin-point zoom for surveillance. The drone also emitted a GPS beacon monitored by a GPS receiver unit. A city map was placed over a grid system which enabled close to pin-point accuracy. At least accurate enough to maintain a hover and allow a visual from the operator.

The operator was a young man with the thickest glasses imaginable. They did not fit well either, and he would have to push them up his nose several times a minute. He had a poor complexion and was gaunt-thin. He was engrossed in his work and could certainly fly the drone well.

The driver of the van was dark in complexion with a short trimmed beard and a shaven head. He was Russian, smoked constantly and was heavily tattooed. They were Russian gang and prison tattoos. Among them were nine strands of barbed wire on his forearm - one for every year served in prison. Further down just above his wrist another four strands wrapped around, indicating another four-year term. Three daggers ran down his neck. One for every man he'd killed in prison. Part of his face was white, like someone had taken an eraser to his skin or bleached the colour away. This had been a forced tattoo. A tattoo given to him to indicate a crime or act he was guilty of, but to serve as a warning to others. He remembered that night well. Five men had held him down after his initial beating, and he had watched the tattooist mix the melted rubber, urine, faeces and powdered pencil lead into the mixture that would make up the ink. The tattoo had taken ten agonising hours. He had also been beaten and humiliated throughout. He had never spoken again of the crime, but he had burned the tattoo out of his skin with magnesium the day he was released. When he remembered the crime he had committed, it made him feel as repulsed as the memory of the ordeal the prisoners subjected him to that night. He had vowed never to speak or think of it again. He had found a new path to travel. A path that made him feel clean and valued once more. A path that had provided him with a brotherhood, a family. He had shunned his previous life, and those who had been a part of it. He had found honour, respect and a sense of being. He knew he could not choose how long he would be on this earth, or a part of this new life. But he was confident in the knowledge that he now served a cause worth dying for. He had one man to thank for that. Vladimir Zukovsky had found him at his lowest ebb. He had given him food and shelter, work and the means to survive without crime, and then a sense of belonging. The Russian pulled to the kerbside and looked at the youth next to him. "Do you have the fix?" he asked abruptly.

The young man was concentrating hard. He pushed his glasses back up his nose. "I have the street. Interesting though, the police escort has split and have parked and entered a house directly at the rear."

"Are you sure?"

"Absolutely. See?" He eased the control unit so the Russian could see. "I think those two houses are one in the same."

The Russian studied the monitor. He could see both SCO19 vehicles and both plain Special Branch vehicles from above. The image was crystal clear, slightly off colour, but not black and white. "And the officers went in the house at the back as well?"

"Yes."

"That is the car Hoist travelled in." He pointed at the screen. "And that is the MI5 deputy director's car."

"Correct."

The Russian looked intently at the image and broke into a smile. It was a savage slit in his face. The eyes were dead, there was no emotion, but the youth knew that this was a moment of complete satisfaction for the man next to him.

21

Detective Chief Inspector Hodges stared at the whiteboard in front of him. There was no pattern. There was, however, a lot of connections. He had four dead MI5 agents. That was what he referred to as genesis. It was the incident that started the investigation. The shootings at Hoist's apartment had given him not only Rafan Betesh as a name, but Alesha Mikailovitch as well, confirmed by her positive identification through Interpol. Charles Forester had assured Hodges that former Russian general Vladimir Zukovsky was involved, but he was waiting for more intelligence. It irked him that the intelligence director had not, or rather would not divulge more. Hodges hated spooks. They always had a bigger picture to look at. Hodges had served as a police officer for twenty years. He had always looked at what was right and wrong. It was called the law. Plain and simple. General Vladimir Zukovsky was former Russian military, and as such, did not appear in the police database. He would have to request further information from MI5 and that would delay matters further.

He sipped some coffee, then realising he hadn't eaten all day he picked up a new packet of chocolate digestives off the table and opened them. He looked at the picture of Solomon as he ate one. The date-rape drug lead had bought up CCTV possibilities and the images were processing through the National Crime Intelligence

Computer database. He made a mental note to be on the Nigerian's case when he was finished here. Hodges had a nineteen-year-old daughter from his first marriage and he would gladly have nailed Solomon to the wall had he not needed to barter a deal. But the price had been worth it. Two young women were still in intensive care, but the product would be taken off the streets permanently. No further cases, no further rapes or assaults. A man like Solomon would slip up soon enough, and Hodges had vowed to send the man down for the rest of his days. It didn't matter that a few offences went unpunished, as long as he was punished for something that was all that counted in Hodges' opinion.

The second shooting had confirmed that Rafan Betesh's brother Mohammed was involved. The safe-house CCTV had positively identified Alesha Mikailovitch a second time and thrown up two more faces for the various databases. There was no knowing how long a match could take. The person would have to have committed an offence previously, or be known to the intelligence community for other reasons.

Hodges realised he had eaten almost all the biscuits and dropped the packet down onto the table.

"Rob will be pissed," the woman said behind him. Hodges turned around and saw Watkins walk in with a sheaf of printed notes. "They're his favourite biscuits. His wife is on low-carb so she sent them in with him from home."

Hodges shrugged. "Maybe he'll bring cake tomorrow."

"Have you eaten? Can't function on biscuits and coffee alone."

"Says the seasoned detective," he smirked. "Listen Watkins, I've solved serial killings and bank jobs, diamond exchange robberies and serial rape cases on nothing more than coffee, chocolate digestives and a couple of pints and a bag of chips on the way home. Week in, week out for twenty years."

"It's a wonder you're still here. Come down to the canteen with me Boss, they do a good tuna salad with mung beans."

"Nah, I'll have a bag of chips and bits on the way home."

"Bits?" Watkins asked incredulously.

"Yeah, all the bits of batter that falls off the fish in the fryer. They scoop them out and save them up."

"Oh, good God!"

"What are those, anyway?"

"New cases, new leads. I'm handing them out."

"What about this case?"

"Nothing new," she said. "We're downloading traffic CCTV from the second shooting. The CCTV from the spook safe-house doesn't catch the vehicle they left in. There are a number of possibilities but those cul-de-sacs are a maze. It's been difficult to find access to the main arterial roads. You'd think MI5 would have thought of that."

"They will now," Hodges mused. "So you're telling me that CCTV hasn't picked up three Asian men and a young dark haired woman driving like a bat out of hell because most of them are practically on fire?"

"Yes. But let's give it a chance," she quipped. "What now?"

"Well, it's not a murder investigation anymore."

135

"No?"

"No. It's a manhunt."

"But…"

"Oh come on! We've got names and we've got connections. We know they did it. What we don't know is why. There's something bigger behind this, something we don't know, or are being kept from knowing. I had reservations about working with these spooks, but I can't see any more progress to be made."

"We haven't got all the cards, have we?"

"No."

"You said Forester seemed like a straight shooter. You really think he's keeping something from you?"

"Absolutely."

"So what do we do?"

Hodges picked up the last of the biscuits, bit it in half and chewed, speaking with his mouth full. "We go national. We get Mohammed Betesh, Alesha Mikailovitch and these two unknowns out there in the public eye so that every bobby on the beat, every shop owner, every dog walker, every neighbour twitching curtains on the house next door gives us a helping hand. MI5 want the killers caught, let's catch them."

***

Caroline Darby looked at her watch. It was a silver Cartier with a leather strap and had been a gift from her late fiancé Peter. Every time she looked at it, she thought about her fiancé. She didn't know whether it was a curse or a blessing. Tonight, it made her sad. She kicked off her shoes and walked into the bathroom. She turned the dial to secure the plug and ran both taps. Dropped in a scented salt bomb and walked back out to the lounge.

The flat was all on one level and plenty large enough for two. There was a spare bedroom that she used as an office-come-storage room. Much of Peter's things were in here, she had not yet built up sufficient resilience to get rid of them. Naturally there were items she'd never part with, but the bulky things – the boxes of clothes and even unpacked boxes from both moving in together from their respective flats were still stacked against the wall.

The kitchen was tiny, but the couple had joked that they were never in enough to cook. Peter would grin lecherously and say: *you'd better show me another room you're good in then.* The occasional Sunday breakfast or brunch, or the odd late night supper had been rustled up, but in truth the couple had eaten either on the hoof, or in one of the three canteens in MI5 headquarters at Thames House. And they had been on first name terms with various delivery drivers of many different cuisines. Caroline opened the fridge and took out the fixings for gin and tonic. She poured a large one, stacked the glass with ice and sliced some lemon into the glass, squeezing some excess juice in as well. She walked back to the bathroom and took a deep sip. She took off her clothes and discarded them on the floor. The bathwater was hot, and the gin and tonic was cold. She sunk down into the water. Her mind played over the events of the day. The only person she wanted to talk to was no longer here, and she played the events over, worked through the possibilities of what these people were up to, keeping her mind full and busy to prevent it from relaxing and taking on thoughts of loneliness, emptiness and an aching sadness she would have never imagined possible.

22

There was no way to approach the cottage other than head on. It's openness, its utter bleakness was its security. The cottage in itself was small. It was squat in design, hunkered down against the elements. Obstinate and stubborn against the harshness of nature for two centuries. There was no garden. Forester doubted whether anything other than grass and heather could grow here anyway. Other than the cottage, a single leafless tree, a gnarled and thorny thing bent over at ninety degrees, was the only other object to obscure the flat and desolate terrain for miles. The waters of the loch were dark, almost black and only interspersed from the grey horizon by a million white horses lapping at the sky. Fifty feet of grey and white shingle surrounded the three sides, the expanse of water stretching out into infinity where it joined the sea.

Forester could see that the lane had been poorly maintained. It left the narrow strip of tarmac and weaved around clusters of granite boulders on its route to the cottage. He supposed that when it was built it had been easier to dig and strip the ground around the boulders than waste days of manpower moving them. The lane looked to have many potholes, all of them filled with water. Forester hoped that they were not too deep for the Ford's wheels and clearance. It was a hire car from the airport. He eased off the tarmac and found out at once that the car was going to struggle. He weaved his way as best he could, dropping into the potholes and grounding the underside of the vehicle as he crawled along. He noted that used hire cars were not the most sensible second hand purchase. After five minutes he was near enough to the cottage to see through the downstairs windows. It was a box with a large window either side of the front stable door and with two more directly above. The side aspect of the house had a small window to each gable end. Forester presumed one belonged to the kitchen and the other had been put in for aesthetics. It was hard to imagine many rooms inside the cottage other than a bathroom, bedroom, living area and kitchen. As he drew near he could see that an old and battered Land Rover Defender was parked close to the other side of the house and a small open fishing boat was pulled up on a trailer and parked in an alcove that had been dug out of the small hillock offset from, but only forty metres away from the shingle beach of the loch. It was less obtrusive than an outbuilding and provided the boat with shelter from the fierce wind coming from the west out at sea.

Forester parked the Ford in front of the cottage. He switched off the engine and studied the cottage for a moment. He was out on a limb. Nobody knew he was here, and nobody would publically condone what he was about to do. He opened the door and instantly felt both the chill and force of the wind. As he got out he could feel the cold cutting through his suit. He looked at the front door, but there was no sign that anybody was in. He hoped he had not had a wasted journey.

"I was wondering how long it would take," the voice was behind him. Forester couldn't see how he could have possibly missed him. The ground was so open.

Forester turned around slowly, his right hand clearly in view, his left on the door frame of the car. It was a casual gesture, but he wanted the man to see he was no threat to him. "For what?"

The man was ten feet away. He was above average height, broad and fit-looking, and dressed in khaki cargo trousers and a well-worn waxed jacket. His hair was short and dark and he had a week-long growth of beard that was salt and peppered with grey. His features were hard, chiselled and his eyes were the coldest blue-grey Forester had ever seen. They reminded him of a wolf. "For the past to catch up," he said. He carried a side-by-side double-barrelled shotgun. It was broken safely over his arm in the manner such weapons were carried, but Forester could see that two cartridges were nestled in the action. The man carried a pair of dead rabbits by their hind legs.

"Mister King, my name is…"

"Forester. Deputy Head of Box," the man interjected.

Forester smiled. MI5 used to have the post office box number address of: MI5, Box 500. Most people in the armed forces or security forces still referred to them as 'Box'. "You know me?" Forester asked.

"Remember you."

"I wasn't sure you would," Forester said.

"We met briefly at Jane's funeral," the man said. He dropped the rabbits on the ground and took the cartridges out of the shotgun. He snapped the barrels closed and tucked the cartridges into his pocket. He picked the rabbits up. "But I think you knew all about me a long time before that. Drink?"

"Please," replied Forester.

The man led the way. He kicked off his boots just inside the door and stood the shotgun up beside them against the wall. Forester started to slip his shoe off and the man laughed. "Don't bother with those, my boots are wet and my feet are cold, that's all."

"How have you been coping?"

"Since when?"

"Since Jane passed, when else do you think?"

"It's been a while," the man paused.

"What are you doing now?"

"Surviving."

"Nice set up here," Forester looked around the living room. "For the quiet life."

The room was clean and tidy, simply whitewashed with sanded wooden floorboards and contained nothing more than a chair, a sofa and bookshelves packed with books of all genres. In the corner was an easel and a stack of canvasses, pots of paints and a jar of brushes. An open fire was the main feature with a pile of logs and kindling.

"I like it quiet."

"That's not what I hear."

"And what else do you hear?"

Forester smiled. "I thought there was talk of a drink?"

The man nodded. "Coffee or tea?"

"Nothing stronger? It's been a hell of a couple of days."

"More reason to stay focused."

"Coffee, please."

"Black with one sugar, right?"

"Yes. How did you know?"

"I know things."

"So do I," Forester said. "That's why I'm here."

"Careful. You don't have to leave."

"Jane was an excellent judge of character you know." Forester said. "She loved you, heart and soul. She was one of my best agents. She dropped the service like a hot potato because of her love for you."

"Or ovarian cancer," the man paused. "She had it a while."

"She knew she had it when she left?"

"Didn't want a desk. She was damned if she was going to have sympathy and looks of concern. Awkward conversations."

"But you would have received her death in service pay. You would have been set up for life."

"I don't care about money," the man said. "I didn't want to sit back and do nothing. I didn't want to find an excuse not to work."

"Alex, that's exactly the reason I'm here."

***

55°N 13°E Baltic Sea, fifty miles South East of Sjaelland, Denmark

Max Clenton had not had any sleep. It had been plain sailing since Estonia but the hardest part of the journey lay fifty miles away in the narrow channel of Oresund, which ran between Denmark and Sweden. The bottleneck of water, dotted with hundreds of tiny islands, was spanned by many bridges and serviced by numerous ferries throughout the day and night. It could work both ways. There could be safety in numbers. *The Lady Majestic* could hide within the flotilla of craft travelling in all directions, or she could be spotted by the increased presence in authority vessels. Both Denmark and Sweden operated coastguard, police and fisheries vessels throughout the strait. *The Lady Majestic* was now called *Bestræbelse,* meaning endeavour in Danish, she also flew the Danish ensign above the wheelhouse. The new livery had been sign written in white paint and scuffed repeatedly to weather the look when it was almost dry. Clenton had to admit the crew had done well and the paintwork looked years old, worn by time and the elements.

The glorious weather of early morning had given way to torrential rain and the lone wiper blade on the screen of the wheelhouse made little impression on the glass. The instruments and two laptops fixed to the cockpit showed radar and sonar readouts as well as depth and the topography of the ocean floor. The fish-finder showed a tremendous shoal of what he guessed to be Pollack or Cod judging from the shoal's shape and mass. If he had been geared up for it he would have relished such a large shoal of fish, but *The Lady Majestic* had other tasks today and he would have to continue steaming on his current heading and speed. He looked at the satellite weather patterns for the North Sea. It did not look good. Three metre seas and building, sixty-mile per hour winds. He would rouse the crew to double check the cargo was strapped down tightly and that the hold was water proof and locked tight.

A wiry hard-looking man in his fifties stepped up into the bridge and held out a mug with a rubber safety lid. "Coffee Boss," he said gruffly.

"Cheers," he took the cup and sipped. "That's 'ansome, mate. Where's Josh?"

"Watching *Deadliest Catch* in the galley."

"Oh, for Christ's sake!"

***

"Who else knows about the missing agents?"

"Nobody yet. Not even relatives. Only the director, my opposite number in administration and three officers in administration. Oh, and my right-hand agent, Caroline Darby."

"And they were all intelligence agents?"

"GIG. Some were undercover agents actually embedded in Islamic extremist groups. These were actual MI5 agents, not assets coerced or turned to spy. Others were General Intelligence Group handlers and liaison officers. Actual assets were not detailed in the file. However, if these agents were to be made to talk…" He shook his head. "Well, it doesn't bear thinking about."

"And the agents who were killed, they were drowned? Not killed and transported there?"

"No."

"That would have been difficult. Drugged would be my bet."

"They were. Toxicology showed up a cocktail of sedatives including GHB mixed with cocaine."

"Still, logistically it would have called for professionals. And more than a few."

"That was Hodges' view."

"I still don't think it is wise to involve plod," King commented. He had listened to Forester's reasoning to involve the police inspector, but he hadn't approved.

"We have a dual investigation in progress, both Special Branch and the Security Service are investigating the shootings. We both lost personnel, it only makes sense. But the investigation into the drownings at the pier are under our control using Detective Inspector Hodges of the Met and his team."

"But the two are linked. No doubt about it," Alex King paused. "You're going to trip over each other, or worse still, not share information that may seem irrelevant to one team, but would join the pieces the other team have started to link together."

"I know. And to be frank, I was going to turn it over to Special Branch and moderate from the side lines. Let them handle the pier killings, maybe even cut Hodges loose altogether. But this new information changes everything. I can't let this get into the mainstream. This cannot ever be reported by the media," Forester looked at King earnestly. "That's why I've come to you."

"What can I do?"

"Exactly what you used to do for MI6."

"I don't do that anymore."

"You're not denying it."

King shrugged. "No point. You know enough about me, so it would seem."

"Jane told me what you did," Forester said. "Or used to do."

"You can find someone else."

"No doubt."

King stood up. "Then our business is concluded."

"It's not just missing agents, Alex. It's not just somebody setting out to destroy MI5 and its effectiveness to defend our country. It's so much more than that now."

"It always is. There's always something more. The public get to know about ten percent of what the intelligence services prevent, deter or delay."

"Tell me Alex, why are you all the way out here? What made you quit MI6?"

King looked at the man for a while. Forester seemed uncomfortable. King's eyes were glacier cold. The MI5 officer looked away first. "Cards on the table, Forester. You know what I did, after my last mission, don't you?"

"I had my suspicions," he said tentatively. "SIS seems to have had a huge regime change, possibly for the better. We'll have to wait and see."

"I know Box aren't fans of MI6. After a dozen years in the world's Hellholes, I can see why."

"You were hung out to dry, weren't you?" Forester commented.

"And then some."

"They turned on you. Wanted to silence you."

"They tried. One of them was taking bribes, used me as a private assassin," King paused. "I did what I did because I'm a patriot. I know in multi-cultural, politically correct Britain words like patriot are often seen as right-wing, sometimes racist, but that's not it. I serve my country, the leadership, for the best interests of its citizens. If I kill it's because it is needed. It is not so some privileged, self-serving, public school educated mandarin makes money out of me and the lives I take."

"And you removed them all. Left a hundred-year-old institution leaderless."

"Big boys' games…"

"Big boys' rules," Forester smiled. "Remind me never to piss you off."

"You won't," King said. "Because you're leaving here after that coffee and we'll never see each other again."

"You quit and moved out here. Have you been expecting a visit? Expecting one of your trainees to come and make a name for himself?"

"Who would they send?" King smirked. "There's only boys left there now. They're not up to doing a man's job. MI6 are changing, the new leadership will rely more and more upon drones and local assets in the flea-bitten, God forsaken countries where they conduct their business."

"True," Forester said. "But there will always be someone like you. A man in the shadows with a gun."

"They'll use special forces. Drone strikes are great for TV. I'm the last of the breed."

Forester drained his coffee, it was lukewarm. King watched him intently, but he did not get up. "A nuclear device was stolen in Belarus ten years ago and its disappearance was covered up," Forester said. "This cover-up has been exposed."

"Better late than never."

"Indeed. A Russian GRU major named Uri Droznedov is trying to trace it. Believe me when I say he's been pulling out all the stops. They're not a faint hearted agency at the best of times. He has discovered that a former Soviet and later Russian Federation general called Vladimir Zukovsky was to have detonated it in the Ukraine, on the Crimea. It was intended to show the world that Russia is strong and does not forgive treachery. It was hatched by an old, bitter and completely deranged former Soviet KGB general who was so prolific, he was part of cold war training lectures when I joined MI5 from university. They all thought he was mad back then!"

"So what did this Zukovsky do with it?" King asked. "Or I suspect if you knew, you wouldn't be quite so worried."

"Exactly. Zukovsky, as it turned out, pulled the wool over Russia's eyes for his entire career. He was in fact from Chechnya and he's a full blooded Muslim with Islamic extremist beliefs. He helped out the Mujahedeen and Taliban no end in Afghanistan during the Soviet occupation and he helped the Chechens to fight the Russians during that barbarous affair. He gave them information ever since. Yevgeny Antakov, this KGB lunatic, hired a bunch of mercenaries who had been fighting with ISIS in Syria. They needed a bit of breathing space and through a few contacts became guns for hire for a very short while. The moment Zukovsky found out what hardware he had at his disposal, and who these fighters were, he had them signed up for his own cause. And what better way to see out his last years than to meet his maker and the seventy-two virgins waiting in paradise than to deliver the mother of all terrorist attacks to the heart of Europe."

"Why here?"

"He's gunning for Britain. The rest of Europe were no real threat to anyone all those years. It's only recently that they've got involved in the fight against Al Qaeda and Islamic State. But Britain and America have been at the heart of it for years. Way before nine-eleven. There is also the belief that our shores make us a fortress. These attacks over Europe are all well and good, but with freedom of movement over the continent, they are relatively simple to execute. They want to rock us at our very heart. Not only prove they can get to us, but get to us with a full blown ICBM. Detonated in a major city means the end of that city. Simple as that. The device is eight-hundred kilotons. Hiroshima and Nagasaki were estimated at fifteen kilotons."

King shook his head. "Okay, so the threat is real. You need a team of thinkers on this fast. You need to run the numbers. Maybe an American target within Britain? A military base perhaps?"

"I'm nowhere near there yet, but that would be my guess," Forester paused. "All we have is a woman called Alesha Mikailovitch. She has been identified from the Special Branch film at the scene of the killings. Further CCTV as she walked from Beak Street through to Kensington was of better quality and matched her on the Interpol database. She is Zukovsky's girlfriend.

Rafan Betesh who died in the shooting was one of the mercenaries that Yevgeny Antakov hired."

"Not Jamil Betesh's brother?"

"Yes."

"Bugger. I killed Jamil in Iraq last year. He was part of the ISIS push into Northern Iraq. A group of Kurdish rebels were holding them back, while the Iraqi army allowed the area to become over-run. I was hoping that one day I'd kill the other two and collect the set," King paused. "Evil people. They beheaded many civilians. Did a lot worse besides."

"I could give you his brother," Forester said coyly.

"Mohammed?"

"Yes."

"Mohammed was part of that same push. I was friends with those Kurds. They were good people."

"I want them all put down," Forester said. "I want this device found, but I want every person involved dead and buried. We are losing this war on terrorism and if it ever comes to light that a nuclear device was posing, or had posed a clear and present threat to Britain, then it would start unprecedented panic. It wouldn't take much to create a financial and democratic crisis. Knowing a likely threat was out there would be like living in the last days before an apocalypse. Law and order would simply break down, society would collapse. And then there's Islamic relations. Decent people will get caught up in anti-extremist paranoia."

"You'd better find it then," King said.

"I have good people to do that. But I want you on board. You are somebody used to working off the grid. You operate with no support, beyond the parameters of MI5's remit. You would be invaluable and you would be the man to shut these bastards down."

"I'm not a gun for hire."

"I'll sign you up as a fully-fledged Security Service officer. I'll have your pension benefits transferred and start you in a new career with MI5. You will be a senior agent, but you will report only to me. When or if the time comes, I want you to cross the line we operate behind and take them out."

"Take them out? Where, to dinner?" King looked at him coldly. "Say the words."

Forester looked him in the eyes. "I want you to kill them," he paused. "I don't want them caught and displayed on TV, I don't want them languishing in prison spreading their twisted interpretation of Islam. I want them dead."

23

Vladimir Zukovsky scrolled through the data on the screen. The laptop was fast and powerful. The file size was over five thousand megabytes of data, equivalent to almost three thousand filled A4 pages and two thousand photographs. Most home computers would have been sluggish opening and accessing a file of this enormity, let alone copying the data but the laptop had been upgraded for the task. Its operating software was minimal and it only needed to open two types of file and connect to the internet. The messages Zukovsky would soon send would be short, edited files. He would store the data on various cloud storage facilities and provide the access passcodes.

He was aware of movement behind him, turned around in his seat. Alesha stood there. She had stripped down to a vest top and was covered in scarlet patches of burned skin. Her breasts looked raw, blistered. Her hands were bound loosely in wet bandages, but it was her face that had been most affected. Down the left side of her once beautiful face the skin had blistered and so many layers had been burned that her cheek looked like a large steak, barely seared blue on a skillet. Her eye had escaped injury, but her eyelids were burned and swollen and she could not see out of her left eye because of the swelling.

"I need a hospital," she said.

"I told you, we cannot jeopardise the operation."

"But look at me!"

"You will heal."

"I am a freak!" she snapped. "I need plastic surgery!"

"Khalil insisted that he needed a hospital," Zukovsky said. "He was blinded. He was burned worse than you."

Alesha frowned, but she regretted the action immediately as the skin pulled tightly. She winced. "Where is Khalil?"

Zukovsky stood. "Come, I will show you."

Alesha followed. "Mohammed has lost his sight in one eye," she said as she followed him out of the room and into the loading bay. "He will need a hospital also."

"Has he asked?"

"No."

Zukovsky unlocked the Jaguar remotely and opened the boot on the key fob. "I did not think he would."

"What do you mean?" Alesha asked. She looked at Zukovsky, who had stopped walking. She turned back to the car, saw Khalil's body twisted and folded into the boot.

"He knows what is expected of this operation," Zukovsky said coldly. "Khalil did not. Khalil bleated on that he needed medical attention, that he would keep quiet. But to enter the system is to jeopardise what we have been working towards."

"But…"

"You were a drug addled whore, when I found you, Alesha," Zukovsky said. "But you had beauty. You also had vanity. Vanity is such an ugly flaw in a person's character. It makes one so very arrogant. Now you are all but repulsive on one side. A true Janus. A person of two faces. Maybe the real Alesha will emerge? Maybe this sudden deformity will provide you with a strength of character you have not yet possessed?"

She looked at him with disdain. Her bottom lip quivered and tears rolled down her cheeks. The left side was so raw the saltiness of the tears made her recoil. "*Svoloch*!" she cursed at him savagely and stormed off leaving him beside the car.

Zukovsky walked back to the office, irritated by the interruption, and looked at the screen. He was about to scrawl through, but hesitated. He had only really seen it with his periphery vision, a flash of recognition. He frowned and clicked on the tiny thumbnail photograph. His heart raced and he read through the details, but it was the photograph that he could not take his eyes from. He felt nauseous, slumped down in the chair.

Tomorrow he would pay a visit to somebody he vowed never to meet again in person.

24

Caroline Darby had run her short route. It weaved through two small parks and a tree-lined avenue and she looped back through the market. It was a three-mile circuit, which she always ran at a fast pace, and it ended at the best bakery stall in the city, where she could buy a *pain au chocolat* and a croissant and eat a comparatively guilt free breakfast. She loved the banter and bustle of the market, loved the feeling of uniqueness it gave off over supermarkets and chain stores. The feeling of community. It shamed her that she was largely voyeuristic, only shopping there occasionally even though it was on her doorstep, but she led a busy life and her work took her all over the country.

    She had put the coffee machine on to the espresso setting, taken a powerful shower and dressed quickly. The pastries were excellent and she sat in front of the television with the volume low, checked her phone for messages and glanced up at the screen as she sipped some coffee. She froze when she saw the tickertape scrolling underneath the feature, then saw the photographs of Alesha Mikailovitch and Mohammed Betesh on the screen. Next came two more photographs, this time with no names, but Caroline recognised them as the men from the safe house attack. All the photographs had been taken from the safe house CCTV footage. Along with this were two short films of what looked like drug deals. One involving one of the unknown men from the safe house attack, the other a tattooed man with a trimmed stubbly beard and a shaven head with five o'clock shadow. His features were typically Slavic. A free-phone number was constantly on the screen. Caroline fumbled with the remote. By the time she turned the volume up the newsreader was ending the piece with, *"... in connection with the murder of four government employees discovered at Festival Pier on Friday."*

She tried Forester's number, but it went straight to voicemail. She dialled Detective Inspector Hodges' number, again it went to voicemail, but she left a curt message, already grabbing her bag and coat as she spoke.

She was lucky enough to have parking to the rear of the apartment block. Not everybody did and the cost of a yearly parking permit, combined with London's congestion charge made her regularly think about selling her Mini Cooper, but she was an independent person and knew she would miss the luxury of motoring if it were no longer an option. Besides, the Security Service had her travelling all over the country, often at next to no notice and pool cars were not always available. They paid a handsome expense and mileage if she used her own car, so she knew for the sake of her career it was never really an option to give it up.

She used Bluetooth to dial Hodges' number again. The detective picked up after a few rings. *"Hello?"*

"Detective Inspector, it's Caroline Darby. Forester wanted me to liaise with you," she said casually. "Are you at the yard or Thames House?"

"The yard," he answered, a little hesitantly. *"What can I do for you?"*

"I need to speak to you regarding that shit you pulled this morning," she said. "I'll be about fifteen minutes. I'll be pulling up outside, arrange a space for me."

"I'm on my way out. Following a lead."

"Be in Hodges. For all our sakes."

She ended the call and wound the Mini through her usual route. She had perfected the route over the years and would bet she knew a way that would beat any taxi driver. Especially as she knew of a large carpark that had an exit and entrance on two different streets, and that merely driving through beat the one-way system and shaved more than five minutes off her journey.

When she drew up outside New Scotland Yard she could see Hodges standing next to a uniformed officer and a vacant parking space. Caroline took a deep breath. She had no authority over the police inspector, it was more a case of mutual respect than protocol, but Caroline had soon come to realise early in her career that being in MI5 carried clout in all walks of life. She decided to bowl Hodges over and she hoped she could keep up the act.

Hodges walked over to her car and stood by the door. She got out and looked at him. "We'll do this outside," she said.

"Do what?"

"You're a good murder detective, I hear."

"If you say so."

"It's your record that says so."

"You've seen my record?"

"Of course," she lied. She'd only had the one conversation with Forester. "What the hell was that this morning?"

"You mean the appeal," he said. "We're getting nowhere finding the killers. It was the next logical step."

"Forester wanted this low profile."

"Does he want the killers caught or not?" he interrupted.

"Not at the risk of them running and going to ground."

"That's just a fact of criminal life," he retorted. "They kill, they hide, we hunt them, sometimes we flush them out."

"There is too much at stake."

"Well how about telling me what else is at stake?"

"I can't. Yet."

"Then I'll ask Forester."

"I'm sure he'll say the same."

"Then I'll try him," he took out his phone and dialled. He looked annoyed when it cut to voicemail. "I'll try him later," he added.

"I'll level with you, Hodges," Caroline said. "There is chance of an imminent attack."

"There always is," he said. "What's the security level threat?"

"I can't say. Because I don't know. All I know is if it happens it will be the worst ever."

"A nine-eleven?"

"No. A lot worse," she said. "You've made a move with that news appeal, and that's done. But you need to get staffed up and follow every damned lead you get. You need to find these people and pray to God they don't go to ground permanently."

"A bit melodramatic."

"No, it's not," she looked at him, then the great building behind. The centre of police enforcement and symbolism of law and order. She did not know why, but she felt her fiancé's presence as she thought about the shady cloak and dagger world she lived in. Maybe he would still be here if there was more sharing of intelligence between agencies. Maybe a lot of people's loved ones would be. "Look, Hodges. You've got a hand tied behind your back. I'll say this once and don't ever quote me. Forester wanted you on this case because he saw a dogged, experienced copper. Someone who would leave no stone unturned, and not get bogged down in bureaucracy. A say it as he sees it kind of man."

"Fair enough," he said.

"Wait, I'm not finished. Imagine the worst kind of terrorist attack. Imagine the worst kind of bomb." She saw the look in his eye, there was a slight flicker as he realised the prompt. "Well, one is missing in Russia and linked to a General Vladimir Zukovsky. He's a former general with the Soviet and then Russian Federation military. He served with the army and then the KGB and FSB when it was later renamed. He cannot be linked to these murders because if he gets wind of being a suspect, he will know that we know about the nuclear device. Alesha Mikailovitch is his protégé and girlfriend. You have named her from her involvement with the shootings. That's controllable, they will assume you're linking the clues, joining the dots. And her getting caught on CCTV is a natural avenue you will exploit.

You must not, under any circumstances, name Zukovsky. If his name comes up as a result of the names you have run on the databases, drop it. Like a hot coal."

"And this threat is real?" Hodges asked, he seemed withdrawn.

"We have to treat it as such," she answered matter-of-factly. "Do not tell a soul. Nobody can know, not yet. But I'm giving you this as a curtesy. The appeal is out there now, but let's make it work. Put more people on it than you normally would. The Security Service will pick up the tab for extra wages, resources and overtime."

Hodges nodded. "Thank you."

Caroline walked back to her car, the uniformed policeman was standing beside it, his eyes on the traffic. She nodded to Hodges as she got inside.

Hodges took out his mobile as he walked back to the building. He dialled his home number. "Hello Michelle," he said quietly. "Look, please don't ask me questions, but I want you to pack enough clothes for a week and take the boys down to your mother's. I'll call you later and explain more. And give Ginny a call for me. Tell her to stay at university next weekend." He held the phone momentarily out from his ear, then he snapped. "Look! Do it now! No arguments. Now, I'll call you in a couple of hours when you're on your way to Devon," he paused for a moment. "Actually, forget that, do me a favour and swing by the office before you set off. I want to see you all before you go."

25

Forester's driver pulled the big Jaguar to the curb and both King and Forester got out. King had taken note of the SCO19 Discovery vehicles and the Special Branch vehicles had both changed to Vauxhall Insignias with the shift change. Both were black with tinted rear windows. Forester had ordered his driver to go down both streets so King could study the houses separately.

"You've got a lot of firepower here," King said. "Do you really think they'll attack again?"

"Who knows?" replied Forester curtly.

"What can this guy Hoist know that has made them want to silence him?"

"I'm hoping we will find out soon. The interview team has been with him all night."

King watched the street both ways before climbing the steps. "Well they'd be mad to attack here. You have armed units both ends, they're alert because of the second attack, and the visuals are excellent. You can see a hundred metres in both directions and there's CCTV at both ends of the street." He had an uneasy feeling, but as he surveyed the security and went over the information Forester had given him, he kept coming back to the same conclusion.

Forester nodded, surprised, but somewhat pleased King had noticed. "I'll introduce you to my agent, and then we'll draw up a plan. Decide where best to deploy your *skills*." Forester said. He looked at King.

The man was dressed in the same cargo pants but had swapped the waxed jacket for a leather jacket. "Do you need to stop off anywhere and change?"

"I've got what I need," he said, hefting the military Bergen over his shoulder. "I'm not a suit man, Forester. I'll need some equipment though. Tools of the trade, so to speak."

Forester nodded, climbing the steps to the front door. "I'll have someone organise that. I'll need a list."

"No, I sort my own kit. I'll need some cash though."

"Very well." Forester knocked on the door, glancing up at the CCTV camera to identify himself. The door opened and a Special Branch officer stood to one side. Forester nodded in acknowledgement. He had already called ahead and told them to expect someone else with him. Forester had also called Caroline, who had already been on route, to meet him here.

Caroline appeared at the top of the stairs. She walked down slowly, eyeing up the new arrival warily. She frowned at Forester. "Did you get your business sorted out?" she asked.

"I have," he replied. "Let's go through to the lounge where we can talk more freely."

Caroline followed Forester, King brought up the rear. The lounge was sparsely furnished. It acted as a briefing room with a large dining table and eight chairs and the suite consisted of three sofas, two three-seaters and a four seater facing each other with a coffee table in the middle. TV and DVD remotes rested on the table and a large-screen television made up the square.

"This is Alex," Forester said. "Alex King. He has worked with MI6 for… I don't know… Fifteen years?"

"Feels like a hundred," King offered his hand to Caroline. She shook it firmly, glanced at Forester. "I'm joining the team," King said. "Until this operation is over, at least."

"And after that?" she ventured.

"We'll see," King said. He pulled a chair out from the table. "You are treading water. Let's talk about how to make some headway."

Caroline scoffed. "We've managed pretty well so far! They've tried to assassinate Hoist twice; they've failed both times."

"Did they?"

"Of course!" Caroline turned to Forester. "What is this?"

Forester held up a hand. "Let's listen."

King shrugged. "What does Hoist know? He was worked over in a honey trap, downloaded the information he was blackmailed to do and handed it over. He is a medium-level analyst and processer and has never worked in the field. He knows nothing, unless he has met someone and can ID them, then killing Hoist has very little to achieve. Unless these assassination attempts and in particular the second one, are merely to waste MI5 resources and prevent further investigation. This Zukovsky is known through his association with the Russian woman, Mikail…" King hesitated.

"Alesha Mikailovitch," Caroline prompted.

"Mikailovitch. Zukovsky's involvement isn't known, but you have a tip-off from a Russian intelligence officer linking him to a missing nuclear device. We can only connect the dots, but we also have the information that he is in fact a Muslim, and he kept this from the regime for his entire service. We know he was introduced to ISIS fighters, one of these was killed at Hoist's apartment, and another, Mohammed Betesh, the dead man's brother has been identified."

"Correct," Forester nodded.

"According to your GRU contact, these men were the same ISIS fighters Zukovsky met in Russia."

"Yes," Forester nodded.

"Hoist met Zukovsky?"

"Yes. But only under his first name," Caroline interjected.

"That's the reason they want him dead then," King said. "They, or rather, Zukovsky is worried that knowledge of his involvement will play their hand too soon. Up until now it's radical Muslims running around taking a swipe at the British intelligence services. They want the details on the data Hoist downloaded, and they want to keep you running around with no clear ground gained. Keep you all busy while they set off the device. But first they have to get it in place."

"So we're still no further ahead," said Caroline.

"But we are," King said. "If the device was ready to detonate, then why are they waiting? It's either not here, or not ready to arm."

"And you're sure of this?"

"There's only one way to find out," King mused. "We make Hoist easier to get to. If they try another hit, we know for sure the device isn't ready."

"How the hell do we do that?"

"Get rid of the security. Send Special Branch away right now. If this place is under surveillance it will create a point of interest. I've got to go out for some shopping. When I get back, we send the armed police chaps home. That will be a second point of interest. After that, we're just a house. No armed guards."

"What shopping do you need?" Caroline asked, somewhat bemused.

"Toys, mainly," replied King. "The kind I like to play with."

26

King had two hours. That was the time he allotted himself. Forester had returned to Thames House and had arranged for a smartphone to be delivered to the house by motorcycle courier. Along with this was an envelope containing ten-thousand pounds for expenses. By the time King returned to the safe-house a car would be waiting for him to use and inside the glove box would be a credit card in his name with no theoretical upper spending limit. A file containing all of MI5, Special Branch and police findings to date would also be in the car, as well as a letter from Forester for King's eyes only. This would be King's warrant, his get out of jail free card.

Caroline had been told to assist King in any way possible. She was not part of Forester's and King's agreement, but she knew that what the two men were doing was unorthodox, and most likely illegal. She was correct on both counts.

Forester had intimated that the nation was in crisis, that desperate times called for desperate measures. He had started to quote Winston Churchill, but Caroline had held up a hand and silenced him abruptly. She could catch the drift, and she had lost the love of her life to terrorism. She was not a fan of law and constitution breaking, but she had to admit to herself that she found the idea intriguing and tempting increasingly so. The British establishment were hamstrung in a world of political correctness and what was considered civilised behaviour. She knew that unless the methods changed, the fight against terrorism would be lost. And ground was never easily won back.

King rode in the taxi, glancing at his watch. The Special Branch protection officers would be gone by now. Another hour and the armed police units would be pulling out. They had been told to do it slowly, drive past the property, pause and then continue. The act had to be visible to evoke interest. Caroline was not happy about being left without the armed presence, but King had reassured her. His words were rebuked when she pointed out that he would not be here to know.

King planned to take Hoist out in the car within the next three hours. Attacks were ten times more likely arriving at, or departing from a location. Nine times out of ten an attack would take place getting into or out of a vehicle. If they were not hit they would try once more. If this brought no response, then it was agreed that Hoist would be entered into the legal system for prosecution. He would be the property of the Crown Prosecution Service and all that entailed.

The taxi pulled up outside the address King had supplied. King got out and surveyed the alleyway, and then the buildings opposite. CCTV pointed down the alleyway from the building across the street. King would not be surprised if the building had been leased solely to fix the camera to and keep the other building looking unsecured, a much lower profile.

King had called ahead, spoken briefly to his contact. He made his way down the alleyway and as he reached the metal door it popped open a few inches on a tight spring. King stepped inside and the door closed. A PIR operated light switched on and King looked up into the camera. He glanced down and noticed a set of double shotgun barrels poking out of the metal lined wall, almost flush in profile. In the close proximity and the size of the small box he was now standing inside, a shotgun going off would be bad news indeed. King imagined lead bird-shot in the breach, which would bounce around the metal box he stood inside. There would be no escaping the blast.

The secondary door buzzed open and King breathed a sigh of relief as he stepped inside. He looked to the right and could not see the rest of the gun. It had been built into the adjacent wall and most likely operated from an electrical switch elsewhere in the building.

"Come up the stairs…" the voice said on an intercom. It crackled slightly, enough to know it was not spoken inside the same room.

King walked up the metal grated staircase. There were fifteen treads. At the top the landing went left or right. He had been here before, many years ago. The security box, the shotgun and the intercom were new additions. He turned left as he had before and ahead of him a cavernous room opened up. It was stacked to the ceiling with cardboard boxes and wooden crates.

"MI6, I'm honoured once more," the man said. He limped towards King, a little wary. King knew the man had prosthetic limbs. He was an Afghan veteran. He did not offer a hand, kept three or four paces between them. The man was cautious. It was a risky business at the best of times.

King did not correct the man. He had supplied MI6 many times and had shipped for them all over the world. "How's business?" King asked casually as he looked around the room. "Your inventory seems larger than it did last time I was here."

"I can't complain," the man said. He waved a hand to the stack of wooden crates to his left. "Brand new SCAR rifles for a security outfit in Afghanistan. All legal. Then we've got AK47's surplus from Iraq. Those guys are using M16s now, supplied by Uncle Sam. These AK's have been cleaned and refurbished in India, thanks to cheap child labour, now they're here to be shipped out to Syria for the boots on the ground. Great Britain PLC is picking up the tab for that one. Arming the locals. I just hope most of them stay out of ISIS's hands."

"So do I," King said coldly.

The man tensed a little. "So why are you here?"

"I need a few items."

"Through the books or black ops?"

"Very black."

"What are you after?"

"Something quiet, something extremely loud and something in between."

"Like Goldilocks?" the man smiled wryly.

"I need a silenced pistol. Quieter the better, ideally .22," King paused. "I want two combat pistols, both nines with large magazine capacity. A couple of boxes of ammo should do, but I want at least three magazines a piece. Preferably the same models so it can all mix and match in a pinch."

"Sensible."

"One of those SCAR's sounds good."

"They're top drawer. They don't come cheap," the man paused. "What sort of range do you want?"

"Five hundred metres, tops."

"Do you want deep penetration? Body armour, vehicles?"

"That could be handy."

"I have a few in 7.62mm. The contractors like a few heavy calibres as a fire-support weapon. It's as close as they get to calling the Calvary. As you know the SCAR comes in 5.56mm NATO as well, all sorts of barrel lengths. M203 grenade launchers can be underslung on Picatinny rails, or a .12-gauge shotgun for forced door entry. You name it and I can build it."

"Time frame?"

"Two to three days."

"You've got an hour."

The man looked at King curiously. "Sounds like a rushed job."

"It's an important job."

"Cash?"

"Of course."

"Paperwork?"

"No."

"Urban or rural?" the man asked, then added, "Or desert?"

"Urban, maybe rural,"

"The 5.56mm should do it."

"No, I'll go big."

"Okay. We'll go short barrel though. Fold-down stock. You'll have a range of a solid six hundred metres, but the short barrel will allow room to room scenarios and be easy to store. We'll go olive. It will be less visual in an urban environment than standard black. A four by forty scope should be okay. I have Schmidt and Bender, naturally…"

King nodded. "I'd prefer two point five through to ten, then by fifty…"

"I think I have a compromise. You like a wide angle then?"

"In urban scenarios I do."

"I have a few armour-piercing rounds that can go astray."

"Perfect. I'll take the rest in green dot."

"Now you're getting picky," the man said.

Green dot ammunition was the first hundred rounds cast in a batch. After the first hundred the finish is never quite as good. Batches run into the tens of thousands and the military reserves the first hundred rounds as sniper issue ammunition.

"I'll take ten magazines. Three hundred green dot, full metal jacketed. Whatever you can get me in armour-piercing will be greatly appreciated," King said.

"You starting a war?"

"No," King said. "Just finishing one."

27

Forester had barely sat down at his desk when his internal email binged and he was met with an array of messages from his secretary. There was an update from Detective Inspector Hodges, simply outlining what progress had been made. Forester had to admit that it wasn't much, although the television appeal had kept him tied to the telephone and his office all morning. Caroline had told Forester of her meeting with the detective, although she had omitted to tell him she had let Hodges know about the device. She had made it clear though, that the police were not to mention or follow on any lead for Zukovsky without informing MI5.

There was a progress report from Commander Anderson of Special Branch. They had good leads from the van hire company and the CCTV from the offices had been shared with Hodges' team. Again, the nation's finest didn't seem to be getting much further either.

The third message was forwarded from Major Uri Droznedov of the Russian Federation GRU. He was on route to London and would be seeking an audience with Forester. He wished to join the search for General Zukovsky and the missing warhead. He would have with him certain equipment and paperwork which would aid British bomb disposal units with deactivating the warhead. Forester quickly messaged his secretary informing her to reply at once. He instructed her to send a direct-dial number he could be contacted on.

There were three messages from the Director. Forester ignored them and scrolled down the list. One was an intel report from a surveillance point in the north of the city. The report would have been filed to operation control, but Forester was an automatic tie-in for this particular operation, meaning that when the information was sent to be updated, the report would split and file itself automatically on Forester's database. It wasn't the only operation to do so, Forester kept personally abreast of at least six at any one time. This operation, however, had been hard-fought and he was not about to lose control anytime soon.

Forester opened the file and read the report. It was a surveillance report on the target and detailed times and locations set out in the log with a timeline, dateline and the location using GPS. The report contained a number of jpegs. Forester opened the first and it showed the target. It was a good quality photograph taken with a zoom lens at a distance. The next showed two men with the target. Both were known bodyguards, two of a potential dozen men the target called upon, depending on the size of the event or the availability of the bodyguards. The third photograph made Forester freeze, his heartbeat rising quickly. His throat tightened and he could hear his own heartbeat pulsing in his ears. General Vladimir Zukovsky wore a heavy coat and a tweed flat cap. He carried himself tall and upright, despite his age. The hat was stylish, more Mayfair than farmer. The sort bought at expensive gentlemen's outfitters and worn on beaten pheasant shoots where champagne was served with canapés between drives. Zukovsky looked comfortable, the other man less so, but over the next five jpegs Forester could see the earnest expression on both men's faces. But why was Zukovsky there? And what the hell was he and the Yemeni Iman Mullah Al-Shaqqaf talking about outside the mosque?

28

King got out of the taxi just short of the street. He paid with a tip and walked slowly, casually. The sports bag he'd been given to stow the weapons was slung over his shoulder. The SCAR had been calibrated with the use of a barrel mounted sight zero. This was a tool that drove a four inch pin the desired calibre into the muzzle and looked like a small rifle scope. Once it was fixed and true, it emitted a red dot. This enabled the cross-hairs of the rifle's scope to be zeroed. You merely dialled the windage and elevation adjustments until the cross-hairs sat directly on the red dot. This was calibrated to one hundred metres. King would know where to position the cross-hairs on the target for fifty metres (around three inches low to compensate for the rising bullet) and for two hundred metres (around two inches high to compensate for flattening of trajectory). From his experience longer shots out to five-hundred metres would require elevating the sights of the weapon by eight inches. This was not a precision sniper's weapon and the sights were utilitarian. They were the best for a multitude of scenarios. All weapons were different and King would have preferred some range time to sight the weapon, but for now it would have to do.

The rifle was loaded, cocked and the safety applied. He carried a 9mm Walther P99. It was loaded and made ready. King had purchased a high-draw leather belt holster and it rode snugly putting the butt of the weapon near his right kidney. He had worked so long in this trade, he felt naked without a pistol with him. The weapon was chunky and made its presence known to him as he walked. He felt comfortable with it.

King surveyed the street. There were a number of cars parked under the trees and the leaves had fallen much in the past week. Piles had blown up, and the dry weather had dried them out to a satisfying crunch when stepped on. The street reminded him of quiet, expensive streets in America. The trees were spaced out every ten paces or so. Here and there the roots had lifted the pavement slabs. The houses were large and the cars were premium brands. It was an exclusive street and he could tell that the people were mainly professionals. Mothers and nannies pushed prams or strollers and a few walked with pre-schoolers. The mothers were older, thirties and forties. They had most likely given up on or taken a break from careers. The nannies were younger, east European.

As King watched them he suddenly wished he had taken more into account when testing the water with Hoist's security. The last thing he wanted were stray bullets from a pitched street battle.

There was no sign of any hostile surveillance. King ventured down the adjacent street. The second safe house was similar in design, but the street looked slightly less expensive. The vehicles were older or down a rung in the premium car ladder. They were still expensive, but there were less of the big three German saloons and SUVs. King marvelled how different one street could be. The buildings were slightly smaller, or had clearly been redeveloped into large apartments or smaller terraced town houses. They were bordered or defined by different shades of paint or fencing and railings. It was still a highly desirable location and would no doubt be unobtainable on the average salary.

There was no sign of anybody watching the house here either. King made his way back into the other street and climbed the steps. He knocked on the door and stared into the CCTV camera. The door opened and Caroline stood in front of him.

"Took your time," she said.

"Shops were busy," he said dryly. "I've got some goodies though."

She looked at the bag as he dropped it down on the floor. "These are for you," she said, holding out a set of electronic key-fobs. "A dark blue BMW parked two down from here."

"Nice," King commented. He had noticed the 5 Series as he walked past. He took the keys from her. "Are you driving?"

"A Mini Cooper," she replied. "Parked one door up."

King took one of the key-fobs off the ring and gave it to her. "Here, just in case."

"Thanks," she said quietly.

"Who else is in?"

"Hoist is in the interview room with two of the service's interrogators. Or should I say, interviewers?" she smiled. "Whatever, they're questioning him."

"Who else?"

"The couple who run the place."

"Send them out," King said. "Tell the interviewers to go. Let's have some time alone with Hoist."

"Why?"

"We need to see if we are under surveillance. I want to see if Hoist is still important to them and I don't want any more collateral damage."

"What about me?"

"You're paid to take risks. Besides, I hear you handle yourself well."

"I'm not armed."

"I'll boil up some sugar."

"Funny."

"I have a P99 in the bag," King said. "Do you want it?"

"I haven't used one before."

"Pull the trigger and aim the other end at what you want to hit. It's a very simple weapon, like a Glock. I can put a pan of sugar on if you prefer."

"Idiot," Caroline said sardonically. "Just give it to me."

King unzipped the bag and passed out the Walther and three magazines. "There's an integral safety on the blade of the trigger. It won't fire unless this is depressed," he said. "Each magazine is loaded and holds sixteen rounds."

Caroline held the weapon and felt its weight, which was not inconsiderable. The butt was made from soft rubber compound and textured. Most handgun manufacturers making modern combat pieces had gone down this route, in combat your hands sweat so you need a more tactile grip than the walnut of the old Colts and Brownings of the first and second world wars, or the hard plastic composite of the Berettas or Sigs of the eighties and nineties. It sat snugly in her hand without having to grip it tightly. She aimed it at a point on the wall, getting a feel for the wide fixed sights. She pulled back the slide and it held back in position. When she inserted the magazine, she depressed the slide release button and the weapon jumped slightly as the slide shot forward and chambered the first bullet. The weapon felt heavier now, but better balanced. King held out a holster for her. She took it and clipped it to the waistband of her trousers, on her left side somewhere between her hip and her belly button. It was conceal-carry holster and all but the clip was on the inside of her trousers. She nestled the weapon inside. She was good to go.

"Look's good," King commented. "I like a woman who accessorises well."

"I bet you do," she said glibly. "I imagine a matching set of bra and panties would impress you."

"Ouch."

"Just coming down to your level."

"You'll have a long way to go," King smiled. "Right, time to let the staff go, I think."

29

Forester had thought about calling in the surveillance chief on the Islington Mosque. However, he had called ahead and arranged to meet at an independent coffee shop nearby. He did not want the man taken away from his job for longer than necessary.

The officer in charge was a fifty-year old called Vernon Keller. He was quiet and unassuming with rounded shoulders and balding hair. He was losing it on top but had not yet realised that cutting it short would look better than accentuating the baldness by growing what he had left. He was ideal in surveillance and worked exclusively as a watcher. He would occasionally lecture and demonstrate counter surveillance drills to new recruits. He was noted for carrying three different pairs of glasses in contrasting styles and changing them regularly while on operations. His counter surveillance drills were perfect. Nobody ever remembered seeing him.

Forester scanned the restaurant for a moment, saw him sitting at a booth in the corner. The man had his back to the wall and watched both outside the window and the other customers with a series of casual glances. He had a large coffee in front of him and a slice of chocolate cake. Forester walked past the counter, asked for a tea and walked over to the operative.

"Hello Vernon."
"Sir."

"The cake looks good."

"Blood sugar levels. Need a pick-me-up."

Forester watched the man take a bite. He wished he's ordered something to go with his tea. "Long shifts?"

"Aren't they always?"

"So, Al-Shaqqaf met with someone outside the mosque."

"It looked casual, grew in intensity and then the Mullah throws a big one. Points the finger, shakes his head and starts shouting. The old man pulled him down a peg or two though. They didn't leave on a handshake it's fair to say."

"Parabolic?"

"We picked up bits and pieces on the directional microphone. We've had parabolic sound on them but they're not daft. They're using ultrasonic waves to screw up the microphones."

Forester nodded. "So they're taking active counter measures?"

"Oh yes," Keller said. "They are sweeping three times daily. They're using their own equipment."

"And have you got anything inside?"

"Not since our stuff was discovered and he did his big civil liberties speech to the press and in court. We've come close. We have had a few assets in there at prayers. They haven't had the chance or inclination to risk getting caught though. We can't get a team in there now, they have people in there around the clock."

"Are the transcripts ready?"

"I have them here," Keller said. He opened his laptop and turned it around so that Forester could see the screen. "It's a mess. Ultrasonic has cut it to pieces."

Forester pressed the play icon on the screen.

"...ood faith. You told me he cou.. .e counted .. you t..d me to trust you. How ... I trust ... now? ... ... me. I need you to put this right." This voice was Zukovsky's.

Iman Mullah Al-Shaqqaf responded: *"Without me there would be no .....tion and you should remember that I have stood by you and .... big ide.. now show me you can .. ..is!"*

Then Zukovsky shouted: *"I have told you where. Just be there!"*

"Is that it?" Forester said.

Keller nodded. "They strolled away from the mosque, came closer to our position. The ultrasonic waves were on the cusp. They couldn't break the parabolic microphone. But they shouted this at one another and the Iman threw his hands in the air and stormed back towards the mosque. The old man shouted as he drew nearer to us. We got his whole sentence."

Forester smiled. "I want a big team on this. I want to know where the Iman has been told to go and I want him and every single one of his heavies followed. Get mobile units on this, both foot soldiers and vehicles. We have a chance of linking him to another investigation and I want the other man in that recording. He is my priority."

30

The tattooed Russian kept his eyes on the scene. The monitor was fixed to the dashboard of the van and he could see the front door of the safe-house and the steps leading up to it. Through his colleague's precision placement and landing of the drone he could also make out the gate of the safe-house garden on the adjacent street. The drone had been landed on top of a church on the street running parallel. The Norman spire provided a flat landing zone in an area of pitched roof tops, and the wide angle feature allowed a tremendous panorama, but it would not be possible to pick out individual faces or features through such a low magnification aperture. It had been an inspired piece of armchair aviation and the young man seated in the passenger seat next to him hadn't been exactly modest as he whoop-whooped his way to a perfect landing. The drone was now shut down and powered to standby.

The tattooed man's mobile vibrated in his pocket. He always kept the phone on silent as a security measure. He looked at the display, recognised Mohammed's number. "Yes?"

"We are on route. Are you sure the police vehicles have gone?"

"That's what I said," the Russian replied indignantly.

"I know what you said!" snapped Mohammed. *"And the undercover vehicles?"*

"Gone."

"And the target is inside?"

"We cannot confirm."

"What do you mean?"

The tattooed Russian grit his teeth and clenched the phone. He did not like Mohammed. But he respected the general and any decision he made, and that was enough for him to remain calm. "To preserve the flying battery life of the drone, and to maintain a visual on the houses indefinitely it was necessary to land. This required the camera to be used solely for manoeuvring. It took five minutes to make the landing safely. We cannot confirm one hundred percent that the target is still inside."

"Where are you parked?"

"Hamilton Street, six streets away, running almost parallel."

"Stay there. We will come to you."

The line disconnected and the tattooed Russian put the phone back in his pocket and kept his eyes on the screen.

31

Jeremy Hoist walked into the lounge with the two interview specialists trailing behind him. Swift looked displeased at the interruption. Barbara looked impassive, but she threw the file down onto the table and a few loose pages edged out.

"Thank you," King looked at both specialists in turn and glanced at the file. "We'll be in touch."

"This is highly irregular," Swift snapped. "Deputy Director Forester will hear about this."

"I'm sure," said King.

"May we speak with you without the subject present?" Barbara asked. She was flushing red up her neck and through her cheeks.

"Have you found out anything other than what you already had at the previous safe-house?" King asked.

Both interview specialists looked agitated. Swift glanced at Hoist then back at King. "Not in so many words," he said. "Look, let me talk to you in private."

"I think we're way past that."

"What do you mean?" Barbara snapped.

"Look, the way I see it, your man here has been coerced into divulging information. He has been caught. I don't think he has anything else to say. You have had him long enough," King paused. "Leave all of your findings here. Take the day off and wait to be reassigned. Forget you ever heard this man's name."

Hoist frowned. "What do you mean?"

King stared at him, watched the man's indignant look soften and confusion set in. King had the ability to make people question their motives and emotions with a look. His eyes seemed to dare, but few ever did. "Change of tactic. When these two leave I will take about ten seconds to learn if you have more information. After that, we're changing tack. We're seeing how much these Russian friends of yours want you and what they are willing to do to silence you." King turned to both MI5 officers and nodded towards the door. "Mind how you go. Keep your wits about you, this place may be under surveillance."

Caroline shrugged and showed the two specialists out. They followed, but they were not happy about it.

"Then I'm little more than bait!" Hoist protested. "I want a solicitor and I want to exercise my right for silence!"

King balled his fist and punched Hoist in the chest. The punch came from King's waist, perfectly straight. At the last moment he dropped his left knee and twisted his right hip. The punch now doubled in power and landed squarely in the man's solar plexus and he dropped to the floor, all of his air expelled and unable to take a breath. Hoist looked up at him, shocked and still unable to breath.

"I could kick the life out of you and there's nothing you could do about it," King said. "So when you get back up, shut up, do what I say and answer my questions honestly. If I suspect you are lying, you'll be on the floor again. Continue to lie and you won't be getting back up."

Caroline walked back inside the room and looked at Hoist on the floor. "Are we okay here?" she asked King.

"Fine."

"He appears to be on the floor."

"You're too bright for 'Box."

"Nothing gets past me," she chided. "Is he getting up anytime soon?"

"It's not important, I can punch him where he is."

Hoist rolled tentatively onto his stomach and performed an elongated push-up until he was on his knees. He got back to his feet and stood unsteadily.

"At least twelve people have died because of you," King said coldly. "I don't mind doing this all day. Let's go over it, just in case you have forgotten. Four dead MI5 agents at the quayside. A dead special branch officer at your flat. Four dead surveillance operatives, two MI5 and two from Special Branch. And three poor souls from Special Branch at the first safe-house. Now there are missing MI5 officers. I'm not going to feel bad knocking you about if I don't like your answers."

"I've told them all I know…" Hoist was cut short by a savage kick to his groin. He cupped the pain but went down hard onto his stomach. King stepped backwards a pace. He looked up at Caroline. "I'll have a tea if you don't want to watch this."

"You can make the tea. I don't mind taking over."

"Milk and sugar?"

"No, I'm sweet enough."

King looked down at Hoist. "Get up. We're going for a drive."

The man looked up at him, struggled to his knees. "Where?" he asked through clenched teeth.

King ignored him. He looked at Caroline. "Have you ever done CP work?"

"I did some close protection in the Army. When I was with intelligence."

"Now there's a contradiction in terms. Army intelligence," he said. "All right. I want you at four o'clock. Hoist is twelve, you're three feet back at four."

"Enough to draw a piece and pull him down by his collar if anything kicks off. I know the drill."

"Good. I'll be at…"

"Ten o'clock, three paces in front," Caroline interrupted.

"Yes," King replied. "Covering a one-eighty-degree arc-of-fire. You'll have the same."

"Your car is the destination?"

"Yes."

"Halfway point?"

"Retreat if the threat is ahead. Past half-way…"

"Push on to the vehicle," Caroline finished his sentence. "Are we okay to engage?"

King nodded. "Forester is black-bagging this. Don't stick around for plod to get involved. MI5 headquarters is out of bounds, so emergency rendezvous points will have to be ad hoc. I'll need your mobile number if we get separated."

Caroline took a business card out of her pocket and gave to him. "Forester wrote down two addresses on the back. Both are safe-houses in the city. The first is emergency rendezvous point one, the second is ERP two."

King read both and handed the card back to her. "If you don't know the addresses, memorise them and destroy the card." He looked at Hoist, who was now standing meekly, his hands still cupping his groin. "We're going on a drive. We have to walk from here to the car, and most likely from the car back to here. If we are attacked, crouch low. Caroline or myself will most likely take you down. You will be pulled or pushed one way, and your feet will be kicked or swept the other. Like a judo trip. If we engage with gunfire, you will be pinned down to the ground. Don't fight this, it's to stop you getting up and being shot. When you need to move, you will be pulled and shouted at. Go with it, it is to get you to cover or safety and to stop you being shot. Are you clear?"

"Yes," Hoist said meekly. "I didn't mean for harm to come to anyone."

"But your actions did just that," King said. "And you had a choice. You made the wrong one, and you knew it was the wrong decision when you made it." He looked at Caroline. "Are the safe-house operators clear?"

"They've gone for the night," she paused. "One out the front door and one out of the back house."

"Good. Hopefully it will have been noticed. I am going to check on the car, I'll take my bag to it first and have a casual look about," said King.

Caroline smiled. "I thought you were getting me a cup of tea?"

32

"What the fuck happened to you?" the tattooed Russian stared at Mohammed's face as he stood next to the open window. "That must smart a bit," he smirked.

Mohammed struggled to speak, the skin had tightened, contracting painfully between movements. "It is of no consequence," he said sharply. "My wounds will not follow me to paradise."

The man looked at the burns to Mohammed's face. The skin was raw and scarring, but in places it looked like it had burned down to the bone. Patches of hair were missing on the side of Mohammed's head. His lips were thick and blistered. "That's if you can see your way there," the man chided. "Your eye looks like a boiled egg. Does the general think you can fulfil your duties like that? I'm surprised he let you out."

"Do you want to call him on it?" Mohammed glared at him with his one good eye. "Call him now and ask if he's made the right decision." The tattooed Russian shrugged, scratching his face. Part of his cheek was a tattooed skull with a dagger through it. The drips of blood from the dagger's tip ran in blue ink down the side of his neck. "I thought not," he said coldly. "What is the situation with the target?"

"I am not sure," the man said, his eyes on the screen. "Look, someone is leaving now!"

Mohammed pressed through the window and squinted, finding it difficult to adjust seeing with only one eye. He watched the man walk down the steps and make his way to a blue car. A saloon. The man opened the driver's door and deposited a bag inside. He bent down and disappeared from view. About twenty seconds later he stood back up and slammed the door shut. He no longer held the bag, but he was holding something else. A book? A map? It was difficult to see.

"Go to zoom!" Mohammed snapped.

The young man in the passenger seat tapped onto the control unit and the image changed. The man was clearly visible now. He was tall and fit-looking. Broad shouldered. He looked like a light-heavyweight boxer. He walked with a casual grace, his movements minimal. His hair was cut short and dark in colour, and the zoom was so effective they could see the day or two worth of stubble on his face. The jaw was strong and he had a pugilist's brow.

"Who is that?" Mohammed asked rhetorically. "I don't like the look of him. He's not another suited policeman. He looks tougher. I have seen men like him before. SAS?"

The Russian stared at the man as he disappeared from view. Unprompted, the young man beside him adjusted the lens to wide-angle and they could make him out climbing back up the steps to the house. "He looks the type," the Russian rubbed his chin thoughtfully. "We'll do it hard anyway. He won't know what hit him. They fight hard, but they all die the same."

"I'll get our vehicle closer," Mohammed said. "Position yourselves at the end of the adjacent street to the north. We'll take the adjacent street to the south. There's no armed support units with them now, they must think they're perfectly safe. Keep the drone where it is and get ready to use it. We can watch their position from a great distance and that means we have the advantage."

33

The autumn afternoon was drawing in. The day had become increasingly cloudy, and although it had not yet started to rain as forecast, the light was poor and Zukovsky drove with the Jaguar's headlights on. Rashid sat in the backseat. Marvin, a Bulgarian Zukovsky had used before on covert missions with the Russian Federation sat in the passenger seat, his window open, chain-smoking foul-smelling Turkish cigarettes. Zukovsky allowed him to continue, he knew the man worked better if he smoked. Otherwise he was an agitated soul indeed.

They had left the M25 circular route and headed towards Epping Forest. Zukovsky felt the familiarity as he drove. Much had changed since he was last here. That had been in the late eighties. Times had been different then. Another world. A world that should have been very different indeed. It had not been as it should have, the world he knew changed so quickly. The wall had come tumbling down. The coup toppled the president and the country he had once loved weakened and became a whoring, decadent nation of worthless morals with the rich and poor separated by such a gulf of wealth that the money left the country and never came back. The poor provided little, and the rich took their money to Monaco, to America and to the far East. And to Britain.

Although the route had changed, Zukovsky still recognised the area and he used the Jaguar's satnav to home in on the coordinates.

Finding it would be difficult. Many trees would have grown; the landscape would look different. The satnav directed them off the main road and after ten minutes they were deep inside the six-thousand-acre forest. There were occasional tracks cutting through the dense forest. Many of these were gravelled and used as service routes for the forestry commission and nature agencies. After half a mile, the satnav indicated they should turn right and their destination was two hundred metres ahead. There was no service road here. Zukovsky remembered there being a path all those years ago, but he knew the landscape would change. He pulled the Jaguar to the edge of the road and switched off the engine. There was no other traffic. He glanced at Rashid in the rear-view mirror, then at Marvin next to him.

"Out," he said. "And get the shovel and pick out of the boot."

Rashid opened the boot, then recoiled when he saw Khalil's body inside. He looked at Marvin. "What has…"

"Shut up!" Marvin snapped. "Grab his shoulders, I'll get his legs."

Between them they heaved out the dead-weight and dropped the corpse on the ground.

Zukovsky stepped out of the big car and smelled the dampness of the forest. The ground was spongy with moss and bracken. There were trees with falling leaves, evergreens reaching high into the collective canopy and spindly bare branches of trees, their leaves long-since fallen. Zukovsky watched the two men carry a tool each, hefted over their shoulders and struggle with the body, each holding a handful of clothing, suspending it just inches above the ground.

"Khalil was too badly wounded to continue," Zukovsky said. "He would have compromised the operation and he was in too much pain and discomfort to leave that way."

Marvin nodded, said nothing. Rashid took Marvin's lead.

Zukovsky led the way into the forest. The ground was littered with fallen pine cones and dead branches and it made progress slow, but as Zukovsky turned and saw the two men waiting for him to proceed further he was forced to concede it was he who made slow progress, and he felt a pang of inadequacy and the realisation that he was indeed old. He shuddered to think what these two men thought of him. One in middle-age, the other not yet thirty and between them hauling tools and a corpse. It was of no consequence, however. He had plans for them, and their lives would not be the same. Nor as long as they imagined, or indeed hoped.

The clearing was smaller, darker. The fringe of the forest had moved inwards on the clearing; the height had most probably doubled over the years. Some trees would have fallen; others would have grown up in their place. The forest was well managed and in places piles of prepared branches had been stacked for logs or charcoal making.

"Try the pick over here," Zukovsky said to Rashid. The young man swung the pick and it sunk into the soft earth. "Try again!" he snapped. "Move the pick around in circles."

Rashid swung less powerfully, but moved the pick around as he had been instructed. After a few attempts, the pick hit something hard around eight inches deep in the earth. He jabbed a few more times, each time the pick hit the same depth, striking something metallic.

Zukovsky shouted, "Loosen the earth! Marvin, get the shovel in there and take the earth away!"

The two men alternated picking and digging. Marvin moved the earth away and started to cut a circle around the hard obstruction. After ten minutes, a circular area had been cleared sufficiently to reveal a cover the size of a drain hole cover. Rashid bent down to prise it open with the pick.

"Stop!" Zukovsky walked up to them and pointed a few feet away. "Get back over there. I will deal with it now." He bent down and took a sturdy-looking lock knife out of his pocket. He thumbed the blade open and worked it gently under the lip of the cover. After a few minutes he rested back on his heels and waved the two men over. "Lift the lid, but by no more than twelve inches. He looked at the Bulgarian. Thirty centimetres, no more."

Both men nodded and Zukovsky slid forwards onto his stomach and looked at the bottom of the cover as it rose out of the earth. He took a pen torch out of his jacket pocket and played the beam around the hatch.

"Stop! No higher!" he warned. He reached out and unhooked the first of two wires. When it was clear, he unhooked the second and checked that there were no more wires attached. "All right, place the cover away from the hole."

The wires dangled down into the hole. Each one was attached to the pin of a grenade that had been wired to the rim of the hatch.

Rashid looked at the opening. He was breathing heavily. Adrenalin building within. He breathed a deep breath and looked at Zukovsky. "What is this?"

Zukovsky smiled. "This? This is history." He eased his feet into the hole and shuffled his legs deeper until his feet found the metal ladder. "Stay here. Marvin, I will pass you some items, place them carefully on the ground. Do not drop them."

Zukovsky noted, as he eased his frame down the hole, that he was both slower and thicker in width as he negotiated the descent. At the bottom he stood, with a metre of clearance above his head. He used the torch, but the light was swallowed in the chasm. Torches lined the walls but he knew the batteries would be dead, long since degraded. A row of AK47 rifles were stacked in a rack, along with magazines. He doubted the springs would be strong enough. Decades of being compressed by the ammunition would have damaged them. He would bet all he had that the weapons would work though. However, he was not interested in these. He shone the beam over the shelves and racks. NBC warfare suits hung, along with the breathing equipment needed in the event of nuclear, biological or chemical warfare. Hundreds of ration packs were packed in boxes along with thousands of litres of bottled water and purification equipment. Maps and files filled a shelf above him, and radio equipment lay unused, and most likely unusable.

Code cards, spare batteries and several generators, along with boxes of spare radio parts were stacked floor to ceiling. The idea had been that a team of Spetsnaz commandos would survive a year spreading chaos and sabotage, with a hit-list of British VIPs to assassinate. Or, they would be inserted into position to strike at the heart of western Europe and the civilised world. To deliver a nuclear attack, undetectable by radar. An attack by the covert planting of a bomb. Zukovsky had overseen the building of this prefabricated bunker, but to his knowledge, no thermonuclear delivery system had been secreted into the country. The construction of the bunker had been no mean feat, covertly assembling it over a year. There were twelve in all, tactically placed over the whole of Britain, and to his knowledge none had been detected. Nor, he reflected as he looked at the lead flasks stacked in a cage at the end of the bunker, were the fifty ten kilo caches of enriched weapon grade uranium that had been stored inside them.

34

The BMW was fully loaded. Unusual for pool cars, with the exception of a few high-end Jaguars and Range Rovers used for driving VIPs and diplomats. The leather seats were soft and the ride was cosseting. The power was delivered seamlessly from its straight six-cylinder petrol engine, yet it cruised silently and effortlessly through the traffic. King thought the ride was set up too firmly though and the car jarred over the speed bumps they encountered on the route. He noted a handling button near the gear lever, but did not bother to adjust it. He had set the satnav to display as a map. They had no specific destination, both he and Caroline used the journey to attempt to spot a tail.

Hoist sat in the backseat. King had told him to position himself in the middle and fasten his seat belt. If they were rammed he wanted Hoist to exit either side quickly, but he also wanted the man secured in place and not flailing forwards and injuring them both if they were hit from the front.

King had taken the Walther P99 out from his holster and tucked it under his thigh. He observed Caroline do the same. He was confident she had experience and she seemed as switched on as anybody he'd ever worked with. He liked her a great deal, even though he had only known her a day, and felt a comfortable banter between them. He was wary of working with women in this environment, his previous experience was that they over compensated in a what was predominantly a man's world. They were wary or tired of being judged. Caroline Darby seemed to exude a 'take it or leave it' aura that emanated confidence in her abilities. And why not? She had fended off two attackers, killing one of them at Hoist's apartment and she had sent four attackers to retreat at the safe-house.

King looked at her as she surveyed the wing mirror on her side. She was concentrating, counting and memorising the vehicles behind them. She had strong features, was attractive, but had kept herself plain-looking. Her blonde hair would drape past her shoulders if she wore it long, but she wore it tied back tightly in a ponytail securing it with a thin black band. She had applied a little make-up, but nothing most men would notice, and her lips were naturally glossy. King had noticed her eyes though. Forester had mentioned she had lost her fiancé in a terror attack. He could see she wore a sadness. Her eyes had glimpsed tragedy. Once they had, they lost some sparkle. He had experienced tragedy too, lost personally but he doubted his eyes showed it. They had lost their shine many years before. They were cold and heartless eyes. Glacier blue and piercing. They had seen many people die. Some deserving; some less so.

They had driven for forty-five minutes. King had taken quiet streets, headed for large carparks and even driven through a large industrial estate with many side roads leading to various businesses. There was nobody following them, no vehicle that became obvious. They parked on a petrol station forecourt for ten minutes, both alert, both watching for any sign.

"Let's head back," King said. He glanced down at the SCAR rifle. Technically it was referred to as a weapon system. Its stock was retracted and the short barrel nestled against the foot rest. King's leg kept it secured against the console and being an automatic transmission, he didn't need to keep moving his left leg to work a clutch. He looked at Caroline and said, "Debussing from a vehicle is the number one time for a hit."

"Good job we're ready then," she replied confidently.

35

The lead flasks were stacked in rows on the forest floor. Zukovsky had been adamant that they should be laid in rows and unable to knock into each other if one should fall over. Rashid had climbed down into the bunker and lifted them up the ladder where Marvin took them from him and carried them over to where he had started to carefully arrange them. It was hard work, each flask weight over ten kilos and the opening of the bunker was narrow.

Zukovsky had supervised. He surveyed the progress. The light had ebbed sooner than he had expected. Transporting them back to the car would be difficult. But he would soon have extra hands.

Rashid handed over the last flask to Marvin and climbed out of the opening. He was flushed and panting hard. Climbing the rungs of the ladder with the heavy flasks had been difficult. He sat on the soft forest floor and rested. Marvin carefully laid down the last flask and looked back at Zukovsky. He seemed resigned to more work. He looked at the flasks and back at the direction they had come. There was movement in the treeline. He looked at Zukovsky, taking the small Makarov pistol out of his jacket pocket.

"Wait!" Zukovsky scowled. "Put that away!"

Marvin re-engaged the safety and put the pistol back in his pocket as the two men pushed through the treeline. They were both big, fit-looking and dark skinned. The next man was shorter, slimmer but equally as dark. All three were bearded. The smaller man wore a *kufi* knitted skull-cap. He was wearing a quilted jacket over a traditional *dishdasha*. The other two wore western clothing. Last into the clearing was Iman Mullah Al-Shaqqaf. He was wearing a mixture of traditional Arab and western clothing. He wore a beanie hat that was pulled low over his brow and down around his ears.

Rashid looked at the group, then over to Zukovsky. He started to get up, but the two large men ran forward and caught hold of him. Rashid kicked one in the groin and the man lost his grip. It was all Rashid needed and he was on the bigger man with such a wild and sustained attack of fists, elbows, knees and kicks that the man was overwhelmed and fell down onto his back, his hands held up to protect his face. Marvin looked at Zukovsky for guidance. He had no idea what was going on. Rashid turned back to the other large man and kicked him in the face as he struggled to recover.

"Get him!" Zukovsky shouted at Marvin, but he obviously misinterpreted the instruction and set about beating the other large man with a hugely powerful descending hammer fist on the back of the man's neck. The man sprawled forwards. "Not him!" Zukovsky screamed. "Rashid! Get Rashid!"

Rashid turned to the Bulgarian and shuffled forwards, his fists up and his guard tight. They parried and squared up to each other, but when Rashid punched, Marvin charged forwards and grappled him, tackling him to the ground. He got most of his body over him, then with his arms bear hugging the man's arms, pinning them to his body, he head-butted him on the bridge of the nose. One of the large men was on his feet now and he rushed over and kicked Rashid in the face with a penalty kick. Rashid went still.

Marvin rolled off him and got up. He had Rashid's blood on his face and his forehead was already bruising, such was the ferocity of the blow. He looked at Zukovsky. "What the hell is going on?"

Zukovsky held up a hand to silence him and turned to Mullah Al-Shaqqaf. "You recommended this man, put him forward for me to use in this operation. He could have ruined everything, jeopardised all that has been worked for!"

Al-Shaqqaf walked forwards to Rashid. The two large men, bloodied and bruised, had him held and subdued. His arms behind his back. The Iman looked down at him and spat in his face. "You pig!" He kicked him in the face.

Rashid recoiled. His head lolled forwards and he spat blood and mucus on the ground. He struggled to speak. "What do you want?" his voice was weak.

"You are on the MI5 database. I am under surveillance, I had to drive all around the city and swap cars twice to lose them!" Al-Shaqqaf paused, shook a balled a fist at him. "Zukovsky has found your file you *kafir* bastard! You, infidel! You, son of a whore!" Rashid's shoulders sagged. Al-Shaqqaf reached forwards and pulled him by the hair, pulling his face up to him as he spat. "You will die like the unbelieving pig you are!"

"I am more of a believer than you!" Rashid shouted. "I am a true Muslim! My faith is not in dispute, especially by someone like you!"

"Like me?" The Iman looked at him in bewilderment. "I perform the great prophet's will. I teach what has to be learned, guide what has to be done."

"You're a sick man. What you preach is nothing but *your* will. Not the great prophet Mohammed's, and certainly not Allah's!"

Al-Shaqqaf slapped him hard across the face. "You will not speak *his* name, *kafir*! You are not fit, not worthy of talking of God!"

"I love my God," Rashid said. "And I will go to him with a pure heart, a clean conscience and my faith unwavering. So do what you have to do, but know that you do your will, not *his*. Know that it is *you* who will be judged, and you will never see paradise."

36

"It's not going anywhere," Chief Superintendent Carter said impatiently. "You're floundering, almost dead in the water. I don't want 'Box putting this all on you, all on us. They're slippery bastards and the smelly stuff will slide right off them and get stuck on us. The Police Service is in enough trouble with cutbacks and political correctness, I don't want a bloody scandal. Not this department, not on my watch."

Detective Inspector Hodges nodded, but he held on to the fact he had information that his boss did not. He knew the gravity of what lay behind this investigation. "We need a break, that's all," he said.

"We all need a bloody break! I need a break filling out my lottery numbers, my wife needs a break when she gets on the bathroom scales every morning and finds positive thoughts are never going to help her lose weight. It isn't going to happen. Life isn't that fair." He dropped the file onto the desk. "This isn't a murder investigation anymore. You want a murder investigation? I've got two in this week. I've got under qualified sergeants heading them up because my best detective has gone off to play spies and taken half of our MIT with him."

"It's still a good murder investigation team without us," Hodges shrugged. "We got a good lead with the date rape drug; it tested positive with what was used on the four dead agents. We have CCTV through that lead and we're working it through the usual channels, but still no luck. Something should come up."

Carter leaned back in his chair, folded his arms obstinately. "What else? What about the appeal?"

"A lot of phone calls," Hodges shrugged. "Same as usual."

"Same nut jobs then?" He sneered. "It's dead. I'll be damned if I'm wasting anymore time and resources leaving this department short. I want you back on MIT in the morning. You have until then to follow what other leads you may have." Carter rocked forwards, picked up a sheaf of paper from his in tray and slipped on a pair of spectacles.

Hodges took his cue and left. He walked back along the corridor to the MIT offices. The first office suite was in use by the acting team. People were at work behind desks and computer screens. There were three briefing rooms with various case briefings taking place. Not many acknowledged him, most were miffed at their extra workload. Hodges walked on and to the second suite which acted as the headquarters for this case. His own personal office was located at the end of the suite and there was a large meeting room adjacent. Calls were being answered on the main switchboard, which was an information gathering and filtering service. Calls deemed useful and genuine were redirected to four uniformed officers who were seated around a hub of phones and computer screens in the corner of the suite.

"Sir!" A twenty-something WPC stood up and walked over to him. Hodges tensed with anticipation. "Five separate calls naming a Sergei Gulubkin, a

Russian immigrant, as one of the men in the CCTV photograph buying the date rape drug."

"When you say immigrant…"

"Russian national, Sir. I checked with immigration and he's here on a visa, has been on and off for five years."

Hodges rubbed his chin thoughtfully. "Have we contacted the Russian embassy?"

"I thought it better coming from you," she replied. "Sergeant Davies said they're prickly bastards and it would be better coming from you. Rank, sir."

He held out his hand for the sheet of paper she was holding. "Right, I'll play diplomat, you get digging. I want to find out everything we can on this," he looked at the sheet. "Gulubkin fellow."

"If he's maintained a visa he should be clean. On our records, at least. You can't stay here on a visa if you get convicted."

"That should be the case. But he looks a proper shit, luv. And he's been buying date rape drugs. Whether he's involved in the killing of those agents or not, he's no boy scout."

"You can say that again," she hesitated. "Two of the tip-offs said he used a local pub in Camberwell. The King's Head." She smiled as Hodges grimaced. "You know it?"

"Not famed for its wine list and tapas menu," Hodges said. "What about the other three?"

The WPC shrugged. "I'm not sure they'd be wholly reliable."

"Why."

"They sounded Russian or East European. They also sounded completely wasted. Like drug addicts, or at least drunks."

"But the name is the thing we're looking at. Five people naming him is what we're after. What else did they say?"

"They said he was involved in prostitution. They said he ran a brothel."

"His own skanks?"

"Sounded that way."

"They must be desperate then. Maybe they've been trafficked? Cry for help?"

"Sounded that way."

"But he'd be known to the local police," Hodges said. "He would never keep his visa."

"Always a chance he's not known. Maybe he's really careful."

"Sure. What about these girls? How did they get to use a phone?"

"Maybe they got brave, maybe their captors got careless."

"Maybe they're not trafficked at all. Maybe it's a wind-up? Maybe Gulubkin does run a brothel. Maybe he looks like the guy in the CCTV photo, maybe he doesn't look like him at all and a competitor has stirred up things a bit just to get him rumbled. We go in, turn the place over, it gets shut down, but it's not the Gulubkin in the photo, it's some other tosser, but now that tosser is out of business. Hell, the girls were probably whores working for this grass." Hodges looked at the sheet, then said decisively, "No. This is our man. We need a break and maybe this is it. Get onto the local boys and get everything they know about Sergei Gulubkin. Get his photo to them and get somebody senior to call me back. Like ten minutes ago."

"Yes sir."

"What about the other bloke in the CCTV? The Asian guy."

"No matches, no calls."

"What, not one?"

"No."

"Get it out to Interpol. Gulubkin too. Maybe we need to cast our net further."

37

The two large men and the smaller-built man in the *dishdasha* worked with Marvin to carry and load the flasks into Zukovsky's Jaguar. They were not best pleased performing the manual task, but Al-Shaqqaf had snapped the order at Zukovsky's request and the four men got the task done in just under an hour. Both large men looked exhausted and sat down on the soft earth. Marvin leaned against a tree nearby at the fringe of the clearing and took out a hip flask. He unscrewed the cap and took a swig. One of the large men gestured for a sip, but Marvin smiled, took another sip and simply said, "Vodka." The man waved him away, disgusted.

Zukovsky held a Makarov pistol loosely in his hands. Rashid knelt in front of him, his ankles crossed and his hands on his head. His arms quivered, he had spent the entire time in the same position, occasionally his arms would drop a little and Zukovsky would raise the pistol, aim it at him until he put his hands back on top of his head. From his position Rashid could barely make out the pistol in the gloom. The light was almost gone.

"Well, Al-Shaqqaf," Zukovsky said. "Our business is concluded for today. I'll leave you to tidy your mess."

The Iman shrugged. "Very well. Are you not staying to watch?"

Zukovsky shook his head. "It is of no interest to me. Just see that you conceal the entrance to the bunker once you have disposed of the body down there. You can put Khalil down there too."

"What of Khalil?" Al-Shaqqaf looked at the body, he had not noticed among all the confusion. "My sister's boy!"

"I am sorry. I did not know." Zukovsky shrugged. "He was a good man, but was killed by MI5. My heart goes out to you and your sister. He was a brave soldier of Allah." He turned and signalled for Marvin to follow him out of the clearing.

Rashid watched them go. There was no weapon aimed at him and he looked at the four men trying to assess his options. The smaller man strolled over. He reached under his robes and pulled out a knife. It glinted in what little light was left. Maybe it was moonlight now, Rashid was unsure. He still ached from his beating, his senses nulled and his arms weak from the continuous stress position.

"You are a pig and you will be slaughtered like one," the man flicked the knife in his hand, the blade glinting as it rotated. "I can push through your throat and sever the arteries and windpipe and you'll know next to nothing about it. Or I can slice and saw my way through and you'll die slowly, drowning in blood and gasping for air that will never come."

The two large men pushed themselves off their backsides and walked over. They stood near, one each side of Rashid, but they had not yet made any effort to hold him. The robed man stepped nearer and Mullah Al-Shaqqaf smiled down at him.

"Treacherous beast! Shame on you! You, son of a whore!" he spat. "You, godless scum!"

The man in the robes stepped closer. He spun the knife again, but Rashid lunged forwards, caught hold of the handle and thrust the blade deep into the man's groin. The large men were caught off guard, but they had started to move. Rashid was slow to get up and he swiped the knife to his side catching one of the men across the kneecap. The man wailed and retreated a step. The other large man was putting himself between Rashid and Al-Shaqqaf. Rashid stabbed the man in his buttock and got to his feet. The man winced, but he had a knife of his own in his hand and slashed backwards and caught Rashid across the cheek. Rashid recoiled, but came back to the fight. The robed man was on his knees cupping his testicles and Rashid sliced the man clean across his throat. A shower of blood spurted out in one hundred and eighty degrees and everybody got some on them. The man fell forwards and lashed about frantically, his limbs kicking or flailing about in all directions.

Rashid backed up a couple of paces. He had the advantage, the shock factor was high. He squared off, looked at both wounded bodyguards. Al-Shaqqaf turned and ran for the treeline, he stumbled and crashed into the undergrowth. He got back to his feet and kept running. Both bodyguards hesitated momentarily, most bodyguards did. They were men of action, physical. But their job is to protect, not merely to fight. One of the men remembered this and took off after his charge. He did not look back as he scrambled into the treeline, a hand clasping his bleeding buttock.

Rashid breathed heavily. It was down to one on one. He gripped the knife tightly, checked his stance. He knew how to fight with a knife. It was important not to focus on the blade, not to rely upon it. You boxed, or fought martial arts style. The knife was an extra opportunity, not the sole weapon. If you focused on using only the knife, you missed a hundred opportunities.

The man was large. He stood six foot one and at least fifteen stone. He worked out. His neck and shoulders were thick, his arms were well muscled, tightening the fabric of his coat. "Are you really a spy?" he asked. He didn't square up, did not seem ready or willing to fight. His knee was badly gashed; it had sliced to the bone. He was losing a great deal of blood. Rashid said nothing. His face was sliced open and blood flowed down his cheek and over his lips. "I'll fight you," the man said. "But this is all wrong."

"Whatever."

"No man, it's all gone too far."

Rashid didn't want to risk another fight, but he could not stay here. If the others caught up with Zukovsky and Marvin, they had pistols. They could be coming back at any minute. "Back away," Rashid ordered. "Do it now!"

The man put his hands in the air and stepped back a pace. "Look," he said. "I got into all this because I genuinely believed in the plight of my Muslim brothers. But in Syria, man? Well, it opened my eyes, that's all."

"Then give it up."

"It's not that easy. They suck you in. This shit here, these containers, it's big, isn't it?"

Rashid nodded. "It's off the scale. It's radioactive at least. Nuclear, maybe."

The man shook his head. "I can't do it anymore. It's wrong, too big."

"Tens of thousands will die, thousands of fellow Muslims." Rashid, lowered the knife a little. He glanced at the treeline. "What's your name?"

"John," the big man said. "John Bahatti."

"So what are we going to do, John?"

The man looked at the treeline again. "I want out."

"Good," Rashid said. "I can help you with that. But first I have to get away."

"You'll help me? Tell the people you work for I helped you?"

"Will you help, John?" Rashid asked.

"Yes."

"Then I'll get you out," Rashid lowered the knife and cupped his bleeding cheek. He looked at his hand and was surprised how much blood he had lost. He walked up to John Bahatti. "Say I ran off and there was nothing you could do with that knee injury. I'll get somebody to make contact with you. They'll get you out when the time is right…"

Rashid did not see the man lunge until it was too late. The knife came up and under, spearing his gut and driving to the hilt. The man cupped his other hand around the back of his neck and pulled him closer. He twisted the blade, ripped it out and drove it deeply inside him once more. "Treacherous infidel," he spat at him, his face right up to him, so close Rashid could feel the warmth of his breath. "Godless whore's bastard…"

Rashid swung his arm and drove the knife deep into the man's neck, cutting him silent. Blood oozed over the back of his knuckles, warm and sticky. As both men fell to the ground, Rashid's knife drew clear and the arterial wound spurted a plume of blood twenty feet towards the edge of the clearing. The sound of the blood hitting fallen leaves sounded like the beginning of rain. Rashid landed on his side, foetal. The knife was still in Bahatti's hand, but it rested still. He looked into the man's eyes, but they were already lifeless. The blood flow had stopped; the man had bled out in seconds.

Rashid rolled over onto his back. He looked up into the bare canopy. Stars were visible, cloud scudded in front of them, but largely the sky was clear. The forest was silent. Calm and peaceful. He felt a wave of tranquillity wash over him as he listened to his own breathing, and it surprised him that a part of his mind told him it was not such a bad place to die.

38

They had been back inside the safe-house for almost two hours. A curious feeling, a mixture of relief and disappointment at not being hit on their expeditionary drive around London. Hoist was most relieved and sat nursing a coffee in a small and secluded lounge area. He had switched on the television and was flicking aimlessly between the satellite channels. His expression was glazed, he was less indignant at his situation, more resigned to his fate. He was going to be caught up in the resulting consequence of his actions for the foreseeable future.

Caroline leaned against the kitchen counter. She felt like drinking wine, or perhaps something a little stronger, but sensibly opted for coffee. King was seated at the kitchen table drinking a second cup of tea. The bag with the SCAR rifle and ammunition was on the table, unzipped, and both still wore their pistols in the belt holsters.

"I felt sure we'd have something, thought they'd nibble the bait," King said.

"I'm just glad they didn't."

"I wish they had."

"How can you want that? I fought them off and it was terrifying. How can you *want* to fight? And with them making the first move?"

King shrugged. "I've done it most of my life."

"Some life!"

"This one is better than the one I had before."
"Before MI6?"
"Yes."
"What were you before?"
"Nothing."
Caroline smirked. "You had to be *something*."
"I was nothing," King replied. "What were you?"
"College, university, army."
"That's something. I was nothing."
"You had to be *something*," she said. "You didn't just leave college or university and go into MI6, did you?"
"No. I didn't go to college or university. I didn't even finish school."
"Really?"
"School of hard knocks, university of life," he grinned.
"Is that on your CV?"
"My CV would be very short. Pre-service, at least."
"So what did you do?"
"I survived. That's all I've ever done."
"You're being deliberately evasive."
"I hardly know you."
"What, you want me to buy you dinner first? See a film?" Caroline shrugged. "It's not a date. You don't want to say, I won't ask."
"Good."
"Still, I don't understand how you can be so matter-of-fact about putting us out there as bait for an attack, and be disappointed when we weren't."

"Our soldiers did just that in Afghanistan every day. Rules of engagement. They had to be fired upon first. Or perceive action as a direct threat. You were in the army, you know that."

She nodded. "Yes, but they had a bit more kit than we had, a bit more support from nice big Apache helicopters. I never served in a warzone, I wouldn't know."

"Army intelligence?"

"Yes."

"That's the most intelligent thing about it; not serving in warzones."

"About five percent are deployed to a forward operating base. One person in about fifty may go into the field. Those briefing rooms get pretty combative over the coffee machine though," Caroline grinned. "No, it was pretty hands-off. I left and applied for the Security Service. Transferred to General Intelligence Group soon after." She sipped some coffee, studied his face for a moment. "You like action, don't you? You feed off it."

"I get bored staying still."

"It's more than that. You like it on the edge. I know your type."

"You do?"

"I do."

"Who?"

She put down her cup and folded her arms. "My partner, fiancé. Peter was in army intelligence but got frustrated at the procrastination. He got himself fit, went for SAS selection. He failed. Got fitter, tried again and went all the way. He was an officer so could only serve a four-year tour, but he loved it. Every minute of it."

King nodded. He instantly respected the man for that. King had trained with the SAS as part of his MI6 recruitment. Start to finish. His fellow recruits were told he was in the Parachute Regiment. He had been given a legend to learn and only the Colonel knew he was an MI6 recruit. He was assigned to D-company and fellow paras on the selection course were sent into the other companies to avoid damage limitation to his cover. By the time most of the directing staff and recruits had worked it out, King was in the top tier of recruits and had been simply accepted as one of the men. The day the recruits were badged with their sand-coloured berets and winged dagger insignia, King was pulled out before the ceremony and sent on his first official MI6 mission. Over the years he had bumped into and rubbed shoulders with many of these same men, but he was not SAS. He was an outsider, a spook. But he had earned the respect of the best fighting unit in the world. He regularly went up to Hereford to hone his skills and keep abreast of new techniques or developments in equipment.

King watched her. Her folded arms had turned into a tight hug, and she rubbed her arms soothingly. King wondered whether Peter had often held her like that when she had been stressed or worried. The motion seemed to calm her. "How did he die?" he asked quietly.

She smiled. "Saving me," she said. There was a moistness to her eyes, but she didn't look as if she was about to cry. "We were tracking a suicide bomber, the result of a tip-off and subsequently detailed investigation. It was good intel and we had been on it for a while. There were two suspected bombers. One did what we thought, the other was a red-herring. Which meant that the terrorists knew we knew and had fed us a sacrificial lamb. When we stopped the first bomber, the second was nowhere near where they should have been. The second was at the site of the first, but was waiting until the whole circus showed up. Police, Special Branch, MI5, SOCO, the press, the public. Then the bomber strolls over and that was it." She wiped an eye with the back of her hand, sniffed. "Peter showed up at the same moment as the bomber. He shielded me. The blast was terrible, so violent. It shook the world apart. My world, at least." There were tears now, but still she did not cry. King knew how grief worked, he'd suffered his own. He stood up and walked to her. He put his arms around her and held her firmly. She resisted for a moment, and then he felt her go weak, almost drop into him. She was sobbing now. She pressed her face into his chest and cried. King could tell she had been in an automaton state for a long time. She would have grieved at first, but her tough nature had pulled her through and she had not allowed herself to finish the process. They stood for a long time. He said nothing, just held her, his hands firm and still. She was first to break away, and he stood back to give her space. Her eyes were red. There was a roll of kitchen towel on a dispenser and King tore off a couple of squares and gave to her. She wiped her eyes and blew her nose. "Thank you," she said quietly.

"No problem," he said.

"You've experienced loss as well?" She wiped her eyes a final time and balled the paper towel.

King nodded. "My wife," he said. "Ovarian cancer."

"Want to cry it out?" She smiled. "It certainly seems to help."

"No," he said. "I don't do that anymore. There's nothing left in there."

39

Zukovsky kept the shotgun aimed at them as Marvin and Professor Orlev moved them one by one out from the cells and into the long-wheeled base Mercedes van. Each prisoner had their arms tethered behind their backs with cable ties, their heads covered with a plain white pillowcase. They moved unsteadily on their feet, cramping from their confined conditions, debilitated by the pillowcase, they were reliant upon their captors to guide them where they were going.

Orlev had protested at helping. He was a scientist, not hired muscle. Zukovsky had persuaded the man with a casual wave of the sawn-off shotgun. Orlev reluctantly desisted. Rashid should have been doing this work, but he had not returned with Zukovsky and Marvin. Orlev had not asked why. He was regretting having taken Zukovsky's money, regretting having left Russia.

Marvin was rough with the men, he beat them around the head and punched them in the ribs. He shouted aggressively. The prisoners were scared, they let out grunts and whimpers as they were pulled and pushed about. Orlev noticed that Marvin was more gentle, though highly inappropriate handling the female prisoners. Again, he said nothing. He did not want to create more problems for himself. He continued to hood and move the prisoners until all twelve were seated in the back of the Mercedes van. They sat cross-legged on the rubber matting that coated the load space of the vehicle. Nobody spoke. There was an air of terror, a feeling of fear and despair among them. They were all trained individuals and their minds were all working hard as they remembered their training and played the long game. A few had protested at first, but Zukovsky had aimed the sawn-off shotgun at them and Marvin had beaten them so violently, that they had to be carried into the van and lay still on their stomachs either unconscious or unable to move. Anybody who knows anything about firearms knows that at close range there is no arguing with a shotgun, let alone one that has had all but twelve inches of its double barrels removed to create a devastating spread pattern for its lead shot. They had shown the intelligence agents that they held all the cards and given them all a show of force. They were now all compliant.

Marvin slammed the door shut and walked over to Zukovsky. "I will contact you when I get there."

"No, there is a change of plan," Zukovsky said.

Marvin tensed. "Which is?"

"Sergei is arranging for three of his men to accompany the prisoners. They will go with you. He is tied up keeping a watch for the target. I thought we would have completed that element of the operation by now. I have called him to send some more help. I feel it will be advantageous for you to have help when you get to Lowestoft. I have instructed Alesha to return to help me with the next phase. Losing Khalil and Rashid has left us at a disadvantage. Sergei's men will level the field once more."

"Sergei is a gun for hire, General. His men are cheap criminals. Forgive me, but can we trust his men?" Marvin's brow was starting to perspire. It was not from the effort in moving the prisoners.

"Sergei spent four years in gulag for me," Zukovsky replied coldly. "He did not talk at his trial, and lost his family while he was in that hell on earth. Four years in the fierce heat of Siberian summers, eaten by mosquitos. Four years of frozen winters, waiting for men to die just to take their clothes, his fingers frostbitten, food and water frozen solid. Still he did not talk. I trust him implicitly. If he recommends men to me, I will trust them also."

Marvin nodded. "But I am still to go with them, the prisoners?" he asked, a little too keenly.

Zukovsky studied him. He had seen Marvin's fear and concern handling the uranium flasks in the forest. "You do not wish to stay?"

"I will perform whatever is expected of me," Marvin said hesitantly. "Use me how you will."

"I intend to," Zukovsky said. "But I wish you to assume command of the hostage transfer. There is much to take care of, tracks to cover. I can trust you?"

Marvin visibly relaxed. He saluted the general. "Yes, comrade."

"Comrade," Zukovsky saluted in return. "It will not be long now."

40

He had crawled through the undergrowth, through nettles and brambles, their stings smarting and the barbs tearing at his flesh. He felt no pain from them, the overriding agony of the stab wounds cancelling out all other pain and discomfort.

He had waited to die. Waited for the blood to empty from him and the coldness to wrap him tightly, or for the others to come back and finish what they had started. He thought of his family; his mother, his father, his two sisters. He was sure he would die, but as he waited for release from the pain and for the stillness of death to wash over him, he realised that it was not coming quick enough. He had time to think. Time to wait.

Time to survive.

Rashid had grabbed great handfuls of earth and rubbed it into the stab wounds, plugging the openings and staunching the flow of blood. He rolled over onto his stomach, wincing at the pain, as acute as if he had been stabbed a third time. He had crawled on all fours at first, gritting his teeth together in determination. He had managed to get to his feet and stagger. He pushed himself from tree to tree to put distance between himself and the clearing, put in time and space to separate himself from his enemies. He had fallen often, but got back up each time. He thought back to his training all those years ago, thought back to the agony of those escape and evasion trials, those excruciating route marches through the Brecon Beacons, cold, wet, exhausted. Fuelled only by the determination to succeed. The will to make SAS selection. He was a Pakistani, an immigrant to the United Kingdom when he was just ten years old. He was a Muslim. And he was one of the country's most elite group of soldiers, an experienced SAS soldier on detachment to MI5 to aid in the fight against terrorism. And he was determined to get through this fight, like so many others he had and he would make it to safety and report what information he had.

He kept up the pace. He knew every ten steps he made created a hundred for his enemy. Every direction he took increased their search significantly. He was running low on strength, but not on resolve. He needed water, needed blood. He knew he had to get clear, but he also knew he had to get help. Without medical attention he would not last long.

41

Forester's driver pulled up outside the Holiday Inn in Mayfair. The hotel was brightly illuminated, modern, yet somehow in keeping with the area. Forester thought its location would be appealing for short-term visits, weekend city breaks.

His driver agreed to wait, but Forester had been accompanied by a member of his diplomatic protection detail. It was a service Special Branch provided that he called upon from time to time. Tonight was one of those times. The man in question was an experienced police sergeant who served in diplomatic protection and carried a Glock model 19 compact 9mm pistol. He was a tough-looking rugby player in a well-tailored suit. He followed Forester at a discreet six feet. He remained to Forester's right-hand side. This kept his weapon hand free and clear.

Forester surveyed the reception area. Some low sofas and coffee tables had a few business types working at laptops and on smartphones. Forester ignored them and headed for the bar. He searched, his eyes pausing on a man at a table in the corner. The man looked up from his smartphone and stood. He buttoned his suit jacket and walked over.

"Thank you for agreeing to meet with me at such short notice," the man said amiably as he held out his hand, his accent thick and guttural. "I did not want to go through the embassy. This is a rather delicate matter."

Forester shook the man's hand. "Major Droznedov."

"Uri, please."

"Uri," Forester said. "Please, call me Charles."

Droznedov smiled. He waved a waitress over. "You will have a drink?"

Forester nodded. "A gin and tonic, please, ice and lemon." He waved a hand to his bodyguard. "A coke for my companion." The waitress nodded, looked expectantly at Droznedov.

"A Budweiser, please."

"Not vodka?" Forester asked as the waitress walked away. He sat down at the table. His protection officer sat at the next table. He was near enough, his back to the wall and he surveyed the room. "Or is that stereotypical?"

"I hate the stuff," Droznedov smiled. "Well, I was practically weaned on it, but I prefer whisky. But I want a clear head, so just a few beers will be all tonight."

Forester smiled. The drinks arrived and Droznedov held up his beer. The waitress had brought a glass with the bottle, but the Russian ignored it. "Cheers!"

"Na zdorovje!" Forester returned.

Droznedov laughed. He drank half of his beer in a large gulp. Foam frothed on the lip of the bottle as he placed it down hard on the table. He looked at Forester. "So, what progress have you made in hunting Vladimir Zukovsky?"

Forester sipped his glass of gin and tonic. "We are following a few lines of enquiry," he said, placing his glass carefully on the coaster. "We have CCTV footage of people linked to him, a few names have emerged. We have a good lead on another named in some CCTV photographs."

"Like who?"

Forester smiled. "What do you have? What are you doing here?"

"Ah, quid-pro-quo, no?"

"Something like that."

"I gave you information," Droznedov said. "You would not know about Zukovsky's intentions if it were not for me. I just want to know what you have found out."

"Well, we like to play things close to our chest at MI5."

"Too close to allow a little cooperation from Russia?"

"Well, we're not too friendly at the moment, are we? There was that random bombing in Syria which made things rather difficult out there, and the radioactive poisoning of Alexander Litvinenko. We're still after some answers on that one. And then there's all the planes crossing into our airspace, almost daily. We're an island twenty miles off the coast of France, you should know by now where we are. One day we'll shoot a plane down. It may be sooner rather than later."

The Russian smirked, held his hands up in mock surrender. "Okay, okay. But maybe I can let you know more now. Help you even."

"I'm sure."

Droznedov leaned forwards earnestly. "Look, Deputy Director Forester, Charles. Let me help you. Let me join your investigation, quietly. Unofficially, even.

Let me be involved. I may be able to help. I have been hunting this warhead, I *have* to find it. My superiors do not know I am here. If we find it, I do not need to be credited. I shall merely return to Russia. I just wish for it to be recovered. If it is not, then the conclusion does not bear thinking about."

42

57°N 6°E, The North Sea

The Lady Majestic was sailing under her own identity once more. The boards bearing her real name and port had been screwed back and the crew had brought up thirty lobster pots from the hold and stacked on her deck. Both the Union Jack and the black background and white cross of the St. Piran flag, the Cornish flag, flew resplendently from the wheelhouse. She was rolling in the heavy seas, the swells at the three-metre mark. The currents were strong here, the English Channel funnelled through and opened out into the North Sea. The current hit them head on and the tide was pulling from north to south with the tide dropping on the English side.

The conditions had been good in the Baltic Sea. They were now eight miles off the west coast of Denmark, halfway into the return journey. After the vessel had passed trouble free through the Oresund Channel between mainland Sweden and Denmark's smaller island of Sjaelland, home to the capital Copenhagen, Max Clenton had managed to snatch a couple of hours' sleep. Leaving the boat in the capable hand of his lead crewman who piloted her around the point of Skagen on Denmark's larger island of Jylland. As they had entered the rough waters of the North Sea and the boat had been hit by the onslaught of three-metre waves, Clenton had awoke with a start and resumed control. He knew his senior crewman was more than capable, but he had thought about the old Russian and his not so much veiled as blatant threats and his insistence upon his cargo arriving on schedule. They were halfway and Clenton could almost smell the money.

***

"Cod and chips, please. Oh, and put a battered sausage on top." Hodges perched himself on the window-sill of the fish and chip shop and picked up a copy of the *Evening Standard.* He was tired and the headline didn't make much sense. He tossed the paper down and breathed in the heady aroma of oil and vinegar, frying fish and meat pies.

"Thought I'd find you here," Watkins smiled at him. "Jesus, this place reeks!"

"Gorgeous, isn't it?"

"Your arteries must flow like treacle."

"They do that too, look," he replied, pointing to a blackboard. "Treacle sponge, dipped in batter, deep fried and then rolled in sugar."

"Oh, dear God!"

"What did you want? Obviously not chips."

"Somebody almost ran over a man in the road on the outskirts of Epping Forest."

"So? That's a long way off our patch."

"He'd been stabbed."

"Spit it out Watkins, I'm too tired for a big reveal. I just want my fish supper."

"Sorry boss. The man had multiple stab wounds, he was in a very bad way. He was rushed into A and E at Brentwood. They've put him into an induced coma and he's going into surgery about now."

"I thought I said spit it out Watkins?"

"Sorry, he's the other man in the CCTV footage buying the date rape drug," she paused. "The police were called, one of the officers recognised him, did a check and is convinced it's him. The man has an officer guarding him now. He will call direct as soon as the man is out of surgery."

"So we've got both men in the CCTV footage, only we have to wait for Sergei to come back to his brothel and hope this guy pulls through surgery?"

"That's about right, boss. An observation post has been set up on the building reputed to be Sergei Gulubkin's brothel in Camberwell. We can't do much until he shows his face, other than knock them up."

"No. Don't do that. We'll wait," Hodges said. He looked up at the man behind the counter who was holding out a cardboard tray piled high with fish and chips. He nodded when offered salt and vinegar, then took the tray from him and picked up the battered sausage and took a bite. It was greasy and hot and he had to suck air in through his mouth as he chewed in an effort to quell the burning. "If he's going into surgery, there's no point wasting the night. Pick me up at seven tomorrow morning and we'll head over to Brentwood and see if this man can talk."

"Isn't that too early? To go to the hospital, I mean?"

"No. Shift patterns rotate at eight. Hopefully we'll get to question him without a doctor warning us off in the interest of the patient's health." Hodges held out the tray, offering her a chip. She declined and he shrugged. "If Gulubkin shows his face call me."

"How will I know if he's back?"

"Because you're going to be at the OP pulling an all-nighter Watkins," he replied curtly. "It'll soon be Christmas and you'll thank me for all that lovely overtime."

43

The area was flat and featureless. It reminded Marvin of the Ukraine. He had once spent a summer on the Crimea as a teenager and had driven through Ukraine and the endless fields of potatoes, corn, sunflowers and tulips. On the return journey, after harvesting, he had marvelled at how the once interesting drive had been repaid by endless baron fields of mud as far as he could see in every direction. Norfolk had reminded him of that. Their destination was Lowestoft, a port, harbour and seaside resort town just inside Suffolk near the Norfolk border. Marvin had pulled over as instructed at the layby, a popular truck stop, and switched off the lights. He smoked, as did the four Russians. Or at least, he assumed they were Russians, for not one of the men had uttered a word since leaving the warehouse in Newington. At first it had unnerved him, but after a while it did not bother him. He was in charge, and they would do what they were told soon enough. They were friends, or at least business associates of Sergei Gulubkin and Marvin did not like Gulubkin one bit. He failed to see Zukovsky's appreciation of the man, failed to see Gulubkin's worth. The man was a criminal. A murdering thief. A mutual associate had once told Marvin that Gulubkin was a rapist of two young girls, and that the man had been marked as such in gulag with a number of tattoos. He had not told Zukovsky, for fear of looking as if he had an agenda. But he thought of the brothel the man ran, the girls there, all barely eighteen. Perhaps younger. It would not stretch the imagination far to see this could have been true. In his opinion acquaintances or associates of Sergei Gulubkin were not men to be trusted and it made him feel uneasy of the task that lay ahead.

Marvin looked up as another vehicle pulled into the layby. This time it wasn't another lorry laying up before the port, but a battered red Toyota pickup truck laden with crab pots and fish crates. The driver got out, flicking a cigarette high into the air. The ash burned brightly in the darkness and hit the ground in a shower of sparks. He walked over to the van and around to the driver's window. Marvin lowered it a few inches.

"Name's Arnsettle," the man said gruffly. He was in his fifties, haggard. He had a trimmed beard and the bushiest greying eyebrows Marvin had ever seen. He could barely take his eyes off them. "You expecting me?" Marvin nodded. "Well then, better follow me. Change of plan, we're going to go to a berthing on the 'Broads. Tide's good for it and there ain't nobody around to stick their beaks in to our business." The man's accent was broad and quite unlike anything Marvin had heard before.

"A change in plan?" Marvin looked at him. "It will not affect my deadline?"

"Make it bloody quicker I expect," Arnsettle leaned against the van and started to roll a cigarette. There was a little moonlight and some ambient glow from the interior lights of the parked lorries. "What are you hauling anyhow?"

"That is none of your business," Marvin said coldly. "My employer has paid you well." He tapped his chest pocket. Arnsettle could clearly see a rectangular bulge under the jacket. "I have the remainder of your fee with me, you will receive it once you get us to Norway."

"No bother," Arnsettle said, lighting his cigarette with a disposable gas lighter. The light showed up the lines in his craggy face. "You follow me. It will take about half an hour."

Marvin watched the man walk back to his truck. He took the Makarov pistol away from the door, where he'd held it pressed against the door lining in line with Arnsettle's stomach the entire time. He made it safe by pressing the de-cocking lever and slipped it back into his pocket. One of the men seated behind him grunted and lit another cigarette. The men smelled feral, unwashed. One of them broke wind and another laughed. Marvin wound down his window and started the engine. He was starting to wish he had been given another task. Even being around a nuclear warhead seemed favourable.

Arnsettle drove erratically, the crates and pots swaying from side to side as he took the pickup through twisting, winding turns that thread through marshland and areas of agricultural land. The Toyota had a brake light out. Marvin cursed the man. Sometimes the smallest of details drew attention. The roads were quiet, but it wasn't until they pulled off the road and onto a gravelled track that Marvin relaxed. The chances of driving past a police car were much slimmer now.

The track was potholed and to the edges of the track there were heavy tyre tracks in the mud, which looked considerably deep and wet. Arnsettle drifted and threw up huge clods of mud which hit the windscreen of the Mercedes van. Marvin tutted and worked the washers and wipers. One of the men in the back said something. Marvin thought the man might be Polish.

The prisoners started to complain at the road surface. The ride was so harsh that the front wheels occasionally cleared the ground. Some were grunting and groaning, most were nauseous and a few had been sick. The stench of vomit had become overpowering. A prisoner had attempted to start a dialogue with his captors and had been swiftly beaten by one of Gulubkin's men.

Marvin could see a boat ahead. It was far larger than he had imagined. The boat was moored alongside a wooden jetty that looked rickety and insubstantial. There was a reflection from the partial moon on the water and by the light it provided Marvin could see the expanse of water was considerable. Whether or not it would have enough depth for the boat to sail at low tide, he did not know. He could not see land on the other side but he supposed there was not enough light for him to see that far.

Arnsettle parked the pickup next to a small wooden shed. There was a small motorbike with a learner's L-plate above the number plate. Next to this was parked a small hatchback. It was an old model with a few dents catching the moonlight. Three men were gathered around the hatchback smoking and joking about. They were laughing, but they stopped as Arnsettle got out. Arnsettle addressed them and they nodded and walked to the gangplank leading up to the boat.

Marvin could see the name *Ebony* written on the prow. She was a large trawler type with a crane mounted at her stern. Marvin had no idea how big she was, but there looked to be considerable deck space and at least a hundred crab pots lashed forward of the deck hatches. There were several hundred crates stacked in rows and lashed together with ropes and chains. Marvin had read about the crab fishing on this coast, especially Cromer crab, a famed port for crab fishing. Although tonight, the captain and his crew would earn considerably more than they would have setting their crab pots.

Marvin got out of the van and looked at the boat. The gangplank was narrow and he couldn't envisage getting the twelve prisoners into the boat without taking off their hoods. In fact, the ramp was so narrow he doubted they'd get up unassisted, and there was barely room for two to walk abreast. They would have to remove the hoods and guide them from behind clutching their shoulders. He would need a guard on the boat, another with the prisoners in the van and one to guide them aboard. He would need to brief Gulubkin's men on what to do. He walked to the side door and opened it. All three men sat on the rear seat smoking. There was a fog of smoke surrounding them which dispersed in the cold breeze. The orders were curt and in Russian and the three men nodded. They picked up their weapons, two had compact AKS 74-U carbines and the other carried an AK47. They stuffed some spare magazines into their pockets and stepped outside.

Arnsettle stood at the gangplank and stared at the weapons. He looked at Marvin as one of the men pushed past him, walked sure-footedly up the ramp and stood at the top on the deck. He held his weapon loosely and confidently, waiting for the first prisoner. Marvin opened the rear door and pulled the first prisoner out and unsteadily to their feet. He pulled the prisoner to the jetty, took the hood off him and pointed him towards the gangplank.

"Up!" Marvin snapped.

Arnsettle shook his head. "What *is* all this?"

Marvin took the pistol out of his jacket pocket and held it loosely by his side. He waited for the prisoner to be guided into place and helped up the ramp by one of the men. "I am from the Norwegian intelligence service. These are terrorists of the state. They were denied extradition by British courts, but are being taken back to face criminal and terrorist charges."

"But the guns? The hoods?" Arnsettle said. "I thought you were smuggling drugs or booze."

"You are being paid a great deal of money," Marvin interrupted. "You do not get to pick and choose. You will take us to Norway and you will return and forget everything you have seen tonight." Marvin took out the wedge of fifty-pound notes and held it out for him.

Arnsettle hesitated a moment, then took it from him. He looked at the money, which was three-fingers thick. He felt the heft of it, ran his thumb over the corner and flicked the notes like a child would a sketchpad, then turned and walked silently up the gangplank and boarded his boat.

44

The atmosphere in the car was tense. Zukovsky had driven to where Sergei Gulubkin was waiting in his van. Gulubkin had shown him the footage of the safe house from where the drone was standing by. The young man controlling the drone had expressed his concern that the battery-life of both the aircraft and the camera would be running low and that it should be brought down from the church spire to switch to fresh packs. Zukovsky had agreed and instructed the man to use the drone for another purpose. The young man had re-started the drone and landed it safely beside the van on the pavement and proceeded to carry out his adjustments. Mohammed had been instructed to drive closer to the house and retain an eyes-on surveillance. Alesha had been ordered to walk back to Sergei Gulubkin's position for new orders. She had been outraged that she should be taken off the surveillance and had started to express this when Zukovsky had snapped for her to wait in his Jaguar. He had given the men their instructions and returned to the car, where Alesha sat in silence. As they left the M3 motorway and travelled along the A303, it seemed the woman would continue her silence unless Zukovsky made the effort. He inwardly cursed using her for this, mixing business with pleasure.

"I am sorry to pull you off the surveillance, my dear," he said. "But you will be invaluable to me on this errand. The most important part of this operation. Khalil and Rashid's deaths have changed matters somewhat. Sergei's reserves have had to take their place with the prisoners."

She said nothing, merely unfolded the vanity mirror in the sun visor. It illuminated and she shuddered at her reflection. "I don't care about the stupid surveillance. Just look at me!"

"Is that what this is about? Alesha, your scars will heal."

"Not without surgery!" she snapped. "It's more than that! It hurts so much. I have been taking handfuls of painkillers every hour. I feel drunk on them. I want that MI5 bitch who did this to me. I want to kill her slowly."

"Focus agent Mikailovitch! We have a mission to think about! This is not the time for retribution!"

"That's *all* this is!" Alesha turned and looked out of the window. She stared out across the moonlit fields of Wiltshire as the car cruised past them at sixty miles per hour.

Zukovsky's phone rang. He had set it to Bluetooth and answered hands free. "Hello?" he did not recognise the number.

"This is Al-Shaqqaf."

"Yes."

"Rashid has got away."

"What?"

"He fought with my men. He got away."

"He beat all four of you?"

"No. He wounded one, killed two."

"Did he wound you?"

There was a long pause. *"No, my bodyguard did his job, got me out of there. We got back to where we had parked, but you had already left."*

"And then what?"

"After a while, we ventured back. Searched the area, but he had gone."

"And the bodies? Rashid, your men?"

"We put them in the bunker and left."

"That would have been hours ago! Why have you left it so late? Rashid knows about the warehouse! The uranium is there!"

"But the device is not yet in place."

"On its own the warhead will knock out twenty streets. It is an airborne delivery system that detonates at about two-thousand feet above the target. The uranium will turn it into a dirty bomb and cause the damage we are after. You must get over to the warehouse and move it. Take it to the target and wait for me. I will call professor Orlev and give him new instructions, tell him to expect you there immediately." Zukovsky ended the call. "Fucking amateurs," he said. He glanced across at Alesha, but could only see her expression in the reflection of her window. The profile he saw from his position was unscarred and the reflection was faint, hiding the horror of her injury. For a moment he had his beautiful Alesha again. The woman who had stolen his heart on the coast of the Black Sea. The moment passed in a heartbeat though, when he realised she had been smiling at the way the call had ended.

45

There was a sliver of light in the sky. It was darker outside now that the streetlamps had switched off, but the natural light of dawn was purer. Alex King loved dawn. Wherever he was in the world he always tried to catch it. He felt the air was fresher, cleaner. It made him aware of something else too – that he was alive and had made it to another day. He had lived so much of his life under such uncertainties and knew he could control very little in life, but he took one day at a time and today was no different.

He sipped some tea from a mug, the liquid was hot and strong. Caroline had made it and had not used enough milk. He did not say anything, but the tea was so hot he nursed it and watched out of the window waiting for it to cool. Already dawn was turning to day and the light was brighter and the sky clear. It looked like it was going to be a rare sunny autumn day. He had decided to take Hoist on one more drive through the city, another test of the enemy's surveillance and intentions. If nothing came of it he would meet with the policeman, Hodges, and see what leads the man had.

"Tea no good?" Caroline asked as she walked into the kitchen. She had just taken a coffee into Hoist, who as instructed, had got dressed and was waiting in the lounge.

"Just hot," he said, taking another sip.

King had just showered and dressed after sleeping for a few hours on the sofa in the lounge. He had wanted to be ready to move, and also provide a guard downstairs. Caroline had taken a room upstairs, but had remained dressed, her weapon nearby as King had suggested. Between them they had slept and showered in rotation.

"Forester called while you were showering," said Caroline. "He's coming round in about half an hour, traffic permitting."

"Did he mention if he had any new developments?"

"No."

"Great."

"Just like my…" she hesitated. "I was about to say ex, but he's not. My fiancé. You're just like Peter. He was a man of action too, hated waiting."

King shrugged. "I can wait all day. All week. I just need to know what I'm waiting for. Forester called me in on this, but there's nothing. We need something more to go on."

"Hodges is following up leads from his appeal. Maybe something will come from that?" Caroline paused. "Why exactly are you here? I mean, there's plenty of agents from General Intelligence Group."

"Forester didn't tell you?"

"No."

"You should speak to him."

"I'm speaking to you."

"You're asking, not speaking."

"Don't be a smartarse," she said. "Why you?"

"I have skills."

"They're not in detective work."

"He has Hodges for that."

"So what has he got you for?"

"To assist you."

"Bullshit," she waved a hand at the sports bag. "You've got an arsenal in there. I mean, pistols yes, but you've got a rifle *and* a silenced pistol. What do you need a silent pistol for?"

"For silent kills."

"So you admit it? You're here to kill, nothing more?"

"There's also my wit and my sparkling conversation."

"I'd stick to killing if I were you."

King drank half his tea in a large gulp. It had cooled a little. "You have a firearm on you."

"So?" she snapped. "People tried to kill me yesterday."

"MI5 don't carry firearms. Not in mainland Britain at least. You could be arrested just like any man on the street for being armed."

"Forester knew you were arming me."

"No, he didn't. I thought you'd need it. I *know* I'll need mine."

"I'm not a killer."

"Tell that to Rafan Betesh."

"You know what I mean."

"Forester has had enough. The country has had enough. The vast majority, who value the country for the free democracy that it is. Take Iman Mullah Al-Shaqqaf for instance. Charged with incitement to murder and incitement to commit acts of terrorism, he is behind some of what is happening here. Nothing sticks to him. He was behind the bombing that took away your fiancé, your colleagues, the police. He's just a cog in the wheel, but he's a cog that needs removing."

"So you're going to kill him?" she shook her head. "What about the judicial system?"

"What about it? It failed *you*."

"But…"

"ISIS terrorists operating in London, an old soviet warhorse smuggling a nuclear device, kidnapping MI5 agents. We don't yet know what they're doing, but they're not going to get away with it."

"And you'll kill them all?"

King shrugged. "Tough times. Tougher measures. We're not talking vigilante justice here; we're talking eliminating a threat that cannot be allowed to succeed. If we are weak now, we will be a target forever. And sooner or later we will be defeated."

"I'm not happy about it."

"You don't have to be happy. You don't have to help me either. Forester wanted you on this because he trusts you, values you. I'm used to working on my own."

"I bet you are."

"Meaning?"

"You'd have to be, in that line of work," she sipped her coffee and placed the mug purposefully on the table. "I'm surprised you ever got close to someone."

"It can happen. And did."

"Forester said your wife was with MI5."

"I didn't hold it against her."

"Funny."

"She was. Attractive too. And smart. Smarter than me, at least."

"You met her working?"

"Joint Intelligence operation."

"I didn't know her. I knew *of* her, but I didn't know her."

"She wasn't a field agent. She was an analyst but often overlapped in surveillance," he paused. "She would have analysed the shit out of this, that's for sure. She had a genius IQ."

"And she still chose you," she smirked.

"She liked a bit of rough."

Caroline laughed, sipped more coffee. "Well, most girls do, unfortunately."

***

"You will have to come back later," the doctor said, not raising his eyes from the clipboard notes he added, "He should be coming round now. But he'll be feeling rather poorly and I will need to examine him. The consultant who performed the surgery will want to see him first, before he talks to anyone else."

Hodges nodded. He'd had this conversation many times before. "I understand that, doctor. But the man is a person of interest in a multiple murder investigation. It's crucial I speak to him, just a minute or so."

"Look, detective, I understand, but I have my patient's interests to consider. Now, if there's anything else?"

"No, doctor, thank you." Hodges took out his mobile phone and the doctor continued down the ward. He had no intention of dialling, he just needed a prop and an end to the conversation.

"Are we off?" Watkins asked. She had just returned with two coffees from the vending machine. They were hot and the cups were thin. She looked for somewhere to put them, but she was out of luck. Hodges took his, and she repeatedly passed her own between her hands and blew on the slick surface.

"No, we're not. I'm speaking to that man in there," he nodded towards the window of the private room.

The window shutters were down, but not folded and the man was clearly visible. A nurse was removing tubes from his nose and reconnecting a drip to a cannula in the back of his hand. He said something and she nodded, pouring a finger of water in a plastic cup and giving to him. She held it while he sipped. He went to drink more and she shook her head, replacing the cup to the table. She marked down something on his notes at the foot of the bed and left the room.

Hodges looked around. There were two nurses chatting to one another at the nurse's station and a contract cleaner was dry-mopping the floor. A junior doctor, looking tired and haggard was writing something on a whiteboard. Hodges looked at the policewoman. "Watch the door, Watkins," he said and opened the door. He reached to his right and twisted the blind rod. The blind covered the window and he closed the door behind him.

Rashid looked at him. He had a pallor to his usual milky-coffee colour. His eyes were moist and his breathing was shallow. "Plod?" he asked, his voice raspy.

"How did you guess?" Hodges flipped his warrant card. "Detective Inspector Hodges, MIT."

"I can't talk to you," Rashid said. "I need you to get in contact with the Security Service. I am an agent and my cover has been blown," he coughed, then continued for thirty seconds or so. He pointed at the glass of water and Hodges passed it to him. He sipped, took a deep breath and passed the cup back. "Please, make contact for me."

"Nice try sunshine," Hodges smirked. "But I've got a nice picture of you on CCTV buying a date-rape concoction. Want to talk about that?"

"No."

"You admit it then?"

"I'm not admitting anything. Get in contact with them, and I'll talk to you."

"Oh yeah. I'll go and have a chat with them right now. Then I'll come back and you'll be gone. I know how it works."

"I'm still not talking to you. And you're wasting time."

"I've got all day."

Rashid fumbled with his left hand, out of view of Hodges. "You'll be out of here in five minutes, detective."

"I wouldn't count on it. My detective constable is outside watching the door. It's really quiet out there."

Rashid shook his head. "Do what I ask," he rasped. "You're wasting my time and yours."

"No, I'm alright pal. Now, what were you doing with the drug? Did you give it to the people you killed? Make them compliant?"

"You haven't a clue what's going on, detective." He looked up as a nurse burst into the room. Behind her the doctor Hodges had spoken to earlier was admonishing Watkins. Rashid dropped the control unit on the bed. The button for assistance was flashing. He looked at the doctor as he bustled into the room. "I am not well, doctor. This man is harassing me!"

"Outside, now!" the doctor ushered Hodges aside, holding his shoulder. "I mean it. I'll have your job if you don't leave right now!"

Hodges frowned, shaking his head. He pushed his way out through the gathering of medical staff and nodded for Watkins to follow him.

Rashid turned to the nurse nearest him. "I need a telephone, urgently."

***

Forester had called when he was two minutes away from the safe-house. His driver pulled the big Jaguar to the kerb and Forester stepped out and walked up the steps. Caroline watched on the CCTV and opened the door as he reached the top step.

"Morning," he said and looked around. "Skeleton staff?"

"Just us," she said. "I thought you knew."

"No," he replied. "Special Branch not here?"

"Nobody's here. And there's no armed response outside either."

Forester nodded to King as he stepped out from the kitchen carrying his sports bag with the rifle inside. "No security?"

"Testing the opposition," King replied. He dropped the bag down by his feet. "We've taken Hoist for a drive about."

"And?"

"Nothing."

"Once more?"

"You're as bad as *he* is!" Caroline retorted.

"That's what I figured," King said. "If nothing comes from it, we'll ditch him off at Scotland Yard and let the anti-terrorism boys pull him apart. Then we'll get with this detective you've got on it and shadow him."

"Sounds like a plan," Forester nodded. "I met with a Russian Major last night. He's trying to find this warhead, knows Vladimir Zukovsky has it. He's offered to help, unofficially mind you, and feels he may be of assistance."

"Couldn't hurt," King commented. "What's his name?"

"Major Uri Droznedov. He's with the GRU."

"Let's see how this pans out."

"Well I hope it doesn't," Caroline said. "Let's just get rid of Hoist and go find this thing."

"By the book, of course," said King.

"What am I missing?" Forester asked.

"I just delved a bit deeper into Alex's remit."

"And?" Forester asked.

"I thought you bought him in because of the missing file compromising our agent's security. I didn't realise he was here to clean up town."

"I can go it alone," said King looking at Forester. "I don't need to babysit."

"Babysit!" Caroline snapped. "You don't need to look after me!"

Forester held up a hand. "Stop! Look, Caroline, I should have told you more."

"Yes, you should have."

"I've been in this game all of my adult life," Forester said. "I've never known a time like this. Through the Northern Ireland troubles, Libya, Saddam's Iraq, Bin Laden's Al-Qaeda. Nothing has come close to the ISIS problem. Coupled to this we have a weak justice system, terrified of being accused as racist and unsympathetic to different cultures within our country. Howard runs the service with one eye on parliament and the other on his pension. Chalmers is an accountant and regularly vetoes operations of national security in favour of keeping within a ring-fenced budget. Which means that MI5 is compromised. The trouble is this isn't a business, it's an agency that looks after the country's security. Elsewhere, the police are forced to operate through cutback after cutback. They are not up to taking on more and more intelligence work. Customs and Excise have been remodelled and side-lined by the Border Force. It is impossible to share intelligence with them and they are barely fit for purpose. It might as well have been tendered by private security companies. This will happen in due course and our borders will be conceded. The military out-sources so much of its budget that the army was recently discovered to be sourcing foreign intelligence from *Wikipedia*. We are in crisis. We need to strike at the heart of this and we need to get out in front."

"So you're taking us to a dictatorship state?"

Forester sighed. "Caroline, we always have been. Decisions are made every day that were not on a political party's manifesto. It's the way it is. You don't want tuition fees? So you vote a certain way. That party merges into a coalition with your sworn enemy and suddenly the no tuition fees policy is flushed down the toilet. One example in a thousand." Forester looked at King. "This man has been doing this for MI6 for years. He's batting for us now, when we really need him. This plot, whatever Zukovsky and Al-Shaqqaf are planning must be stopped. We don't have the resources, don't have the intelligence data to mount a long-term investigation. But above all else, we don't have the time. Not with a nuclear device in the mix. I won't take the chance of them detonating it. And I won't have them martyred or copied for ever more. If you are not up to this, then let me know now."

"I never signed up for killing."

"You don't have to," King said. "Not in cold blood at least."

"The SAS have orders like these," Forester said. "Peter would have been a part of operations, or known others to have been ordered to do so."

"Oh come on! Don't sink so low as to bring my dead fiancé into this!" Caroline snapped. "Look, I want to stop this device going off and I want my colleagues found and released. But I'm not walking up to someone and shooting them in the back of the head! Not when I can arrest them, or call in the police."

"No," said King flatly. "Just help me find them and leave the rest to me."

Forester fumbled in his pocket for his mobile phone. It was set to vibrate and he held up a hand to the pair of them as he took the call, walking into the kitchen for privacy.

"You can live with that?" Caroline asked King. "With killing people who may or may not be armed, who may have surrendered?"

"Yes," King shrugged, then added, "You have to know how to compartmentalise. They're terrorists. They are ISIS. They are planning to kill thousands, maybe millions of British citizens. Babies, children, women, the old, the infirm. Pacifists. Charity workers, medical workers. Decent people," King looked at her coldly. "Now, I was in northern Iraq not long ago. I saw the carnage left behind by an ISIS raid on a region. Babies and children beheaded, not cleanly, a good proportion of spine ripped out along with the head. That's what happens when blunt gardening tools are used. Men castrated, women raped, people burned alive in cages. It goes on and on. These people, people like Al-Shaqqaf's supporters, or his bodyguards have been out there, and in Syria doing all of these things. Now they strut around in our country preaching hate against the west. Well we can't allow that, can we? They'll never stand trial for those raped women, those beheaded children, those castrated men. Well, we skip the trial and go straight to punishment that's all."

Caroline remained silent. She looked up as Forester walked back in.

"We have a significant break," he said. "An agent we had with Al-Shaqqaf has had his cover blown. He's been stabbed and he's not in great health, but he called in and a debrief and security team are on route to his hospital. Hodges is already there following a lead and I've told headquarters to instruct the agent to start speaking to him. I've called Hodges to send him back to the hospital. Seems he was sent packing with a flea in his ear by the doctor. He's going back to start debriefing and sit in on the debrief team when they get there."

"How did Hodges find him?" Caroline asked.

"A uniformed officer who was called to the hospital after staff reported the stabbing recognised him from an internal bulletin, resulting from Hodges' appeal. Seems it worked after all," Forester smiled. "I'm going to head down there now."

"You had someone in Iman Al-Shaqqaf's mosque?" Caroline asked incredulously. "But weren't you worried his details would be on the files Hoist downloaded?"

"Yes, I was," Forester said matter-of-factly. "But we're not the bloody boy scouts here. It took us five years to get an asset in place and when we finally did we couldn't jeopardise him. Likewise, we couldn't risk compromising him for his own safety. We couldn't go out of our way to observe him either. We put a watch list out with the surveillance team in residence, but even they didn't know he was an asset." Forester walked to the door, put his hand on the handle and turned back to them. "This is the break we need. Get Hoist out there again and let's see if the enemy are going to make a move. It feels wrong that they didn't try anything last time." He opened the door. "Like Hoist wasn't a target at all…" Forester stopped in his tracks and looked in bewilderment at the drone hovering above his Jaguar, just metres in front of him at head level. He hesitated for a moment.

A moment too long.

46

The detonation was blinding, the explosion so loud that neither King nor Caroline could hear anything in the aftermath. Both were hurled backwards by the shockwave and the windows on the side facing the explosion shattered, showering them both with glass. King had landed on his back, but instinctively rolled onto his front. The sensation of soundlessness was similar to diving deep into water. There was pressure in his ears. Gradually, the sound of his heartbeat returned, thudding in his chest and pulsating in his neck and ears. He rolled on his side and looked at Caroline. She was staring at the ceiling, glass on her chest and face and blood weeping from cuts to her neck and cheek. She turned to him and opened her mouth to say something. King couldn't hear what she said, but was aware of a popping sound outside. He pushed himself up and looked for Forester. Again he heard the popping, this time louder. He'd heard the sound before. Muted and distorted after a similar explosion.

Gunfire.

"Get up!" he screamed at Caroline. He was reaching for his weapon when the man came in through the shattered doorway, the AK47 aiming down at Forester's still form on the floor. King's muscles were tight and slow, aching from the violent blast. He gripped the rubber butt of the Walther and snatched it clear of the holster as the muzzle of the AK47 flashed and Forester's body arched and danced on the floor, hit repeatedly by round upon deadly round of 7.62mm copper and lead.

The flashing muzzle stopped and turned in slow motion, swinging around towards King and Caroline. King had the 9mm pistol up and started to fire, not yet on target but firing away as he came up to aim, hoping to put the gunman under pressure. The gunman broke left and dived into the kitchen, his weapon blasting away as he moved, King's rounds going wide and striking a tight pattern of holes into the plaster. Sound was returning, and as if a switch had been flicked, time caught up and slow motion was merely an illusion. Caroline was up and moving towards the lounge. Her pistol aimed at the doorway of the kitchen. An explosion rocked the house, but deep within. King looked in the direction, but it seemed to come from upstairs.

The adjoining doorway!

"They're entering both houses!" he shouted to Caroline. He sprinted to the stairwell and leaped the first three stairs but there was an almighty eruption of automatic gunfire and the plaster and wooden bannisters were cut to shreds. He fired straight into the muzzle flashes and was reaching for a spare magazine as he leaped the rest of the stairs and crouched on the landing. The sights of his weapon searching desperately for a target.

Caroline had made it to the lounge where Hoist was crouching behind the leather sofa. He was trembling and had dropped his coffee on his lap. She looked at him, but didn't have to tell him to get down. If the pile of the carpet were any deeper he would be hidden from view.

Caroline turned towards the wall separating the kitchen from the lounge. She aimed and fired a line across the plaster, each shot approximately three feet high and ten inches apart, until all sixteen rounds had gone and she started to change over to her spare magazine.

The wall exploded in plaster and wood fragments as the gunman returned automatic gunfire with five times the muzzle energy and three times the velocity. He changed magazines quickly too and started to answer Caroline's sixteen rounds with sixty of his own. Caroline threw herself to the floor and rolled into the fire place. The space was tight, thankfully unlit and surrounded by bricks and mortar. She was covered with soot and had smashed a glass vase and display of dried flowers, cutting her leg in the process, but she was shielded from the onslaught of sustained gunfire.

Hoist had taken several of the rounds in his chest and stomach and lay still. There was blood, but not much. The bullets had hit more than one vital organ and death had been close to instantaneous.

Caroline heard gunfire deep within the house. She checked she had reloaded correctly and that a bullet was chambered. Her hands shook and she realised she had been holding her breath the entire time. She breathed in a huge lungful and breathed out slowly. She was safe in her hide and she had a good view of the doorway. She would have the advantage.

King could see the sports bag with the SCAR rifle inside. It was loaded, cocked and the safety on. He could go for it down the stairs, but the man with the AK above him may make a move, and the man with the AK below might chance a look. Either way he was exposed and under-gunned. He fired three shots above him and tore down the stairs. He got to the bag, dropped the Walther on the floor and got the SCAR out. He flicked the selector to fully automatic, and realising what had been going on downstairs, he turned towards the lounge. He could see Hoist's body on the floor. "Caroline!" he shouted.

"In the lounge! X-ray in the kitchen!"

King fired the whole magazine into the doorway and trailed it along the wall. The 7.62x51mm was far more powerful than the AK and the bullets smashed through the kitchen units and the saucepans within and through the range and slammed into the wall beyond and far into the second adjoining building. For a moment there had been return fire, but as King reloaded, there was an eerie quiet within. It didn't last long and gunfire erupted from upstairs once more. King trailed the SCAR under the landing above his head and heard a solid thud of somebody hitting the floor. He took the stairs two at a time and dived prone at the top. A young man of around twenty with thick glasses and a poor complexion was struggling to bring his rifle round to aim. King aimed, but a flash of light and roar of gunfire resonated from the end of the landing. He ducked under the top step and slid down a few treads for good measure. When he raised his rifle and head above the step again, the man on the floor was steadying his aim. King fired three rapid rounds and the man jolted and rested still. The bullets had entered through his head and exited out of his backside. It wasn't the prettiest thing King had seen, but it wasn't the worse either. He got up and made his way carefully down the landing. He could hear running footsteps. He wanted to pursue, but chose Caroline instead. He hesitated at the top of the stairs, kept the weapon trained on the hallway and kitchen doorway.

"Caroline!"

"I hear you!"

"Moving down the stairs. One X-ray dead! Another exiting out of the adjoining safe-house!"

"Go after him!"

"No. We'll do this," he paused, looking at Forester's tattered and bloody body on the parquet floor. "Cover me at the door." He looked at the lounge doorway and saw Caroline easing herself out on her belly. For a moment he felt a pang of desperation that she had been wounded, but almost as soon as he felt this he could tell that she was keeping low and approaching tactically. Her weapon was steady, as was her nerve.

King stepped off the staircase and crunched the glass under his feet. Whoever was in the kitchen would hear his approach, but then again, they would have heard him communicating with Caroline. He just had to do this and not get shot. He stepped over Forester's body and peered into the kitchen. It was covered in debris and tiles had punched off the wall and smashed on the stone floor. Cupboard doors had opened as pots and pans had been blown out and plates had disintegrated into shards and dust. There were numerous empty cases, but still no sound. King edged inside, shouldered his weapon on the form on the floor and closed the gap.

Mohammed Betesh lay on his back, his hand still on the grip of the AK47, but the weapon was pointing away from King and the man's grip was loose.

He was breathing irregularly, his torso strewn with holes, each trickling a steady flow of blood. King could tell the man's limbs were useless, paralyzed. A couple of the bullet holes were low, but dead centre. They had shattered the man's spine. The man looked up at King belligerently.

"Where is the bomb?" King asked.

Betesh smiled. There was a faint smudge of blood at the corner of his mouth. "You think… I would… tell you?" he rasped.

"This isn't about religion," King said. "You'll kill thousands of Muslims. Decent people."

"They… made… their choice… they… can… die by… their decision… to live… among… the godless… pigs…"

"I killed your brother," King said coldly.

Caroline entered, her pistol held down by her side. "Me too," she said. She glanced back at Forester's body. Her boss, her friend, her mentor. When she looked back at Betesh she had tears in her eyes. She raised the pistol slowly, deliberately and fired.

47

King caught Caroline by the arm and pulled her out of the kitchen. He picked up his Walther and holstered it, grabbed the sports bag containing the spare magazines and the silenced pistol and ran to the door. "Come on!" he shouted.

Caroline hesitated over Forester, looked at King bewildered. "We need to be here when the police arrive."

"We need to get that gunman!" He peered outside, saw the bomb-damaged Jaguar, the dead driver inside, the bullet holes through the windscreen. There was no sign of the attackers' vehicle, no sign of the man with the AK47. He glanced back at her. "Stay if you want but I'm going to find him!"

He ran down the steps and made for the BMW. Ahead he saw a red van, someone getting into the driver's side. All he saw was khaki combat trousers and a desert boot. He thought back to the stairs, saw the muzzle flash and the man retreating. He remembered boots. It was close enough. The van took off rapidly and erratically took the bend at the end of the road at speed, and on the wrong side. That decided it. He got the door open and threw the SCAR rifle onto the passenger seat.

Caroline opened the door, pushed the rifle aside and dropped into the passenger seat. "Well move then!" she shouted. She dropped the used magazine into her lap and reloaded, then tucked the partially full magazine into her pocket.

King pressed the start button and slammed the gear selector into drive. He floored the accelerator and the car surged forwards, its traction control cutting in and avoiding wheel spin. It juddered as the 'box went up through the gears and within seconds they were heading towards eighty miles per hour. Hard on the brakes, a slight drift around the corner and the morning traffic was already congested in the street ahead. King pulled out into the traffic without hesitating and a van sounded its horn. A cyclist slammed a fist on the roof and swore as he pedalled onwards.

"I see it!" Caroline shouted excitedly. "Five, no six cars in front. I can get out, run to him and take him now!" She went for the door handle and King grabbed her thigh.

"Wait!" He looked ahead of the van and saw the traffic lights. "We follow him for a minute and see where he goes."

"Fine," she said. She looked at him. "You don't need to hold my leg anymore."

King looked down, removed his hand. "Sorry."

"Dinner first," she smiled. "Jesus! My bloody heart is going to come out through my chest!"

"Serious adrenalin rush. What the hell was that back there?"

"I don't know. It was seeing Forester. I saw red." She shook her head. "Oh my god! Charles!" She started to sob. She wiped her eyes with her sleeve. "I can't believe it!"

"Don't think about it," King said. "We need to stay on this guy."

"I should call it in."

"Yes, you should. But don't give too much away. Don't tell them you shot Mohammed Betesh and don't volunteer to come in for questioning yet."

"Why?"

"You killed him, and not in self-defence," said King. "A post mortem will show he was paralysed, if anybody pushes for one. There's plenty of people out there who would want to stick an execution on the British establishment."

She stared at the floor and shook her head. "What was I thinking?"

"Give them the salient facts only. Nothing more," he said. "Forester mentioned a Special Branch commander called Anderson. Call him. It should be someone he had a professional relationship with."

Caroline was trying not to sob as she dialled. She wiped her eyes with her sleeve and held the phone to her ear. King opened the window, keeping his eyes on the van in front. He didn't listen but heard Caroline speaking softly.

"I should call headquarters now," she said, looking at the screen of her smartphone.

"No. Anderson will take the lead now. The police have to be involved in this, nothing MI5 can do at a crime scene like that other than shadow them."

"And Hoist?"

"Screw him. He was a traitor, he got the traitor's kiss."

"Jesus, you're black and white."

"It's all there is."

"He's turning left!" Caroline said suddenly.

"On it."

The traffic drew to a standstill ahead and King mounted the pavement. He gave a short burst of acceleration and swung left. The van was already a long way ahead but King did not jump on the accelerator. Now, more than ever he had to hang back and not risk drawing attention to their vehicle.

Just another vehicle. Just another street.

"He's turning right."

"On it." King floored the throttle and slowed before the turning. He eased through the turn just in time to see the van turning left. "I'm not sure if he's made us."

"Do you think he's doing some counter-surveillance?"

"It's possible." Again he floored his right foot and the car surged forwards on a wave of power. "He's turning right." King suddenly accelerated up to forty miles per hour, swung the wheel and pulled the handbrake.

"What are you doing?" Caroline shouted as the car swung through one-hundred and eighty degrees.

King floored the accelerator and swung left and brought the car up to sixty in the quiet residential street. He threw the car left at the junction in front of a taxi and settled into the traffic. "One… Two… Three… Four…"

Caroline stared ahead. "There he is!"

"Knew it."

"He's only four cars ahead now."

"Perfect."

"He won't be too bothered about what's behind him now," King said. "If he was on to us, he'll never expect us to be on this street already."

Ahead the traffic was thinning and the pace was quickening. King kept back as much as he could, but it was a balancing act. He needed to maintain a visual, but if the cars in front turned off in a short space of time, they'd be right behind the target vehicle and sticking out like a sore thumb. The van stayed on the road for a mile, crossed Waterloo bridge and headed southeast. King allowed a taxi and a few motor scooters past him, lengthening the gap. The road was wider and the van threaded its way in a little more relaxed manner. They were driving through Camberwell. The traffic was lighter. Many of the vehicles were trades vehicles and public transport. Before long they were in a less desirable area with tall tower block social housing and a series of lock-ups and closed-down shops. Graffiti adorned the walls of many buildings and the doors to the garage lock-up units were kicked in and buckled. Youths in hoodies swaggered and loitered, skaters performed tricks on railings and old people walked among them with discount supermarket chain shopping bags.

"Nice area."

"You'll see where I grew up soon."

"You're joking?"

"Yeah, this is nice compared to where I used to live."

"Really?"

King nodded. "A tower block not dissimilar to that," he said, pointing to a monstrosity covered in satellite dishes and drying laundry hanging from the windows and balconies. "Broken lifts, drug dealers on the stairs, people pissing in doorways, cars on fire outside. All the desirable features you look for in a family home."

"I don't believe you," she said lightly.

"My mother would throw us out at midnight. So she could shag some bloke for a day's worth of crack," King shook his head. "We were taken into care. Some pervert wanted some time with my younger sister, my mother almost caved," he said quietly. "She would have for the right amount of blow. It was only a matter of time. My sister was ten."

"Jesus."

"A neighbour spoke up, we got taken into care. My mother later died of a heroin overdose," King paused. "I think he's parking up."

King pulled the BMW into the side of the kerb and selected neutral. He would have kept the engine running but start/stop eco technology was here to stay. He knew it would restart the moment any of the controls was touched. He watched the van park up ahead. The SCAR was down beside Caroline's feet in the foot-well. King reached for it and held it across his lap.

"We need to take him alive," Caroline said. "We need information." She looked at the compact rifle and shook her head. "That's overkill."

"He has a Kalashnikov."

"Then let's get him now and take him by surprise. Look, he's using his phone. We need that, we need to know who he called."

"So we snatch him?"

"Yes."

"Might end up messy."

"He probably won't get out with an assault rifle. It's broad daylight."

"You *really* don't know the area."

"Let's do it now. He's obviously going into one of the buildings, if he does we may lose him. Too many exits, too many variables. But we better do it quick, a smart car like this will attract attention here."

"So you *do* know the area."

Caroline took her pistol out and checked the breach. She holstered it and reached for the door handle.

King caught hold of her thigh again. "Wait," he said sharply. "I have an idea."

"I'm listening," she paused. "And yet, your hand is still there." He moved it, but not too quickly. "Go on, what's the idea?"

King watched the van as the door opened and the man got out. He looked around the buildings, appearing to watch the windows and casually closed the door. King pressed the footbrake, put the selector into drive and the engine fired up quietly. He eased the car forwards slowly. The man turned and looked at them, walked slowly, yet purposefully towards a building which looked like an old mill. It was largely derelict-looking with many broken windows. King speeded up and the man turned, looked and then continued, quickening his pace.

"So, what's the plan?" Caroline asked. "Because he looks a little spooked."

King floored the throttle and the BMW lurched forwards. The man had passed the point of no return and he was caught halfway. He instinctively ran and he was doing well until the very edge of the front bumper slammed into the back of his knee and he was thrown both forwards and upwards as King snatched the handbrake, spun the wheel and the car slid through one-hundred and eighty degrees and the rear bumper slammed into him as he landed on the concrete. This time he was thrown ten feet forwards and landed on his stomach.

"That was the plan?"

"Well it worked," King said, getting out.

"Yeah, if killing him was the plan, well done!" Caroline followed suit, her pistol held down by her side.

King reached the man, dropped to one knee and pressed his fist into his neck. "You hear me?"

The man groaned.

Caroline bent down. "Well he must be breathing if he's groaning."

"Armed police! Remain where you are! Show your hands!" The warning was clear and loud and came from behind them. *"Armed police!"*

"Stay still!" King snapped. "Pass me your pistol."

She dropped it on top of the man. He was still groaning. She started to raise her hands slowly.

"Let me see your hands!"

King ejected the round in the chamber and another took its place. A storm drain was three feet away and he flicked the 9mm round over towards it with his foot. He slipped the weapon into the man's hand and clamped it tightly around the butt.

"He has a gun!" King shouted, twisting around. He looked at the two armed officers, held up one hand, but kept the other on the man's hand. "I can't get him to let go of it!" he shouted, then whispered to Caroline out of the corner of his mouth. "Hands up, stand up and step away." He kept his left hand raised, looked at the officers and with his own finger covering the man's trigger finger he squeezed. The gun fired, rocked in the man's hand, and King snatched the weapon out onto the ground, raised both hands and kicked the pistol a few feet away. "I've got it! It's clear, don't shoot! Don't shoot!" He was standing to one side and said, "Caroline! ID and pull rank now!"

The armed officers were moving forwards, their pistols aimed at them, both shouting who they were and what they wanted. Caroline had her ID out of her pocket. Behind the armed officers two plain clothes police officers were on site and moving towards them.

"Caroline Darby, Security Service! Lower your weapons and stand down at once! You are interfering and corrupting an MI5 operation! I said, lower your weapons, now!"

The closest officer kicked the Walther further out from the man on the ground. He kept his weapon aimed on King.

King stepped around the man and kicked the 9mm round down the drain. He lowered his hands and, ignoring both armed police officers, walked towards the approaching officers. "This man attacked an MI5 building. Three MI5 employees were killed and this man killed his wounded accomplice before fleeing the scene."

"It's true," a man walked over. He was tired looking and scruffy, dressed in a crumpled suit. "I've just had a call from Commander Anderson over at

Special Branch." He looked at King and Caroline in turn. "I'm DS Mathews. I'm part of the Metropolitan Police task force assigned to MI5 for the investigation," he paused. "I'm sorry about your boss."

Caroline nodded. "So am I."

The two armed officers had cuffed the man and rolled him onto his side. He was coming round, tersely complaining about his treatment and injuries.

As a certified weapons officer, one of the armed officers donned a pair of rubber medical gloves and made the Walther safe by unloading it and leaving the slide locked backwards. He placed it in an evidence bag and handed it to one of the CID detectives. "Two rounds fired by the looks of it," he said. "Mag takes sixteen. There's fourteen there and the empty case from the bullet discharged here."

Sergei Gulubkin groaned and looked up at them. "Bastard pigs," he mumbled. "I'll have your jobs for this."

King looked at DS Mathews. "I need to speak to him," he said. "Once he enters the system, he'll clam up."

"I don't know," Mathews said. "These things tend to have a habit of biting us in the arse. Later in court."

"Just ten minutes, until the ambulance arrives."

Mathews looked at the armed officers, who were now standing and chatting.

Caroline nodded. "We've got multiple personnel down, twelve missing. We need to know."

"Five minutes," Mathews relented. "It's cold here and the suspect looks to be in shock. Put him in your car until the ambulance arrives. I'm going to make a call." He walked a few paces away and took out his mobile phone.

Gulubkin was stiff and in pain, battered and bruised, but nothing seemed broken as he limped, supported by both King and Caroline, to the BMW. King pushed him into the rear seat and sat down beside him.

"You're looking at life."

"That's not my pistol."

"It's got your prints on it. And gunpowder residue on your fingers. And DNA on the butt and trigger."

"Fuck you."

"As far as people are concerned, you killed Mohammed Betesh. ISIS fighter and Islamic activist. Many people would want to make you a saint. But this is Britain and if you're guilty of murder, you're guilty of murder. You'll go to prison and one of those Islam extremist boys in there will cut your throat with a shiv."

"You know shit."

"I've been inside. I know what I'm talking about. They'll hold you down and do it slow. They'll saw down to the bone and then some." King pulled down the man's collar and looked at his neck. "You've seen a lot of cell-time. You've got the tats. Siberian gulag?" Sergei nodded. "Our prisons are still tough here despite what hardened convicts like you may think. Sure you get three hots and a cot, but the people are exactly the same. And for committing an armed attack on MI5, being caught up on CCTV buying a sedative that was used on four MI5 agents before they died and possessing an illegal firearm you'll do close to life. That's without all that DNA, powder residue and upstanding eye-witness accounts of a cold-blooded murder. You'll go away forever. But like I said, they'll get to you first."

"But I didn't kill anybody!" he snapped. He did not want to go back to prison, King could see it in the man's eyes.

"I'll do a deal," King said.

"Bullshit!"

"Right here, right now."

"What deal?"

"You bought the drugs that were used on the agents murdered at the pier."

"You can keep me out of jail?"

"You get us to that missing warhead and I'll give you my word."

"Really?" He looked at Caroline.

"We haven't really seen you kill anybody," she paused. "I'm sure we can swing you getting off an abduction and possession of a firearm charge. But we need all you've got."

"Protection?"

"Naturally," said King.

"And I won't go to jail?"

"No jail," King nodded.

"I do not know where the warhead is. I promise," Gulubkin paused. "It is still on route here."

"What route?"

"Estonia."

"To where?" Caroline held her iPhone up, recording everything. "And by what means?"

"Fishing boat. Or small freight ship."

"Where is it coming in?" King asked.

"I do not know. Zukovsky has gone to meet it."

"You'll have to do better than that."

"I do not know," he paused, then added, "But I know where the prisoners are."

"Where?" Caroline asked. She looked up, the ambulance had arrived. "Tell us, this deal expires in less than a minute."

"A fisherman. Joseph Arnsettle. He runs a large fishing boat out of Lowestoft. I do not know the name of the boat, but I gave him his initial payment. I went there and paid him the cash, recruited him."

"To Lowestoft?" Caroline checked.

"Yes."

"Where are they going?"

"Norway. They are being met there and taken to a secure location. I do not know where."

"What for?"

Sergei Gulubkin frowned. "For revenge, why else?"

"Revenge for what?"

"You do not know?"

"No," King looked at the approaching ambulance crew. They were being led by DS Mathews.

"I thought everybody knew," Gulubkin smirked. "You know Zukovsky is behind this?"

"Of course."

"Then you know what he plans to do," he sneered.

"What?"

"To kill them."

"For revenge?" Caroline looked bewildered. "I don't understand." She glanced up at the approaching detective and the two paramedics. "What does he want revenge for?"

Gulubkin looked at her and smiled. "You can't cut me a deal," he sneered. "You're stuck for time and reaching out in the darkness." He laughed. "You are pathetic! I'll take my chances with the police, I think. I reckon I'll cut a deal with them just fine."

"You'll enter the system and never leave," King commented flatly. "Even if you tell them all you know and they find the warhead, you'll still do some serious time."

"And if they don't find the warhead?" Caroline continued. "Well, you won't know anything about it because you'll be in the blast radius."

"Or will you?" King stared at him. "What is the target?"

"Fuck you!" Gulubkin glared back. "You know, I think I will be all right in your liberal, weak-willed system. A few years inside a holiday camp you call prison and I'll be back in Russia."

King punched him hard in the face. The man recoiled and looked at him in astonishment. King punched him again and he slumped forwards.

"Oh great!" Caroline snapped. "We're out of time and he's bloody unconscious!"

King got out of the car, nodded at Mathews as he reached the passenger side. "I'm sorry detective sergeant," he said.

"Sorry for what?"

King walked around to the driver's side, looked at him over the roof. "I need more time."

"Wait." Mathews stepped forwards, then froze when he saw the pistol.

King rested it on the roof. Casually, but the noisy end was facing the police officer. "I don't know how much you know, detective. And we'll cross paths again soon, I am sure. But we need a few hours with this man and if he enters the system, we can forget about getting the right answers."

"I can't let you take him," Mathews said. The two paramedics were already backing away. "Don't do this."

"Don't *you* do this."

"You won't shoot a police officer."

"I've done worse," King stared at him, his cold blue eyes unwavering. "A few hours, that's all."

"It's not worth it," Mathews took a step forwards, but stopped when the weapon came up to aim.

"Speak to your boss. There is a nuclear device on route to this country and this man has answers." King looked at him and shook his head. "Walk away. You'll get a call telling you where to find him." He got into the car and started the engine.

Mathews grabbed at the passenger door handle, but froze when he looked into the muzzle of the SCAR rifle in Caroline's hands. She shook her head at him and he stood back as the BMW roared off and swung a tight right at a row of graffiti covered garages. Within seconds it was gone and all that could be heard was the building sound of engine revs, before it just as quickly trailed off to silence.

48

Detective Inspector Hodges scribbled in his notebook with a pencil. He was old school and used reporter's shorthand. He listened intently, interrupting occasionally to clarify the man's account.

Rashid was tired and weak but he wanted to get everything out. He had been undercover for more than a year and the experience of being discovered, of being back on the grid was proving cathartic, he shook as he spoke and looked close to tears at times.

Hodges had been informed about Forester's death and had been saddened. He did not care for many of the people he had met from the intelligence services, but Forester had been different. The man did not seem to have an agenda or ulterior motive. He had wanted the death of his agents investigated and had freely admitted that the police, and in particular Hodges was best placed to do so. Hodges continued to question Rashid as Forester had called and asked him to, but he expected to be pulled off the case as soon as the security service reconvened and somebody else was brought in to replace Forester and take over the investigation.

"Can you describe where this place was?" Hodges asked.

Rashid nodded. "I had my mobile with me," he paused, pointing at the bedside unit. "If it's in there, you can take a GPS reading of both the bunker in Epping Forest and the warehouse."

"Perfect." Hodges opened the cupboard door and took out a clear plastic zip lock bag containing a phone, belt, wallet and some loose change. "Now we're talking. Give me the warehouse address."

"Fleet business park in Newington," Rashid said slowly. "A building still registered and signed as DDS Distribution Ltd. They went bust, Zukovsky has it on a short lease, I understand."

Hodges scribbled madly on his pad. "So who gave you your orders, Vladimir Zukovsky?"

Rashid sipped some water and rested his head back against the stack of pillows. "Iman Mullah Al-Shaqqaf *supplied* me, if you will. Both Khalil and I. Zukovsky has something planned with Al-Shaqqaf, but I have no idea what. At first I thought it was going to be a series of random attacks, but as soon as we hit the safe-house I knew it was a government building."

"And you didn't think to try and apprehend them?"

Rashid shook his head. "Deputy Director Forester told me if I got in to the Islington mosque and close to Al-Shaqqaf, then I was not to break cover at any cost."

"Including taking innocent lives?"

"I bought the GHB, but I did not know what for. That was Marvin, Alesha and Sergei who killed those agents. I did not know what was happening at the safe-house until it started. I didn't fire a shot, and I got Khalil down the alley and away after he was wounded, instigated a retreat."

"And you didn't know about the agents at the pier?"

"No."

"What about the warhead."

"Warhead?"

"You don't know about the warhead Zukovsky acquired in Russia?"

"No," Rashid replied emphatically. "But at the bunker, those lead flasks had radio-active labels on them. I thought they were planning a dirty bomb. I knew I would have to break cover, but they were on to me, that's when they confronted me."

"And they tried to kill you." Hodges said flatly.

Rashid nodded. "They were going to cut my throat. I fought them off."

"All of them?"

"Yes."

"Who?"

"Zukovsky and Marvin had already left. They had what they came for. Al-Shaqqaf is a coward, he ran."

"Figures," Hodges sneered. "Talks kids into wearing suicide vests, taking up jihad, then runs away himself at the first sign of a fight."

Rashid nodded. "I don't know how they found out about me. I had been so careful. I was so embedded in Al-Shaqqaf's organisation, it wasn't until the attack on the safe-house, or when they challenged me in the woods that I seriously had to remind myself who I really was," he paused. "It's weird how being deep undercover affects you. My biggest fear is a single slip up word or sentence, or talking in my sleep."

Hodges nodded. "So Al-Shaqqaf runs away. Who else?"

"Malik, his main bodyguard. I stabbed him in his arse cheek with the knife that I got off of Suad. He was Al-Shaqqaf's spiritual enforcer. Malik was in a quandary, but chose to take care of Al-Shaqqaf."

"Suad?"

"Small man, lethal. He is, or was as extreme as they get. He was the man who would whisper in the Iman's ear. He was all too ready to kill me."

"But you killed him?"

"Stabbed him then slashed him, yes."

"And then what?"

"That just left John. A Brummie. He was a big guy, but he fooled me. I was stupid. He said he'd had enough, that Al-Shaqqaf was going too far. Then he stabbed me. I got him though."

"You killed him?"

"For sure."

"And these bodies will be there, in the woods?"

"I imagine so," Rashid said. "Can't imagine Al-Shaqqaf returning, but maybe someone did. They were going to dump me down the bunker. If someone cleaned up, then the bunker would be the best bet. You'll have to get somebody there soon though, Khalil is down there and there's a shed-load of AK47s, pistols, ammo and who knows what else. Oh, and the lid is booby-trapped with two grenades."

"We'll need to get you checked out for radioactivity. And get a HAZMAT team over there. The Russians are not famed for their health and safety. I'd hate to think what was in those flasks."

Rashid looked worried. "Send the doctor in when you leave."

"Can't just go telling him about radioactive materials," Hodges said. "I suggest you speak to your MI5 debrief team when they get here. Should be any minute now." He turned away from Rashid and answered his mobile phone which had vibrated on its silent setting. "Hodges." He listened, nodded and started to pace around the tiny room. He read out the address of the warehouse in Newington, told the person to get over there, then ended the call.

Rashid watched him. "Problem?"

"You could say that," he paused. "Your friend Sergei Gulubkin has been arrested."

"He's not my friend," Rashid glared. "I am an SAS soldier on secondment to the Security Service who has been long-term deep-cover. Don't you mix it up in your head Inspector Hodges. I'm one of the good guys, and don't you ever fucking forget it."

Hodges nodded. "Alright, fair enough. I'm sorry. But I'm not used to working with 'Box, and you spooks have unravelled a whole load of shit for me to clear up. You do all your James Bond shit in the woods and I've got two more murders on my hands."

"Self-defence."

"It's still got to go to the CPS, still got to go to court. I can't just lose bodies, and wouldn't anyway. Now I've got my sergeant phoning me and telling me that two MI5 agents have taken my prisoner. Just upped and drove away with him. It's all too irregular."

"Well, Inspector, you mentioned a warhead. And there's some radioactive shit in a lot of flasks. Perhaps there isn't time to go by the book. Perhaps those days are over."

49

Professor Orlev was panicked. He had not dealt with the Islamist group previously and had been viewed with suspicion. The men had taken the flasks, but they had been undisciplined and smoked and talked, laughed and joked all through the task. He had received instructions from Zukovsky in the early hours, but had been drinking heavily and had spent the night with a prostitute. He thought he had more time, enough opportunity to move the flasks, but had not banked on a number of things – falling asleep after his assignation, and Al-Shaqqaf's men being so delayed in turning up and so slow in their efforts in moving the flasks. Orlev still had to bleach everything they had touched during their time in the warehouse and take the computers away to dispose of in the river.

The bleach had been watered a little, but as long as a film of the solution coated the surface, then DNA would be destroyed, as would hair fibres become discoloured, enough to be inadmissible in an investigation or court. It sounded a relatively inane task, but Orlev had not realised how time consuming it would be, nor how many possibilities of detection there were. As he cleaned and wiped, he remembered that the rubbish they had disposed of still lay in the bins outside. He would have to empty those also. His heart raced, his nerves getting the better of him. Rashid had got away and he knew of the warehouse. It would only be a matter of time before the police or MI5 knew about their primary location. Orlev looked at his watch. He had been cleaning for nearly an hour. He dropped the cloths in a plastic rubbish sack, but kept his rubber medical gloves on. He would get the computers, the router and printer and load them into his car. There was still so much to clean and think about, but he could not risk being here any longer.

The noise made him freeze. A solid rapping on glass. He ran as best he could, hampered both by age and excessive weight, and looked at the CCTV monitor. The man stood there, hammered the door once more and stared through the glass, his hands cupped to shade his reflection. Orlev was shaking.

He only needed a few more minutes and he would have been clear!

He needed to think, but he was an academic, a man used to thinking-over formulae and systems, sequencing and combinations. He needed his office, his books or his long walks on the Baltic coast. He could not cope with spontaneity and reaction. But he knew that he could not get caught, could not face life inside prison, a life without drink and women. He looked down and saw the case containing various firearms. He had used them in basic military training before specialising in weapon delivery systems with the USSR and later with the Russian Federation. He looked at the man again. If he was a policeman, the chances of him being armed were slim. Britain was a ridiculous nation. A country who armed their police with pepper spray and batons while the criminals came up with more ingenious methods to smuggle guns and ammunition in from the rest of

Europe. He picked up the CZ75 pistol and looked for a magazine. All the magazines for the weapons were pre-loaded and when he found the right one he quickly loaded the weapon and made it ready. He walked out to the foyer with the pistol in his pocket, his jacket concealing it. When he entered the foyer he could see the man staring in, but he had not yet seen him. The man got a shock when Orlev walked up to the door.

The man tapped the glass and held up a warrant card. "Detective Sergeant Mathews, CID. Can you open the door? I have a few questions."

Orlev shrugged like it was no problem and unbolted the lock. "How may I help you?"

"You're Russian?"

"Err, no Polish," Orlev lied. "I am caretaker." He held up his gloved hand. "I am cleaning." Mathews stepped inside, Orlev took a step backwards. "What can I help you with officer?"

"Do you know these men?" Mathews held up a printout with a photograph of Rashid and Sergei Gulubkin both taken from the CCTV. Orlev shook his head. Mathews said, "Are you sure? Sorry, mister?"

"Err, Nazwisko," Orlev said hesitantly. "I do not know these men. Now, I very busy."

Mathews frowned. He looked around the foyer. "Funny, you sound more Russian than Polish."

"I am Polish!" Orlev snapped, then softened his tone. "Sorry, I have much work to do and must be at my next property to clean soon."

"Oh really?" Mathews said, moving through the foyer and into the corridor. "Where's that?"

Orlev frowned. He did not know the area, he had only driven from the warehouse to his rented flat and back. Much of the time Alesha or Marvin had driven him. "About two kilometres away."

"Where?" Mathews looked around the corridor and headed for the open doors of the loading bay. "You know; my wife is Polish."

"Small world."

"Lots of Polish people here now."

"I know."

"Good workers."

"They are."

Mathews stopped. "They?"

"We."

Mathews nodded. "Good workers, strong work ethic. Like yourself, no doubt?"

"Yes."

"Hard work, cleaning."

"It is."

"You are knocking on a bit, for cleaning," Mathews said, smiling. "Sorry, but it must be quite hard at your age."

"It is," Orlev agreed. "But I must get on with my work, officer."

Mathews looked at the rubbish sacks, then saw through the open door of the office. The two laptop computers sat on the bench. They were open. One was running an algorithm, flagging up names on the MI5 personnel list matching core words Orlev had entered and storing it to a cloud. The other was displaying a diagram. Mathews was too far away to see what was on the screens, but he turned to Orlev and frowned. "They left their computers here?"

"Who?"

"Whoever you're cleaning up after."

Orlev shrugged. "All I have to do is clean and empty the rubbish."

Mathews nodded. He walked towards the loading bay. "Yeah, my wife is Polish. We've been together seven years."

"I am happy for you, officer," Orlev said tersely. "But I will lose my job if I do not finish my work."

"Who do you work for?" Mathews asked. "An agency?"

"Yes."

"Which one?"

Orlev hesitated. "Several agencies. More work that way."

"Yeah, my wife works with an agency. Secretarial. Just one agency though. Most agencies like it that way. They don't like people signing on with multiple agencies." Mathews stopped walking, looked around, took in the size of the loading bay. "Do you know, it's funny but I swear that Nazwisko is just the Polish word for surname. And not actually a name at all." He turned around and froze when he saw the pistol levelled at him.

Orlev flicked the pistol towards the storage room just off the corridor and the loading bay. "Move," he said coldly.

"Now don't be silly," Mathews said to him. "This will not end well for you."

"Be quiet and move," Orlev said. "It is you this will not end well for."

Mathews walked ahead of him. "Look, put down the gun. This situation doesn't have to escalate."

Orlev stopped walking, kept the pistol aimed at him. "See those bin sacks?" Mathews nodded. "Take a few and spread them on the floor."

Mathews shook his head. "Put down the gun."

Orlev walked towards him and flicked the gun again. "Get back!" Mathews took a few swift steps backwards and Orlev snatched up a handful of the rubbish sacks. He dropped them down on the ground and spread them out with his feet. He pointed the pistol at the young detective and shouted. "Get on there! Now!"

Mathews flinched. "Don't shoot!" He took a few tentative steps. He didn't know why, but he found himself complying. "Look, please!"

"Be quiet." Orlev stepped around. He aimed the pistol at the man's head.

"Please! My wife is having a baby! It's due in six weeks. Please!" Orlev lined up the pistol with the man's head. Satisfied there was nothing behind Mathews but the vast chasm of the loading bay, he stepped forwards and took deliberate, careful aim. "Don't do this!" Mathews looked at him pleadingly. Orlev took another step forward. He was now approximately seven feet from the young police officer. "For god's sake! Don't…" Mathews begged, but he did not hear the shot, nor finish his sentence. The gunshot rang out in the chasm of the loading bay, reverberating like canon fire. The shrill, metallic jingle of the spent cartridge case bouncing and rolling on the concrete echoed and sang long after the gunshot.

And then silence came. Ominous and final.

50

The sunlight reflected off the water, golden yellow and glistening like the spent embers of a log fire. The sun was low in the autumn sky, above the headland of The Roseland Peninsular, casting its light across the Carrick Roads. The body of water was tranquil today, but could soon whip up to white water at this time of year. It was made up from numerous rivers, primarily the Truro river which ran slow and wide developed from many tributaries filled from water rushing off the rolling hills. The waters ran into the mouth of western-most end of the English Channel where it met the powerful waters of the Atlantic. The Carrick Roads was a haven for sailors and boat users and already at this early hour yachts were heading out, their owners taking advantage of the last week of clement weather before they hauled out for winter storage.

Zukovsky turned back from the window and watched Alesha walk naked to the bathroom. They had arrived at the cottage in the early hours and gone straight to bed. They had made love too quickly. Zukovsky had buried his head into Alesha's neck throughout, a glimpse of her disfigurement enough to kill his desire. She had known. She had sobbed afterwards. They had lain in silence until Zukovsky had got up to look at the sea view overlooking Loe Beach. The boats had already been hauled out here with only the mooring buoys remaining to bob up and down in the choppy swells. Many of the boats had been stored by the beach, their masts and rigging jangling in the wind.

"We will go out for some breakfast," Zukovsky shouted towards the bathroom. He could hear Alesha running the bath. She had put some camomile lotion in the tepid water to ease the tightening skin and blisters. "There is a good place to eat, apparently, at the marina. Then we will take a reconnaissance run."

Alesha walked in, draped in a towel. "What is wrong with right here? There is nobody around now, in the early hours it will be deserted. It was when we arrived. There is a slipway of sorts on the beach."

Zukovsky looked out of the window to the far right extremity of the view. The shingle beach was covered in weed and driftwood. There was indeed a slipway, and a gig rowing club were launching down it. Sturdy-looking women in shorts, rugby shirts and wellington boots. "The port of Falmouth lies at the end of the waterway, where it becomes the sea. There is the coastguard, the fisheries agency, harbour master and marine police. Simply too many authorities to contend with. A large fishing boat sailing past the port and up the waterway may, or most likely *will* attract attention." He started to pull on his trousers and gave his shirt a shake to get rid of the creases. "The place I have chosen will work well. As long as the swell in the bay is no more than a metre or so. Conditions are looking favourable at the moment."

"Is there a plan B?"

"Plan B is a small slipway in the Percuil River, near St. Mawes. But the tide has to be favourable and that means no more than an hour later. It will be tight."

Alesha nodded. "What are the police like down here?"

"Understaffed. The small and winding roads make it difficult to respond to emergencies quickly, but there are enough of them, and they have armed officers patrolling the A30, the main arterial road running through Cornwall. The thinking being that when they are needed they can race to the emergency," Zukovsky paused. "It's likely the port police will have a very rapid access to an armed response unit."

Alesha shrugged and walked back into the bathroom. Zukovsky heard her step into the bath, gasp in pain as she eased herself into the water. He picked up his mobile phone and dialled Orlev, cursed at the lack of signal and put the phone in his pocket. He called out to Alesha, told her he was going to walk around and see if there was a signal outside.

The cottage was a four bedroomed property but was a cottage in name only. Zukovsky imagined that people conjured up an idea of Cornwall and cottages rented well. It was in fact a largely glass-fronted waterside house with its own boathouse and small slipway accessible at an hour each side of high-tide. Two hours on spring-tides. For an extra three-hundred-pounds a week a fourteen foot dingy could be rented along with the cottage. Zukovsky walked along the garden parallel with the water. He took out his phone and cursed at the one bar signal. He knew if he dialled it would miraculously disappear. The end of the garden was at least ten feet higher than the rest of the garden and he walked to the top of the mound, which afforded an excellent uninterrupted view across the bay. At the top he looked again, but there was no signal at all. There would be a signal between Loe Beach and the marina at Mylor. He would pull in as soon as he picked up a signal and call Professor Orlev then.

51

"You really don't know what this is about, do you?" Sergei Gulubkin stated smugly. "For all your resources, all your intelligence gathering capabilities, MI5 hasn't got a clue."

King shrugged. "I've only been with MI5 for two days."

Sergei looked bemused. He looked around the room, if it could be called that, at the pipes suspended from the ceiling, the water running in the open drain below the grate in the floor. "What is this place?"

"End of the line, sunshine," King said. He had brought the silenced Ruger .22 pistol in from the car, given his own Walther P99 to Caroline. He rested the pistol on his leg, the large bulbous suppressor counter-balancing the heavy butt. Sergei was seated on the basic wooden chair opposite his own. His eyes were on the pistol. It was a specialist weapon, and its specialism had made the man think. "I imagine that drain runs out into the Thames. It's a few feet deep and flowing at quite a pace. Should wash a body away easily enough."

"Fuck you!" Sergei sneered. "You're not going to kill me." His eyes flickered. If it were a game of poker, he would have lost his bluff.

King smiled. His mouth looked cruel, his eyes cold. He ran a hand through the four-day-old stubble on his jaw. "I wouldn't bet on it."

Caroline came down the metal steps and walked towards them, pocketing her mobile phone. "Director Howard wants us to come in. He said that Forester's death has changed things."

"It would," King said.

"Meaning?"

"Me, for starters."

"How so?"

"Forester wanted to bring me in on this, but keep my brief to himself. He wanted me to tidy the loose ends," he said. "That means kill. Break all of the links in the chain. I agreed. Hell, it's what I did all those years for MI6. But Forester isn't here anymore. My remit isn't only going to change; it's going to be cancelled altogether."

"So what now?"

"Carry it on," he said. "If you want to honour Forester's memory then stay on the investigation. Feed me the intel. I will shadow you. Shut this lot down. You let me know the target and I'll do my job. Afterwards, I'm out of here. Until then, I'll play my part closing these terrorists down. Starting with this guy here." He pointed the pistol at Sergei who shifted awkwardly in his seat. "If he isn't going to talk, then he's of no further use."

Caroline looked thoughtful. "What if they don't keep me on it?"

"You were Forester's go to girl. He used you when he could have used anybody else. You move heaven and earth, raise bloody hell to stay on it. They'll keep you on the investigation, you've been on it from the start."

She nodded. "I spoke to Hodges as well. He's pissed off. I mean royally so."

"His guy contacted him then?"

"Yep."

"And?"

"He wants his prisoner," she tapped Sergei on the head and he flinched. "They were staking out the brothel he ran after he was grassed up by people who had seen the police appeal."

"It's all closing in, sunshine," King smirked at him.

"I've passed on the information about this Joseph Arnsettle fellow in Lowestoft. I've told Howard *and* Hodges. That way there will be two investigative angles. They'll have all there is to know about him soon. And if they can get that, then they can get the name of the boat."

"We need to meet with Hodges, but I want to avoid 'Box. Did Hodges mention the asset whose cover was blown?"

"He did. The man has information that could prove vital. He didn't go into it, as I said, he's pissed off about matey here." She tapped Sergei around the head again, smiled as he flinched. "We need to drop him in, mend a few bridges so to speak."

"You said you'd keep me out of prison," Sergei reminded them.

"Well you better get singing then. Think about all you know and you can tell Detective Inspector Hodges. The question now is; how much do you want to stay out of prison?"

52

50°N 2°W The English Channel

Max Clenton flicked his cigarette stub into the bow wake below him and watched it float towards the stern. Before it reached the propeller wake a seagull swooped in and took the stub away, gulping it down greedily as it flew. The gulls had been with them since the swell had died down off Dover. He had known that the boat would have been monitored, but he carried different GPS beacons rented in cash from other vessels that fished the Cornish coast and he knew that at times of busier ferry traffic, as long as he sailed steadily, following the rules of the sea he should be left alone. He had relaxed a little, drifting closer to the French shores than the English coast, and was now approximately fifty miles off the coast of Dorset.

Clenton lit another cigarette and watched the gulls dip and rise on the wind. He wasn't used to plain sailing. The crew had dropped some lines earlier and hauled some cod and bass. Bass were prohibited from being caught in the English Channel from boats this year, so they packed them on ice and stowed them below decks in two purpose built smuggling holds. After this business was over he knew an expensive restaurant who would take them off him for cash, no questions asked. Clenton would drop the cod on the market when he moored *The Lady Majestic* back at port. It would keep him in beer money while he worked out what to do with the small fortune the Russian would pay him tonight.

***

Alesha had eaten Eggs Benedict and Zukovsky had sampled a Full English. They had taken a window table overlooking the marina. Judging by the many buoys bobbing in the swell it was evident that many of the boats had been hauled out for winter. Zukovsky noted that only large yachts remained. Except for an older couple struggling to uncover a sleek speed boat named *Diva*. The boat was blue and white and Zukovsky estimated it to be twenty-five feet. It looked fast, from what little the Russian knew of pleasure craft. But it was the only boat of its type in the moorings and he assumed the couple were wringing the last out of her before winter. The process of launching from the open water mooring had not looked enjoyable in the cold wind and building swell. But they had finally completed the task and were taking the boat out into the marked channel. Once clear of the channel the boat rose quickly and left behind a terrific wake as she powered out across the water and aimed for the horizon.

Alesha had fashioned a headscarf across her face. She was subdued. Zukovsky sipped his Americano and looked at her. "It will be better when you return to Russia. I know a man who will make it all better."

"I want to kill her," she said emphatically. The waitress had chosen the wrong time to ask if the food was to their liking. She hesitated between them. "I want to kill the fucking bitch who did this to me!" She looked up at the young waitress. "What do you want?"

Zukovsky held up his hand. "Everything is wonderful, my dear. Please, leave us alone." He nodded and smiled at the perplexed young girl and she busied herself at a service table, folding napkins. He turned to Alesha. "Enough. You will draw attention to us."

"I mean it," she said. "If this is about revenge. I want *mine*!"

Zukovsky nodded. "And you will get it. But we have to complete this. Maybe our paths will cross again."

Alesha pushed her plate away. "I'll see that they do."

After they had paid, Zukovsky drove the winding series of roads that led them to the King Harry Ferry. This took them across the narrower end of the Carrick Roads across the River Fal, a hundred-metre expanse of water to The Roseland. The ferry only took five minutes. It operated on chains that were sunk in the deep water. The ferry dropped its ramp and they followed a small procession of vehicles onto The Roseland Peninsular. When they cleared the woods and reached the top of the hill the expanse of rolling fields dotted with farmhouses and distant villages was breathtaking. The traffic thinned, each vehicle taking various smaller roads and tracks until they were alone on the narrow road travelling around tight corners and up and down with the hilly terrain. They followed the signs towards Gerrans and Portscatho and after a series of turns they drove down a narrow track and the sea appeared in front of them. The road swung right and there was a small concrete slipway to the sea ahead of them and a sandy parking area to their right.

"This is it," Zukovsky said.

"I noticed the last ferry was nineteen-twenty hours. Winter timetable."

"Yes. We will come by road through Truro. It apparently takes twenty minutes longer. We shall return by that route today to familiarise ourselves with the road layout."

Alesha got out and walked to the edge of the slipway. She looked out at sea which was green and slick-looking, then turned and looked at the steep earth bank behind her which led to the farmland beyond. She turned to Zukovsky when he stood next to her. "Ideal," she said.

"Perfect, isn't it?" He looked out at sea and the endless horizon.

She reached and held his hand. "It will not be long now," she said softly. "You have been so patient, my love."

53

King pulled the BMW to a stop behind Hodges' car. They had dropped off Sergei Gulubkin at Scotland yard where he was being processed until Hodges could get there to question him. Hodges had agreed to meet them at a service station in Newington and lead the way to the warehouse Rashid had informed him about.

"My man hasn't reported anything," Hodges said walking up to King's open window. "I can't get hold of him either."

"What was his brief?" King asked.

"I told him to get down here and check it out," Hodges dialled DS Mathews' number again, then put the phone back in his pocket tersely. "There's a good signal here. We're all on the same network. It's not like him not to pick up."

Detective Constable Watkins walked over. "I'll scout about, see if I can see his car," she said. "Maybe he's parked around the back?"

"All right," Hodges said. "But be casual, don't get seen."

King opened his door and Hodges stepped back a pace. "Look, let's clear the air," he said. "Caroline told you about the missing warhead. It's a big deal. I needed all I could get out of Gulubkin before he hit the system."

"We have laws. It's the thin end of the wedge when we start to ignore them."

"You're not used to my world."

"But you're operating in mine!" Hodges shook his head. "If it goes to trial, then the fact Gulubkin was refused medical treatment, was questioned improperly and then abducted means the odds are stacked against him being found guilty of anything. In fact, the CPS will probably fail to even bring it to court. The best friend of the criminal is a police officer who doesn't go by the book. And in your case, MI5 don't even have the power of arrest."

Caroline, who had got out and walked around the car to them, added, "But in our defence, Inspector, we have a duty of care to ensure that further terrorist activities do not take place. We were using our powers of exclusion to ascertain the threat was no longer clear or present."

Hodges shrugged. "It's a different world. But mark my words, your actions this morning will not see justice done." He took out his ringing phone, his words hanging in the air. "Yes?" he paced away and spoke quietly. He put his phone back in his pocket. "That was Watkins. Mathews' car is parked to the side of the building. She said she can hear a metal door unlocking to a loading bay."

"We need to cut off the exit," King said. "It doesn't sound good."

"I'll call for back up," Hodges said. "We stay put for now. I don't want any escalation."

King shook his head. "If they failed to kill Rashid, then they know it's only a matter of time before he informs the authorities about this place. We have Sergei Gulubkin but if he clams up, then we have nothing. This place is the only lead we have and if there's somebody in there, they cannot be allowed to escape."

Hodges looked indecisive. He shook his head. "No. We wait for back up." He turned, started to dial on his phone.

King got into the BMW and started the engine. Hodges turned and waved his arms, but King had the car reversing rapidly and he swung the wheel hard, engaged drive and the car J-turned smoothly without any loss of momentum. He accelerated quickly and took the left turn into the carpark at speed, the tyres squealing and the car juddering as the traction control cut in. He could hear the gunshots over the engine noise, recognised them as pistol rounds. As he rounded the building he could see Watkins taking cover precariously behind a sign advertising the previous business. It was wood and PCV and she was dodging the splinters as the bullets smashed through with no real loss of velocity. King swung right and put the car in front of the sign, slamming on the brakes.

"Get in the back!" he yelled. Watkins needed no further encouragement and got the door open. She struggled at first, but King remembered the automatic locking and pressed the button on the dash. Watkins flung herself across the rear seats and the gunfire continued, this time the copper-coated lead tearing into the steel, aluminium and fibreglass of the BMW. The passenger window blew out and both of them were showered with tiny square fragments of safety glass, glistening like diamonds in the bright light of day.

King still didn't have eyes on the threat, but he knew the approximate direction, and as he slung the car into a U-turn, the rear wheels powering the car and swinging it around like a pendulum he could see the man crouched by the side of the rising corrugated door of the loading bay. The man jumped wildly as gunfire broke out to his right and King saw Caroline crouched down, firing double-taps with the Walther P99 he'd given to her earlier.

The man ducked back inside the warehouse and the door started to come back down. King got the BMW out of the arc of fire and yelled at Watkins. "Get out!" She struggled with the door and rolled out onto a stretch of grass near the pathway to the warehouse. King slammed the BMW into reverse and shot back the way he'd come, straightening up and then speeding up at a forty-five-degree angle towards the lowering corrugated door. The BMW struck the door at its reversing speed limit, the valves of the six-cylinder engine reverberating from under the bonnet. The door folded like baking foil and the sound boomed and echoed around the interior of the warehouse. The side and rear impact airbags inflated and King was thrust deep into the seat. There was no shock factor, however, because of the deliberate nature of the manoeuvre. King opened the door and rolled out to present a smaller target. He brought the Ruger pistol up to aim, but the man had disappeared. Caroline appeared at his shoulder, her weapon up. Watkins peered around the edge of the doorway. She was unarmed, but she was brave.

King turned to her. "Wait outside. Liaise with back-up. They need a clear picture of what's going on." He moved forwards, keeping the Ruger trained in front of him. He could hear Caroline moving behind him. She had his back.

Ahead of them they could hear breaking glass. An alarm sounded and above them a red light flashed and spun like an old fashioned police light. King reached the end of the loading bay and cautiously rounded the edge of the corridor. Caroline shuffled close to him, her weapon aimed past King's shoulder.

The man was old, in his seventies and his hair was white. He was short in stature and overweight. He was dressed in an old fashioned tweed suit. King studied him, studied the grip on the pistol aiming at the back of Hodges' head. Studied the grenade in his hand, the pin removed. The man's hand gripped the lever tightly, his knuckles white and his hand shaking minutely.

"Get back!" he shouted. He pressed the barrel of the pistol harder against the detective's head.

"Put the weapon down," King said coldly. "The police are on their way. Armed response units. You'll never get out of here alive."

Hodges was on his knees. His hands were on his head and he looked scared. He had a look of contempt towards King, like he was willing him to know that waiting for back-up was the way to go. King ignored him, stared at the old man instead.

"I said get back!" Orlev shouted.

Caroline moved across the corridor and stood in the open doorway of a lavatory and changing room. She gave Orlev more to think about, but she had lost King as cover. But King could see what she had achieved. Orlev had the weapon not just aimed at, but touching Hodges. If he moved the weapon, he had two guns aimed at him.

To take the gun away from Hodges was to die. To shoot Hodges was to lose his only bargaining chip, and with two guns on him he had no chance. It was check, but not yet checkmate. Hodges was holding it all in the balance. Orlev was clever though, a scientist. He looked at both of them for a moment, then as quickly as he had assessed the situation, he threw the grenade between them.

The grenade was a canister about the size of a drinks can. The grenade spun through the air and the spring-loaded handle sprang off and travelled alongside the grenade as it arced and tumbled towards them. King dived across the corridor and cannoned into Caroline taking her to the floor. Orlev took the pistol away from Hodges' head and fired twice at King. Both shots missed and carried on into the loading bay. King landed on top of Caroline and the pair slid on the newly mopped floor. They looked at each other momentarily, their faces inches apart. The grenade detonated and they heard the whoosh of smoke being released under the pressure of compressed air. King rolled off her and brought the Ruger up to aim at the doorway. Caroline was up now too and the chunky 9mm pistol was covering King from his right and rear.

"Smoke grenade," he said.

"Well, duh!" Caroline countered.

King edged his way out of the lavatory. Smoke filled the corridor, but already he could see that Orlev and Hodges were gone. "Come on!" he shouted.

"Where?" she asked, but followed him as he ran. He was sprinting through the loading bay towards the BMW. King got in and Caroline jumped in the passenger seat next to him. The airbags were deflated and hung from the sides of the seats and the headrests like uninflated party balloons. "Where are we going?"

"The man's car is in the warehouse. He must have gone for Hodges' vehicle out the front." He drove out, disconnecting from the twisted metal of the ruined door. There was a series of gunshots. "Oh shit!"

The BMW rounded the loading area and powered into the carpark. Orlev was bundling Hodges ahead of him towards the vehicle. He had the pistol in front of him. DC Watkins lay on the ground, a still and foreboding figure.

"Oh no!" Caroline gasped. "The bastard! She wasn't even armed!"

Orlev looked around, aimed the weapon and fired three shots at the approaching vehicle. Hodges tackled him, but Orlev smashed the barrel of the pistol across the man's mouth and he went down. Hodges looked up into the muzzle of the pistol, his hands in front of his face in a vain attempt to protect himself. King slammed the car to a stop and got out, the Ruger aimed at Orlev and the open door providing some cover. He fired twice and the .22 silenced pistol merely coughed. Both bullets hit Orlev in the right thigh, a mere inch apart. Orlev spun like a top and fell. Hodges scrambled away on his back, pumping his legs like pistons to get clear. King ran the ten paces or so and stepped on the pistol, with Orlev's fingers still wrapped around the butt. The man was moaning, his leg was sprung back with his heel touching the back of his thigh. Part of his hamstring was severed and the bleeding was spurting in time with the sporadic muscle cramps he was experiencing. King bent down and retrieved the pistol. He held it out to

Hodges, who was nursing his mouth with a bloody handkerchief.

He looked at King and said, "If only we had waited."

"Bollocks!" King cut him off. "We've got a nuclear warhead targeted for somewhere in Britain and not a clue where it is. We've got a dozen missing MI5 agents and if we lost this guy, then it's one less lead and we haven't got many, in case you hadn't noticed. Plus, you've got a missing officer."

"Where's your back-up?" Caroline asked, walking up the grass embankment from where Watkins lay.

"I never finished the call," Hodges said. "You took off around the back, I thought I had better go in through the front, or risk losing him." He shook his head. "Oh Christ, Watkins!"

"I'm sorry. She's dead," Caroline said. "I just checked."

King bent down and pulled Orlev to his feet. He dragged him to the rear of the BMW and shoved him inside. He was bleeding and screaming, but he could barely move.

"What are you doing?" Hodges asked, bemused.

"You said earlier that I was operating in your world," King replied. "Well, you're in mine now. So you can walk away, or you can get some payback for Watkins and find out what has happened to DS Mathews. King got into the BMW and looked at him coldly. "Which is it to be?"

Hodges mopped the blood from his mouth and looked around. The warehouse was at the end of a road and it was a Sunday. It was deserted. Hodges looked back at King for a moment, then walked around and got into the backseat next to Orlev.

54

King pushed Orlev into the wooden chair and stood back. He tossed the roll of duct-tape to Caroline and kept the silenced Ruger pistol aimed at the man's chest. Caroline pulled out a length and wrapped it around the man's wounds. Two small bullet holes front and back. Orlev winced as she bound it tightly. Next, she fastened his right ankle to the chair leg. She wound it round twice and tore it off. She repeated the process with his other ankle, then with both wrists and the sturdy chair arms. She was mindful not to get into the line of fire with King's pistol.

They had disabled the alarm, but the red light still spun and threw crimson shadows on the walls and ceiling. King had taken a look at the control panel and was confident it was not a monitored system.

Hodges stood at the open boot of Orlev's car. Just a few feet aside on the floor rested Watkins' body, where they had moved it and covered with a wrap of polythene sheet. The sheeting was opaque, but after it had been folded three or more times it was not easy to look through and hid the young police woman's features from view. Hodges was staring at Mathews' body in the boot. It was twisted and already pale and stiffening. The tiny hole in the forehead was at contrast to the gaping chasm of the rear of the skull. The boot lining was matted in thick, sticky matter. Blood had drained and pooled and congealed. Hair was matted to the fabric of the lining, when the body was eventually moved, it would be a messy and undignified affair.

Caroline looked at King. "Do you think he's okay?" she asked, nodding towards the detective. "He looks broken."

"Not a good day for him," King replied. He looked at Orlev. "But it's going to get a whole lot worse for you."

"Idle threats!" Orlev snapped indignantly. "Look in my wallet! I have diplomatic immunity!"

Caroline reached inside the man's jacket and pulled out a thick, tattered leather wallet which looked decades old. She tossed it to King. He tucked the pistol into his waistband then thumbed through the wallet. King had seen the Russian Federation diplomat card before, and this looked original to him. He frowned at Caroline and she walked over and looked at it. She turned to Orlev. "What are you doing with this?"

"I'm a diplomat, sweetie," he sneered. "I could fuck you here and now and if you cried rape, I'd still go free and be allowed home."

She slapped him across the face. It was hard and fast and would have hurt less had it been a punch. Orlev recoiled and glared at her. "You'll pay for that. You will all pay for this."

Hodges walked over. He had seemed broken moments before, but as he walked he had regained his resolve. He seemed possessed. "He was about to become a father!" he shouted, pointing back at the car. "His wife was expecting!"

Orlev sneered. "Yes. He mentioned it. He seemed to think I'd care somehow," he paused. "Now, get me untied and call my embassy. You are breaking the convention of international diplomacy. If you do not release me this minute, you will have started an international incident, of which there will be no good outcome for yourselves. Call my embassy, chalk it all up to a learning curve and get on with the rest of your lives."

Hodges was on the man like a rash. He struck him and hit him, but with no control or thought to his intentions. He was in a rage and the blows were both clumsy and ineffective. King pulled the man off of him by his collar and when he tried to attack him again, he hooked the man's foot with his own and he fell to the floor. Orlev stopped flinching, he had a small cut to his brow and his eyes were watering. He smirked and shook his head in disgust. "I have whores hit me harder and I pay them for it," he sneered.

"Hodges," King said, releasing the man's collar. "See if you can find a kettle or a jug. We will need some material – a towel or blanket. And a bucket of water. A lot of water."

Orlev looked at King. "You can't be serious?" he said. "I have told you of my diplomatic status. You are making a grave error."

Hodges walked away down the corridor. Caroline looked at King, but he looked away. He took off his jacket and put it on a chair. He placed the pistol on top of the jacket and rolled up his sleeves.

Hodges came back into the loading bay. "There's a roll of jay cloth. Will that do?"

"Perfect." King walked a pace towards Orlev and kicked him in the chest. The chair toppled backwards and the man crashed down, cracking his head on the concrete floor. He was winded and dazed, but King took the roll of cloth off Hodges and wrapped it several times around the man's head. He tried to protest, but the words were both slurred and then muffled as the cloth covered his face. Hodges put the bucket of water down and King reached for the kettle, dipped it in the bucket and waited for it to fill. He started to pour the water in a steady stream over the man's face. Orlev gagged and choked and coughed, but still King kept up the steady flow of water. It was icy cold and as Orlev gagged it splashed King in the face. He refilled the kettle and continued to pour. After about a minute King put down the kettle and roughly unwrapped the cloth. Orlev gasped and hungrily mouthed for air like a fish on a riverbank. "What is your role? What are you doing with Vladimir Zukovsky?"

Orlev fought for breath. He was about to speak, but rather than give the man chance to scorn or lie to him, King wrapped his head again and tightened the cloth. Orlev tried to protest, but water was already filling his mouth and lungs from breathing through the cloth alone. King poured more water and the man rocked and jerked in the chair, his body arching so violently the movement threatened to damage his spine.

Caroline stared on in horror, but to her surprise, she did not protest. She thought of Forester, her mentor. She thought of her dead and missing colleagues, of Watkins and Mathews, of the sergeant's unsuspecting wife, now widowed; their unborn child now fatherless. She watched King as he poured the water. His expression calm, determined. He neither enjoyed, nor hated what he was doing. He was merely performing a task. He refilled the kettle and poured. Unwrapped the cloth, asked again, but did not give time for the answer. After five times repeating the process, with Hodges fetching water twice more, King left the cloth off long enough for an answer.

Orlev spluttered, turned his head and vomited heavily. He looked pleadingly at King. "Wait, wait! Give me time, more time!" he coughed and took in huge gulps of air. "I am a scientist, a physicist. Weapon delivery systems. I specialised in nuclear and conventional warheads." He gulped more air. King picked up the soaking cloth. "Wait! I will tell you what you want to know!"

"I know you will," King said, and wrapped the man's head again with the wet cloth. He started to pour the water and Orlev struggled, choked and spluttered. "I know you will."

"He was going to talk," Caroline commented quietly.

"Drown the bastard," said Hodges. He looked a different man. He had a thousand-yard stare like a seasoned soldier with multiple tours, kills and dead comrades behind him. "Kill the son of a bitch."

King refilled the kettle and poured, Orlev was gagging less, struggling less, he was gargling. Drowning. "He will talk now," he whispered. "When I take this off he will sing like a bird. Write down everything. Better yet, get out your iPhone and record it. Film and audio. He's reached the point."

Caroline did as he said, took the phone out of her bag. "What point is that?"

"Dying. He only has enough strength in his lungs to do this one more time. He knows it too. He will talk now. He will tell the truth." King emptied the last of the water in a final wave and pulled off the cloth.

Orlev vomited, gasped and cried. His eyes were bloodshot and a thick goo ran from his ear where the eardrum had perforated under the pressure of holding his breath for so long. "There is uranium... Weapon grade." he gasped.

"I know that," Hodges said. "Rashid told me about the bunker." King and Caroline looked at him and he shrugged. "We need a pow-wow later."

"The uranium has been taken by Iman Mullah Al-Shaqqaf's men."

"Where is the warhead now?" King asked.

"On route."

"We know that, Sergei Gulubkin told us," King looked at Hodges and shrugged. "We'll talk more in our pow-wow."

"I do not know the location, but I know it is in the west country."

King picked up the cloth. "We need more than that."

"No! Wait! The uranium is to be initiated by the detonation of the warhead. The warhead is an aerial burst delivery system." He fought for breath, he was light-headed. "It detonates two thousand feet above its target and disperses. Detonated on the ground, it is only twenty percent as effective. But with the additional uranium the fallout becomes forty percent more effective than if it was air dispersed." King rang the cloth out over Orlev's face and the man writhed around. "Wait!" he spluttered and strained against the tape restraints. "Why! You don't know why! Why he is doing all of this!"

"Because Zukovsky is a radical Muslim. A fanatical son of a bitch," King replied.

Orlev scoffed. "Hah! That's what he has crafted, what he has created as a persona. It's all to do with his son. He's no Muslim. He fought the radical ragheads for decades. First in Afghanistan, then in Chechnya. He's as Muslim as you are!"

"What about his son?" Caroline prompted. "What has he got to do with this? Where is he?"

Orlev laughed. "You really don't have a clue, do you?" King refilled the kettle. Orlev looked at him pleadingly. "His son is dead! He died in an airstrike in Syria. He was Spetsnaz – that's Russian special forces, but you know that. He was held captive by ISIS. The Russian government told Britain, told MI6 and MI5 that they had an asset on the ground and they were going to perform a rescue mission. British bombers were operating in the area and Russia wanted a temporary lifting of RAF sorties. MI5 discovered the location of a major ISIS cell with British connections and had intelligence that important and wanted individuals were gathered in one place. MI5 also knew that there was a Russian hostage, Zukovsky's son as it turned out, but they still went ahead and gave the order for an airstrike. They only needed to wait a few more hours and the Spetsnaz brigade would have been on target. They ignored the request, called in the RAF and Zukovsky's son was killed."

"So this is all about revenge?" Caroline asked. "On MI5?"

"The dead agents were all connected at the time, as were the twelve missing agents. Zukovsky found out through the information that Jeremy Hoist supplied. Charles Forester was the last in the chain. He knew there was a Russian asset on the ground. Russia has been widely criticised for the approach it took in Syria, the widespread bombing and collateral damage. It was a power play."

"But the radical Muslim link?" Caroline asked. "Al-Shaqqaf?"

"Betesh," King said. He looked at Orlev. "Al-Shaqqaf had operators in that ISIS cell, didn't he?"

"He *is* the ISIS cell," Orlev said. "Every man in that ISIS brigade was recruited by Iman Mullah Al-Shaqqaf, right here in Britain. They were the most barbarous of the lot. And your government does nothing, can't even try him in court successfully."

King nodded, said to Hodges and Caroline, "I hunted Jamil Betesh. He left a brutal and bloody trail to follow in Iraq. MI6 were not aware who recruited him. The fact both of his brothers were here and connected to Al-Shaqqaf makes the picture clearer."

"What are they planning to do with the warhead?" Caroline asked.

Orlev hesitated. He looked at King, the dripping cloth in his hand. "Please, don't do this again."

"Answer the question then," said King.

"Zukovsky has conned Al-Shaqqaf into thinking he will be detonating a mildly dirty bomb. Hence the flasks of uranium. Al-Shaqqaf thinks its iodine in the flasks. Massive disruption, huge publicity, many casualties. They agreed on the target together. Zukovsky wanted central London, but Al-Shaqqaf wouldn't consider it. Too many Muslims, too much destruction. They agreed on a mutual target for maximum damage to the establishment."

"Where?" asked King.

"I don't know," Orlev shrugged. "I was to be taken there to complete the set-up of the device."

"And it's a dirty bomb?" Caroline asked.

"If I put it together I could make it a thermonuclear chain reaction. At a rudimentary calculation I would estimate about five times Hiroshima. But there's a sting in the tail, when Al-Shaqqaf sets the timer, we were to have it configured for instant detonation."

"Just like that?" Hodges commented. "Five times Hiroshima on a British target. All these years after we avoided nuclear war, you just set up a bomb for a religious fanatic to have at his disposal."

Orlev shrugged. "Zukovsky was paying well. But I have not started work on it. If Zukovsky can set it off, and he is more than capable, it will still be more powerful than Hiroshima, but the uranium will make it a dirty bomb. In essence, it will be worse. There will not be the same amount of vaporisation. The dirty element will stay for decades. Just look at Chenobyl."

Caroline looked down at him and said, "So Zukovsky's son dies, and he gets retribution by unleashing unprecedented destruction on innocent Britons?"

Orlev smiled. "Think deeper, my dear," he tutted. "Look, if it is seen that radical Muslims blew an entire city to pieces with a nuclear device; what do you think the rest of the world will want?"

"They'll wage war on Islam," she stated flatly. "But…"

"But nothing!" Orlev snapped. "Every government in the world will want to destroy all radical Islamic groups overnight. The Muslim countries will clean house, or they'll be seen as a potential target. One bomb and radical Islam will be under attack like never before, and it will not stop until they are obliterated. Wiped off the face of the earth."

"I'm going to ask you one more thing," King said. He bent down and held the cloth up to him, dropped it on his face and pulled it across his mouth slowly. "You don't want more water, do you?"

"No."

"Where is Zukovsky?"

"Gone to the west country to meet the boat. It is coming in tonight."

"Where?"

"I do not know."

"And the MI5 prisoners?"

"They went with Marvin and Gulubkin's men. I do not know to where." Orlev did not take his eyes from the cloth. "I beg you, don't do it again. Everything I have said is true."

King grabbed Orlev by the shoulders and pulled him up, he slumped in the chair. He was drained and pale. His eyes were still red. King whipped out a folding lock knife and flicked the blade open with his thumb. He sliced through the tape around Orlev's ankles and then slashed the man's wrist bindings. Orlev rubbed his wrists, bringing the circulation back.

"What now?" Hodges asked. "Shall I take him in?"

"Yes," King said. He pulled Orlev up and pushed him ahead of him. The man nearly fell, his leg was near-useless. King slipped his jacket back on and picked up his pistol. They walked across the loading bay and Orlev stopped just in front of the open boot, where Mathews' body was staring out at him, his eyes wide and glazed and vacant.

Orlev seemed nonchalant. He turned to King, unsure where to go. King's BMW was parked just inside but it was a wreck of bullet holes, twisted metal and broken glass. The airbags hung limp and deflated.

King stopped short and took the CZ75 pistol out of his jacket pocket. He bent down and placed it carefully on the smooth concrete floor, then slid it across to Orlev with his foot. Orlev looked down at the weapon, then raised his eyes to King and the bulbous suppressor of the silenced Ruger. King fired once and Orlev dropped to the ground, a tiny .22 of an inch diameter hole in his forehead. His legs twitched for a moment then went still.

Hodges looked down at the professor's body. "Son of a bitch," he said. "I hope you go to hell."

"He's already there," King said, tucking the pistol into his waistband. He looked at Caroline. "You need to report back to headquarters. Regroup. Share what Orlev said about Zukovsky. You need to reiterate what Sergei Gulubkin said about the hostages. If they sailed last night, we're running out of time."

"Where are you going?" she asked.

King ignored her, looked at Hodges. "You need to question Gulubkin."

"We need to secure that uranium. If it's in that Islington mosque, it needs to be seized and arrests made," said Hodges.

"No." King shook his head. "Not until tomorrow morning. You get things in place to take the mosque. You'll need a HASMAT team, and armed police. But don't move until tomorrow at dawn."

Hodges nodded. "What else?"

"Give me details of this fellow Rashid in the hospital. I need to go speak to him."

Hodges took out a notebook and scribbled with a pencil. He tore off the piece of paper and handed it to King. "What about here? What am I going to say about this guy?" He nodded to Orlev's body on the floor.

"Leave me out of it. Say that Orlev did what he did, but one of Zukovsky's team killed Orlev to stop him talking further and then got away. You'll need to scrub the CCTV system."

Hodges nodded and looked at the carnage. He nodded to both of them and walked out through the broken door of the loading bay.

"You never answered my question," Caroline said. "Where are you going?"

"I have a few errands to run."

"Like what?"

"I'm going to talk to the deep cover agent," King said. "Rashid will have crucial information for me."

"Why you?"

"Because I'm going to finish what Forester started. This has all gone too far, on too big a scale. If Al-Shaqqaf fails, he will try again. He has a hunger for this that won't be satisfied until he does something big. Zukovsky has fed the man's appetite with the warhead. Okay, Al-Shaqqaf thinks it's a smaller dirty bomb, but that is as big as he could ever dream of. If he gets arrested, he'll slip through the net again, I'm sure of that. And so was Forester," King paused. "Forester knew that there are no failures for these people, merely rehearsals. Down the line they'll get it right and life in the west will never be the same. I see that, and I'll do what it takes."

"And then what?"

"And then I'm gone."

"Just like that?"

"Just like that."

"Where will I meet you?" she asked. "After I've checked in with headquarters and probably been arrested."

"Your place."

"What?"

"What do you have, a house, a flat?"

"A flat."

"Where?"

"Why?"

"It should be secure."

"Yes."

King shrugged. "I'm going to do my best to stop this threat. And I'm going to do it how Forester planned it."

"Forester was no better than anyone else," she commented flatly. "He wouldn't wait, wouldn't give the

Russians a few more hours. If he had, Zukovsky's son might not have died and Vladimir Zukovsky would not have been tipped over the edge. The man is obviously quite mad, but Forester's actions were the trigger."

"Forester did his job as best he could, in the best interests of the country he served," King looked at her. "What's some Russian he didn't know compared to an ISIS cell he knew would kill and terrorise? It's a shitty job and terrible decisions have to be made."

"It *is* a shitty job."

"And I thought I was out of it."

"So why my flat?"

"I'm not going anywhere near Thames House. I'll do what I do, then I'm gone. Until then, we need a place to meet and if you don't mind, I need a place to crash before tonight."

"What's happening tonight?"

"I'm shutting down Mullah Al-Shaqqaf," King said. "Permanently."

55

King drove the BMW into the middle of the high-rise assisted housing complex and left it with the key-fob in the ignition. It was battered, the windows smashed and the airbags deployed, but he knew it would be gone within the hour. Either to a body shop or for a joy-ride to end its short life a burned out shell on an estate much like this one. As he swung the sports bag containing the SCAR rifle over his shoulder and walked away the local "chavalary" was already riding near. These children wearing hoodies and riding BMX bikes, were pre-teen scouts who had already singled out the premium car and were on their mobile phones, no doubt to older brothers or the drug dealers they couriered for.

King had reloaded the Ruger pistol back at the warehouse and taken the remaining Walther P99 from Caroline, who was now clean. The weapon she shot Mohammed Betesh with was in police possession with Sergei Gulubkin's finger prints and DNA all over it, and he had gun powder residue on his hands. It was crude and contestable, but it tied him to the weapon and drew attention away from Caroline. The CZ75 pistol Professor Orlev had shot both DS Mathews and DC Watkins with was on its way to forensics. Again, he had his DNA and prints on it, but was not around to deny it. It was a locked tight case. Scenes of crime officers (SOCO) were now pulling the warehouse apart and both Caroline and Hodges had worked out their stories to corroborate. King would be left out of their accounts and a mystery gunman responsible for Orlev's death would be replaced. All evidence of Orlev's waterboarding had been cleared away and the CCTV had been wiped. Following their investigation, Caroline and Hodges had merely walked into the carnage that had been left behind. Mathews had arrived first, followed by Watkins. Neither Caroline nor Hodges claimed to have seen the person who had shot Orlev.

King stopped at a minicab firm three streets away from the assisted housing complex. It was an undesirable street with a launderette, several halal butchers and grocery stores, a betting shop and two cash-converter type stores. The rest of the shops were boarded up and covered with graffiti. He knew the system and stood beside the waiting ten-year old Toyotas and Hondas and dialled the firm's number in the window. He booked his taxi, turned around and was greeted by the nearest driver. Mini-cabs could only be booked, not flagged.

The driver took him swiftly to the Avis Prestige vehicle hire at City Airport where he had phoned through and booked a car. King had both the money and credit card that Forester had issued to him. He made his selection, but his next request was unusual and the salesman referred him to his manager. They took his payment and instruction, added a hefty premium, but fulfilled his request. King slipped the salesman a fifty note and the manager three fifties after the paperwork had been completed.

King left in a silver Mercedes E class. An executive saloon with a slick six-cylinder engine and a silky smooth automatic transmission. London traffic was terrible as always, but King glided through the experience from a luxury seat.

The drive down to Epping Forest and then on to the hospital in Brentwood took almost two hours, but once he had cleared the city traffic the journey had been swift and uneventful.

King parked the Mercedes in the visitor car park and made his way to the ward. Hodges had agreed to call ahead and let Rashid know to expect King. Rashid had only just finished his interview with the MI5 investigators. He had been tired, almost terse on the phone.

King bypassed the nurses station. He walked confidently through the ward and counted the doors and wards as he went. He looked at the uniformed police officer perched on an uncomfortable chair outside the room. "Detective Inspector Hodges called ahead," he said. "I'm Alex King, I'm here to see the patient."

"He's a busy boy," the officer commented.

"Are you armed?" King asked.

"I'm not at liberty to say."

King shrugged. He peered through the window and saw Rashid propped up on his pillows, his eyes closed. He opened the door and the man woke instantly. King guessed he had merely been dozing. Rashid looked at him warily.

"I know you," Rashid said. "Hereford. Am I right?"

King walked in and pulled out a chair. He slid it across and sat down next to the bed. "I've been to Hereford, yes."

"Stirling Lines."

"You were in?"

Rashid scoffed. "Still am. On detachment with 'Box."

King nodded. "I'm sorry, I don't remember you."

"You were in my selection. No offense, you were an older guy and you were there one minute and gone the next. I figured you were binned. But I remember you, your eyes."

"I worked for MI6. They had a shitty sense of humour. They would just send me for part of selection to assess my operational fitness. I did all of SAS selection to get in to MI6 as a specialist operative. I must have completed it in separate stages about ten times over the years."

"You're right. A shitty sense of humour," Rashid smiled.

"So you were deep cover?"

"The plan was to get me into Iman Mullah Al-Shaqqaf's mosque. Everyone knows he's an extremist. He's been lucky, had smart lawyers, played the racism card so many times its stuck like shit to a blanket. The CPS can't get anything to stick to him though, and 'Box, Six and The Met have all tried to get a UC into his organisation, they kept being made," Rashid reached for a plastic cup of water. King passed it to him. Rashid drank thirstily. The air was dry and stale. "So what was your angle?"

"Hereford sent me out to Iraq. 'Box helped me with travel arrangements and told me who to contact.

From there I made my way to Syria, hooked up with some extremists and fought along ISIS."

"Holy shit…"

"It was. I fought against Assad's regime and made a name for myself. I didn't aim wide or anything. You can't soldier that way. You fight to win or get the hell out of there. It's all fucked up there anyway. Assad's lot are the ones we should have backed but we were supporting rebels with no hope of winning or ruling Syria if they did win. Just like in Libya. The Syrian government are better than ISIS, and that's who'll be in eventually if anti-government forces take control." Rashid handed King the cup. "Give us a top-up, mate."

King poured him another cup and handed it to him. "Do you want a coke out the machine or something else?"

"No, I'm alright," Rashid drained the glass. "The nurse told me not to have much, but I'm chewing air here."

King smiled. "So you were in deep with ISIS, came back and made contact with Al-Shaqqaf?"

"That's the short version, yes. But it was more like putting myself in position and getting recruited. I had to prick-tease a bit, play hard to get, like. But 'Box arranged for a family member to die, not literally, just a cover. I came back and before I left I asked my ISIS commander for a contact to help me out. 'Box chose the right corpse, an old man in Islington with no other surviving relatives. This guy was supposedly a mentor to me when I was young. A proxy uncle. He worshipped at Al-Shaqqaf's mosque. I had to gen-up but got the story straight. Al-Shaqqaf gave me some spiritual guidance and held a remembrance at morning prayers. I thanked him, walked away. He knew of my involvement in Syria, couldn't wait to get me. He had a great reference from the ISIS commander. It was a coup. I spent six months fighting alongside ISIS, then almost another six months doing odd jobs for Al-Shaqqaf. Then they made me. Bastards. All that work."

"I'm shutting Al-Shaqqaf down."

"Sanctioned?"

"Grey area."

"They're the best."

"It was sanctioned," King said. "But then the guy died. I haven't been pulled off."

"Charles Forester. He was a good man. He was different to a lot of the spooks I met."

"I thought that. He knew there was a high tide on the way. He wanted it held back a while, that's all. Al-Shaqqaf and his reach needs shortening."

Rashid nodded. "And Zukovsky?"

"The same," King said. "What happened there? How did you end up working for the Russians?"

"He was meant to be an Islamist extremist."

"When did you know he wasn't?"

"He never prayed. I did, for cover mainly. I am a Muslim, but I'm like you lot who wander into a church at Christmas or give up something for Lent. I do it when I need it or visit my family in Bradford. I prayed and Zukovsky watched. I later saw him pray at Iman Al-Shaqqaf's mosque. But he only followed the lead."

"And the agents killed at the pier, were you involved?"

"I bought a batch of the Rohypnol drug," Rashid shook his head. He was despondent.

"What about the missing agents?"

"I helped, yes. It was snowballing by then, I needed an out."

"What does he want with them?"

"They were all in the chain. The events which led to the sacrificing of Zukovsky's son. He wanted nothing more than for them to admit it on tape, I don't know for what purpose, but after that he wanted to kill them."

"So how did you meet Zukovsky?"

"He had built up a relationship with Al-Shaqqaf. He wanted a good man to make up the numbers, by now they had a plan for a strike. I was hired help, that's all. I never contacted control to inform them, mainly because my infiltration was so perfect. Sometimes I forgot who the hell I was. Sometimes I worried 'Box would think I'd gone rogue."

"You're going to find it hard to adjust."

"No doubt."

"I want you to tell me everything about the mosque and Al-Shaqqaf's movements."

"It will take a while," Rashid paused. "How long have we got?"

"I'm going in tonight."

56

An interview without coffee. Caroline Darby knew it was stacked against her when the tea ware didn't make an appearance. She'd had one in the army too. She'd left shortly afterwards.

Director Howard looked at her coldly. "You kidnapped a prisoner."

"I secured a witness. Someone in a chain of hostiles who knew of a plan to use, and therefore the possible whereabouts of a missing Russian nuclear warhead. He was also one of the attackers on a Security Service safe-house which resulted in the death of Deputy Director Forester. I wanted to ascertain the facts before he got himself lawyered up."

"Well, he *has* lawyered up and as he's a suspected terrorist the police have four days to question him before he is charged instead of the normal twenty-four hours. The Crown Prosecution Service has already stressed that his abduction means it's unlikely they'll get a successful case built against him."

"So he'll walk?"

"It looks that way."

"For theft or armed robbery, maybe!" Caroline snapped. "But he attacked the safe-house. Property belonging to the Security Service. He killed someone!"

"Did he? You know that for a fact."

Caroline stared at Howard. "Yes," she lied.

"There's more CCTV in that house than you are aware of Miss Darby. Who's the other man? The man with the assault rifle shooting the hell out of my safehouse?"

"Mohammed Betesh."

"No. The man on *your* side."

Caroline hesitated. "A contact of Forester's. With the missing data Forester wanted someone helping whose cover wasn't blown wide open."

"Name?"

"Smith."

"Really?"

"That's what he said."

"Where is he now?"

"I don't know."

"And this warehouse. You and Inspector Hodges followed up a lead from the deep cover agent and walked into a gunfight?"

"No. Hodges sent two of his coppers to take a look. We found it the way it was."

"And this *contact* of Forester's; he was there?"

"No."

"Bloody mess," Howard commented. There was a knock at the door and Howard raised his eyes above Caroline. "Ah, Elizabeth, thank you."

Caroline turned and saw Deputy Director Elizabeth Chalmers with a tall, beady-eyed man. He had slicked back jet-black hair and a hooked nose. He smiled and sat down on the leather chair next to Caroline. Caroline eyed him warily.

"This is Major Uri Droznedov of the Russian Federation GRU. He has been liaising with Charles

Forester. He is hunting the warhead, and therefore Vladimir Zukovsky. He will liaise with you, work *with* you in fact. Is that clear?"

"If you say so," she replied.

"I feel it will be advantageous," Droznedov said, his accent was thick but his English was good. He stood up, seemingly full of nervous energy, and paced across the room to the window, his back was towards them as he spoke. "What a gorgeous view. I like this building, it is more discreet than The River House. I find it amusing that you can see MI6 on the other side of the river. But you have just as good a view of the Thames."

"Thank you," Howard said. "We're closer to the action here. Whitehall, Downing Street, the Houses of Parliament. We like to feel the SIS act as a tourist attraction. Everybody recognises their building, but drive right by Thames House." He stood up, held a hand towards the empty seat. "Major, if you don't mind?"

Droznedov continued to stare out across the Thames for a few moments, then turned wearing a thin smile. "I have some ideas that might throw something up. Maybe give us a few avenues to explore. I know the man's habits, the habits of his people also." He walked over to the desk and held out his hand for Caroline.

"Very well," Caroline shook the man's hand. It was sweaty, clammy. She wiped her hand casually on her skirt. She stood up, looking down at the Director. It was a trait; a tactic she had seen Forester use. "If that's all?"

Howard glanced at Chalmers first then looked up at Caroline. "I want regular reports, updates of your location, mainly."

"Track my mobile phone," she replied. "Anything else?"

Howard turned back to a file in front of him. He did not raise his head. "Tell Debbie tea for two, and close the door on your way out."

Caroline walked ahead of Droznedov. She closed the door but walked past Howard's secretary without a word. He could tell her himself.

"Your boss will not get his tea?" the Russian smiled.

Caroline stopped in the corridor and looked at him. "What can you bring me? What use are you going to be?"

Droznedov smirked. "I know the man. Not personally, but I have walked his footsteps. I have gotten closer to him. I started out with nothing, now I'm in the same city and his team have been identified. That is progress, no?"

"We discovered his team. Put names to the faces. We captured and killed members of his team. A deep cover agent gave us their base location. You seem to have brought nothing to it at all."

Droznedov smiled. "I like you. Sassy, woman. You have boyfriend?"

"Forget it," Caroline said sharply and walked on down the corridor.

The Russian jogged a few steps to catch her up. "Okay, I get it. Not interested. Look, I filled the gaps with Forester. It was I who informed him about the missing warhead in the first place. I will help you, like your boss said I would."

"So tell me what else you have."

"Let me talk to this man you have captured. An interrogation may well bring up something fresh, something of importance."

"Interview," Caroline corrected him. "We don't call it an interrogation; we call it an interview."

Droznedov laughed. "No waterboarding for you Brits, hey?"

"No," Caroline lied. "We don't go in for that sort of thing."

57

Hodges walked into his office and wound down the venetian blind. He loosened his tie, pulled out the top button of his shirt and sat down heavily at his desk. He closed his eyes and breathed deeply. He had experienced palpitations earlier, an aching in his arms and chest. The moment had passed, but he noted to visit a doctor soon. He already knew his blood pressure was high, today wasn't going to make it any better. He kept picturing his young detective sergeant. The twisted limbs, the vacant expression, the third eye in his forehead. He would have to call in on the man's wife soon, but he did not have the time and had dispatched a family liaison officer and an older sergeant who had attended the couple's wedding. The young widow was pregnant. Her world would be in tatters.

He thought of Watkins. She had a boyfriend in the navy. He was on a six-month posting patrolling the Caribbean for drug smuggling. He hoped to leave the navy next year and join the police service. The couple planned to marry once he successfully changed careers. Again, Hodges had handed it over to family liaison to deal with, but there would be no visit for him, just a protracted meeting with a senior officer aboard his vessel and a cup of tea. The couple were not yet engaged and did not live together. Hodges doubted whether the young man's situation would even qualify for compassionate leave.

Outside of his office he could hear the urgency, the purposeful workings of the police on full speed with one brief. Leave had been cancelled. Anything other than the search for the missing MI5 agents and the whereabouts of the nuclear warhead was being directed to other stations. All other stations in London and the home counties were to use twenty-five percent of their resources to aid in Scotland Yard's investigation. The genie was well and truly out of the bottle now, there was nothing clandestine or discreet about the search. And now Hodges feared, as Charles Forester had, that Zukovsky would go off the grid entirely. They may not know any more about the warhead now, until it was too late. All he had held back was the uranium in the lead flasks held at the mosque. He had granted Alex King until the following morning. After that, Muslim race relations would most likely never be the same again.

Hodges opened the desk drawer and took out the quarter bottle of whisky. It had been in the drawer for nine-hundred and forty-two days. The seal was unbroken. The contents amber and glossy, strong and smooth. Seventeen years old. He looked down at his hand and noticed it shaking. His heart had started to race. He was closer to cracking the seal than he had been since his last drink. Only he had no recollection of his last drink, because truthfully there had been fifty last drinks on a bender that had left him hospitalised, his marriage in pieces and his children despising him. He had fought for everything since. His job, his wife, his children, his sobriety. He knew if he took one small swig, one tiny mouthful to steady his nerves, to deaden the pain and anguish inside it would make him feel better. But he also knew that it would not end there and it would cost him everything and more, because it would cost him what he had fought to win back, fought daily to retain. There were no more second chances, from his family or from the job. It would be gone in that moment. But it was worth the risk. He had to numb the feeling, had to sacrifice all for that feeling of warmth and comfort. He twisted the seal, his hands shaking. There was no going back, but he was already experiencing the taste on his tongue in anticipation. The door opened and he threw the unopened bottle back into the open drawer and slammed it shut. A young female detective had stuck her head through, not opening the door beyond the width of one of her slender shoulders.

"Sorry Boss," she said. "There's a lady and a bloke here to see you." Her accent was twangy, London. The east-end or south. "It's the bird from MI5 you've been working with, and some Russian bloke."

Hodges regained a little composure. "Where are they?"

"Downstairs. Family room."

"Tell them I'll be right down," he hesitated. "Scratch that, I'll go now." Hodges stood up, not looking at the drawer. Better to leave now than to stay there accompanied only by temptation.

Caroline Darby stood up as Hodges entered the family room. It was a quiet place for victims of sexual assault, or for people to hear of a tragic loss. It was a simply furnished room with pastel colours, soft sofas and a coffee table with magazines that were five years old. A coffee machine sat on a table near the door. Caroline and the Russian had made good use of it. Both had military in them, and had developed the habits of eating or drinking anything on offer and resting when they could. Droznedov was eating a biscuit. The kind hotels give away in rooms with cheap teabags and UHT milk.

"This is Major Uri Droznedov of the Russian GRU," Caroline said. "That's military intelligence," she added.

"Charles Forester mentioned you," said Hodges, shaking the man's hand. "You informed him about the warhead."

"That's correct," Droznedov said without getting up. "You have a prisoner. I wish to question him."

"A suspect in custody," Hodges corrected him.

"Whatever," Droznedov spilled a few crumbs as he spoke. "I feel I could glean something from the man. Maybe he will speak more freely in his mother tongue?"

"Perhaps."

"Then take me to him," Droznedov stood up and brushed crumbs off his shirt. "If you please?"

"He'll need his brief."

"Brief?"

"Solicitor. A lawyer."

Droznedov tutted and shook his head. "You will find they talk better without such representation."

"No doubt," Hodges said. "Anti-terrorist squad are with him. They might want a break. I'll see if they can give us a few minutes."

"Maybe a quick word with yourselves present?"

"Anything he says will be scrubbed from evidence. Inadmissible. Unless a brief is with him and we officially validate his audio."

"I am not after a successful prosecution. I merely want to know where Zukovsky is and get that warhead back. Gulubkin can walk or rot, for all I care."

"Five minutes," Hodges said. "Five minutes with me in the room." He looked at Caroline. "Perhaps you won't mind watching from outside?"

Caroline shrugged. She had spent enough time talking to Sergei Gulubkin already with King. She would prefer to stay away and not get caught up in procedurals from now on.

The booth was standard one-way glass. It looked into the interview room which was a floor below the family room and a dozen rooms further inside the labyrinth which was New Scotland Yard. There was video and audio recording equipment running continuously. Sergei Gulubkin sat back in his seat, arrogant and unthreatened. His eyes on the wall behind the anti-terrorist officers questioning him. His solicitor sat beside him, making notes and whispering into his client's ear.

"He's a fucking no comment all day long," the detective in the booth said as Hodges peered inside. "Look at him. Hard as nails. He's not afraid of us or the system. I don't know what else to do. He cooperated and gave information up when it was off the books. Told MI5 what he knew, but he's as tight as a clam's arsehole now."

"I have a Russian intelligence officer with me," Hodges said. Droznedov peered over Hodges' shoulder into the booth. The detective nodded by way of acknowledgment. "He thinks he might get something out of him. Might be worth a shot. This is Caroline Darby from MI5. She's the one who Gulubkin spoke to, she's sitting this one out. We don't want to mess things up with the CPS."

The detective gave Caroline the same nod. "We'll take a break. Better keep his brief in there."

"Thanks," Hodges said. He turned to Droznedov. "All right son, follow me in, but don't you dare touch him."

Hodges led the way and the two Special Branch officers walked past them, one raising an eye to the detective. Hodges looked at Sergei Gulubkin as he sat down. He glanced at the solicitor, recognised him from other interviews. He was a touchy one with a love of making the police look heavy-handed and bullish. If he'd known who the suspect's lawyer was beforehand, he may well have declined Droznedov doing this.

Droznedov pulled out a packet of cigarettes. It was strictly speaking a no smoking building, but a grey area. Many suspects loosened up with a smoke. Droznedov tapped one out and offered it. Gulubkin shook his head. Droznedov shrugged and helped himself to one. He lit it and blew a plume of smoke across the table, where it dispersed and wafted into the two men's faces. The lawyer looked at Hodges and Hodges stared back. The lawyer looked away.

Droznedov started to speak in Russian and the lawyer held up his hand. "In English please," he said. "Unless my client requires an interpreter."

Sergei Gulubkin responded and rattled through seven or eight sentences. His lawyer frantically tapped his client on the shoulder. Gulubkin lashed out and knocked the lawyer's hand aside, physically hurting him as well as shocking him.

The lawyer stood up, held his hands up. "I can only give advice if you are willing to accept it! Please, stop this and wait for an interpreter."

Droznedov and Gulubkin seemed to be arguing, but it was Gulubkin who stopped talking and sat back in his chair, his arms folded, wearing a scowl. He was agitated and started tapping his foot, his heel clipping the floor.

Droznedov picked up the cigarettes, offered Gulubkin one again, and the Russian took it. Droznedov reached across the table and lit the cigarette for him. He sat back, tucking the lighter into his pocket. He spoke once more in Russian but Gulubkin looked away. Droznedov shrugged at Hodges and stood up. "Nothing more to say here," he said. "Not unless we get rid of the lawyer and start to throw him around the room."

Hodges knocked on the door and it opened, he led Droznedov out and the uniformed officer stepped inside the interview room and closed the door, guarding both the lawyer and the suspect and continuing the constant police presence the law dictated.

"What the hell was all that about? I thought you'd open with some questions in English first," Hodges said. "You two seemed to be arguing, the bloody CPS will love that!"

"I asked, but he just started to tell me what my mother does with goats," Droznedov smirked.

"Anything else?"

"Besides other farm animals?" The Russian shook his head. "No. He's going to take his chances, I fear."

Caroline stepped out of the booth and looked at the Russian. "That was a waste of time."

"Don't sugar coat it, honey," Droznedov sneered. "Be quiet and let the men talk."

"Call me honey once more and I'll drop you on your backside."

Droznedov bent down, prodded a finger into her, just above her cleavage and pursed his lips. "Honey…" He didn't see it coming but he was on the floor staring up at her, his legs swept out from under him. "What the?"

"I warned you!" she shouted.

Two uniformed officers loitered nearby having seen the exchange, Hodges stepped over Droznedov and blocked Caroline. He eased her backwards. "Look, that's enough. There's a bit more going on here, if you haven't noticed. I think maybe you need to get your head down for a bit. Take a shower, eat something," he suggested. He ran a thumb over her shoulder. There was a bloodstain. Crimson and dried. It looked like a rose. "Maybe get a change of clothes? A few hours and then you can get back to it."

She nodded. "All right," she said, realising the need to back down. She looked at Droznedov as he got back up. "Sorry, but I warned you."

Droznedov was angry, humiliated. He smirked, tucking his shirt into his trousers. "My mistake," he said. "No harm done." He was flushed, and had started to perspire. "You should listen to the detective. I will go back to my hotel. I will make some enquiries and get back in contact with you."

"Okay. Do you need a lift?"

"No," Droznedov answered curtly.

Hodges escorted them to the door and agreed to keep Caroline informed of further developments. He had both her mobile and landline numbers, and she had quietly conceded to the fact that a sandwich, a hot shower and a couple of hours' sleep would make a new woman of her. Droznedov followed Caroline down the steps. She could feel the tension. She turned to him, needed to straighten things out. "Look, I'm sorry about in there…"

Droznedov reached around and grabbed her by her ponytail. He wrenched her head backwards and pulled her into him. She tried to counter, but his height and strength held her at bay. She felt he would pull all her hair from her scalp. She tried to move, but couldn't. Her head was pulled so far back, she could barely breath and her neck felt like it was about to crack. Droznedov grabbed her right breast with his left hand and squeezed so hard she gasped. "You pull shit like that again, honey and I will take my knife and peel the flesh from that pretty little face of yours. Understand?" He squeezed her breast again, she could feel his fingertips ripping something inside, separating muscle. "Understand?"

"Yes!" she wailed. "Please, let go!"

Droznedov released her breast, but circled the nipple with his finger as he spoke, "Very good, now you know your place. I don't expect to have to remind you again." He carried on with his finger and smiled. "That's better. You like that, don't you?"

Caroline could not see his face; her head was still being wrenched too far backwards. She cupped his hand with both of her own, felt out a finger and wrenched it until it snapped. "Fuck you!" she screamed at him.

Droznedov wailed and released his grip, Caroline fell backwards to the ground. She was lightheaded and her vision was going in and out of focus. Her legs were weak and she struggled to her feet but dropped onto her knees. She looked up, a couple were approaching and doing their best impression of having not noticed. A cyclist rode past her, eyeing her as he pedalled. He didn't stop. She got back to her feet, looking around, feeling vulnerable and defeated.

Droznedov was nowhere to be seen.

58

"I see you've made yourself at home," Caroline said as she stepped in through the front door of her flat.

King had heard her key in the lock and had got his feet off the coffee table just in time. He stood up, a mug of tea in his hand. "Fancy a cuppa?"

"No," she said. "Something much stronger."

"Coffee?"

"Funny," she said, opening the fridge door. She took out a bottle of gin and a case of tonic water. She had an ice dispenser in the fridge door and put a glass under it. "Want one?"

"No. I need a clear head. Driving."

"Where?"

"I'm going to do some shooting."

"Well, it's important to have a hobby." She poured two fingers of gin into the glass, opened a little bottle of tonic and topped the glass up. "Anyone I know?"

King smiled. He liked Caroline, felt completely at ease with her. "So, why the need for a stiff drink at four-thirty?"

She sighed. "It's six-thirty somewhere." She hacked off a large wedge of lemon, dropped it into the glass and waited for the froth to settle. She drank thirstily. "Shitty day. Shitty fucking day…"

"There seems to be a few of those lately," King said. He muted the television, he had switched on to *Sky*

News out of habit. He walked over to the counter, placed his cup carefully on the floral coaster. It was a feminine touch, but he felt it was at odds with the MI5 agent. Maybe the set had been a present.

He noticed her soothing the back of her head, her expression distant. "What happened to you?" he asked.

She raised a hand to her breast, then seemed to think better of it. "It's nothing."

"Doesn't look like nothing," King said. "Looks like somebody hurt you."

"Expert in mind-reading, are you?"

"No. But he seems to be in pain, and you appear distracted."

"Well, it's nothing to worry about," she insisted, but King stepped closer. He placed a hand on her shoulder. "It's nothing. Really," she said. She looked at him, then relented and rested her head on his shoulder, she hugged him, and he wrapped his arm around her shoulders. "That Russian shit, Major Uri Droznedov. He was a patronising bastard. He told me to be quiet while the men talked. He called me honey. I told him I'd put him on his backside if he called me that again."

"And he did?"

"He did. Peter always said you had to do what you say in a confrontation or you'll be seen as weak."

"He was right. So you put him on his backside?" King ventured.

"Just a simple trip. I hooked out both feet with my foot. He was off balance anyway, I just sent him the other way."

"And he didn't like that? Strange."

"Oh shut up!" she laughed. She nuzzled in a little closer. His arms were strong and firm. She had missed being held. "He lost face. When we were back outside, he found it again."

"Are you going to report him?"

"No. He's liaising with us. I'm not going to start something. But if he tries anything again, I'll certainly finish it. I broke his finger this time. I'll break his bloody neck if he tries anything else."

King held her away and looked at her closely. "I believe you."

Caroline looked up at him, holding his gaze. She moved a little closer and he reacted immediately bending his tall frame and kissing her on the lips, softly at first and then more firmly. Their tongues explored each other's, their hands reaching and touching, King's down to her buttocks, Caroline's over his firm chest.

Caroline's heart was racing. It had been almost two years since she had been intimate with someone and although she felt a slight pang of guilt, the overriding passion was difficult to ignore and she wanted this moment more than anything. It enveloped her, consumed her, fuelled her. She kissed harder, wetter, her hands wandered, smoothed over King's chest, her fingers probed between the buttons of his shirt and brushed through the short hair of his chest. She fingered the buttons and let her hands smooth over his tight stomach, her nails tracing the lines of his muscles, his scars the ridges of his abdomen.

King had not expected the kiss, but he was not going to turn it down. He had spent three years without physical contact after the death of Jane. He had been intimate with another woman recently, but there had been no future in it. The experience had finally helped him put the death of his wife to bed. He missed her terribly, but he also wanted to move on. The kiss with Caroline was about as charged and passionate as he had experienced and he needed her as much as she needed him. His hands wandered slowly, cupped her firm breasts, but she winced, both at the pain and the reminder. She cupped his hand and she ran him down her flat, but soft stomach. He worked at the buttons of her blouse, unfastened the zip of her skirt. She pulled at his clothes and in a few moments they were both naked. She pulled away from him, took his hand in hers and led him confidently and purposefully into her bedroom.

59

"You'd better get down here!" An over-weight, middle-aged detective had barged the door open and Hodges looked up from his desk, startled by the intrusion. There was and always had been a two knock rule. He had overcome his demons, for now, and had ignored the bottle in the drawer. Something was eating at him, gnawing at the furthest-most recess of his mind. And he wasn't going to find it now.

"What the hell?" Hodges snapped, but the detective had already gone. When he got to the door he could see the detective running out of the office and barging his way into the corridor. Hodges looked at the staff at their desks. They looked as puzzled as he did. He gave chase and although he kept the man in sight, he didn't get close until they were down two flights of stairs. "What's going on?"

The detective was breathless, but he kept running as he panted. "Russian suspect," he heaved. "Gulubkin. He's having a fit!"

"Has somebody called a medic?"

"First-aiders are on him and an ambulance has been dispatched!" the detective shouted.

They hit the corridor together and Hodges got out in front. He could see a gathering of people ahead and they saw him too, they parted and allowed him through. A uniformed male officer was straddling Gulubkin's prostrate form and pumping out the rhythm of *Staying Alive* on his chest. The Russian wasn't moving. A female uniformed officer was panicked and attempting to unfasten a single-use respirator. It was complete with a clear plastic sheet fixed to it to avoid blood or vomit or saliva. She gave up on the package, handed it to a detective to try and pinched Gulubkin's nose. She leaned forward to start mouth to mouth.

"Stop!" Hodges shouted. The woman glanced at him, but continued to lean in. "I said stop!" Hodges pushed through the crowd and sniffed the air. He bent down, the man pumping his chest halted while Hodges sniffed Gulubkin's lips. He grabbed the first-aid kit and took out a pair of surgical gloves. He slipped them on, then with his forefinger he opened the Russian's mouth and bent down to sniff once more. And then that's when two things hit Hodges at once; the nagging feeling of doubt, something intangible that he could not place, and the smell of bitter almonds which was overwhelming. So much so, it burned his eyes and nose like mustard. He backed away and shook his head at the two first-aiders. "Cyanide," he said quietly. "Just stop." He looked at the floor near the table and saw the cigarette butt. It was burned down to the filter. He picked it up, cautiously smelled it and then placed it next to the corpse.

"Bag that," he said, pointing at the cigarette butt.

Hodges pushed his way out of the crowded room and rubbed his face as he walked back down the corridor. That nagging, gnawing feeling that had played on his mind and kept him from focusing on anything else had gone, replaced by the realisation of what now seemed obvious.

It was in the family room. Not two hours ago. Droznedov had said, *Gulubkin can walk or rot, for all I care.* But nobody had told Droznedov the suspect's name.

Hodges sat back at his desk. The bottle was still there, for now. He picked up the telephone and called the central desk. "Hello, Detective Inspector Hodges, I need a Russian translator asap."

60

The .50 BMG calibre Barrett rifle is the sniper's anti-personnel and anti-material rifle of choice for ranges in excess of one-thousand metres. It has a kinetic muzzle energy of fifteen-thousand foot pounds. It has an effective range of more than three-thousand metres, although sniper's serving in Iraq and Afghanistan have claimed anti-material strikes of five-thousand metres, or three miles. At these ranges the bullet takes approximately eight seconds to reach its target. It is a truly awesome weapon.

It must have been a comforting thought when the planning committee chose the glass for the top floor of Thames House for its resistance to parabolic microphone surveillance. That it could also withstand a bullet from this leviathan would not have gone unnoticed. No glass is rated to a higher ballistic performance.

The Anzio 20mm anti-material (tank) rifle is exactly three times more powerful than .50 BMG. Its kinetic energy is thirty-eight thousand foot pounds. Or, seventy-five times more powerful than a 9mm handgun bullet.

Vauxhall Bridge measured two-hundred and forty-seven metres in length. Thames House, or MI5 headquarters sat thirty-nine metres back from the riverbank and the sniper's position was one-hundred and fifty-four metres from the bank on the Lambeth side.

Four hundred and forty metres with a downward trajectory of sixty-two feet.

The window was open, the curtains partially drawn and the light was switched off. The street lights had just illuminated, they were sporadic, not all yet lit. Certain sensors were more sensitive. In a matter of minutes, it would be dark outside as dusk gave way to night and an orange gloom would envelop the outside world. The sniper had set up the 20mm anti-material rifle on a table a week previously and weighted the bipod down with five kilo sandbags. He had loaded the heavy 20mm Vulcan rounds. The first and second rounds were depleted uranium. The heaviest naturally occurring element, and at these kinetic energy values, capable of penetrating not only the ballistic glass, but the building and the next three buildings behind it. The third, fourth and fifth bullets were incendiary rounds. Each incendiary bullet contained phosphorus which would disperse upon impact and burn and stick to everything in a twenty by twenty-foot room.

The sniper got down behind the weapon and sighted the post and cross reticule on the eighth floor. The first and second windows from the left were clear. The light of the office was on but the smoked glass made it impossible to see inside. The sniper took out his mobile phone and dialled the direct line.

"Director Howard, please."

"Certainly. Who is calling, please?"

"Major Uri Droznedov. Russian Federation GRU."

"One moment."

There was a short pause followed by a clicking as the line was transferred.

"Howard speaking."

"Ah, Director Howard, Major Droznedov. Thank you for your time."

"How may I help, Major?"

"I wanted to talk quickly about the operation in Syria. The one where Forester called in the air strike on the ISIS cell. There was a Russian spetsnaz operative being held captive. Russian intelligence called for a pause in the bombing, a chance to get their operative back."

"Major, I am certain I cannot discuss such matters with you."

"I think it was a tipping point for Zukovsky. I think it was the reason he is here. The reason he wants revenge."

"We are aware of that," Howard paused. *"But I cannot discuss past operations with you, Major. It is a confidence too far, I'm afraid."*

"I understand," Droznedov said. "Are you in your office? I am nearby and maybe we could talk more discreetly."

"I am at my desk, but I have to meet the Prime Minister in an hour."

"Director Howard, I am sure you know. In fact, I am sure that it was both you and Forester who made the decision to sacrifice a young man in order for you to kill an ISIS cell which could have been killed at a later date. Another time and place."

"Major Droznedov, you are GRU. You know how it works. Now, I appreciate your cooperation but I have a pressing matter to attend to."

"One more thing, if you please."

"Yes?"

"I work for Vladimir Zukovsky. I have done my entire career. The agent you sacrificed was his son. How pathetic you are, you and your Security Service. You even let me into your office. What a wonderful reconnaissance opportunity it was. Goodbye, Director Howard..." He put the phone down and sighted in on the first window from the left. The window with the smear of invisible ink, the kind used for security marking valuables, that was showing up clearly in the infra-red sight. The ink he had smeared on the glass as he admired the Thames and the landmark building belonging to MI6 on the other side of the river. He fired and the massive weapon erupted like a volcano, its muzzle flash scorching the curtain six feet away and the pressure wave rattling the window on its hinge. He moved his aim to the next window and fired. With the 5.9x75 scope it was an easy shot. Both windows were out and he fired the next round through the second window cutting off any potential escape. He moved the weapon back to the first window and fired twice more, working the bolt smoothly between shots. The office was burning white and yellow. A thousand or more degrees of burning phosphorus consuming the room and burning everything and everyone within.

61

King lay on his back. His breathing had returned to normal and he was in that wonderful post-coital dreamlike state of exhaustion, satisfaction and contentment. Caroline was curled into him, her left breast resting on his chest, her chin nuzzled into his neck. When she exhaled he had to fight the temptation to flinch like a child resists a tickle. He could put up with it.

They were hot, the covers riding low on them. Caroline had been wild and passionate, King had matched her mood accordingly. Both had been completely satisfied, and the other had been sure of it.

"I'm going to fall asleep if I stay like this," Caroline whispered. The whisper tickled more than the breathing, but King still resisted. It was a snapshot moment, and he didn't want to be the first to move, to break it.

"Then sleep," he replied. "You need it."

"Can't. Too much to do."

"The police are out all over the west country looking for Zukovsky. By now the boat carrying the hostages should have been identified. There'll be something in place soon. The Norwegian coastguard should have been informed as well. There's nothing direct for you to do," King said. "Get some sleep."

"You get some sleep," she said, running a hand down over his stomach and resting it tantalisingly close to his groin. "I haven't finished with you yet."

"Well, I need a drink," King said. He moved her hand and slid out of bed.

"There's beer in the fridge."

"No, like I said, I'm driving later."

"Good point. There's fresh orange with added vitamins. Drink that, it'll get your strength up," she grinned.

King padded out into the lounge. He picked up his clothes and draped them over the back of a chair. He hated not being ready to move. It was a habit, but those were the habits which had kept him alive. He walked towards the kitchen. It was an open-plan flat with just the kitchen counter to separate the kitchen from the lounge. He glanced at the television, froze in his tracks. "Caroline!" he shouted. "Get out here and see this!"

Caroline appeared moments later fastening an ivory silk dressing gown. She looked at him, then looked past him at the television. King was turning the volume back on. They could see Thames House burning. The eighth floor, first and second windows from the left. The Sky News reporter was looking flustered and she was adlibbing, but she had no information to hand and was clarifying that Thames House was the less obvious spy building on the other side of the river. The ticker-tape scrolled along the bottom of the screen: MI5 BUILDING UNDER ATTACK, MULTIPLE CASUALTIES. DIRECTOR HOWARD AND DEPUTY DIRECTOR CHALMERS BOTH CONFIRMED DEAD. MI5 DEPUTY DIRECTOR CHARLES FORESTER

CONFIRMED KILLED IN GUN ATTACK EARLIER TODAY AT AN MI5 PROPERTY. MI5 NOW DECLARED LEADERLESS. JOINT INTELLIGENCE AND SIS (MI6) TO TAKE TEMPORARY CONTROL OF THE SECURITY SERVICE...

Caroline rushed to her handbag and picked up her mobile. "Shit! It was on silent. Nine missed calls." She dialled her voicemail and listened intently, pacing the room as she waited.

King picked up her clothes and put them on the back of the chair next to his own. He got dressed quickly, walked over to the counter and switched on the kettle.

"Switchboard recalling all personnel," she said, thumbing through the menu options and messages. "Oh Jesus! Hodges called – Sergei Gulubkin is dead. Cyanide by the looks of it. In a cigarette that he was given by Droznedov! That bastard! Hodges says that a translator listened to the tapes. Both Droznedov and Gulubkin knew each-other, that the two were arguing about Gulubkin being caught. Droznedov offered Gulubkin a way out. That's when he took the cigarette. It makes sense! He refused the cigarette the first time he was offered."

King poured the boiling water onto the coffee granules and handed it to her. "Get that down you before you go. That was a big gin. You're going to be busy tonight."

"Thanks," she said as she took the cup. "What about you?"

"I'm paying Al-Shaqqaf a visit." He looked at her as she sipped the coffee. "We need Droznedov. If he did that, then he's tight with Zukovsky. We need Zukovsky, Droznedov may be our only lead. Where did Forester meet him?"

"At his hotel, I don't know which."

"Forester's driver died at the safe-house," King said. "As deputy director he would have taken a security detail, surely?"

"Usually an armed bodyguard."

"Pull the records, find out who the BG was and get him to tell you where they met. I doubt Droznedov is still there, but it's a place to start. The manager can pull his bill, check the CCTV. Get round there as soon as you can. Work it, don't allow SIS and Joint Intelligence to bog you down with busy work or a new assignment. The Security Service has suffered unprecedented losses overnight. There'll be a power play. Contact Hodges, you need manpower to find Droznedov, but you need to do it now." King went to the sports bag, took out the Walther P99 and gave it to her, along with the spare sixteen round magazine. "Take this," he said. "Don't let anybody know you've got it. But rest assured, Droznedov will be armed."

She took it, placed it on the counter and looked at it. "Thought you were going shooting?"

"I'll get by."

62

Thames house was in chaos. The fire had burned fiercely, but due to the security measures in the building's architectural design it had been localised and contained. The fire brigade was still damping down, and Howard and Chalmers were the only two fatalities. There were a dozen casualties from both the fire and debris caused from over-penetration by the 20mm bullets. Adjoining offices were scattered with a shrapnel of bullet fragments, concrete and wood splinters. The whole top floor had been sealed off and a HAZMAT team were sweeping and monitoring for radioactivity after it was discovered weapons grade depleted uranium projectiles had been used. Office staff on the top floor were being treated with anti-contaminate.

Once Caroline had got through the security cordon she made her way to the records and personnel office suite on the second floor. She had pulled up Forester's travel schedule on the mainframe computer using her ID and security clearance number, and after making some checks with the head of security she found out the name of the bodyguard who had escorted Forester and pulled the security report.

Caroline left her Mini in the parking lot and called up a security officer and a pool car. The man was called Frank and he was a quiet ex-RAF warrant officer who had a wide ranging career and ten-years of service before applying to MI5. He had applied for a security post as a way of coming through the backdoor. Twelve years in and he had learned to be a cog in the machine. He was never going to be the intelligence officer he hoped, but he was a good driver, security officer and had been on watcher detail in the past. He was a solid character and had provided security for Forester many times. He drove the Ford Mondeo swiftly away from Thames House the short distance to Mayfair. Away from the embankment the traffic was flowing and apart from many traffic lights, there were no further delays.

"I'm sorry to hear about Charles Forester," he said as he drove, his eyes not leaving the road or mirror. "I know he meant a lot to you."

"Thanks," Caroline said. She'd barely been able to think about it. Time had been a blur since they left the house and chased Gulubkin. She suddenly felt an ache inside as she thought about her mentor's last moments. "It's been crazy, hasn't it?"

"No word yet on who was behind the attacks tonight. It's like something the IRA would have tried. Back in the day," he paused. "But I expect it's ISIS."

"It's highly likely it's a Russian attack. I'm going to try and find someone who might well be behind it."

"What, now?"

"Yes."

Frank floored the accelerator and the car surged forward. "Better get a bloody move on then," he said.

"When I get to the Holiday Inn, you wait outside with the car."

"Bugger that, love. I'll be right behind you."

"I'm armed," she said. "I shouldn't be. I'll be okay."

"Too right you'll be okay," he said, swerving and overtaking two bicycles, frighteningly close. "Because I'll be there with two weapons of my own." He clenched his fist between gear changes. For the first time Caroline noticed how big the man's arms and fists were. His forearm looked like a leg of lamb straining under his jacket, his fist like half a ham. "RAF boxing champion," he said. "Four years on the trot and left the service undefeated. I want a shot at the bastard behind this."

"Well do what I say. Because we have to play the long game. If the man is there, he is our only lead to our principal target."

"Is this to do with the warhead?"

"Yes. You know?"

"It's public knowledge, well, within Five that is, as of late this afternoon. The police are being cautious. Scotland Yard are handling that aspect, a percentage of each force is looking for this Zukatsy fellow."

"Zukovsky."

"Right." Frank swerved again, this time around a bus. "And this attack is to do with these Russians?"

"I'd bet my life on it."

"So what does this man at the hotel look like?"

"Six-two, slim. But wiry, fit. Very black hair, slicked with gel. Or maybe just greasy. Hooked nose, sharp eyes. Two day's black stubble."

"Typically Slavic, a Rusky?"

"Just needs one of those fur hats and a bottle of vodka."

They pulled up to the entrance of the Holiday Inn and Frank mounted the curb. Caroline was out and making her way into reception while the engine was still running. Frank switched off, locked up and followed her in. Caroline was already showing a receptionist her ID and had the computer monitor angled around while the receptionist searched. The manager came out and asked if she could help. Caroline and the manager talked animatedly. Frank stood discreetly nearby, his eyes all over the foyer.

"And the CCTV?"

"Maybe you should come round to the office?" The manager suggested.

Caroline turned to Frank and waved him over. "The bastard's still here! He hasn't checked out yet, but has ordered a car for tomorrow."

"A taxi?"

"No. A hire car, to be delivered here at eight o'clock."

"And he's definitely still here?"

The manager interrupted as she looked up from the CCTV monitor. "He's a strange one. He's stipulated no room cleans, make-ups or anything else. He has highly sensitive work spread all over the place and wants no interruptions. His car is ordered from Hertz in the morning. Concierge service, delivered to the door. Look, this is him returning this afternoon."

Caroline watched the man at the reception. It was Droznedov. He looked flustered. She looked at the time. Seventeen-thirty-five. Forty minutes after the attack on Thames House.

The manager looked at the screen of the hotel booking platform. She typed into the CCTV keyboard. "That's him at the desk when he ordered a taxi. She looked at the notes on the platform and typed again on the CCTV keyboard. That's him at the bar last night," she paused, typing again. "And that's him checking in, oh wait…" She frowned, looking at the screen. He checked in, so it should be… Sorry, it's not him."

Caroline looked at the man checking in. Jet black hair cropped short. Wide shoulders, average height. It definitely wasn't Droznedov. Nowhere near tall enough. "Who the hell is that?" She watched the man sign the form at the desk, put his card back in his wallet and put his wallet back into his pocket before turning and walking away with his travel bag.

"Hold it!" Frank said urgently. "Rewind!" The manager did so and the man walked backwards to the desk. "There!"

Caroline frowned. "What?"

Frank pointed to the man behind. He was checking his smartphone. "That's him. Blonde hair, but that's him. Same gait as the bloke ordering the taxi and at the bar."

"Play it again," Caroline said sharply. She studied the man, all two seconds of screen time. "Jesus, I think you're right!"

"Shall I call the police?" The manager asked.

"Good God no! Don't say a word to anybody. In fact, I'd like you to go off shift right now. I don't want you to chance seeing him and him seeing your reaction." She looked at the screen again, watched the footage and studied the man she knew as Droznedov, but without the extremely dark hair. "So if that's the real Major Uri Droznedov checking in; who the hell is this guy?"

63

Max Clenton waited on the starboard deck, he smoked and watched the shoreline. The boat rose and fell with the swell, but was anchored securely. The tide was dropping and the prow of the boat faced the shore. He had seen the vehicle's headlights more than ten minutes ago. They had cut a swathe of light across the shore break as the vehicle had turned off the road and into the carpark. The lights had gone out and the shore was in darkness once more.

His eyes were accustomed to the dark and he could see the mound of earth rising up from the beach. Not quite a cliff, but it rose fifty-feet or so and was topped with a sporadic barrier of trees. The southern Cornish coastline, although still open to the elements, did not take the brunt of the Atlantic swell or wind like the north coast did. It was rare to find trees within a mile of the craggy cliff-line on that coast. While along the southern coast trees would often grow along the shoreline, in some cases so close as to cast fir cones and pine needles upon the shore.

The single beam of the torch shone from the beach. Five short pulses, and then three longer ones. A five second gap and the process repeated. Clenton responded as he had been instructed. He dropped his cigarette butt into the water and walked to the stern. The two crewmen waited on the deck. They had previously lowered the wooden tender into the water. It was a large tender, but also served as the *Lady Majestic's* lifeboat. Stowed inside it was an inflatable survival life-raft with survival suits, supplies and flares, oars and fuel cans. Fixed to the stern was a five-horsepower outboard engine. The crew had removed everything except the engine and the oars and lowered the crate somewhat precariously into the middle of the boat and strapped it down securely. Neither had wanted to remain on the tiny boat as it chucked itself about in the swells, but both men climbed down the rope ladder and positioned themselves while Clenton untied the rope from the cleat and left it trailed through. He dropped the other end of the rope down to the younger man at the tiller and climbed down. As Clenton sat down on the bench seat, the younger man released the rope, casting off and started the engine. Clenton gathered up the wet rope, coiling it with a lifetime's practise and dropped it into the boat as they moved steadily away and towards the shore. The swell was slow but sizeable and as they approached the shore they could see the rollers break and the offshore wind blew the spray back towards them. Clenton nudged the young man out of the way and took the tiller. He adjusted the throttle and slowed the boat until they matched the speed of the rolling wave and started to surf in. The wave was approximately four feet and at the last minute Clenton throttled back and the wave broke in front of them, he then gave the tiller a twist and aimed at the beach at full speed. The wave behind them loomed up and broke, but they were far enough in front to avoid it breaking on them and the wave, losing most of its energy simply washed them up the shore. Clenton turned the tiller and steered to port and they came up at the base of the slipway, grinding the bottom of the boat on the concrete. Both crewmen jumped out up to their knees in the water and pulled the boat clear of the waves. The older crewman pulled a rope attached to the prow and heaved the boat higher. He took an anchor out and ran up the beach, jamming it into the shingle and then ran back to the boat and wound the rope around a cleat, securing the boat to the shore.

Zukovsky walked down the steep shingle beach towards them. "Well done, my friend," he said, holding out his hand warmly to the captain. Clenton shook his hand and grinned. Zukovsky said, "If you will please carry it to my car."

Clenton shook his head. "How about some money first?"

"Of course," Zukovsky replied. He reached into his jacket pocket and took out a folded parcel envelope that was approximately four inches thick. He tossed it to Clenton, who caught it quickly and peered inside. "But please hurry. Get it into the boot of my car and we can all go our separate ways."

Clenton nodded to his two crew and they unstrapped the crate and heaved it between them. They struggled, putting it down twice before Clenton hurried forwards and caught the other side. Zukovsky conceded and between the four of them they got it up the beach, over the mound of shingle and onto the sand of the carpark. The crate was heavy and cumbersome, but the ground was easier above the beach and it just fitted into the boot of the Jaguar. Zukovsky closed the lid carefully, and the crate touched the lid. He had measured and planned perfectly.

He smiled at the three men. "And that," he said amiably, "Concludes our business."

Clenton shook his hand and the two crew walked back down the beach in front of him. The older crewman pulled the anchor out of the shingle and fell forwards. He crashed down onto the ground and lay still. Zukovsky could hear the other two men laugh, but not for long. The younger crewman walked towards his colleague, then he too fell. He struggled up, but fell again. This time he did not move. Clenton bent down and tried to help the young man, then looked up in the direction of the carpark. He tried to pull on the boat, but it was far too heavy for one person to move on their own. He tried to run, but the steel-toed wellington boots he was wearing were cumbersome and he found the shingle too deep and unsteady. He fell onto his rear, clutching his stomach. He tried to get back up, but merely fell forwards and lay still.

Alesha rose up out of the line of bushes on top of the embankment and slid down the muddy slope. She held a rifle in one hand, the barrel tilted upwards and resting on her shoulder. It was a semi-automatic Ruger 10/22 with a suppressor fitted and a 3.9 x 50 night-vision scope mounted on top. The .22 subsonic rounds had been virtually silent in conjunction with the suppressor, and coped well at the two-hundred-feet range. The elevation had helped. In all she had fired five rounds. She walked past Zukovsky, her breathing rapid. She was flushed and her expression was one of heightened pleasure. She walked across the shingle and stood over the first body. She fired into its head. Then repeated this with the other two. She picked up the bundle of money beside Clenton's body and walked back to Zukovsky. She kissed him on the mouth, hard and passionately. He smiled and they walked back to the car.

64

King eased the Mercedes into the nearest space along the street. He had driven around the block three times, ignoring the spaces further along. This space backed onto double yellow lines, and the car's rear wheels were illegally parked. However, this space was also in view of what King guessed to be the MI5 watcher vehicle across the piazza style open ground in front of the mosque. The area was largely concreted with park benches and a water feature. A group of youths were skateboarding and using some steps near a streetlamp for performing tricks. They were wearing hoodies and using their phones to film. Most probably uploading to *YouTube* as they went. Other than that, the piazza was deserted.

    King had left Caroline's flat and driven a mile north. He had found what he had been looking for next to an Asian mini-market that specialised in halal meat. He admired the busy independent stores opening all hours and the locals' patronage. There were all nationalities, but it felt like a community nonetheless. From there he had driven southeast to Brentwood and the hospital. Rashid had been ready. He had not been discharged, but he was willing to assist in King's plan. He had dosed up on painkillers and had a dressing on his wounds, as well as a cannula in the back of his hand. But the drain had already been removed from his stomach and he would reconnect to the antibiotic drip when he returned. He had briefed King on the layout inside the mosque on the drive to Islington. As they parked, King noticed the man wince. The painkillers were wearing off.

"I need to make it look convincing," King said.

Rashid looked at him and smirked. "I can see that."

King looked down at the kaftan smock and baggy Islamic trousers he was wearing. He put the *kufti* skull-cap on and shrugged. "What?"

"It's a look."

"It'll serve a purpose." He passed Rashid the cotton sack and said, "Over the head and walk quickly. We'll be on camera and I want to be in and out before the cops arrive."

"What about my hands?"

King held up the roll of duct tape. "Sorry…"

They got out and King walked around the car and onto the pavement. The street was tree-lined and dark. It appeared that every other lamp was out. Perhaps it was cutbacks and the council had removed the bulbs. There was no light over the Mercedes, or the three cars in front. Rashid held out his hands, but King shook his head. "Behind your back, I'm afraid," he said. "The more convincing, the better."

"Figures." Rashid turned around and King moved him in towards the wall. King wound the tape around twice. "I need to be able to get them off."

"You will."

"I won't," he said, struggling with his hands. "They're too tight."

"Well, I didn't think you'd like the next part." King spun him around and punched him in the face. Rashid recoiled backwards and King stepped on the man's instep and held his arms to stop him countering. "Relax!" He looked at the blood dripping from the man's nostrils and the split lip. "All done."

"Bastard!"

"So true. Never knew my Dad."

"Good. Hope your mother charged him double."

King smiled. "Depends. Maybe it was free for my shot. By the time my sister was born she'd have taken payment in drugs." He pat Rashid on the cheek. "You won't upset me by downing on my parents. Now, time for the hood." He slipped it on over his head. He checked Rashid over. Satisfied, he took out a folding lock knife and put a tiny cut in the inside of the tape near Rashid's wrist. "That's the best I can do."

"What the hell have I signed up for?"

King caught hold of him and they walked swiftly down the pavement, out into the relative light of the gloomy piazza and across the open ground to the mosque. The main entrance was directly in front. There was a sort of open porch with a pitched roof at the main entrance complete with a large hand wash trough and a dozen rows of racks for shoes. Past this and halfway around the building was a municipal entrance used between prayers and for deliveries, post and people seeking counsel. The mosque acted as a help centre for Muslims and Islamic guidance, and in this sense the door was open to all, at all hours.

King reached the door and banged with his fist. He glanced back across the piazza and could see the youths staring. Past them, he could see the static van on the other side of the street. It was too far away to detect movement, but he would bet that inside there were at least two people panicked and unable to decide what action to take. He hoped they would call it in. Tonight was not the time to be a hero.

The door opened a few inches. It was on a chain, but King took the initiative. "Open the door! I have Rashid here, the treacherous pig! Zukovsky has told me to bring him here to our Islam brothers! He said the Iman would like to get a second chance with him. Now come on, open up!" The man peered out at them. King's dark hair and half a weeks' stubble, combined with a semi-year-round tan worked in favour with the Islamic clothing. Rashid struggled, putting on a good show, King gripped him firmly. He pulled up the hood. "See? Recognise this pig?"

The man nodded, unsure. He turned around and spoke to someone. And then the man was gone and a large figure loomed into the six-inch gap.

"Let me see," the man said sharply.

King lifted the hood, Rashid struggled some more. "Come on," King said. "I'm exposed out here!"

"Shut up!" the man thundered. "Leave him there."

"No. I have a message for Iman Mullah Al-Shaqqaf from Vladimir Zukovsky."

"Give it to me."

"No."

"I said…"

"I don't care what you said. Zukovsky is my boss, he told me Al-Shaqqaf would want this man and I was to give a message only to him."

"That's Iman Al-Shaqqaf!"

"Forgive me," King nodded. "My apologies," he said, bowing his head.

The man pushed the door shut, unfastened the clip then stood back, opening the door. King pushed Rashid roughly inside. The man pushed King up against the wall. He was the same height, but a good two stone heavier. At least sixteen stone and he seemed muscular and fit. King had to fight his urge to resist. The man patted him over, found the knife and put it in his own pocket. He spun King around and patted him down the front. Satisfied King was unarmed, he turned to Rashid and ripped off the hood. Rashid flinched. He recognised the man as Al-Shaqqaf's bodyguard.

"Oh, we're going to have some fun with you," he said. "You won't be getting away this time." He beckoned the other man over and told him to hold Rashid still.

Rashid looked at him coldly. "How's your arse?"

The man smacked Rashid with an open hand. It made a huge slap and Rashid recoiled. He smiled, looking at King. "Maybe you want in on this?"

King shrugged. "Sure. I have a message for the Iman first."

The man nodded. He took out his mobile phone and dialled. He started to talk, walked across the foyer for privacy. He nodded, looked at the man who had opened the door and nodded his head towards a thick oak door off the other side of the foyer. "Downstairs."

65

The Hercules C130 banked hard to port, its engines wailing all the way through the ninety-degree turn. The pilot acknowledged the message from the AWACS radio operator and tipped the starboard wing slightly bringing the plane onto its new course.

Scott MacPherson tapped the co-pilot on his shoulder. "How far now?" he asked.

The co-pilot glanced at the map strapped to his thigh. "Five minutes and we will be passing over her."

MacPherson nodded. "Right, give us the red light when we're over her and the green light when we're five miles clear. Keep on her heading."

The co-pilot nodded. "When do you want the ramp down?"

"Sixty seconds. We'll switch over to our personal air supply now." He tapped both the co-pilot and pilot on the shoulder and held up a thumb. He walked back into the cargo hold and signalled his sergeant. The light in the hold was a dull red gloom. Red allowed the men to maintain their night vision.

Sergeant Peters got up from the bench seat and thread his way through and over the men's legs and equipment. "Do we go now Boss?"

"We go. Get the men standing by, we go in three minutes."

Peters turned and signalled the men. As he disconnected his air supply and switched to his own tank, he saw the men do the same in unison. Their own air was cooler than the central supply. It was mixed with more oxygen.

Four men went to the rear of the plane, just short of the ramp. They dragged the three rubber bundles into position, then stood aside for the men who had made ready first. They moved past them and checked their own equipment. The RAF loadmaster connected his lifeline to the wire above and made his way past the men to the control at the base of the ramp. The loadmaster turned to the men and raised his hands above his head. He dropped them slowly in front of him, indicating the men should form two lines and make their way towards him. The ramp started to open and the cargo bay was engulfed by cold air and a tremendous hum of engine noise. The ramp opened slowly and the red light above flashed briefly before remaining on.

The three lead soldiers each pulled a length of para cord on the rubber bundles and a flashing beacon activated on each one.

MacPherson shouted, "Equipment check!" He was standing at the front of the line on the port-side. His 2IC, Sergeant Peters was standing at the end of the line on the starboard-side.

Each man checked over his equipment in an order which personally suited them, although their primary weapons and ammunition were all stored in waterproof containers inside the rubber bundles. They all carried a diving knife strapped to their legs and a Sig P225 pistol strapped to their thigh in a low slung holster. Each pistol was loaded but not made ready.

The dull red light in the hold switched off. The whole rear of the plane was lit just by the single red bulb at the base of the ramp. The loadmaster pressed his earphones tighter to his right ear as he struggled to hear the cockpit communication over the wind noise as the plane cut through the night at two hundred miles per hour. He looked up at MacPherson and held up his right hand with all five digits extended. He counted each one off. The plane slowed considerably as the pilot neared stall speed, the engines lowering in tone, but sounding as if they were struggling. The speed dropped to just under one hundred miles per hour as the loadmaster's thumb folded and he pumped his fist in the air, the light beside him switching from red to green in the darkness.

MacPherson stepped aside and the four men nearest the ramp, two men from each line, pushed the rubber bundles off the edge of the ramp and followed them out into the night. MacPherson followed, diving straight ahead, barely a metre behind the four men, but thirty metres behind them once he cleared the ramp. The engine noise vanished in an instant and within seconds he was reaching terminal velocity and plummeting towards the cold, grey North Sea twenty-five thousand feet below.

They were using the HALO technique. High Altitude Low Opening. Falling almost all of the way and using their skydiving abilities to travel towards the target. The three lead men would tip themselves forward, increase their speed to catch up with the bundles and guide them forwards. The rest of the men would fan out and follow. At that height it would be possible to travel three miles in any direction of their choosing. At fifteen hundred feet, using their wrist mounted altimeters, they would open their chutes, then decelerate until they were twenty feet from the water, break free and splashdown. Their chutes would drop away from them without dragging them underwater. If there was a failing, if they sustained an injury during descent by colliding with another soldier, or made an error in judgement, the parachutes were calibrated to open automatically at twelve hundred feet.

The men filed off into two groups, falling together in the buddy system, a circle with their heads close together. Both groups remained close. Regrouping after the jump would be easier if they were closer during the descent.

The three bundles, although heavier than the men, fell at the same speed. They were automatically calibrated to open at five hundred feet to avoid colliding with them.

Sergeant Peters checked his altimeter. It indicated four thousand feet. He released his grip on the man next to him and gave the signal to break. The group of six broke free to give themselves room. MacPherson's group did the same simultaneously. Seconds later the canopies trailed and reached full canopy at eleven hundred feet.

Peters braced for the shuddering, gut-wrenching jolt as terminal velocity was broken from one hundred and sixty miles per hour to approximately eighteen miles per hour in a second. He looked around him and counted eleven canopies. Less than three seconds later, he detached and dropped the last twenty feet into the icy water.

The swell was two metres. Peters pulled off his helmet and mask, detached the personal air supply system and unfastened the rest of the parachute harness. He inflated his life vest a little using the manual fill mouthpiece. He chose to fill it only half way so he could swim faster. He shuddered with cold, the immersion was a shock to his system, the rubber dry suit kept him warm, but some water had leaked through the cuffs, neck and ankles, and the cold on his face was painful. He could see a flashing beacon and swam towards it. Head down, front crawl, kicking hard. Hampered by the dry suit, equipment and swell, he still made the twenty metre swim in less than a minute. When he got to the bundle and flashing beacon, he manoeuvred it until he could reach the pull tab and pulled back with all his might. The carbon dioxide canister inflated the Gemini rubber boat in less than three seconds. The boat was the right way up and Peters used the loops that ran all alongside the craft to pull himself out of the water. Once inside he took out his PNVGs and strapped them to his head. The passive infra-red night vision goggles turned everything green, but had a range of only two-hundred and fifty metres. He scanned three-hundred and sixty degrees searching for the other boats.

Men were at the boat now and getting inside. There were more than there should have been, but they would pull the crafts together, headcount and even out the numbers before they moved out. Peters started the virtually silent four-stroke engine and headed for the nearest boat. He could see two more inflated and taking on men. The night was lit by a quarter moon and starlight. The cloud cover around fifty percent. It allowed reasonable visibility to one hundred metres unaided vision. The swell was considerable, but it was slow and there was a distinct rhythm to it and a distance of fifty metres or so between the troughs. A directional swell coming from the north. The wind was light. White water was at a minimum. Peters rubbed up against the nearest boat. The men tied on, and before long all three craft were a bound flotilla rising and falling in the swell.

The men spread out and started to piece their kit together. They were using Heckler & Koch .45 calibre UMP machine carbines. Chosen for their compact dimensions and heavy-hitting round. The .45 had tremendous stopping power at close range but did not over-penetrate human targets or walls. A useful trait for a hostage rescue weapon. It was also deemed a one-shot-stop calibre. Not many people remained standing and fighting after being hit. All of the UMP's were fitted with a suppressor making them virtually inaudible from fifty metres away. Each man checked their pistols, ejecting the magazine, tipping out water and reloading. They made them ready and holstered them. They were well-oiled and would work fine. It wasn't the best way to treat a weapon, exposing it to salt water, but MacPherson had insisted they all jumped with them. If anything had happened to the dry weapon canisters inside the boats, or indeed if one or more of the boats were lost or damaged, he reasoned they would at least have a pistol and a knife and take on the task regardless.

"I didn't think the swell would be as big as this," Peters said. "Going to be tough boarding."

MacPherson nodded. "It is what it is." He took his night vision goggles off and used a large thermal imager to scan the horizon. It looked like a stubby telescope but allowed the operator to see everything in a dull red hue. It picked out heat sources and showed both distance to the target and a digital compass reading overlaid the image. "Got her. Two-thousand metres south-east. Almost on a direct course with us."

"The RAF boys did well," Peters commented. "So we wait-out and they should sail right past us."

"Sounds like a plan."

"Get the ladders assembled!" Peters barked. "Same as the briefing. Mac's boat takes starboard-side. Chubs' boat takes the stern and my boat takes port-side. That's left, dickheads!"

MacPherson smiled. Peters was a good sergeant. An officer's trusted right-hand man, but also one of the men. He was never afraid to call MacPherson on his decisions and the SAS captain respected him all the more for it. MacPherson was a rare breed. He had completed his four-year term; the maximum any officer could serve in the SAS. However, occasionally an officer would be invited back with a permanent posting. MacPherson had served in the SAS for almost ten years.

Peters had showed his concern for this mission. There was no stand-down. No communication with Hereford. Once they left the plane they either succeeded or failed. They needed to secure the ship's radio to communicate with control, and they needed the ship to get home again. There was only ten miles range in the silent engines' internal fuel tanks and they were two hundred miles from land. A navy rescue operation would be called in after a zero-hour deadline, but the nearest frigate was over a hundred miles away. Until then, the men were on their own. *Bloody suicide mission*, Peter's had remarked. *I want double time for this!* he had smirked.

"Remember," MacPherson said, looking at the men in turn. "Twelve confirmed hostages. Intelligence has confirmed four x-rays, but the number of crew remains unconfirmed. We do not jeopardise the hostages or each other by taking prisoners."

"So we shoot everyone and hope we don't need *Lawyers 4 You* later on," Peters commented flatly.

The men chuckled and MacPherson looked at them all in turn. "It's your call. You know how it works. But this is a tight mission and anything going tits-up means we may not get back home."

"We'll do what needs to be done, Boss," said Peters.

MacPherson looked through the thermal imager again. "Okay lads, she's eight-hundred metres and closing fast." He looked at the trooper at the tiller of the outboard. "Get us out there and into position."

The men unlashed the boats and they broke away from one another as soon as the next swell hit them. MacPherson's boat shot out across the path of the *Ebony* and carried on for another two hundred metres. The swell met them broadside, and the helmsman played with the revs and direction to put the prow of the rubber boat into the trough. He turned a wide circle and dropped the revs. The fishing boat sailed onwards. The SAS soldiers ducked down under the sides of the boat keeping their silhouette profiles to a minimum.

MacPherson stowed the thermal imager and put on his own night vision goggles. He stared in the direction of the *Ebony* and breathed deeply, steadying his nerves. The boat came into view somewhat mystically as she broached the two-hundred and fifty metres limitation of the night vision goggles. The men remained silent. Noise could carry easily on the wind, even with the monotonous drum of the boat's slow turning prop shaft and noisy diesel engines. She lolled slightly in the swells, but her prow rose high out of the water and crashed down the back of each trough. Boarding the craft in these swells was going to be difficult.

When the boat was one-hundred metres clear, MacPherson ordered the helmsman to go and the other boats followed suit. MacPherson could see the red spot of a glowing cigarette as his boat drew near. Soon the silhouette of a man appeared leaning on the railing. He smoked, looking at the white water which broke along the *Ebony* and trailed off as wake. MacPherson raised his UMP and sighted on the centre of the man's chest. He felt the Gemini ride high on the swell then drop down the trough. He breathed out, held his breath and squeezed the trigger. The weapon had been set on its two-shot burst. Both rounds struck less than an inch apart. The man fell and MacPherson kept the sight on the railing to see if he got back up. He didn't.

Chubs was a big man. He came from Fiji and was as black as coal. He was also extremely fit and a semi-professional bodybuilder. He was obsessed with fitness and maintaining a low body fat percentage, and ate egg white omelettes and grilled salmon for breakfast. Naturally his SAS colleagues called him Chubs because it annoyed him so much. He positioned himself at the prow, ready with the ladder. It had two large hooks on one end which could find purchase on the edge of most boats and ships. The ladders had been built according to what intelligence they had. The intelligence was wrong as usual and as Chubs hooked his ladder over the stern it was evident the men would have to pull themselves hand over hand for four or five rungs until their feet would find a rung. Chubs heaved himself up and those extra hours in the gym paid off as he scaled the twelve feet or so to the deck in seconds. He unslung his weapon and did not look back. He was on board and the rest of his team were left to their own devices. He eased himself around the crane fitted on the stern and saw MacPherson pulling himself over the rail and the body lying face down on the deck. MacPherson saw him and moved closer.

"Where's the rest of your team?"

"Still climbing," Chubs replied. "Peters and his team are struggling with their ladder. It's higher than we thought."

"Tell me about it," MacPherson said, panting from the exertion.

Peters appeared over the guardrail on the port side. He rolled over the top and got his weapon off his shoulder. The three men moved forwards, MacPherson in the lead, the other two behind and to each side like an arrowhead formation. They headed for the wheelhouse. A few feet short, MacPherson crouched low and signalled Peter's past. The SAS captain kept his weapon covering the area ahead, while his sergeant creeped past him and opened the door. There was a lone man sat in front of the wheel. He was rolling a cigarette.

Joseph Arnsettle looked up in surprise as he saw the SAS solider step inside - clad in a black dry-suit with a bulletproof vest under his life vest, his pistol low-slung, a diving knife strapped to his calf, ammunition pouches and wearing night-vision goggles, his UMP carbine aimed directly at him, the man dropped his half-rolled cigarette, his mouth agape. He didn't hear the silenced shot that went straight in his open mouth. It had been an intentional shot, the brain stem nestled right behind the back of the throat. It was the surest way to switch off the lights. The body slumped down in the seat, completely still except for its right foot which shook slightly, quivering as the nervous system shut down.

Peters crouched low and aimed his weapon at the top of the stairs. MacPherson eased himself up to his sergeant's shoulder.

"Good shot Dave," MacPherson said quietly. "Chubs is on the door. Three of ours are working their way up the front."

"The prow."

"Fuck off, sergeant. The bloody front," he grinned. "We'll take the quarters."

"We're three down then. Three of us here, three going up front. Are the others coming or staying in the bloody boats?"

"The three short-arses probably can't reach the bloody first rung, with the swells."

"Ah well, bollocks. Let's do it." Peters edged forwards and aimed his weapon down the stairwell.

MacPherson took out a flash-bang, pulled the pin and lobbed it down the stairwell. Both men turned their heads and covered their ears by tucking the right ear into their right shoulder and cupping their left ears with their left hands. This kept their weapon ready and aimed in front of them. The flash was brilliant white; the bang was a hollow thump that shook their insides. Both men were up and moving with well-honed precision. MacPherson saw the man attempting to get out of his bunk. He aimed and fired two single shots. The man dropped back into his bunk. He was still moving, groaning. MacPherson stepped forwards a pace and pressed the muzzle against the man's head at the same instance he fired, did not bother to check as the head rocked forwards and he continued to move onwards, his weapon up and scanning everything he looked at through the sights.

Chubs had taken the decision to throttle back the engines and steer the Ebony on a course heading towards the swell. With no one steering, the boat could well change course as it rose and fell in the swells and be left broadside to the two metre waves. Slowing the boat down would also give the other three men tasked with the assault, but still in the Geminis, an opportunity to board and allow the three assault boats to back away as planned. The helmsmen were to protect the boats and provide covering fire if necessary from the belt-fed 5.56mm Minimi support weapons each boat carried. Chubs kept his weapon close to his shoulder and watched the foredeck. He knew that the area behind him was clear and from his vantage point high up at the rear of the boat he could provide fire and tactical support.

There was gunfire ahead of them as they made their way through the engine room and into a storage hold. MacPherson held up his hand at an open door way and Peters crouched low and eased his weapon's muzzle through resting it against the door jamb. MacPherson moved through the doorway and ducked as wood and debris splintered just inches from his head. The sound followed, a short burst from an automatic weapon. The SAS captain knew he couldn't fire back without acquiring a target, but he moved forwards into the unknown to change position. The gunman would swing back and aim at where he had his near miss. MacPherson unpinned another flash-bang and threw it hard at the wall just in front of the door opening opposite. It struck at a forty-five-degree angle and rebounded into the next hold. He turned his eyes away, shielded his ears and waited the terrifyingly long three seconds. The moment it detonated he was up on his feet and charged at the opening. Ahead of him, a mere five metres away, a man stood bent over, his hand still on the grip of a compact AKS 74-U carbine, his other hand shielding his eyes. MacPherson aimed and fired, but his weapon merely clicked.

"Stoppage!" he screamed and in one fluid motion he dropped the weapon to one side and drew his pistol, dropping to one knee as soon as he started to bring the weapon up to aim to present himself as a smaller target. The man started to bring the weapon up to fire, not believing his luck at hearing the click. But MacPherson was faster and fired twice, double-tapping the man twice in the face at the same moment that Peters fired a short burst of automatic fire over his captain's head and hit the gunman in the centre of his chest.

MacPherson got to his feet and ignoring the UMP on the floor, moved forwards with the pistol held firmly in both hands, looking at everything through the sights.

Peters put a hand on his shoulder. "I've got this, Boss."

MacPherson let the man move in front, he now had the greater firepower. Standard operating procedure with a misfire was to discard, go to secondary weapon and keep moving. Hostage rescue was not a battlefield scenario, it was something that needed constant and unbroken momentum. Once the first shot is fired and stealth is compromised, the real threat was that hostages could be executed. Speed is of the essence. The stoppage could merely have been a shell casing caught in the ejection port and easy to clear. However, it could also be a damaged firing pin, a weak casing that had expanded and welded itself in the breach or a fault in the spring and blowback mechanism and that would require a repair with tools and a bench. There was no time to look, no time to be caught staring down the wrong end of a weapon and get shot by the enemy.

"On me! On Me!" An SAS trooper called as he came down a set of stairs and into the hold. "One down at the top of the stairs! Looked like crew!"

"Three crew, one armed x-ray!" MacPherson replied. "That's three more x-rays!"

Peters moved forwards followed by the trooper. MacPherson fell in and covered the rear using his pistol. They made their way through the hold which was packed full with nets, rope, coils of wire, crab pots and lobster pots. Buoys, flags and markers were stacked in wire cages and there were multiple sets of waterproof clothing, boots and life jackets hanging from the walls, which were merely the steel sides of the inside of the hull. MacPherson was confident that the copper-coated lead bullets of the .45 UMPs and his own 9mm Sig Sauer pistol would not penetrate the hull, but the high velocity rounds of the AKS the dead gunman was using might well have been a different matter. To add to his concern, he could hear a sudden and unmistakable clatter of an AK47 on fully automatic ahead of them. The AK47 was even more powerful than the AKS. In the confines of the hull it was near-deafening.

"Man Down! Man Down!"

The words made his heart sink and he could hear a huge retaliation in return fire, the quiet whump of silenced .45s, the clatter of their working parts audible over their silenced gunshots. The UMP was a specialist hostage recovery weapon and the cyclic rate had been lowered considerably to just five-hundred and fifty to six-hundred rounds a minute. Compared to many machine carbines that would spit their bullets out at nine-hundred to a thousand rounds a minute. The result, however, was an extremely controllable and accurate weapon.

"We need to get up there!" MacPherson shouted.

Sergeant Peters grunted something as he eased his weapon's muzzle around the next opening. He was not going to rush in for anyone. He respected and liked Captain MacPherson, and would follow the man anywhere, but he wouldn't be rushed and the younger captain tended to be a bit cavalier. Old bull, young bull he would often joke. But he felt the adrenaline rising and he desperately wanted to get to the downed trooper. He ducked through a bit quicker than he otherwise might have and heard the zing of bullets past his ear as the gunfire erupted ahead of him. He dropped to one knee and aimed, but there were hostages everywhere. Their hands were bound behind them and they had been forced to stand and act as cover for the terrorists. Some had dropped to the deck upon hearing the gunfire next to them, others were standing confused. All were hooded.

"British Security Forces!" Peters bellowed in his parade ground voice. "MI5 Hostages! Get down now!"

He sighted the nearest gunman and fired. He kept firing until the man fell. MacPherson was pushing in with his pistol blazing and the other trooper was engaging with a gunman to his right.

"X-ray right down!" The trooper shouted.

"X-ray front down!" Peters copied.

MacPherson had hit both too, the second as he was falling, but he didn't respond. He ran over to a man on the ground in the middle of a cluster of five hostages. The man looked up at him. He had a hood partially covering his eyes and his hands were behind his back.

"Hands! Let me see your hands!"

The man reached around and showed them and MacPherson shot him once in the forehead, snapping back his head and spraying the deck and hostages around him with a crimson smatter.

"Shit!" Peters screamed.

"Count them, now!" MacPherson shouted back. There was a surge in gunfire towards the prow. He looked at the trooper. "Get up there!" The soldier ran and MacPherson rolled the body over onto its front. The grip of a 9mm Browning HP-35 pistol poked out of the waistband. The SAS captain took it out and tossed it a few feet away.

"Twelve Scott, all accounted for."

"The bastards put a sleeper in," MacPherson said. "Stay and guard the hostages Dave, I'll go and get this last bastard out of his hole."

"Here, take this then," Peters handed him his UMP and took out his own pistol. He kept the weapon aimed at the hooded forms on the deck. "Stay exactly where you are. Do not move or I will not hesitate in shooting you. It will all be over shortly."

***

The AK47 was empty. He had used all three thirty-round magazines and he had hit one of the SAS soldiers. He was confident that the soldier was either dead already or soon would be. He had pinned the elite soldiers down, but he could hear them communicating and was aware they were getting ever-closer. He had the Makarov pistol in his hand now and had used all but three of the punchy little 9x18mm bullets. He was an experienced soldier and had served in the Russian army for twelve years and he had fought terrorists in Chechnya. He knew what was about to come. They would lob grenades soon, now that he no longer had them pinned down with the AK47. Then, when he was shielding his eyes and deafened by the explosion they would make their move.

Marvin cursed. He had wanted this. He had wanted to be part of the operation that did not keep him in London and near the risk of the nuclear device. He wanted to be back in his beloved Russia. He wanted to be back among his people, eat, drink and breath its air. He could hang on, maybe if he could charge at them, use his three shots and get a weapon from one of them and keep fighting… He cursed again. This wasn't the movies, he'd seen mightier men than him fall and he knew he was outnumbered at least five to one, simply by the arcs of fire slamming into the lobster pots and fish crates he had taken refuge behind. He knew he was done. Thoughts raced around his head. How could they have found them? Had somebody talked? Was Zukovsky dead, the operation finished? He would never know. Marvin took a deep breath, placed the muzzle of the Makarov under his chin and closed his eyes.

***

The hostages were checked over, unhooded and untied. They were drinking from mugs of hot, sweet tea; sharing a cup between three. There was plenty more being prepared. The SAS soldier who had been hit had been stabilised. The wound was a nasty gash, slicing through the meaty part of his upper arm about six inches long, and because of muscle contraction, about as wide. It looked horrendous, but the medic had given him morphine, doused the wound in antiseptic powder and closed the wound with two-dozen sutures and a whole load of adhesive stitches. A gauze pad was placed over the wound and then bandaged. He was nursing a mug of steaming hot tea. No doubt he would be out of action for a month, but such was the medic's training and experience in Iraq and Afghanistan, it was unlikely to require follow up treatment, although it would be inspected by a doctor upon his return to Stirling Lines base in Hereford.

The Geminis were pulled on board and their equipment stowed inside of them. A detailed and thorough search of the *Ebony* proved to be clear and the coded call to report operation success was made on the ship-to-shore radio on the designated channel.

Finally, the bodies had been laid out, herringboned on the deck and covered with a tarpaulin.

"Well done lads," McPherson said, sipping tea and taking a bite of a digestive biscuit. They were in the wheelhouse and someone had plugged in a fan heater. Now they had cooled down, their nerves and adrenalin subsided, they all realised they were cold, wet and tired.

"Duff round in your UMP, Boss," Peters said. "Didn't have enough powder to work the blowback. The case wouldn't eject." He had checked the weapon and nodded to the pile of UMP carbines in the corner of the cabin.

"We'll dump the ammo back at the quartermaster and do some more testing at the killing house when we get back." MacPherson put his mug of tea down and patted the wheel. "Now, who knows how to drive a bloody fishing boat?"

66

Caroline kept her eyes on the reception area and foyer through the security mirror from the manager's office. She had dispatched Frank to park the car in a more discreet spot while she called in a surveillance team from Thames House. The team leader walked into the foyer and straight behind the reception desk via the dedicated door. He entered the manager's office like he worked the desk every day for the past five years. Caroline had described the reception in detail so he would make it look natural.

"Brannan. Surveillance," he said. He eyed her carefully. "You're Forester's girl."

"Not anymore."

"Sorry. Tactless."

She could tell Brannan was not big on small talk so she went straight to the brief. "Suspect of extreme importance in room five-fourteen. He has a car being delivered at zero-eight-hundred. Firstly, I want to ascertain he is in fact still in his room. Secondly, I want to find out where he goes."

"Thirdly?"

"Lose him and there is the very real chance of a nuclear weapon being detonated on British soil. Fact."

Brannan nodded. "Don't fuck this up, then."

"Correct."

"Right. Firstly, we can put a call up from reception, ask him something about his room. Is he happy? Or housekeeping is not sure they replaced his towels. But we risk spooking him. This is a Holiday Inn. Functional and well-appointed, but not the sort of place to chase opportunities to provide service. So we need an eyes on. Micro-fibre-optic camera under the door, two-forty-degree aperture. In, visual, out. Job done."

"What if he sees it?"

"He won't. Rotten luck if he does."

"Rotten luck won't cut it. What about a lens from across the street?"

"We can do the micro-fibre. I'll do it personally; he won't see it."

"Let's come back to that," Caroline said. "The car. It's a concierge service from Hertz. We need a tracker on it."

"What if he's canny? What if he gives the car a thorough counter-surveillance check?"

"We need to be cannier," Caroline countered.

"If we can have the car for an hour we can make the tracker invisible."

"We can use the records here, go direct to Hertz and commandeer the vehicle."

"Good. If we can do that we can get audio and visual *inside* the vehicle as well. But you'll need an order, the Official Secrets Act, on the staff in the chain at Hertz. We can't afford to have a tip-off. I'm sure they would be clean, but one never knows."

"Perfect."

"We can hook it up to our receiver vehicle. It's down the street with a full tank. Land Rover Discovery. A big cruiser that copes with everything we may come up against. We have a GPS system that uses a cell phone frequency and if we have an hour with the target vehicle we rig it to the wiring and it has indefinite power. It's coupled to a rechargeable battery with an additional seventy-two hours' life."

"If he moves I'll be following in another vehicle. Can you relay the tracker? *And* the visual and audio."

"Yes. Easily," Brannan said. "We'll hook you up with a dedicated receiver and a laptop."

"Right. Well let's get on it."

Brannan nodded. "And about the eyes on. He won't see the micro-fibre. Trust me."

Caroline smiled. "Well if he does, don't bother coming in tomorrow."

The team moved swiftly, taking up a vacant room at the end of the corridor on the fifth floor. Room five-zero-two. A laptop and dedicated receiver were hooked up. The dedicated receiver prevented the frequency being interrupted and tapped into. Wireless broadband systems were easily corrupted.

Brannan changed out of his suit and into a fleece tracksuit and soft-soled basketball trainers. Caroline tried not to laugh. It was the sort of fleece worn by people who frequent pound shops.

"Smirk all you like," he said seriously. "But there's no rustle, no rattle and if I get compromised I just jog off down the corridor and do a few lunges while I wait for the lift."

"A fitness freak would take the stairs," she commented dryly. "But then again, a fitness freak wouldn't be seen dead in those."

"Maybe you're right. But nonetheless, these clothes are silent. And silent is vital."

"If you say so Mister Bond," Caroline smiled. "Just don't get caught."

Brannan turned to a man and a woman perched on the edge of the bed. "Right, walk past the room and be casual, but don't be too quiet. Don't be too noisy either."

"So, normal then boss?" The man said.

"Yes."

"And we walk to room five-thirty and open the door," the woman said.

"Yes. But give it ten minutes and come back out. Have a giggle and walk past the room. Again, act normal."

The pair nodded. Caroline looked on, slightly bemused. Brannan had the fibre-optic camera out and was testing the picture, which could be viewed on the laptop. The wire was stiff and pliable with the camera and inbuilt infra-red light about the size of a quarter carat diamond. He tested it sliding it along the floor. It picked up the aspect of most of the room.

Brannan nodded to the couple and they picked up an overnight bag and left. Brannan held his finger to his lips and everyone was silent as the pair walked down the corridor. Caroline heard the woman giggle and the man laugh heartily, a little lecherously. They were a couple and couples going into a hotel room usually had one thing on their mind. "So far, so good," Brannan said. He started flexing himself and stretching. "Ten minutes and it's a go."

Caroline walked over to the technician hovering over the laptop. Brannan seemed somewhat comical. She was worried she'd made the wrong call. But it was too late now, too late to abort.

Brannan was stretching his hamstrings and touching his toes. He held the micro-fibre-optic down by his side and kept the transmitter in his left hand. He nodded to Caroline, "Get the door please," he asked. "Leave it off the latch." Caroline did as she was asked and stood back next to the coat rail. The two MI5 watchers left room five-thirty and chatted and giggled their way down the corridor towards them. Brannan walked out into the corridor and Caroline let the door close.

"He's a complete dickhead," the technician commented from behind the laptop. "But he is one hell of an operative. Nobody better in surveillance, that's for sure."

Caroline nodded, a little relieved, and studied the laptop display. She could see the two operatives walking towards the camera. Brannan arrived at the door moments before them. The camera went low and dark for a moment, then picked up the view behind the door.

"Oh Christ! He's there!" Caroline gasped.

The man they knew as Droznedov was leaning towards the door with his eye against the peephole. He was wearing trousers and a shirt, and was barefoot. His eye was a few inches from the door staring through the peephole. The camera pulled back and the corridor came back into view. The couple were near; Caroline could hear their approaching chatter.

"But he wasn't looking at the floor," the technician said. "Brannan and his belly shuffle. He was lower than a dead snake at the point they crossed paths and the target would not hear him because of the diversion, nor be far enough back to see the camera. The target is edgy though, hence the spying through the peephole."

The technician was already packing up his equipment when Brannan came back in. The couple did not return and Brannan started to change swiftly back into his suit.

"I take it we got him?" he asked.

"Perfectly," Caroline said. "I'm impressed. And relieved."

"Now we'll work on the car. The operative I sent ahead to Hertz will have smoothed the way by now. I'll stay in reception with you, make sure the target doesn't leave. The rest of my team will go and work their magic," Brannan looked at the technician. "You okay with that?"

"Absolutely boss."

67

The basement was cold and dark. The lighting, however, when it illuminated the room, was complete and soft, with no shadows cast up the walls or upon the ceiling. The reason for this became evident as King's eyes adjusted to the light. The reflector screens were positioned to cast pure light onto the wall behind the bank of cameras.

The large man smiled as he saw King looking at the camera equipment. "Impressed?"

King turned and looked at him. "At what?"

The man bent down and opened a laptop on the table. He switched it on and after a few seconds he tapped on the keyboard. A series of primary coloured bulbs shone on the wall, where a thin, slightly curved interactive television screen was sliding slowly down on silent electric motors. "This is fifty grand's worth of equipment," he said. "But wait and see why."

Two men entered the room ahead of Iman Mullah Al-Shaqqaf. They were all big and hard looking. They looked like they spent a lot of time in the gym lifting weights. More bodyguards. Along with the small man who had opened the door to them, the big man at the laptop and Al-Shaqqaf that made five.

Al-Shaqqaf looked at Rashid for a long time before saying anything. "I am pleased to see you again. We shall make up for lost time soon." He turned to

King. "I am surprised Zukovsky made no mention of you."

"We operate a cell system," King replied. He edged nearer to Rashid, but stopped when the bodyguard nearest pulled out a sawn-off shotgun out from under his long leather jacket. "What's this?" King protested vehemently. "I've brought you the traitor! Do what you want with him and let me out. I've got things to do before Zukovsky gets back with the warhead."

Al-Shaqqaf laughed. "Zukovsky is not the only one to operate a cell system! Your information is old news!" He looked at Rashid and smiled. "There's no bomb going to go off in London! Fellow Muslims dying for Islam? For retaliation to the west? Fool!"

The guard with the shotgun stepped closer and the other two men stepped around and each caught hold of King's shoulders. King did not try anything, he knew what the sawn-off shotgun would do at close range. He had seen people cut in half with them.

Al-Shaqqaf walked up to Rashid and swiped him across the face. Rashid recoiled, then smiled. "Pussy," he said. The Iman punched him hard. Rashid fell back against the wall, righted himself then spat a glob of spit and blood into his face. "Like I said, pussy."

"We will see," smiled Al-Shaqqaf, wiping it away with his sleeve. "We will see." He looked at the largest of the four bodyguards, the man who had shown them down to the basement and nodded towards Rashid.

The big man came at Rashid and grabbed him around the throat. He pulled him in front of the screen and pushed him onto his knees. He went to a shelf opposite and pulled out some cable ties. He stood in front of King and without a word punched him in the face. King fell backwards, but the two men held him firm, pushed him downwards and the big man walked behind him and fastened his wrists tightly. All the while, the shotgun remained just inches from his face.

Al-Shaqqaf went to the laptop and the screen behind switched seamlessly to a scene of the desert. It was a moving image with clouds, a vehicle in the distance traveling on a dirt road some two miles or so away. "We use this one for Syria," he said. He nodded to the guards and one of them twisted King's head around to see. "We had the CIA and MI6 looking for preachers of our faith out there for months, years in fact. They were here right under MI5's nose." He flicked the mouse on the laptop and the scene changed to film of a bombed-out city. Our ISIS brothers film as they conquer, send the footage back digitally and we use it for our films of spiritual enlightenment."

"For propaganda," King corrected him.

"Depends," Al-Shaqqaf said. "One man's terrorist is another man's freedom fighter. Your ITV, BBC or Sky News play propaganda every minute of every day."

King watched as the man with the shotgun took a step backwards and lowered the barrels to the floor. King turned to look back at the screen again but one of the men behind him slapped his face. He looked back at Al-Shaqqaf, blinking as his eye watered from the blow. "MI5 are outside. Across the street in a van."

"Yes. Sometimes a van, sometimes an SUV. It's also been a removal lorry and a broken down mini-bus," the Iman smirked. "I expect it will be an ice cream van one day," he laughed. "We have our own parabolic microphones on them. We know their every move. They were concerned when they saw you hurrying over. They haven't called the police. They were in discussions with their team leader on what to do. But I understand MI5 is a little busy this evening. *Let it play out* was the last instruction I heard over the airwaves." He pulled a vicious-looking knife out from a belt sheath underneath his robes. "We are planning to hold executions down here. They can be filmed and sent digitally to our brothers in Syria and Iraq. It will keep the British and American intelligence agencies busy hunting for people to martyr. You two can be the first." He looked at the knife, gave it a little flick in his hand. "This is a halal slaughter-man's knife. You will not receive the *Shahadah* our ritual prayers before killing an animal. You are not worthy. You will be spat on as the pigs you are, as you bleed and choke on the ground."

King looked at the Iman and asked, "Why was it old news?"

"What?" Al-Shaqqaf looked bemused.

"The warhead going off in London. Why was it old news?"

The Iman fiddled with the laptop and the screen behind turned to woodland, a clearing on a dry, but cloudy autumnal day. "Yes, that's quite fitting," he said of the film. "We worked out where to do more damage, that's all."

"Can't damage a nation more than hitting its capital."

"We don't want to damage the nation! This is my nation as well!" He felt the edge of the blade with his thumb, then walked over and stood in front of them. "We will strike at the heart of the intelligence community. At their ability to thwart our brothers' best efforts in the east."

King frowned, but it was too late. Iman Mullah Al-Shaqqaf pulled on a balaclava mask and gripped the knife tightly and walked around behind them.

King glanced at Rashid. Their eyes met. Both were scared, but still determined.

"This is what enemies of Islam can grow to expect," Al-Shaqqaf announced loudly and clearly for the benefit of the camera. "We see our Muslim brothers persecuted daily. Bombed by the west. Refused asylum by countries dedicated to eradicating Islam and westernising our brothers and sisters, our sons and daughters and eroding standards and values long fought for by our ancestors to keep. From the crusades England waged upon our faith a thousand years ago, to the frequent bombing of Syria and Iraq today, the west has fought in vain to marginalise us, to defeat our will and our faith." He brought the knife around in front of King and caught hold of the tuft of hair on his forehead, pulling his head backwards and exposing his throat. "And like my esteemed Muslim brothers before me…"

King powered upwards, driving through his powerful legs and smashed the back of his head under the Iman's jaw. He grabbed the man's balls with his bound hands and wrenched them savagely, twisting left and right, up and down with all of his strength. Al-Shaqqaf screamed and dropped the knife and King pushed backwards, barrelling the man into the screen smashing the glass and turning the image to blue and green liquid and a distorted and flickering woodland image. He turned and head-butted the nearest guard, but the second guard was already on him. Great bear arms hugged him close. King smashed his head backwards. There was a bone-crunching snap and he kept going, two, three, four times. The bear hug weakened and the man started to sag. The guard had the shotgun up and was trying to find a target, but if he fired at that range he'd hit everyone in front of the screen, and he knew it. King saw the man's quandary, and as the man started forwards King kicked the table and the cameras and laptop toppled off as the table rammed into the man's legs and drove him backwards.

Rashid rolled out of the way. Bound and laying on the floor the smaller man ignored him and made for King. He punched King, but the blow glanced off as King ducked and bobbed and weaved. A second punch found its mark, but King lashed out with a well-aimed front kick and the man dropped forwards clutching his groin. King brought his knee up hard into the man's face, but was pulled backwards by someone. The blow was glancing and King fought to regain balance. The first guard that he had head-butted was getting to his feet, but King took an unskilled penalty shoot-out style kick and connected under the man's chin. He was either unconscious or dead before he hit the ground. The shotgun was getting nearer. Al-Shaqqaf was getting back to his feet, his face a mess and the balaclava had ridden up on his head like a child's ill-fitting bobble hat. His beard was matted with blood and mucous. He was unsteady, falling back into the screen as if he were drunk.

The man with the shotgun had recovered, had the weapon held steady and had covered the ground around the table quickly. He aimed it at King then flinched, a look of surprise on his face. A small red hole appeared in the centre of his forehead. Blood seeped out and then ran swiftly over the perspiration on his brow. He fell forwards into King then tipped sideways and lay still on the floor.

Rashid had the silenced Ruger .22 pistol aimed at Al-Shaqqaf and the remaining two men. He was sat down, his back pressed against the wall. He looked in pain, but the weapon was steady enough not to argue with. The tape was dangling from both wrists, but he had finally torn it free.

King kicked the knife over to Rashid, then walked over and turned around. Rashid aimed the pistol one-handed and sliced quickly through the cable ties around King's wrists with the knife.

King rubbed his wrists. They were bleeding, his hands purple from the pinch. He bent down and took the Ruger off Rashid. "Well done."

"I thought you had cut through most of the tape?"

"I did."

Rashid shrugged. "Could have fooled me."

"Well it had to be convincing." He stepped forwards and levelled the pistol at Al-Shaqqaf. "Where is the uranium?"

"Fool! I'll never tell you! Do you think you can threaten me, scare me into talking? Arrest me now. Let me tell my solicitor how you broke in here, threatened me with a weapon, shot my assistant using illegal force…"

King pulled the trigger and the Iman dropped lifelessly to the floor. There was a messy hole the size of a pound coin in the back of his head where the tiny bullet exited and both men left standing had a crimson splatter pattern on their faces. King aimed at the two unconscious men on the floor and fired a single bullet into both men's heads. One man's legs shot out and twitched for a moment before resting still.

He looked at the two remaining men, aimed the pistol in their direction. "I want to know where the uranium is."

The larger man nodded, his eyes wide and full of terror. "I know! I know!" He stepped a pace forward, shielding the smaller man from view. "I loaded it onto the van, I delivered it personally, had instructions to return with…"

The blade flashed in front of him, then slashed his throat wide open. Blood sprayed out and hit both King and Rashid ten feet away. The big man fell forwards onto his knees, his hands clutching his throat. He keeled over onto his stomach and struggled on the floor, gargling loudly as he breathed nothing but blood.

The smaller man held the knife by his side. It was a classic flick knife with a four-inch-long blade. He looked at King with malevolence. King hadn't noticed before, but the man had a thick scar which ran from his temple to the tip of his chin. "Allah Akbar!" he wailed. He held the knife out in front of him and charged towards them. "Allah Akbar!"

King shot him in the forehead and he fell forwards smashing into the table, spun around and lay still on his back. He stared blankly upwards. King picked up the knife, wiped the blood off the blade on the dead man's collar, then folded it and put it in his pocket. He took the butcher's knife and wiped the blade in some of the guard's blood, then placed the handle in the smaller man's hand and squeezed the man's hand tightly closed. He then put the pistol in the guard's hand and squeezed the trigger. A silenced shot thudded into the wall and King let the man's hand go and turned to Rashid. He helped him up from the floor. He was unsteady, his dressings were seeping.

"Let's get you back to hospital," he said. He ripped off the robes and picked the nearest sized guard to himself. He hastily undressed the man, then dressed in his clothes and redressed the man in the set of robes. It was difficult, but he knew it would be. He had done it before.

He looked at Rashid and said, "Get undressed, I'll get the smaller guy undressed, then you put his clothes on while I redress him in yours."

"And the rest of the plan?" Rashid asked, struggling with his top over the stab wounds.

"Well, we were filmed entering the mosque. Our clothes will identify us. Hopefully this will confuse the hell out of the police."

"Hopefully."

"They've got a lot of bodies and a lot of blood. They have enough confusion, contradiction and assumption here to write a thesis. They've got something going down that went wrong. No man left standing," King said.

"Well it will keep them busy," Rashid commented.

"There's a service entrance to a yard. They keep some containers in the yard for aid work donations. Then the bastards take it out to Syria and slip off to do a bit of killing, then come back with the aid convoy. It's a gated entrance which I'm sure 'Box have under surveillance, but if we can get on top of one of those containers we can jump into the garden of the neighbouring house at the back. That will get us back into the street where we parked."

"Jump?"

"Yes."

"Fifteen feet into a garden?"

"More like eighteen. The containers are on blocks."

"With twenty-two leaking stitches? And that's just the stitches on the *outside*. I'll take my chance with 'Box and the police."

"Well they've got to stitch you back up anyway."

"You're a real bastard, you know that?" Rashid laughed. "Oh, what the hell."

King stood back and looked at the bodies on the ground. "Got your wallet, anything that could identify you?"

"Sorted."

"Let's go then." King led the way up the stairs and into the foyer. He hadn't noticed the collection of clocks and brass nautical compasses on the oak-panelled walls. The clocks had different cities written underneath them and underneath each one written in English was the Arab interpretation. The central clock was marked *Mecca*. King turned left and found a dining room with bench seating. The floor was parquet wooden blocks with a scripture cast in the middle using pieces of ebony. King had seen the scripture before. On ISIS flags. The service hatch in the wall ahead told him where to find the kitchen. "This way. Kitchens always have outside access." They walked quickly and King pushed open the door. The kitchen was well-appointed and could easily cater for numbers in the hundreds. The outside door was easy to spot, there were coats, aprons and overalls hanging from pegs, indicating people arrived and got changed. The key was in the lock and King opened the door and made his way out into the yard. The containers were further down the length of the building.

Rashid was panting, clutching his side. King hooked his arm around him and together they jogged the short distance. "I can hear sirens," Rashid said.

They stopped for a moment.

"So can I," King said. "Quite a few. Let's get going."

King stood at the container and beckoned Rashid forwards. He cupped his hands together and Rashid used them like a stirrup. They counted a silent three and King heaved as Rashid pushed and the man shot upwards. He was only ten or eleven stone and was up the side of the container and easing himself on top in no time. King put his foot on the side of the container where there was a lip. It was high off the ground and took a bit of effort, but he was able to get his hands on top and pull himself up slowly. King weighed about fourteen stone and the going was slower without the added shunt, but Rashid hooked his arm under his own and helped him up as he reached the top.

"That's a fucking long jump," Rashid said, heaving for breath. "Four feet out and a long way down."

The sirens were getting louder as the vehicles raced near. MI5 had made the decision ahead of seeing how it played out. Or maybe they had heard something on the parabolic microphones. Either way it looked as if they were going to be compromised shortly.

"Got to do it!" King said sharply. Rashid took a few paces back and ran at it. As he leapt King shoved him hard and he sailed off into the night. He just cleared the fence and then disappeared from view. King heard the crumple and roll and Rashid curse and cry out in pain. "How was it?" King called out.

"Just jump, I don't want to ruin the surprise for you," came the hushed reply.

King took a run at it and jumped. His stomach rose towards his throat and he felt the hair blow around his head as he headed towards the ground. He couldn't see the ground and brace, but rolled as soon as he hit. The landing was hard and he got up slowly. Both men limped towards the end of the garden and the dull hue of the streetlights beyond. Rashid opened the garden gate and turned right.

"No, this way," he said, catching Rashid's shoulder. "That car's a decoy. It's been reported stolen already and I've left the keys in the pocket of the man's clothes I swapped."

"Your flashy Arabic pants?"

"Those are the ones."

"Authentic. I'm surprised you didn't bring a camel," Rashid smirked.

King led the way to the end of the road where the second hire car had been delivered. "This is us," he said.

"Nice wheels," Rashid said.

"Well, it was on expenses," King said. He reached around into the inside of the driver's side front wheel arch and felt for the key fob where he had instructed the manager to leave it. King opened the door of the Jaguar F-Type and dropped down into the snug leather seat. Rashid eased himself in a little more tentatively.

"Nice expense budget," Rashid said, looking around the dashboard and the array of switches. He looked down the long bonnet. "This car is just a giant cock," he said. "I guess we're the balls holding it down."

King started the five litre supercharged V8 and gunned the throttle. The engine and exhaust note resonated around the parked cars and quiet houses, and as they sped down the road he could hear the sirens of the police vehicles arriving in front of the mosque and see the flashing blue strobes dance off the trees and reflect off the windows of the houses in the otherwise tranquil street.

68

Droznedov, or the man claiming to be Droznedov, ate from the buffet breakfast at seven o'clock. He drank black coffee and ate bread rolls, cheese and ham, ignoring the traditional cooked English breakfast buffet. He took a bottle of water from the buffet table as he left the restaurant and went back to his room. The man and the woman from MI5 posing as a couple called through on a hidden microphone. The woman reported that the target had left the dining room and that he was heading for the stairs. They had taken breakfast together since the dining room had opened, refilling their coffees and toasting their own toast and croissants on the conveyer grill and reading the complimentary newspaper at the table. They appeared unhurried, and because of the rapid turnaround of guests at breakfast they did not draw attention.

 Droznedov walked past the tiny middle-aged Asian woman cleaning the glass on the stairwell. He stood aside to allow a man past. He was a curious looking man with striking features and severely parted hair. It looked like *Lego* hair. He seemed to look fit, but wore a cheap fleece tracksuit and dated basketball shoes. He stopped at the top of the stairs and performed a few lunges before jogging down. Droznedov walked on. The cleaner used a spray and cloth to clean away the fingerprints guests had smeared on their way down to breakfast. When Droznedov stepped out of the stairwell and onto the landing of the fifth floor she spoke into her concealed throat mic and informed the next unit that the target was heading for his room.

The hotel was a transient place by its very nature. But throughout the week business people tended to stay only one night and housekeeping were already pulling carts laden with bedding and sheets and towels into the corridor, set for a rapid turnaround in rooms to be thoroughly remade. Droznedov pushed past one such cart and swiped his door with the key card. One of the women stacking towels pressed a contact button three times in quick succession on her concealed radio. She pushed the cart on past room five-fourteen and continued to stack towels further down the corridor with her eyes on the target's room.

The noise created by pressing the contact button three times was known as a coded burst and Caroline noted that the target was back inside his room. She looked up at Brannan as he came into the office. "The target is static. That must have been bloody close."

"Too close by far. But I have a tracker in his overnight bag and another in the lining of his coat." Brannan pulled the tracksuit off and started to pull on his suit trousers. "We have to get ready for him to leave. My team are in place. Your driver knows the score, doesn't he?"

"He will do as I say," Caroline said. "We let the equipment do what it does and we follow from a distance of about a mile. Never in sight. And I have called my police contact, he will be here with SOCO as soon as we leave. I just have to give him the word."

"Excellent." He turned around and answered his mobile which was ringing to the *Mission Impossible* theme tune. Caroline smiled and turned back to the log to give the man some privacy. He listened intently, paced, then cursed loudly. Caroline looked up, but he was muttering instructions quickly and urgently. He ended the call. "Sod's law. The Hertz driver has been hit by a bus. Badly. The vehicle is a write-off. They're sending another right away, but now we only have time to put a locator on it. It's the same as I have secreted in his possessions, but only transmits to a maximum of three miles, weather and atmospheric conditions permitting."

Caroline closed her eyes. Not good. She stood up and smoothed her dress down over her legs. "Will the receiver you fitted in my car still pick up?"

Brannan nodded. "We'll make sure the locator puts out on the same frequency. But you will have to keep fairly close. If you're at the extremity of signal and he floors it to a junction, you could sail on past and lose him. And you don't want that, do you?"

69

The table was sturdy, made from thick pine, but even so he had reinforced it with concrete blocks purchased from a local home improvements chain store based on an out of town shopping complex. The blocks ran from the floor to the underside of the table around all four legs and in the centre. The warhead had been disassembled and the delivery system, the cone shaped warhead, had been set aside.

The initiation system for the warhead consisted of two kilogrammes of thermite explosive. This was detonated in much the same way as any plastic explosive or IED by use of a detonator which would explode into the explosive compound by means of electrical current. Only in this case the two kilogrammes of thermite explosive would act merely as the detonator. On its own enough to take down a row of houses or turn a battle tank to hulk of twisted metal, but it would take an explosion of this magnitude to drive the three kilogramme polonium rod down into the five kilogramme segmented honeycombed plutonium chamber to initiate fission and in turn, create the cataclysmic reaction to create a thermo-nuclear explosion. The devastation created would destroy the intended target one hundred times over, but the weapon grade uranium would do more damage. It had been Zukovsky's intention to use the resources he had been aware of, stored deep below the earth in Epping Forest, to create a devastating explosion and shockwave throughout London. But he had needed both Iman Mullah Al-Shaqqaf's involvement and Professor Orlev's expertise in the construction of the device. And although Al-Shaqqaf had wanted to strike at the heart of the British establishment and claim a victory for Islam, he had vetoed the centre of London. Orlev had explained the warhead's relatively limited footprint when detonated at ground level. The weapon had been designed as an aerial delivery system, to be initiated and detonate between one thousand and two thousand feet above the target. Al-Shaqqaf had been happy with that. But it was Zukovsky's talk of the uranium stores to create a larger and deadlier weapon that had given the Iman his doubts. The cleric was not a foolish man. He knew that total annihilation of the city centre would cause more threat to Islam than it would to strengthen his Muslim brothers' resolve and take up arms against the west. Professor Orlev had ventured that if the uranium were to be stored next to the device, but still sealed in the lead flasks and not directly detonated in the same manner as the plutonium, then it was highly probable, at least eighty-five percent, that it would create a dirty bomb. The initial explosion would be vast, destroying almost everything within a two-mile radius, but it would render the area, at least a fifty-mile radius, off limits for the next forty years or more.

A British Chernobyl.

Once that had been established as a possible scenario, both Zukovsky and Al-Shaqqaf could finally find plenty to agree on. There was a wealth of targets to choose from, but there was also the big picture. The future. Zukovsky had a list of detailed targets for the first strike of a Soviet Union nuclear attack on Britain. It was an old paper dating back to 1985, but it was clear that not much had changed. He had picked one of the targets for its proximity to an important Soviet area of interest. Not just Soviet, or indeed now Russian, or other enemies of Britain, but for the wound it would inflict upon British security.

Zukovsky had hired Professor Orlev for his superior expertise in nuclear weapons and delivery systems. Orlev had gone off the radar. Something had happened. He knew the old professor was out of the game. But Zukovsky had served in every unit in the Soviet and Russian Federation army. He had been a medic, and scout and sniper, an artillery spotter, had performed a stint in Spetsnaz specialising in urban warfare and hostage rescue and as a bomb disposal specialist. And people who took bombs apart knew how to build them. And what he had in front of him was a bomb. He understood all of the components and he was competent with the process of electrical initiation and timing delays. He had studied Orlev's notes and had learned all he could by researching the internet on the stages of nuclear reaction. He did not have the knowledge required for detonating the uranium, but as Orlev had explained, it needed merely to be in close proximity to become a dirty bomb.

Zukovsky wore an NBC mask and non-porous rubber gloves to handle the honeycomb of plutonium into place. The base plate of plutonium sat on a piece of steel drain cover he had taken from the side of the road. He had drilled the plutonium plate using a water-cooled drill bit on an extremely low speed, high torque setting. The plutonium plate was then bolted through the drain cover and the table and reamed tightly with washers and wing nuts. He then heated the nuts with a blow-torch, fusing the threads. He had built a sturdy cradle out of a cut-down step ladder to hold the polonium rod just above the plutonium. The first few inches of the rod were inside the honeycomb with a half-centimetre gap all of the way around. The thermite explosive had been shaped around the other end of the rod using the funnelling method. The explosive was shaped like a triangle, the thinnest part at the end of the rod and the thickest part packed closest to the plutonium. Detonation from the RDX detonators inside the thermite would grow in intensity, millisecond upon millisecond, but the greater the explosion at the end of the chain acted as a driving force much like the slow burn explosion of a bullet from a case inside a rifle breach. The polonium rod would accelerate into the plutonium honeycomb at thousands of feet per second and at hundreds of thousands of foot pounds in kinetic energy. The honeycomb would absorb and spread the energy and create the highest temperature from the reaction creating fission. It was the exact opposite of nuclear energy or fusion, an uncontrolled and erratic breakdown of stability.

Alesha entered slowly, cautiously. She was dressed the same as Zukovsky and carried another of the lead uranium flasks. She was flushed, breathing heavily through the thick rubber mask. She placed the flask next to the others under the table and looked at him earnestly.

The mask hid her terrible burns, but it rubbed them and she was irritable. "Are you finished?"

"Not yet, my dear," he paused. "I have to fit the detonators and the timing device."

"How long?" she asked. "I'm freaking out with that thing here."

"Just keep bringing in the flasks. It will not be long now."

"We need Professor Orlev for this. How do you know we have not been irradiated?"

"Orlev is either dead or has been captured. Along with Sergei Gulubkin, he is finished." Zukovsky nodded towards a box on the table which sat amongst the components. It was constructed from orange plastic and the size of an early nineties Nokia phone. "Geiger counter, commercial grade," he said. "See the readout? It detects the beta pulses. It's not ideal, we're in the high end of the safe zone. I wouldn't have an x-ray for a few years, but we are not close to radioactive threat."

Alesha backed away nonetheless. "Well hurry up and get it done," she said and walked out for the last flask of uranium.

Zukovsky turned back to his work. He would fit the timer last and would not set it until he had met with Al-Shaqqaf and his men. They wanted to film a propaganda video in front of it before a known and wanted ISIS fighter was to detonate it. Zukovsky had met the man before, a small but evil looking character with a large scar on his face. He had felt uneasy in his company, and given his hatred of Islamic extremists, it had been difficult to talk to the man about the weapon. This particular extremist was wanted for his part in the execution videos of several western aid workers in Syria during the early days of the war.

Zukovsky looked up at the window. He had a clear but distant view of the principal target, but the far reaches of the weapon in every direction were of equal importance in striking at the heart of his enemy. He had waited so long for this, and now he was so close he could barely breathe with anticipation.

70

"Where are you?"

"I've dropped Rashid off at hospital, I'm in your flat. Just had a shower and change of clothes. Where are you?"

"I've just merged with the M40 from the A40, heading northwest. We're following Droznedov, but he's not Droznedov. The real Droznedov checked in, but has disappeared. What were you doing with Rashid?"

"Complicated. I'll tell you later. He was a stalking horse for me."

"A what?"

"A way of bringing in something I would need," King paused. He was attempting to dress with the phone to his ear. It had reached the point for a hand change. *"Turns out he was a bit more helpful than that."*

"Do you have a vehicle?"

"Oh yes."

"Well I hope it's a fast one because you need to get up here and see how this plays out."

"Shouldn't be a problem."

"Well get going and call me when you're on the M40. I'll let you know where we are."

"We?"

"I have a security officer driving me. And a watcher team is up front. We have a tracker on the target and his vehicle, but last minute problems meant it's nothing more than sixties technology."

"I'll be with you shortly," King said.

Caroline turned in her seat and leaned in towards the window. She spoke softly, quietly. "I wanted to talk to you about yesterday afternoon," she paused and whispered. "At my place."

"We'll talk later. No problems my end. But I'd better get going if I'm to catch you up."

Caroline felt a little flushed. King had ended the call. She had not even considered a date since her fiancé's death, let alone imagined being intimate with another man. And she had never done what they had so soon after meeting someone. Not even with Peter. Maybe it was the threat of the warhead hanging over them, the missing agents or the death of so many innocent people around them, but being with King had made her feel so alive. For a brief while, all had been forgotten and she felt safe and warm and needed. She had felt guilt too, but to her surprise not at having finally moved on, but for Watkins, for Mathews, for the Special Branch officers, for Forester – people who would never feel again.

"You okay?" Frank asked.

Caroline nodded. "Hell of a week." Frank slowed the car considerably and moved over to the inside lane. Caroline looked at the laptop resting on her lap and realised what he was doing. "Well played," she said.

The intermittent dot had slowed and was entering the slip road of a services. Frank held back and eased into the carpark in the first space he saw.

Caroline dialled Brannan's number. The surveillance team leader picked up on the first ring.

"Hello, we saw it too," Brannan said. "Have you pulled in or carried on past?"

"Pulled in."

"Well, it won't matter because he can't get off the motorway for another eight or ten miles. You can wait out, or get back on the motorway and stay under fifty in the inside lane. From how he's been driving he'll sail right past you before the next exit."

"No way, he's seen me, remember? We've spent time together." She thought of how he'd grabbed her by her hair, humiliated her. The threat he had made to her. Maybe he would forget her, but she knew she'd never forget the man's face. "One unlucky sideways glance and he could recognise me. Besides, we don't know how long he's stopping for. And anybody travelling that slow will get a look from most people as they pass."

"Fair enough," Brannan conceded. "I'll send one of my team in for a peek."

"Well just don't spook him," Caroline said and ended the call.

***

Hodges opened the door to the hotel room and turned to the scenes of crime officer. "I'll check it over first, then you can go do your thing. Finger prints and DNA swabs on whatever you can get."

"I know what to look for," the SOCO woman said curtly. "Just don't touch anything. And this is a hotel room, there'll be tens, if not hundreds of trace elements from previous guests."

Hodges reached into his pocket and retrieved a pair of latex medical gloves. He slipped them on and held them up for approval. Smiled when he got no reaction at all from the dour woman. "Well let's just hope the Holiday Inn staff do a thorough clean on a changeover and got rid of a lot of previous traces," he said and stepped inside.

The room was tidy. The man claiming to be Droznedov had been thorough. He had even made the bed, which Hodges guessed was to eliminate the chance of leaving anything behind under the sheets or the bed itself. There was nothing to look at, nothing out of place. The room was not that big to start with and Hodges could see all there was to see from where he was standing. He dropped down and looked under the bed, but it was clean. He opened the door to the bathroom carefully and saw the body straight away. After all his time as a homicide detective it still made him flinch. "Major Droznedov, I presume," he said quietly.

The body stared back at him, the eyes dry and dull. It had slumped low in the bath and the legs had bent upwards and outwards. There was a faint swelling and bruising on one eye and the nose was bloodied. The right arm looked to be broken at an impossible angle. *That would have been the game changer,* Hodges thought. Whatever fight the two men had had, the arm would have meant the end for Droznedov. Hodges looked the body over and could see the neck was distorted. He could imagine the two men fighting, Droznedov was a Russian GRU major. He would have been through a great deal of specialist training at some point; he would not have been an easy opponent. The other man had dealt a savage blow to the arm, most probably a striking forearm block or a kick, then snapped the Russian's neck as he had writhed in agony.

Hodges took out his phone and dialled. It answered on three rings. "Caroline, Hodges," he said curtly. "I have a body who I suspect to be the real Major Droznedov. Broken neck, most likely. SOCO are going to go over the room now. I'll get a pathologist on it right away, but the injuries are pretty obvious."

"Thanks," Caroline said. *"Any ID to confirm it?"*

"Not yet. I'll check and call you back." Hodges ended the call and pocketed his phone. He reached into the inside pocket of the man's jacket. Nothing. He tried the other one and felt the thick wallet and pulled it out. He looked at the jacket curiously, something seemed to snag, pulling the material of the shirt underneath. He looked at the wallet and frowned at the length of wire and the ring pin fastened to it. It looked like the wire had been twisted around many times to keep it in place. He had never seen a security measure like it, and it seemed to have little effect as he had managed to pull it clear. It did not even dawn on him when the blinding light hit him a millisecond before the shockwave of the explosion which lifted him off his feet and threw him through the plastered and tiled partition wall and out into the bedroom where his body fell at the foot of the bed. Lifeless, broken and still.

71

"Moving on."

"We're on it," Caroline said. "We'll maintain our rear position. Give him half a mile or so. Any eyes on at the services?"

"He went to the men's room, bought a bottle of water and some cigarettes."

"I do hope he hasn't been spooked."

"My man was invisible, walked out ahead of him and back to the car without looking back."

"We could do with topping up the tank," Frank interjected.

"Brannan, we're going to do a quick fuel stop," she said, leaning across and looking at the gauge. "Half a tank, so we'll be about five-minutes tops."

"Have that, will call and update as we go. You may need to get a foot down though."

"No problem," Frank smiled.

"Will do," Caroline said and ended the call.

Frank pulled up to the pump and got out. Caroline watched the screen of the laptop and saw that from being stationary, Droznedov was moving across the map at an alarmingly swift rate. She looked up at Frank through the rear window and saw that he was hanging up the pump. There was no pay-at-pump facility and she watched the man walk swiftly to the kiosk. He was less swift as he perused the confectionary aisle. Caroline hit the horn, but it did not work without the keys in the ignition. She cursed inwardly, then relaxed a little as she saw him pay. "Come on, don't wait for a bloody receipt!" she said, then watched as he walked back across the forecourt. She caught his eye and beckoned him to hurry.

"What's up?" he asked, dropping into his seat.

"He's off the bloody screen," she said sharply. "Come on, let's get going. Foot down!"

"Yes, my lady," he smirked. The car sped forwards and he glanced over his shoulder as he entered the exit, floored the accelerator and kept changing up through the gears. They left the slip road and entered the slow lane at one hundred miles per hour and kept on their course to the outside lane where the car touched one-hundred and twenty. "There's been a major ECU remap on this vehicle's engine. It does about one-forty but gets there pretty damned quickly."

"Well let's see how long it takes to get him back on the screen." Her mobile started to ring and she answered it, seeing that it was Brannan from the caller ID. "Yes?"

"He's got his foot to the floor. We're up around one-twenty. It's right at the top of our vehicle's speed limit. We stand to lose him if he goes much faster. If plod see this and get involved we're in the smelly stuff."

"Do you think he's trying to shake you off?"

"I'm not sure, it seems a bit erratic behaviour."

"I can't see him yet," Caroline said, finding it difficult to keep her eyes on the screen as Frank slowed for a last minute manoeuvre from a car drifting across the lanes in front. "Where are you?"

"Just past Junction Five."

"We're at Four. That's eight miles or so on the map," she turned to Frank. "Foot to the floor!"

"He's slowing up," Brannan said. *"He's shifted lanes; it looks like he might be coming off at Six. Either that or he's seen plod up ahead."* Caroline kept the phone to her ear and her eyes on the screen. She said nothing and nor did Brannan. *"No, he's gone past. He's doing around ninety, and so is everyone else by the look of it."*

"Call if there's any change, I need to save my phone's battery." She ended the call, but the phone rang instantly. King's mobile number. She felt her heart skip a little. Then she blushed feeling like a teenager. "Hi. Where are you?"

"Junction Five."

"Jesus! What are you in, a rocket?"

"As good as. Where are you?"

"A mile or two in front of you. Blue Ford Mondeo. Registration ending CMB," she recalled from memory.

"I'll pull in behind you."

"What are you driving?"

"Red Jag. An F-Type sports car."

"Subtle."

"Well, it was on expenses." King said dryly. *"And sometimes being a bit noticeable can actually make you go unnoticed."*

"Like Magnum PI and his Ferrari?" she laughed. "Whatever. I'll scrutinise your receipts from now on," she said and ended the call. She turned back to the laptop screen and frowned. The display finally showed an intermittent red dot, but the moment it had appeared there was suddenly two and one veered left, the other carried on along the motorway. Her mobile rang. It was Brannan. "What's going on?"

"I'm not sure. It can't be equipment failure, all I can say is that the suspect is going one way and the vehicle is going the other."

"Or the suspect *and* the vehicle are going one way and his tracker is going the other."

"Look, I'm pulling off and going after the beacon on the minor road. You stay on the motorway. See if you can catch up and get a visual. You'll stand a better chance than we will. The roads off the motorway will be twisty single lanes or dual carriageway. He won't test our top-end speed. And if we try for a visual, he may well make us. We'll keep back a mile and see what happens."

"Okay, but keep me posted," Caroline ended the call and looked around. She could see the gleaming red Jaguar with King behind the wheel. He was following closely. She scrolled down her phone and dialled his number. "That was quick."

"I might not be handing this back."

"Droznedov's signal has split. The watcher team leader thinks it might be a case of target gone one way and the vehicle has been taken another. He stopped at Beaconsfield services, it looks as if he had someone waiting there. They've kept close enough to appear as a single signal. But they've played their hand now," she said, then felt a pang of grief as she thought of Forester and his habit of card game or gambling comparisons.

"I'll shoot on ahead, take a look, then drop back. How far ahead is your signal?"

"A mile. A white Audi A4 saloon. We're right on the cusp of the signal, but that way the target won't know we're following. I think this may just be an elaborate counter-surveillance measure." King powered past, accelerating the car with its big V8 engine and whirring supercharger to over twice the legal limit. The exhausts bellowed, the sports car shot forward and the Ford seemed to be going backwards. "Alex, he's taking the junction. Back off, it looks like he's going to Oxford. He's on the slip-road now. Can you see him?"

"No. I'm not there yet," King paused. *"Right, I see the slip-road now. There's a lorry on it. No car. One small hatchback just pulling onto it."*

"No, he's off the slip-road now. Back off, we'll come past you and you follow us. It will be less obvious than that penis substitution you're in…" She leaned towards the window, shielding the phone. "…Which, by the way, you don't need." She glanced towards Frank, who was grinning. She felt herself flush red.

King hammered on the brakes and slowed all the way up the ramp and pulled in onto the gravelled shoulder before the lights. Two cars passed him, then Caroline and Frank in the blue Mondeo. King pulled back out and they took the exit off the roundabout in unison. King backed off a few car lengths and the two vehicles settled to fifty miles per hour. The next twenty minutes were spent weaving through roundabouts and taking various roads until they ended up on the A44 travelling towards Chipping Norton.

Caroline answered her phone. It was Brannan. "Yes?"

"Just to advise you, we are on the hire car. The white Audi. We've drawn close enough for a confirmed visual. We can't see if it is the target inside. My gut feeling is that you are with the target and we have been following a vehicle switch. I personally stitched the tracker into his jacket and the lining of his travel bag. I can't see him discovering it in the time frame."

"Where are you?"

"Just hit the A41 travelling towards Hemel Hampstead. It seems like we're doing a big loop back to London."

"Well stay with it. We need a visual on the target. *Not* just his vehicle."

After forty minutes or so they had taken a right-angle south-west and were on the A436 via a winding route. They had yet to have the opportunity for a visual. Brannan had called to say that he was travelling clockwise on the M25 circular. He was making calls to access the traffic control cameras and attempt a visual on the driver.

Small towns and villages came and went and still they could not see what make of vehicle they were following. After Bourton-on-Water they turned off the main road and took a series of country lanes. Frank closed the gap to half a mile. There did not seem to be any other vehicles in front.

"Be careful Frank," Caroline said. "Out here he'll spot a tail if we show ourselves."

Frank looked at the screen and the road ahead. The map on the screen showed a series of turns. Frank started to close the gap in the bends, then backed off for the straights. All the while they could hear the Jaguar behind burbling as King took his foot off the throttle.

"Can you bring up the scale on that map?" Frank asked.

Caroline looked at the operating tool bar and clicked on the magnifying glass icon. The screen display enlarged. "It looks like he's pulled off the road and is travelling down a track. That looks like a farm." She pointed at the map. "The track is definitely a dead end," she said, looking up at the hedges and sweeping fields beyond. "Pull in, I want to talk to King."

72

The farmhouse looked old and unkempt. The house itself was large. Two storey with six windows on the top floor. King could see that the building went back a way too. He imagined six or more large bedrooms and a large bathroom on the top floor and two or three large reception rooms downstairs. Maybe a kitchen with a range. Certainly the house looked to have seen better days. There were various outbuildings and a large shed that was like an aircraft hangar approximately one hundred metres from the house.

"Vegetable packing station," Caroline said. "That's what it reminds me of. My uncle had one in Devon and I used to stay for a week or so in the summers when I was a girl."

"Doesn't look busy packing vegetables now," King observed.

"Looks to me like a bankruptcy. Hence the lack of crops in the fields or animals," she said, pointing to the stretch of empty fields beyond the house. "The fields are fallow. I expect this farm felt the pinch from supermarkets either not paying enough, or holding off from paying altogether for too long, and sooner or later it was too late."

"So do you think they're squatting in there?"

"No. I imagine they're renting it, or have a short term arrangement with the bank or agents representing the claimants. The plaintiffs are long gone."

"You know a lot about such things," King said, studying the house through the binoculars.

"My uncle went bust the same way. It was very sad."

"Did he get over it?"

"No. He shot himself. Highest suicide rate of any profession, and most farmers own a shotgun," she shook her head. "We all eat, but we don't ask the right questions or want to pay enough for our food."

King didn't answer. He could see it was still raw for her. "Droznedov, or whoever the hell he is has just gone inside."

"Do you think the device is here?"

King looked across the fields and at the fringe of houses in the distance. Beyond it he knew the target. He had thought as much when they were twenty miles out. He had walked its corridors, eaten in its cafeterias and been briefed in the many briefing rooms. "Without a doubt," he said.

Caroline nodded. "Why are you so sure?" King stepped down from the hedge and walked back to the Jaguar. Caroline followed. She stood on the uneven grass verge. "Why are you so sure?" she repeated.

"I should have seen it sooner," he said. "It's not just the proximity, it's what lies at the very reaches."

"I don't understand," Caroline looked at him earnestly. "What is the significance?"

"That's Cheltenham down there," King replied. "Or the suburbs."

"GCHQ, oh Christ!" she exclaimed. "I didn't pick up on it, didn't realise quite where we were."

"We didn't exactly come by the most direct route." King took a road atlas out of the foot well of the Jaguar and opened it to the relevant page. He walked around and placed the map on the vehicle's sleek bonnet. "Here's Cheltenham." He pointed, then drew his finger out two miles. The explosion would take out everything in here." He drew a circle around with his finger.

"Here," Caroline said, taking a pen out of her handbag. She glanced expectantly at her mobile. "Hodges was going to call me back. He discovered a body in the target's room. The real Droznedov no doubt, but he hasn't updated me."

"Doesn't seem like him. But you've been on your phone non-stop." King circled the area a few times. "That is the blast radius. And if it's here, on this farm, then there is nothing much in the way to stop it. GCHQ will be gone for sure. Along with it the cleverest people working in intelligence, some would say the country, if not the world. With them is the infrastructure, databases and equipment only they know about. This is a serious target, it will take Britain back fifty years in terms of our hold on the world stage in intelligence, both criminal and foreign and domestic terrorism and counter espionage." King drew a point about forty miles out circled the radius. My guess is that would be a dirty bomb's reach going on the amount of flasks of uranium that Rashid talked about. It's an estimate but a fair one."

Caroline looked at the area inside. "The SAS base at Hereford," she said, pointing inside the circle.

"You've got about ten military barracks, bases or airfields at a quick estimation," he ran his finger over the map. "There's Cirencester there. Bristol docks, that's commerce killed right there."

"Oh my God, look!" Caroline pointed to an area in Gloucestershire. "That's the source of the River Thames. Contamination will flow right through London."

"We need to move," said King.

He folded the map and walked around to the rear of the Jaguar and opened the boot. He reached inside and opened the sports bag, started taking out the remaining spare magazines for the SCAR rifle. Caroline checked her Walther.

"We should call for some back-up," Caroline said. "Armed police or the SAS."

"We don't know what time we've got. And this is the end, right here. Everything Forester wanted done, for good or bad. If the police come in at this stage, then the truth will come out. Islamic extremists directly involved with ISIS on British soil were behind an attempt to use a nuclear weapon," he said, shaking his head. "And with the involvement of Russians? Nobody will believe it was one man's vendetta. Taking down MI5 and GCHQ in an act of ultimate vengeance? Killing hundreds of thousands of people? The public will see it as a direct Russian attack."

"So we just go in and kill them?"

"I don't think it will be that easy."

"You can bet your ass it won't be." The woman's voice carried behind them. King started to move but a gunshot rang out and he froze, a large clean hole punched through the boot lid and shattered the rear window. "Hands! Let me see them!"

Caroline dropped the pistol in the boot and raised her arms slowly. King gave her a look, but she shook her head adamantly. The SCAR was still in the bag. He'd never make it. King followed suit, slowly turned to face the direction of the voice. It was slow, guttural. He could see the barrel and front sight of the Kalashnikov, the eyes of the woman lined up behind it. She rose slowly and King could see the shapely face, the attractive features of Alesha Mikailovitch. She kept the weapon trained on them as she stepped unsteadily on top of the hedge. King could see the burn marks across her cheek. As she sat down and slid down the hedge he could see the nasty scabbing burns and scarring on one side of her face. The burn had been so fierce it had cratered and changed the profile.

"There is a God," she said, looking at Caroline. "How I prayed I'd meet *you* again."

"Third time lucky," said Caroline coldly.

"For me, but not for you," Alesha smiled, then frowned. "Third?"

"We met at Hoist's flat. I just missed you," Caroline smirked. "Just before you ran away."

She glared at her, then shrugged. Like it was of no consequence. The ball was now back in her court. She moved around them, keeping an expert four paces of distance between them. She kept the weapon held tightly into her shoulder, although she was no longer aiming, but at this distance she could not miss. King noticed she had flicked the selector up a notch to full-auto. One move and she would make strawberry jam of them. "Put your hands on your head and walk in front of me. Down the lane. Do it now!"

73

"I expect by now you're wondering what all of this is about?" Vladimir Zukovsky smiled.

King stood against the wall of the kitchen. It was as he had imagined. Long and wide and heated by a wood-burning range. Alesha, standing to the side of Zukovsky, covered both Caroline and King with the AK47. Droznedov placed his Makarov pistol on the kitchen work surface, stepped forwards and grabbed hold of Caroline. He pulled her away from King and pushed her against the kitchen counter. He frisked her, patting her down over her back and stomach, under her arms, down her legs to her knees, back up. He lingered near her crotch, then ran a hand over both breasts. She flinched and he smiled. "Ah, is it still sore? I was looking forward to seeing you again."

"Your boy done?" King said. Droznedov turned and King stared at him. The Russian sneered, but he was the one who looked uncomfortable. He held the stare for a while, then looked away.

Zukovsky smirked. "Now, now. Play nicely."

Droznedov pushed Caroline down into a chair which was turned out from the table. He walked over and stood in front of King.

"Turn around," he said.
"Make me."
"I'll shoot you."
"Your gun's over there."

Droznedov backed away, smiling. He picked up the pistol.

"Enough!" Zukovsky snapped. "Dimitri, cover them. Alesha, search him."

"Dimitri. Not Uri Droznedov then?" King smirked.

"No, alas, the real Major Uri Droznedov was unfortunate collateral damage," Zukovsky said.

"Unfortunate?"

"Yes. How you say, a terrier? He just kept digging."

Alesha patted King down his sides, she tried to turn him around but he resisted. She heaved at him, but he remained firmly in his stance. She concentrated on moving him, not wanting to lose face, reached around him and patted his back around the waistband. She retrieved the flick-knife from his pocket.

King eyed her closely. "Nice face," he whispered, almost in her ear.

She glared at him, went to slap him then thought better of it. She backed away, smiling. She walked past both men and took a pan out of the cupboard. She reached high up on a shelf and retrieved a large kiln jar of sugar, poured it into the pan and then lifted the lid of the range and placed the pan on top. She walked back to the table and picked up the AK47. She smiled down at Caroline, gave her a wink.

"So, as I was saying, you were wondering what all of this is about." Vladimir Zukovsky said.

"Not really," said King.

Zukovsky tried to hide his surprise. "No?"

"Well, I'm wondering how your man here did the car switch."

Dimitri smiled. "One of Gulubkin's men. I wasn't sure you would be on to me, but we are professionals. We take that sort of thing into account."

"And Gulubkin?" King asked.

"I gave him a simple out. He never knew where we were going to detonate the device, but he realised there was no way out for him. Not even if he talked. The filter of the cigarette was packed with cyanide."

"Anything else?" Zukovsky smirked.

"No. I think we have the gist of it." King looked at Caroline. "Nothing really for them to add?"

Caroline was staring anxiously at the pan on the stove. She looked back at King, her face ashen. "No, I think we have it worked out."

"Indulge me," Vladimir Zukovsky said. "Let me see how close you got."

King shrugged, leaned back against the counter. "Your son gets killed in a British attack on ISIS in Syria. You blame British intelligence, you find out who was involved and you make your own hit-list."

Zukovsky nodded. "Good. And?"

"You blame ISIS. Islamic extremists. You want them eliminated at source and you find out who recruited, indoctrinated and financed the ISIS cell or group. You want them not only dead, but you want to stoke the fires of the west, get them behind the cause of seeing Islamic extremism wiped out. How's that?"

"Good."

"They're not coming," King paused. "Iman Mullah Al-Shaqqaf and his mob. They're all dead.

Including the suicide bomber that was to have set off your warhead."

Zukovsky smiled. "I expected no less. Thank you."

King frowned, he glanced across at Caroline, who in turn was watching the pan of boiling sugar on the stove. She looked terrified. He looked back at Zukovsky. "Okay, we're missing something. Are you going to indulge us?"

The old man smiled. "You have deduced your theory, and you have done well. It was exactly what we wanted you to believe. You followed the breadcrumbs, joined the dots, fitted the missing pieces." He patted the man Dimitri on the shoulder. "This is Dimitri Zukovsky," he said. "My son."

"Son number one, or son number two?" asked King.

The old man smiled. "Number one," he patted Dimitri on the back. "I've only ever had one son."

"So there was no Russian Spetsnaz soldier sacrificed by British intelligence."

"Oh, there was, but not my son. That was a nice touch, don't you think? Dimitri was there, went missing in action for a while but got out, escaping into Turkey. He was injured, but made his way back to Russia. We gave the dead soldier Dimitri's identification, his life. This allowed Dimitri to disappear, lay the plans for this. Work behind the scenes. My team, apart from Alesha that is, all thought Dimitri was dead."

"I even told your boss Howard about it before I killed him," Dimitri Zukovsky said. "All calls are recorded; it will all add to the deception."

"So what was your motive for all this, if not revenge?" asked Caroline.

Zukovsky smiled. "Many, many motives... But nothing you will have considered. You see, I worked for most of my life to do two things. Prevent an attack on Russia from the west, or attack the west. There were wars and insurgencies in between, but primarily that was what the Soviet Union trained for. And then we became as bad as the west. We found money and western values, celebrity culture and unearned entitlement. But not all of us feel this way. Look at the Ukraine for example. Separatists aided and funded by a hard core of true patriots. We have given enough away and we will give no more. We are not only strengthening our borders, but we aim to weaken our enemies."

"A few demoralised underachievers? You'll have to do better than that," King scoffed.

"We have led you a merry dance! Destroyed your so called Security Service!"

"You killed three people due to retire within five years. We know about the hostages, where they were heading, the name of the boat. If we don't have them back yet, we soon will."

"A decoy! Some busy work for you to worry about, to draw pointless conclusions, to waste your time while we brought in a nuclear device under your noses!"

Caroline took her eyes off the pan. The steam was rising steadily, the burnt caramel filling the room with a bitter odour. "So your plan was to set off the bomb and get away?"

"Of course!"

"But we know your identity," she said. "You'll be hunted down."

"By whom? We will be rewarded, receive new identities. Medals, even!"

"Medals?"

Zukovsky grinned, nodded emphatically. "Of course! This is sanctioned! This directive has come from the Kremlin itself. It was carefully conceived, even the GRU were tasked with investigating so there was always a trail and if the operation was pulled, nothing would stick to the men in power. Major Droznedov was sacrificed for authenticity, to cover the government and lay a false trail. This is the culmination of a task I was given in the mid-eighties. Then the wall came down, the Iron Curtain, as your prime minister at the time called it, and suddenly there were no more operations to plan, no more ground to be gained. I have waited half my life for this moment. This operation was Russian policy!"

"It can't be," Caroline said quietly.

"Every day, Russian aircraft probe your borders, stray into your airspace. You send an interceptor as a show of force, we move away. But every day, we go a little further, a little lower. Every week we send more," Zukovsky smirked. "After the warhead wipes out your global communications at GCHQ, irradiates and contaminates your SAS at Hereford, all of the personnel in ten military installations within the fallout of our dirty bomb, including a US airbase, these Russian aircraft will be full of paratroopers. One hundred thousand troops dropped all over your feeble little land, they will target the police and have details of all your politicians, your local government. They will kill or capture anybody in a civil service role."

"And the president is behind this?"

Zukovsky scoffed. "Not likely! But if we are successful, he will be assassinated and the man who will take his place orchestrated this mission. We will have a strong leader and a dominant presence on the world stage."

"You'll have war!" Caroline spat at him.

"Which we will win!"

Alesha walked over to the range and placed her AK47 on the worktop. She picked up the pan and smiled. Dimitri Zukovsky aimed his pistol at Caroline. Alesha walked over slowly, held the pan low. "Look what we have here," she said. "You see what you did to me? You bitch!" Caroline glanced at King, then looked at the pan. She could see the froth of brown foaming caramel continuing to boil even though it was no longer on the stove. Alesha came closer. "You will not believe how much it hurts." Caroline backed into the chair. Dimitri kept the pistol firm and steady. He was smiling. "It burns for hours afterwards," Alesha teased. "And you will look far worse than I do!"

King straightened up, but Zukovsky senior shook his head, his pistol held loosely at waist level.

Caroline shook her head. "Don't! Please!" She backed up further in the chair, it almost toppled but the heavy farmhouse table behind her held it firm.

"Beg, bitch!" Alesha said through clenched teeth. She held it out for Caroline to see. "You will wish you were dead when it eats through your pretty pale skin…"

Caroline flung herself forwards and kicked the pan. It upended and hit Alesha full in the face, her eyes and mouth taking the brunt of molten sugar. Every person in the room felt her scream reverberate within them. Dimitri and Vladimir stared on in horror as Alesha fell to the floor and wailed, but the wail became a gargle as the sugar in her mouth started to set and blocked her burnt airway. Her throat swelled, slowly but steadily closing off her air supply.

King took the kitchen in three strides and punched Dimitri in the face. The Russian started to go down, but fired his pistol as he turned. Caroline screamed, but soon regained composure and was out of the chair and heading towards Vladimir Zukovsky, only she was sticking to the floor on the cooling caramel. Dimitri fired again, but King had control of the man's arm and was dragging it with him to the floor. Vladimir Zukovsky ran for the internal door and slammed it shut after him. Dimitri and King were fighting for possession of the pistol. King managed to get the gun hand out straight, then slipped his left forearm around Dimitri's chin and onto his throat. He pushed down with both arms, and his upper-body strength advantage soon had the Russian groaning, but he pressed his knee deep into the centre of the man's spine to unbalance him further. Simple physics meant something would soon give, and King shunted his position a little to make sure that it was the man's neck which gave out first. Dimitri's head started to turn upwards at an impossible angle and he grunted more as his neck was forced simply too far. There was an audible 'crack' and the man went limp.

King let him drop to the floor and stepped towards Caroline.

"Oh my God! You're hit!" she exclaimed.

King looked down and saw the blood on his shirt, he started to look unsteady on his feet. The wound was under his ribcage. Caroline stepped over Alesha. The woman was in the death throes. She was no longer visibly breathing, her scalded eyes were completely white with no colour and her hands had stuck to her face as the sugar started to cool. Only her feet moved, thrusting out in spasm every so often.

"Has the bullet gone through?" he asked, propping himself on the table.

Caroline checked, felt with her hand. She looked at her fingers and the thick blood covering them. "Yes."

King nodded. "Get me some cloth, a tea towel. Preferably clean."

Caroline rushed over to the drawers. She came back with two clean tea towels. She folded them and placed them over the wounds. King held them in place, wincing at the effort. Caroline unbuckled the dead man's belt and pulled it through. She wrapped it around King and fastened it tightly. Dimitri Zukovsky was thin and the belt just caught on the last hole. He shuffled forwards and picked up Alesha's Kalashnikov.

"Get his pistol," King said, nodding towards Dimitri's body. "We need to stop Zukovsky."

The door had been bolted shut. King stepped back a pace and fired two shots at the lock. Caroline tried the door but nothing happened. He flicked the selector up a notch, took aim at an approximation of the hinges and fired a short burst. Wood splinters spat out of the wood. He aimed at the lower hinges and fired another burst of about ten shots or so. He shoulder-barged the door and it gave way. He struggled to keep on his feet. Caroline steadied him. "We need to get you to a hospital," she said.

King nodded, but he walked onwards. They heard gunfire. Four shots, medium calibre. Three shots a little louder. Two more quieter shots. Less echo, a sharper pitch. Now the sound of a car and some erratic acceleration and the sound of gravel under a wheel spin. They made their way through a scullery. Through the open door and into a large lounge area, empty except for an eight-foot long pine table, reinforced with blocks. King froze. Caroline stood behind him, pushed around his shoulder to see.

King quickly surveyed the area, then walked tentatively to the table. The warhead stood three-feet high and almost as wide. There was a timer on the side. It was counting down.

"He's killed us all," Caroline said from behind him.

King studied the timer, the wires coming from it. The timer looked to have its own internal battery supply. He could see the power source for the initiation, a series of laptop batteries. They only needed to hold enough charge on a standby setting, the timer would activate them to power-up and send their supply to the ignition, or detonation system. King recognised the thermite as Czech-made plastic explosive. A variation of Semtex. He looked at the wires feeding in. The heads of two RDX detonators were visible, but almost flush.

"I need some plyers, nail clippers, anything that will cut through electrical wires," King said. Caroline bolted out of the room. King bent down and studied the plastic explosive. He ignored the timer. It was only going to interrupt his thoughts. After two minutes, but what seemed like thirty, Caroline came back in. She was pale, ashen. She held out a red Swiss Army knife. "Brilliant," King said as he took it. He opened the scissors and clipped the first of four wires on the detonators. "Where did you get it?"

"It doesn't matter," she said quietly.

King snipped the wires, coiled them backwards and gently eased the detonators out of the plastic explosive. His brow was perspiring, he wiped it with his sleeve. He felt nauseous. He knew he was losing blood. He started to lift out the plastic explosive, but stopped suddenly.

"What's wrong?"

"Too easy. I mean, these things tend to be less technical than in the movies, but all the same..." He walked around the table and crouched down, looking up at the underside of the warhead. "Now this is more like I'd have expected."

"What is it?" she asked, then said, "King, there isn't much time."

"Don't tell me," he said and started to dig at the explosive. "He's put another one in here, but I can't see the power supply. Oh, no..."

"What?"

"The power supply is set within the plastic explosive. The explosive is moulded around it. It's a bundle of rechargeable batteries and a synchronised timer. There's another electrically initiated detonator but the electrical current is also rigged to an old fashioned type fuse wrapped in some kind of abrasive paper – like a match and striker. If I simply pull it out it will light like a taper."

"And that's not good."

"No. If I get the detonator out from the explosive and it explodes, it wouldn't normally threaten the plastic explosive, but the old fashioned type fuse is highly combustible. It will be enough to detonate the plastic explosive. He's got three in here by the look of it, he's just hedged his bets."

"King, I don't want to worry you, but time is ticking."

King pulled at the detonator, but it did not budge. He dug at the explosive, channelling out the detonator until he could see the wires. He started to clip them, but the scissors would not cut the wire. It seemed tougher than the previous wires, like titanium. He dug at the plastic explosive again and got most of the detonator clear. He looked up at Caroline earnestly. "I can't cut this wire. Okay, tell me the time!"

"Seven seconds!"

King yanked at the detonator, but it didn't move. He ripped the blood-soaked pad from his stomach and wrapped it in his hand, closed it around the detonator and squeezed as hard as he could. The timer counted out and the explosion sounded like a shotgun going off in the room and King fell to the floor. He couldn't hear Caroline's screaming because of the ringing in his ears. He looked at his hand, the cloth was in tatters and his burned flesh was stuck to the material. There was the smell of charred flesh and hair in the air.

Caroline looked at him, then turned her eyes to the timer and the warhead in front of them. She seemed to be waiting for an explosion she would never see or hear. She seemed to realise this and she dashed around the table and started to help King to his feet. "Are you okay?"

"No."

"Does it hurt?"

"Like you wouldn't believe," he sucked air through his teeth. "I need to get it in water."

Caroline helped him back out into the kitchen. Both Dimitri's and Alesha's bodies lay still and twisted on the floor. It was a strange, macabre scene; they had almost forgotten about them. Caroline got the cold water running and put the plug in the sink. King put his hand in the water. He cupped some in his other hand and lapped at it thirstily. Caroline called an ambulance and the police on her mobile. She rubbed a hand over his shoulders, turned him toward her and they kissed. It wasn't the prelude to anything more, simply a release.

"Let's go outside."

"You'll be better inside. The ambulance will be here in ten minutes or so."

"No, King said. "I need to go outside."

Caroline helped him across the room. He was heavy against her, growing heavier as they walked. She opened the door and they shuffled out into the glare of the sun. The wind was cold, but the sun was warm. King shivered. Ahead of them the service's blue Ford Mondeo was parked with the door open and the driver's window shattered. Frank lay face up on the ground, his stomach and chest were bloodied from gunshot wounds and the Walther pistol was still in his hand. She helped King down onto a bench seat that had been made out of part of a wooden trailer. She hurried over to Frank and bent down, checked for a pulse in his neck. She stood up and walked solemnly back. Shook her head at King.

"Frank must have got worried, or bored waiting for us. He saw the damage to the Jaguar, took that Walther out of the boot. He managed to fire back at Zukovsky," she paused. "It was Frank's Swiss Army knife. He was dying when I got to him. He wanted me to stay with him, to pass a message on to his wife." She rubbed tears from her eyes. "I had to ignore him. I knew we didn't have the time."

King nodded. His breathing was shallow. "I like you a lot," he said. He looked down at the blood seeping out of the bullet wound. He knew the exit wound would be bleeding more. They were usually larger because the bullet deformed and changed shape, lost velocity.

Caroline took off her jacket, folded it over and pressed it into the wound. She smiled at him. "I like you a lot too." She shifted closer into him. "It will be okay."

The ambulance siren was audible, the police too. It looked as if the police vehicles had come from one direction and the ambulance had come in from another route. The flashing lights congregating at the entrance to the lane and filing down.

"Thanks," he said.
"For what?"
"For getting me outside."
"Why?"

King rested his head on her shoulder. He was heavy, becoming heavier all the time until she felt he was completely rested against her. "I never wanted to die inside. I always wanted to be able to see the sky one last time."

74

Six Months later
Moscow

Dzhokhar Ivanovich closed the file in front of him and looked at the eleven men around the table. Each man had given their opinion and each man had drawn the same conclusion. There was no practical way to revive the operation known as *Probuzhdeniye-Medved,* or Awakening Bear. Sanctioned by the four most powerful men in the government, beside the president himself. Spoken of in whispers the operation was now being blamed on separatists within the military. The same separatists who had never given up on the Ukraine. Former army general Vladimir Zukovsky was originally to be named and blamed, but he was to be confirmed dead. FSB director Dzhokhar Ivanovich had made plans to award Zukovsky the highest service honour, the *Geroj Rossijskoj Federatsii,* or Hero of the Russian Federation. Of course, with a new identity and an award that would never leave the Kremlin, Vladimir Zukovsky would not be able to live as a national hero, but he would live out his retirement on the Georgian coast, a secret hero of the federation and in permanently funded comfort.

That was before the failure. Agents of the Russian Federation had been killed, the nuclear warhead was in British possession, funds were unaccounted for, and although Vladimir Zukovsky had escaped capture, his whereabouts was still unknown. Zukovsky was capable of finding the means and opportunity to return to Moscow and make a report. He had simply chosen not to. His failure to capitulate and throw himself on the mercy of the FSB was telling. The funds placed in various European Banks had all been withdrawn. The accounts now lay empty. Zukovsky had accepted that he was now a wanted man. He had been blamed entirely and was now considered an enemy of the Russian Federation and would be treated as such. The directive had come from the president himself, and all twelve men at the table had agreed and sanctioned his termination. They had an ulterior motive though, and hoped Zukovsky would be killed before he could talk.

Dzhokhar Ivanovich stood up, bringing the meeting to a close, their business concluded.

75

Mallorca, Balearic Islands

They had taken the mountain road from Porta Pollensa. The road twisted back on itself more times than they cared to remember. A twenty-five-mile route that had taken over an hour and a half. They had stopped a few times for photographs, but the road climbed high through the mountains and the straightest section was no more than one hundred metres. She had started to feel nauseous at one point, so he had pulled over and they had sat and taken in the dramatic and quite beautiful view. Sat together on a large rock, their arms around each other, comfortable and complete.

It was late May and the temperature was a comfortable 26°C. They had spent the first few days swimming and snorkelling at a secluded cove, walking along the marina and dining at a different restaurant twice a day. This was the first excursion they had taken so far and they only had two days' holiday remaining. He hired the Opel Astra and promised to take her on a scenic drive she would never forget.

Port de Sóller was a curious town. On a Spanish island, it looked more like a town in the south of France. The French architecture was obvious, and by no means understated. The result of its people finding it easier to trade with France across the ocean, than to trade with the rest of the island on the other side of the mountains. The horseshoe cove was fringed by a dirty-yellow beach and a promenade that wound around the bay separated from the open-fronted restaurants and hotel facades by a tram line and regular trams running to the town of Sóller some three kilometres inland.

"I'm really hot," Caroline said. She tugged at her wrap. "Fancy a dip?"

"Sure," King said.

They walked down the slope and Caroline pulled the wrap over her head. She was already wearing a white bikini, and against her tan it looked magnificent. At least, in King's eyes she looked more so. Perfect in fact. She kicked off her sandals and walked into the water, turned around and waited for him.

He tugged off his shirt and waded out. He was slim and toned, returning to fitness slowly. He had lost weight after the shooting, but was steadily rebuilding his muscle mass. He had lost over a metre of intestine and part of his stomach and now ate far less than he used to. The bullet had passed through, but required comprehensive surgery to repair the damage inside. His stomach looked as if a shark had bitten half of his torso, then let go. The scars had turned white against his tan.

They swam out, the mountains to their left, million euro yachts and powerboats to their right and the mouth of the horseshoe bay ahead of them. King drew her close, kissed her and they laughed as they started to sink and splash and were forced to break free of each other. They swam back and sat in the tiny shore break.

"I'm not hungry yet," King said. He stood up and picked up his shirt. "Why don't you chill here, take a decent swim while I check out the gift shops."

"I'll come."

"No, I want to buy you a gift. This town is going to have some nice jewellery and things. Better than the typical tourist stuff elsewhere."

Caroline smiled. "I like the idea of jewellery."

"I'll be back in an hour." He bent down and kissed her tenderly. "Don't go finding yourself a millionaire playboy while I'm gone."

"I'll try not to. Don't be too long though, I can't promise anything."

King walked briskly down the promenade. There was no service on his mobile, but the last text message he'd received on the descent down the last part of the mountain pass into Sóller town had the target on site. King had read the message in the carpark whilst Caroline had paid for the ticket at the pay-and-display point.

At the end of the promenade he followed the road around to the right, crossing the tram tracks and past an expensive jewellery boutique. He noted to go in on his way back. Past the row of gift shops there was a bicycle hire shop which looked to specialise in repairs. King had seen many professional looking road racer cyclists on the drive, they obviously tested themselves against the arduous hills and mountain passes that had cut the town off from the rest of the island.

He saw the bicycle chained to the railings. It was a bright yellow Dawes. The saddle bags were made from lightweight fabric with zip fasteners. King bent down, opened the main zipper, removed the lightweight Beretta, the loaded magazine and the six-inch long suppressor, and distributed them in the pockets of his damp shorts. His phone vibrated. He had rounded the cove and was between two mountainous outcrops. The signal was intermittent, but had returned.

Four words.

Hostiles on route - hurry.

He walked the steep gradient. Cobbled street. His fitness was coming back, but he noticed his breathing was rapid and his chest pounded. Adrenalin, but also exertion.

Caroline had been helping with his fitness, and so many other things besides. After being discharged from hospital he had stayed with her and gone for regular physiotherapy, stomach drains and later for skin grafts to his hand. Caroline had helped him physically and they had helped each other emotionally. Caroline had been sent on emotional leave and had been monitored for PTSD. During the restructure of MI5 and the subsequent reviews and briefings both had been called to bear witness. Forester had left a file in his personal records running King as an unofficial agent for years. King had been remunerated and extended every curtesy, including private healthcare and an allowance during his recuperation. Like it or not, he was now with MI5.

The house was typically French, a southern style chateau. It was painted cream with terracotta accenting and tiled roof. The garden was mature, mainly potted plants or borders of typical Mediterranean appeal. It was May, so many of the species were flowering in colourful blooms of yellow, orange, pink and red. King stood back and studied it from across the road. He watched an ambulance crawl down the hill and park. The driver had a clipboard and was talking on his phone, while the passenger studied the houses on the hillside. They seemed unhurried.

The two men walked up from the port. Both were tall and lean and fit. Both wore their dark hair slicked back. They each wore a day sack on their shoulders. When they reached the chateau opposite, both removed the sacks and opened them. King pressed himself into the doorway. It was a residential building of apartments. There was an awning over the doorway and a few chairs scattered on the pavement. A place the residents sat at night and smoked and drank and watched the lights in the port or the glimpses of sunset out at sea through the opening of the horseshoe cove.

King inserted the magazine into the Beretta and screwed the suppressor into the custom-made bushing which had been fitted to the muzzle of the weapon.

The men both surveyed the street, cast their eyes over the walls of the chateau, then pulled their weapons out of the sacks and climbed the steps to the garden gate. King waited until they entered the property, then made the weapon ready as he crossed the road. He sprang up the steps and followed. The terraced gardens each had a patio or strip of lawn and a garden border with either chairs or sun loungers. The highest paved terrace led straight to the sliding glass windows of the house, the lowest featured the tiny swimming pool and alcoves of seating with pergolas above, covered in vines which were now in full growth and spreading their leaves to provide ample shade in the mid-day sun.

Vladimir Zukovsky sat reading a newspaper. His skin was red and peeling, and he wore a Panama hat to cover his head and face from the sun's rays. He looked up at the two Russians, stared at their matching Glock 17 pistols with extended magazines. He placed the newspaper carefully down and raised his hands. King made his way silently down the steps and could hear Zukovsky pleading his case, quite desperately in Russian.

The nearest man raised his pistol. He did not hear the gunshot from King's Beretta, merely fell into the pool as the bullet hit him in the head. The Beretta had made next to no sound and both Zukovsky and the second gunman were momentarily confused. King reached the terrace, held the weapon up just three paces from the gunman.

"Drop it!" he said. "Drop the weapon and you can walk away."

The gunman had half turned, his pistol was pointing at the ground between King and Zukovsky. "Thank you," the man said. "Thank you for the professional curtesy. But you do not know my employers…" He turned and brought the pistol up on King. The move was quick and well-practised.

King fired twice and both bullets hit the man in the face. He fell backwards and writhed on the ground, the pistol still in his hand. King aimed and fired once more and the man went still.

Zukovsky stared at King. "You?"

"It was always going to be."

"Before you kill me, tell me what happened to my son?"

"You didn't wait for him."

Zukovsky shrugged. "I did what I did. What I had to do."

"You set the timing device off, you thought you'd get the hell out of Dodge. You'd never have made it."

"It was a mistake. In my haste, I set it on the timing meant for Al-Shaqqaf's suicide bomber. Once it was set, there was no going back. I was hoping to lure you away from the bomb, let it run its course. Do you have my son?"

King stepped closer, keeping the weapon aimed at him. "Your son is dead. And that crazy whore Alesha Mikailovitch."

"You killed them?"

"Alesha choked on the boiling sugar," King looked into the man's eyes. "I killed your son." Zukovsky's expression dropped. There was genuine sadness there, amongst the craziness. "Wasn't worth it, was it?"

The Russian shook his head. "So now you kill me? Why not let my countrymen do it for you?"

King looked around. The two men dressed as paramedics carried the empty stretcher between them. They hesitated at the foot of the steps. One carried a medical pack containing the drugs and tape needed to subdue and secure Zukovsky on his drive to the private airfield where a plane was waiting. King looked back at the Russian. "Because you are going to tell some people everything you know about this invasion lunacy. And after you have told them everything you know, you will tell our American friends. And they'll record and review everything you say and analyse it back and check for holes and lies and patterns, until you can only remember the truth and the lies fall away and the truth is all there is left in your world."

***

Caroline had swum out past the buoyed-off area and to the headland beyond. She was now laying on her back in the sand, drying off and warming in the sun. King watched her. She looked glorious in her white bikini, her tousled blonde hair hanging long and golden. She looked around and waved. He smiled, she'd known he was there. Coincidence of course, but when one is so in love the coincidences become the norm. Something that only they would ever share. He walked down the ramp and kicked his sandals off as he stepped onto the warm sand.

"How was your swim?"

"Good," she smiled and kissed him. "No millionaire playboys bothered me, but it's early yet."

"Maybe after lunch then?" he said.

"How was your shopping?"

"Good," he smiled. "Couldn't find a keyring in the shape of a penis that works as a whistle."

"Damn."

"But I found this." He held out the box and she took it slowly.

"Thank you," she said and opened the box carefully. She took out the ring and the sunlight caught the cluster of three diamonds and threads of white gold interwoven with the yellow gold. "What kind of ring is it?"

"Mainly gold."

"Knuckle head," she smiled. "I mean; which finger does it go on?"

"Whichever. But ring finger will be the best fit, from my estimation."

"And which hand?"

"Whichever feels more comfortable," he said, and patted his heart. "Here, that is."

"I'd like the left, I think."

King smiled at her. "I was hoping you'd say that."

Author's Note

Thanks for reading and I hope you enjoyed the story. For those who did not know this was a sequel to The Contract Man, I hope it read well as a standalone novel. For those who did, I hope you like what I've done with Alex King and appreciated a few nods to his past.

We modern writers rely so much on reviews, Amazon in particular. I hope you can take a couple minutes to log on and leave a review and rating. It helps keep our work visible in a competitive market. Here's a link that will get you there - www.apbateman.com

I plan another outing for Alex King very soon. Either way I'm currently working on something. You can keep up with me on Facebook: @authorapbateman to find out what.

Thanks for reading

A P Bateman

Printed in Great Britain
by Amazon